"DO YOU S___ **THE MAN WITH THE** ___**,**
THE BLADE MOVING SLIGHTLY
AS SHE SWALLOWED.

She gave him a nod.

"El Jefe wishes to see you. Someone will call, let you know when and where. You will say nothing about tonight. No police, you understand?"

She managed to nod.

"Go home, *querida*." The mustached man ran a gloved hand over her cheek in an intimate caress, and nausea rolled in her stomach. "We will meet again soon."

"Hey, you! Get away from her!"

Carly's heart jerked. She knew that deep voice, knew it belonged to Lincoln Cain, and for once she was glad to see him.

Also by Kat Martin

BEYOND REASON

KAT MARTIN

ZEBRA BOOKS
KENSINGTON PUBLISHING CORP.
http://www.kensingtonbooks.com

ZEBRA BOOKS are published by

Kensington Publishing Corp.
119 West 40th Street
New York, NY 10018

All Kensington titles, imprints, and distributed lines are available at special quantity discounts for bulk purchases for sales promotion, premiums, fund-raising, educational, or institutional use.

Special book excerpts or customized printings can also be created to fit specific needs. For details, write or phone the office of the Kensington Sales Manager: Attn.: Sales Department. Kensington Publishing Corp., 119 West 40th Street, New York, NY 10018. Phone: 1-800-221-2647.

Zebra and the Z logo Reg. U.S. Pat. & TM Off.

First Printing: June 2017
ISBN-13: 978-1-4201-4315-7
ISBN-10: 1-4201-4315-8

eISBN-13: 978-1-4201-4316-4
eISBN-10: 1-4201-4316-6

10 9 8 7 6 5 4 3 2 1

Printed in the United States of America

Chapter One

Iron Springs, Texas

For the second time since her return to Iron Springs, Carly Drake stood in a graveyard. On the opposite side of the coffin, between rows of granite headstones, the Hernandez family huddled together, a wife weeping for her husband, children crying for their father.

Carly bowed her head, her heart aching for the loss of a man she had known only briefly. With her grandfather's recent passing, she understood the pain Miguel's family was suffering. Joe Drake, the man who had raised her, the only father Carly had ever known, had died just five weeks ago.

But unlike a heart that had simply worn itself out, Miguel Hernandez, Grandpa Joe's number-one driver, had been shot in the head, the criminals who had committed the truck hijacking still on the loose.

In the weeks since her grandfather's death, Carly had been doing her best to run Drake Trucking, to keep the company afloat and its employees' checks paid. She was putting in twelve-hour days, but Miguel had been killed on her watch and Carly felt responsible.

The harsh Texas wind kicked up, whipping blades of grass in front of the casket draped with a blanket of bloodred roses. The end of September weather was fickle, hot and humid one day, rainy and overcast the next. Strands of heavy blond hair tore free from the tight bun at the nape of her neck. As Carly smoothed the strands back into place, her gaze paused on a man at the far edge of the mourners, a head taller than the men in Miguel's Hispanic family, taller than most of the truckers or any other man in the crowd, big and broad-shouldered, with dark brown hair, and a strikingly handsome face.

Carly leaned over and spoke quietly to the woman beside her, Brittany Haworth, a willowy brunette who had been her best friend in high school. As if it had been just days instead of years, their friendship had resumed the day Carly had returned to Iron Springs.

"The man across from us . . ." Carly said. "The tall one? He was also at Grandpa Joe's funeral. I remember him going through the line to pay his respects, but I was hurting so much I barely paid attention. Do you know who he is?"

Brittany looked surprised. "You're kidding, right? You don't recognize him? Obviously you don't read the gossip rags. He's in the newspapers all the time. That's Lincoln Cain. You know, the multimillionaire?"

Carly's gaze swung across the casket on the mound above the grave to the big man in the perfectly tailored black suit and crisp white shirt. "That's Cain?"

As if he could feel her watching him, his eyes swung to hers, remained steady on her face. Carly couldn't seem to look away. There was power in that bold, probing stare. She could actually feel her pulse accelerate. "So what's Cain doing in Iron Springs?"

"He owns a ranch here. He was born close by— Pleasant Hill, I think. He left to make his fortune, came back a few years ago megarich. It's a fascinating story. You'll have to Google him sometime."

"I still don't understand why he was at Joe's funeral, or why he's here today."

"For one thing, he was one of Joe's competitors. Texas American Transportation is one of the biggest trucking companies in the world."

She nodded. "Tex/Am Transport. I know that, but—"

"Cain credits Joe Drake as one of the people who put him on the path to success. The *Iron Springs Gazette* published a couple of articles about him and Joe."

Guilt swept over her. She'd been gone so much. Off to college at the U. of Texas in Austin ten years ago, which her grandfather had paid for, then a job in Houston as a flight attendant.

She had always wanted to see the world, so instead of coming home to help Grandpa Joe, she'd gone to work for Delta. She'd been transferred here and there, worked out of New York for a while, come back to Iron Springs a couple of times a year, but her visits never lasted more than a few days before she was gone again, flying somewhere else, off on another adventure.

Six weeks ago, she'd quit her job, given up her apartment in San Francisco where she had been based, and come home to stay. Joe's heart condition had worsened. She'd started worrying about him, decided to come back and help him run Drake Trucking, take over some of the responsibilities, and lessen the stress he was under.

She'd only been in Iron Springs a week when Joe

had suffered a massive heart attack. He'd died in the ambulance on the way to the hospital. By the time she'd received the call, rushed out of the office, and driven like a maniac to Iron Springs Memorial, Joe was gone.

She hadn't been there for him when he needed her.

Just as she had so many times before, Carly had failed him.

"Carly . . ."

She glanced up at the sound of Brittany's voice. The service had ended. The mourners were breaking up, people walking away.

"He's coming over," Britt whispered. "Lincoln Cain."

Carly honed in on him, at least six-five, a man impossible to miss. She straightened as he approached.

"Ms. Drake? I'm Lincoln Cain." He extended a big hand, and as she set hers in it, felt a warm, comforting spread of heat. Since being comforted only made her feel like crying, she eased her hand away.

"We met briefly at your grandfather's service," Cain said, "but I doubt you recall."

His eyes were green, she realized. The color of money, she thought, with gold flecks in the center. He had a slight cleft in his chin and a jaw that looked carved in stone. "Yes, I remember seeing you there. I don't recall much else. It was a very bad day."

"Yes, it was."

She turned. "This is my friend, Brittany Haworth."

He made a faint nod of his head. "Ms. Haworth."

"Nice to meet you," Britt said. She'd always been shy. The way she was looking at Cain, as if the year's sexiest man alive had just dropped by for a visit, Carly was surprised her friend was able to speak.

Cain's gaze returned to Carly. "I realize how difficult

it must be, going through all of this again so soon. Once more you have my condolences."

"Thank you. It's been difficult. But my grandfather lived a long, full life. I can only imagine how terrible this is for Miguel's family."

A muscle in Cain's jaw tightened. "Maybe catching his killer will ease some of their pain."

"You think they will?"

"Someone will."

There was something in the way he said it. Surely he didn't intend to involve himself in catching the men who'd murdered Miguel.

"I didn't realize you were a friend of my grandfather's."

His features relaxed as if a fond memory had surfaced. "Joe Drake was a good man. One of the best. He gave me my first job. Did you know that?"

Her eyes burned. That sounded so like Joe. Never a hand-out but always a hand-up whenever one was needed. "I wasn't around much after I got out of high school. I should have come home more often. You'll never know how much I regret that."

His expression shifted, became unreadable. "We all do things we regret." Up close he was even better looking than she had first thought, his dark hair cut a little shorter on the sides, narrow brackets beside his mouth that only appeared once in a while, not dimples, but something more subtle, more intriguing. "Your grandfather loved you very much."

A lump swelled in her throat. She had loved him, too. She'd never realized how little time they would have. "Thank you for saying that." She needed to leave. She was going to cry and she didn't want to do that in front of Cain. "I'm sorry, but if you'll excuse me, I need to say good-bye to Miguel's wife, Conchita, before we go."

He nodded. "There's something I need to discuss with you. After Joe died, I waited. I wanted to give you time to grieve, but after what happened to Miguel, it can't wait any longer."

She tried to imagine what Cain wanted. Something to do with Joe, she thought. "All right. You can reach me at the office. I'm there every day."

"I know the number. I'll be in touch."

She watched as he turned and walked away, wide shoulders, narrow hips, long powerful legs striding across the grass as if he had something important to do. What could one of the wealthiest men in Texas possibly want to talk to her about?

Carly watched as Cain slid into the back of a shiny black stretch limo waiting for him at the edge of the graveyard.

"I wonder what he wants," Brittany said, voicing Carly's thoughts.

"He's in the transportation business, so it must have something to do with Drake Trucking."

"You're probably right. But Tex/Am Transport is only a small part of his company. Cain owns half of Texas American Enterprises, which means it could be anything. Or maybe it's something personal, something to do with your grandfather."

"Maybe. I guess I'll find out." Carly started making her way through the tombstones. Up ahead, Conchita Hernandez and the rest of Miguel's family stood on the church steps, accepting condolences. Carly squared her shoulders and kept walking.

* * *

She wasn't what he had imagined. Oh, she was as pretty as the pictures her grandfather had proudly shown him: late twenties, taller than average, with big blue eyes and wavy golden blond hair past her shoulders. Joe had shown him a photo of her playing volleyball on the beach so he knew what she looked like in a bikini, knew she had a dynamite figure.

She didn't seem concerned with her appearance the way he'd expected. He thought she'd be more aloof, more self-absorbed. He hadn't expected her to be grieving her grandfather so deeply.

He'd been sure he wouldn't like her. Not the young woman who had accepted so much and returned so little.

And yet as he had watched her with Miguel's family, as he read her sorrow, the depth of her concern, he had been surprisingly moved. She felt responsible in some way for her employee's death. She blamed herself, and he couldn't allow that to happen.

Linc had made a vow to her grandfather. He'd promised Joe Drake he would look after Carly, make sure she was okay. Linc planned to keep that vow. And the best way he could take care of Carly was to send her packing—before she ended up as dead as Miguel Hernandez.

Carly turned the corner and pulled up to the curb in the white F-150 pickup she was driving. DRAKE TRUCKING gleamed in dark blue letters on the doors, along with the logo of a stylized male duck in flight—a drake.

"Thanks for the ride." Britt cracked open her door. "Thanks for going with me."

"Miguel was a really nice guy. I can't believe someone killed him."

Sadness rolled over her. Such a senseless murder. Why hadn't Miguel cooperated with the hijackers? A piece of equipment, no matter how valuable, wasn't worth his life. Or maybe he'd given them what they wanted and they had murdered him anyway. Maybe they were just cold-blooded killers.

"I'm calling Sheriff Howler as soon as I get back to the office," Carly said. "I need to see if he's made any progress on the case."

"I hope they catch whoever did it."

Carly hoped they sent the bastards straight to hell, but she didn't say that. "So do I."

"You want to come in, have a glass of iced tea or something?" Brittany asked.

"I need to get back. I've got a ton of work to do." Including writing paychecks. Not easy when you had to juggle accounts, borrow from Peter to pay Paul, try to keep all of the balls in the air so none of the checks would bounce.

"Okay, I'll call you later." Britt slammed the pickup door, turned and headed up the sidewalk to the front door of the small gray brick house she rented. It had a white picket fence, white shuttered windows, and a perfectly tended lawn. Flower beds overflowed with yellow and purple pansies.

Britt was a homebody, always had been. As a substitute teacher at Iron Springs Elementary, her dream was to marry and have a family. So far that hadn't happened.

After a five-year engagement, Britt had come home early to find her fiancé—what was the legal term?—in flagrante delicto with the voluptuous neighbor who lived down the block.

Britt had been devastated, but Carly hadn't been all that surprised. Being a flight attendant, she had met and dated men from all over the world. In her experience, guys were fun for a while, but as soon as you fell in love with one, he was gone, looking for another conquest.

Britt might seem as if she'd weathered the heartbreak, but inside she was still hurting. Carly wasn't sure how long it would take her tender heart to mend.

It wasn't going to happen to her—not again. She'd been engaged two times. Both had ended in disaster when the man she thought loved her had found someone to replace her.

For the last several months, she'd been taking a break from men. She'd had enough disappointment to last a lifetime. She wasn't ready to jump into the dating world again.

One look at Brittany told her she had made the right decision. Add to that, the fact she had inherited her grandfather's trucking firm, a fleet of fifteen Peterbilt tractor trucks and an assortment of trailers. With a company that grossed in the millions each year and employed twenty-eight people, she didn't have time to date.

Thinking of the afternoon ahead and the pile of work she faced, Carly pulled the pickup onto Highway 67 and headed back to Drake Trucking.

Returning to his office in Dallas, Linc loosened his tie as he stepped out of the elevator on the executive floor of Tex/Am's corporate headquarters building, a six-story, mirrored glass structure on the North Central Expressway.

The receptionist, Leslie Bingham, sat behind a sleek teakwood desk that matched the low wooden tables in the contemporary seating area. The smooth, rust-grained wood posed a warm contrast to the nubby texture of the oatmeal fabric on the sofa and chairs.

Linc walked past the desk, heading for his private office.

"Good afternoon, Mr. Cain."

He smiled absently, his mind still back in Iron Springs. "Afternoon, Les."

She smiled in return, a perky, freckle-faced redhead in her late twenties with a pleasant disposition and plenty of ambition, just what he liked in an employee.

There were only two offices on the top floor of the building, his and that of his partner, Beau Reese. Each of them had a personal assistant who worked in a private area behind the receptionist desk. Staff worked in cubicles nearby, serving both him and Beau.

Linc waved at Mildred Whitelaw, a brunette in her early forties who was one of his most valuable employees, the lady who had kept him organized and on track since he and Beau had first started building the company.

He pulled open the door leading into his private office and walked inside, his gaze going to the wall of windows that wrapped around the room and looked over the busy Dallas streets.

The teakwood theme he had personally chosen for the executive floor continued in here, though the sofa and chairs were caramel leather instead of fabric.

Linc stripped off the black suit coat he had worn to Miguel Hernandez's funeral, draped it over the valet along the wall, sat down behind his desk, and went to work. He had a four o'clock conference call with the mayor of Ruidoso regarding a road construction project in New Mexico on Highway 48 north of the city. The job was just getting started. He didn't want any glitches so he needed to be prepared.

He picked up the file Millie had set on his desk, but instead of flipping it open, his mind went back to his graveside encounter with Carly Drake. He hit the intercom button.

"Millie, I need you to set up a meeting with Carly Drake at Drake Trucking. Tomorrow would be best. Whatever time works in my schedule, but the sooner the better."

"I'll take care of it," Millie said.

Linc turned back to the file, but his thoughts strayed again to the pretty little blue-eyed blonde, Joe Drake's granddaughter. She wasn't a slender woman, not overly buxom, either. She had more than enough curves to look feminine, but there was something solid about her that gave the impression of strength.

He remembered the first heart attack Joe had suffered. Linc had gone to the hospital to see him, been surprised at how frail the tough old man had looked. Lying in that hospital bed, Joe had stared at his mortality and faced it head on, the way he did everything else.

He had asked Linc a favor that day, as he had never done before, asked that if something happened to him, Linc would look after his granddaughter, make sure Carly was okay.

Joe didn't give his trust lightly and Linc didn't make promises he didn't intend to keep. The day Joe had died, Carly Drake had become his responsibility.

He owed Joe Drake more than he could ever repay. This last small favor was the least he could do.

Chapter Two

Carly sat behind the metal desk in Grandpa Joe's office, a plain twelve-by-fourteen-foot room off an open area out front where the scheduling, record-keeping, and customer service took place.

Attached to the building in a big metal warehouse, there was a truck service department that held replacement and repair parts: tires, batteries, oil, fluids, and anything else a big eighteen-wheeler might need, as well as a maintenance bay where the mechanics did the actual work on the rigs. A huge asphalt yard, surrounded by a chain-link fence, faced the road out in front.

Carly studied the computer screen on her desk, going over account records, scrolling down one column after another, trying to find enough money to pay the employees their two-week checks.

When she'd arrived in Texas, she'd had no idea the terrible financial straits Drake Trucking was in. Joe had been a successful businessman all his life. He'd run the company with a firm hand and an eye on every dollar.

But apparently his bad health had taken its toll.

He'd been so busy with doctor visits and trips in and out of the hospital that the business had gone downhill. And though he had been on Medicare, there were still outstanding medical bills that had to be paid.

Having only been in Texas a week when Joe died, Carly hadn't had nearly enough time to figure out what was going on and start trying to solve the problem. Not enough time to save Drake Trucking or her grandfather.

A familiar deep pang reminded her of the loss of the man who had raised her. She should have come back sooner. If she had been there, she could have relieved some of Joe's stress. She could have made sure he was taking his meds, that he kept his medical appointments. Maybe he would have lived a few more years.

Carly shoved the guilt away. She didn't have time for that now. She had responsibilities, people to worry about, a company to run.

Late in the afternoon, by holding off on some of the utility bills, some of the suppliers' invoices, a bill from Joe's attorney, Willard Speers, for settling Joe's estate, and a lot of miscellaneous debts she didn't yet understand, she managed to round up enough to make payroll and had all the checks written.

Tomorrow she would get on the phone and start making cold calls, see if she could stir up some business. She'd do whatever it took to make the company profitable again.

She had failed her grandfather before.

No matter how hard she had to work, Carly wasn't going to fail him again.

A quick knock sounded and the door swung open. It was Donna Melendez, a Latina who had been Joe's office manager for years. Donna was in her fifties, with long black hair turning silver and the kind of work ethic money alone couldn't buy.

"I just got a call from Texas American. Lincoln Cain's secretary wants to make an appointment."

Carly thought of their meeting at the cemetery. Cain's tall, broad-shouldered build and amazing face popped into her head, and a trickle of warmth spread through her.

Recognizing that warmth as attraction, she firmly tamped it down. She wasn't interested in Cain or any other man. At least not now or anytime in the near future. "I saw him at the funeral. He said he wanted to talk to me."

"Well, he certainly didn't waste any time."

"He didn't look like a man who wastes time."

Donna chuckled. "I put him down for two P.M. I told his secretary I'd call her back if that was a problem."

"Two is fine." That would give her all morning to make calls and spend a little more time going over the books. There was a lot she didn't understand about running this business—way too much she needed to learn.

As a teenager, she'd spent hours after school and on weekends with Joe at the yard and she had picked up a lot. The summer of her eighteenth birthday, he had taught her to drive a big rig, which had been a thrill, though she had never left the field they pretended was a road.

Back then Joe had wanted her to work with him, maybe take over the business after he was gone. At the time she hadn't been interested in staying in Iron Springs. But years had passed; things had changed.

The phone rang. Joe's direct line. When she pressed the receiver against her ear, the voice of Emmett

Howler, Sheriff of Howler County, came through the earpiece.

"Sheriff Howler, I appreciate your returning my call," Carly said.

"No problem, little lady. I know you're worried about catching the men who killed your employee. We all are."

Little lady. The words grated on her feminist nerves. She didn't mind the *ma'am,* a respectful term used by half the South, but *little lady* was pushing it, as far as Carly was concerned.

"So there's still no sign of the men who murdered Miguel Hernandez?" she asked.

"No, missy, there sure ain't. But the department's on top of it. We'll find 'em sooner or later."

"What about the truck and trailer?" It was insured, of course, but there was a steep deductible, which at the moment she couldn't afford to pay. There'd be one less big rig in the fleet for a while.

"No sign of it. Like I said, we're on it. I'll be sure to let you know if anything new turns up."

"Thank you, Sheriff." Carly hung up the phone. *If anything new turns up.* So far the cops didn't have squat, just a plausible theory based on a .45 caliber bullet wound at the back of Miguel's head and the disappearance of the truck and semi-trailer it was hauling.

The door swung open again and Donna stuck her head in, her stick-straight, silver-streaked black hair tied neatly at the nape of her neck. "So what did the sheriff have to say?"

It wasn't really Donna's business. Carly definitely needed to set some rules—or what the hell, maybe not. Before he'd gotten sick, Joe had been extremely successful. He treated the company like one big family. She'd stick with his tried-and-true methods for a while.

"So far, Howler has come up with a big fat zero. There's not a lot of crime out here. I think he's in over his head."

"Too bad the murder happened in the county." Which was the sheriff's jurisdiction. "Oh, Gordy asked if he could have tomorrow off to take care of some personal business. What do you think?"

Her shop foreman had worked for Joe for twenty years; he was the man who helped her keep things moving along.

"He's been a real trooper. A day off shouldn't be a problem."

"Okay, then." Donna swung the door closed and went back to work.

Carly returned to scanning the computer screen. How had her grandfather lost track of his finances so badly? She began scrolling through old accounting files. She needed to go through every month of the past year. If she still didn't have an answer, she'd keep going back month by month until she did.

With a sigh, she went back to work.

The pilot landed one of two Tex/Am Bell helicopters on the pad outside the main house at Blackland Ranch, Linc's property north and east of Iron Springs. The rotors slowed, but didn't completely stop spinning.

"Have a good weekend, Mr. C," the pilot said.

Linc slid open the heavy door. "You, too, Dillon. I'll see you next week." Jumping out of the chopper onto the asphalt, Linc kept his head low as he ran toward the palatial mansion.

Fifteen thousand square feet constructed entirely of stone, the house stood more than two stories tall, with arched, paned windows and formally landscaped grounds broken only by the long ribbon of driveway leading up from the road.

Linc hated the place.

A monument to extravagant bad taste, the mansion had been designed by his ex-wife, the former Holly Springer, a Miss America beauty pageant finalist. Linc loved the ranch, had hoped that building Holly a house would convince her to spend more time at the 2,500-acre property that was his personal retreat.

The house had taken two and a half years to finish—just six months shy of their three-year, completely unsuccessful marriage.

Linc didn't bother to go inside, just skirted the house to the seven-car garage, passing one of the gardeners in a floppy-brimmed straw hat along the way. Linc waved and Pedro waved back.

Standing in front of the gray stone garage that matched the house, he punched in the code to bay number three and waited for the door to slide up. A black, fully loaded, extended-cab Sierra Denali 2500 GMC pickup gleamed in the sunlight streaming through the open garage door.

Linc tossed his briefcase into the backseat, opened the driver's door, slid in behind the wheel, and fired up the big diesel V-8 engine. He didn't want to be late for his two o'clock meeting with Carly Drake.

It was Friday. After the meeting, he planned to work the weekend from the ranch, which he did as often as he could.

Linc hit the gas and headed for the Drake Trucking yard at the edge of town, not too far away. He wasn't sure exactly what he was going to say, only that he'd let Carly know her problems were solved.

Linc was sure she would be grateful.

Sitting behind the desk, Carly pressed the phone against her ear.

"You've always been a loyal customer, Mr. Jensen. But I've been going over the freight contracts for the last few months and I don't find any recent deliveries for Jensen Manufacturing. If there's been some sort of problem, I'd certainly like to get to the bottom of it."

"The freight hauling business is highly competitive," Mr. Jensen said. "I found cheaper prices somewhere else, that's all."

"Was the service as good? Because you know you can count on Drake to get your products delivered on time and in excellent condition."

"Times are tough, Ms. Drake—"

"Carly, please."

"Like I said, Carly, times are tough. I had to make a decision and I couldn't get hold of Joe."

"Well, I'm here now and available whenever you need me. And we'll match whatever terms you got on your last contract."

Silence fell. Carly closed her eyes and crossed her fingers.

"I feel bad about Joe. He was a really good guy. I'll tell you what I'll do. I've got a couple of loads coming up the first of the month. We'll see if Drake can do as good a job without Joe as it used to do when he was there."

Carly grinned. "Thank you, Mr. Jensen. I promise you won't be disappointed." The line went dead and Carly leaned back in her chair. Her hands were shaking and she was perspiring. The ceiling fan rotated above her. She lifted her hair up off the back of her neck to catch the breeze, took a deep breath, and slowly released it.

She had made calls all morning and again after lunch. Jensen Manufacturing was her first real success.

She glanced at the clock. Crap, it was almost time for her two o'clock appointment. She'd hoped to have a chance to run back to the house and change into something more professional than jeans. No time now.

Instead, she hit Google Chrome, typed in Cain's name, clicked up one of the many links that mentioned him, and began to read, starting with Wikipedia.

Lincoln Cain, no middle name. Entrepreneur, developer, investor, philanthropist. Born in Pleasant Hill, Texas, on July 4. He was thirty-five years old, six years older than Carly.

Co-owner of Texas American Enterprises. His partner's name was Beaumont Reese. She'd heard of Beau Reese, son of a wealthy Texas family, famous for his flashy lifestyle and his expensive hobby—driving Formula One race cars, kind of a Texas Paul Newman. Though apparently he just drove for fun these days. When she had a little more time, she'd Google Reese, too.

Carly glanced down the page. There was a ton of stuff about Cain. One sentence caught her eye: net worth estimated at over five hundred million. *Oh. My. God.*

Mother deceased. No mention of his father. She went back to the Web links, spotted the word *prison*, and clicked on the link. It was an article in *People* magazine.

She didn't have time to read it all so she skimmed the page, paused halfway down the article. An entire section was devoted to Cain's teenage years, which mentioned a stint in juvenile detention when he was a junior in high school and another stay as a senior.

At age eighteen, he'd been arrested for the attempted armed robbery of a convenience store along with two other youths, all three were apprehended at the scene. Having just turned eighteen, Cain was sentenced to two years in prison while the other two kids, still seventeen, received lesser sentences and their juvenile records were sealed. Cain had never revealed their identities.

According to the article, after prison Cain had turned his life around and set himself on a course that had made him the multimillionaire he was today.

A knock at the door ended her reading. Instead of bursting in as she usually did, Donna waited for permission, which meant Lincoln Cain had arrived.

She shut down the computer and answered the knock. "Come on in."

Donna opened the door, her cheeks flushed and her eyes bright, the same effect the man had had on Brittany. "I'm sorry to bother you, Ms. Drake, but Mr. Cain is here to see you."

Cain walked past Donna, wearing a charcoal suit today, Armani or Gucci, or some equally posh designer. At Delta, she had worked the first-class section. She knew high-dollar clothes. The briefcase he carried was expensive belted leather.

Carly stood up behind the desk in her jeans and T-shirt. Suddenly remembering what was printed on the front, she froze. Cain's gold-flecked green eyes ran over the words BAD MOTHER TRUCKER, and his mouth edged up.

Carly hadn't expected the jolt of heat that faint smile created. She hadn't expected to notice his lips at all, the slight tilt, the sexy way they curved. She wished to God she hadn't.

She looked down at the bold white letters. "I . . . umm . . . spilled coffee on my blouse and one of the guys loaned me this. I thought I'd have time to change, but . . ." She shrugged. She was babbling. It was ridiculous. She didn't owe Cain an explanation.

"No need to apologize," he said. "I don't always wear a suit and tie."

One of her eyebrows went up. "Just most of the time?"

"Only when I have to."

"Which is most of the time?"

His faint smile broadened. Those faint grooves appeared and her stomach lifted. For God's sake, he was only a man. Good-looking, but so what? He was also rich and powerful, undoubtedly controlling. She'd dated men like Cain. She had no interest in doing it again.

He said, "Too damned much of the time—that's for sure."

She relaxed a little. Maybe he actually had a sense of humor. "Why don't we sit down?" Carly walked over to the round Formica table and metal folding chairs in the corner, and both of them sat down.

"So what can I do for you, Mr. Cain?"

"Linc would suit me better. If I can call you Carly. I feel as if I've known you for a while. Your grandfather talked a lot about you."

She wished Joe had talked about Lincoln Cain. Why hadn't he? But then they never seemed to have enough time to really talk at all.

"All right, *Linc,* what can I do for you?"

"As I said before, your grandfather and I were friends. He helped me when I needed it. In return, I'm here to help you."

She studied the strong, masculine lines of his face, noticed the beginnings of a beard shadow along his jaw. She wondered if she could trust him. "Help me how?"

Cain opened his briefcase and pulled out a sheaf of papers, set the thick stack of pages down on the table. "This is an offer to buy Drake Trucking. I expect you to take it to your financial advisor as well as your attorney, but you'll find the offer is extremely generous and the transaction will hold you harmless from any problems from the day we close the deal."

She couldn't believe it. Lincoln Cain was there to buy the company. Damn, she wished she'd had time to read more about him.

"What makes you think I'm interested in selling?"

One of his dark eyebrows went up. "I assumed that would be your first priority now that Joe's gone. You're telling me you don't want to sell?"

She didn't have to think about it. She had known almost from the day Joe died. "That's exactly what I'm saying. My grandfather's health issues left Drake in less than perfect financial condition, but with a little hard work—"

"Why go to all the trouble? If you take my offer, you can do whatever you want. You moved back here from San Francisco, I understand. As a flight attendant, you traveled all over the world. I can't imagine you'd want to stay here in Iron Springs."

He was beginning to annoy her. "Then you're a man of little imagination, Mr. Cain. Because that is exactly my plan. I've traveled. I've done the things I wanted to do. Now I'm ready for a change. I need a new challenge and I've found it right here. I'm going to rebuild Drake Trucking, make it the successful company it was before."

"It's just Linc, and that's a fine ambition, but how much experience have you had running a trucking firm?"

Not enough, but that was beside the point. "I learned a lot from Joe. I've forgotten some of it, but it's beginning to come back to me. I'm a fast learner and a hard worker. I'll figure things out."

Cain shoved the paperwork across the table. "At least take a look, see what I'm offering."

Her irritation mounted. Carly stood up from her chair. "I'll be blunt, Mr. Cain. Drake Trucking is edging toward bankruptcy. It isn't worth whatever you're offering—which you would find out as soon as you looked at the books. So I'm saving you a lot of grief by simply saying no."

Cain stood up, too, his towering height putting her at a disadvantage. "Buying companies in trouble and turning them around is what I do. I'll cut you a deal that will cover your debts and let you walk away with half a million dollars."

Half a million dollars! And all her worries over. For one crazy instant, she actually considered it. Carly shook her head. "Thank you, but no." She had a debt to repay. And she needed a purpose in life. She had found it here in Iron Springs.

His deep voice softened, rolled over her like a caress. "This deal isn't just about money, Carly. It's about friendship. Mine and Joe's. Look at the paperwork, give yourself some time to think it over, then call me. My card is in the envelope."

Carly slid the paperwork back to him. "I'm not interested. I appreciate whatever it is you think you're doing, but I'm not selling. Drake Trucking is not for sale."

He studied her for several long moments. "You're not what I expected," he said softly, making a little curl of heat slip into her stomach. Picking up the papers, he put them back in his briefcase and closed the lid.

He pulled a card out of his inside coat pocket and set it down on the table. "If you need anything, call me. It's what your grandfather would want." Grabbing the handle of the briefcase, he turned and walked out of the room.

As soon as the door closed behind him, Carly sagged down in the chair. Her hands were trembling. A shaky breath whispered out. Just being in the same room with Cain made her nervous.

She hoped he wouldn't come back again.

Chapter Three

Iron Springs was a small, typical East Texas town, with a long main street, slant parking in front of the stores, and several side streets, each a few blocks long.

The businesses were mostly flat-roofed, false-fronted buildings that hadn't changed much in the last hundred years. The most memorable feature of the town was the courthouse, a massive, gray and red stone structure with turrets and arched windows that looked like a combination Victorian mansion and something out of a Harry Potter movie.

Just for the hell of it, Cain drove past the building that morning, felt the pull of a smile at the fantastical architecture. He slowed to a stop in front of a crosswalk, waited for two gray-haired women and a kid on a beat-up bicycle. People were already out, even this early on a Saturday.

He continued down the road, not looking forward to the conversation he meant to have, pulled the big GMC up in front of a plain beige, single-story structure. As he turned off the engine, a white Ford-150 with the Drake dark blue bird-in-flight logo on the door pulled in and parked a few spaces away.

He recognized the pretty blonde who stepped down from the cab and started toward the office. She was wearing jeans and sneakers, a soft coral blouse that showed the shape of her breasts. Since she was Joe's granddaughter, he tried not to notice how perfectly they suited her feminine curves, or the way her stretch jeans drew his eye to her long legs and perfect ass.

When he started getting hard, he silently cursed.

It didn't take long to catch up with her, just outside the front door.

"Morning, Carly. I didn't expect to see you again so soon."

She turned to face him, took in his brown slacks and yellow Oxford shirt. He considered telling her he was dressed for a video conference call or he'd be in jeans, but didn't.

"I thought you'd be in Dallas," she said. "You live there, right? What are you doing in Iron Springs?"

"I've got a condo in Dallas. I like to spend my weekends at the ranch as often as possible."

"I see." For whatever reason, she didn't look happy to know he was that close by.

"You're here to see the sheriff?" he asked.

"That's right. I've called him a dozen times, but I never get any answers. I thought maybe if I came in person it would force him to tell me what's going on."

Linc thought of Emmett Howler and ignored the bad taste in his mouth. "Maybe if we talk to him together he'll get off his ass and find the men who killed Miguel Hernandez."

"That's why you're here?" she asked, clearly surprised. She was really sexy, more cute than beautiful like a lot of the women he dated. With a few pale freckles across her nose, eyebrows a little darker than her long blond hair, top lip slightly bowed, a little fuller on the bottom.

His groin stirred for the second time that morning. *Sonofabitch.* "That's right. I'm here to see Howler, just like you."

"You were at the funeral. I should have realized Miguel was a friend."

"Miguel was a friend of your grandfather's. Joe would want his killers brought to justice. I plan to make sure that happens."

"Why? I know you worked for him a long time ago, but—"

"Your grandfather gave me a job when no one else would. He stuck up for me when the whole damn world had turned against me. If it hadn't been for Joe . . ." He shook his head. "If you're really interested, we'll talk about it sometime."

Before she could press him for more, he reached for the door and pulled it open, held it so Carly could walk past him into the office.

She cast him a this-isn't-over glance as she sailed on by and he almost smiled. She wanted to know more about Joe. He liked that. She really was different from what he'd expected.

Linc followed her into an office as plain as the building itself, just a counter with a pair of desks behind it and a couple of employees.

A smaller office opened off the main room. The door stood open. He could see a pair of worn cowboy boots propped on top of a wooden desk, a battered cowboy hat resting beside them.

Howler was the cliché of a country sheriff, beer belly

and all. He'd been in office for twenty years. Emmett's great-great-granddaddy, Silas Howler, had founded Howler County and the family still wielded plenty of power.

The clerk walked up to the counter, gray-haired and slightly bent. Daisy Johnson had worked at the sheriff's office since Linc was a kid.

"Well, if it ain't Lincoln Cain," she said. "I saw in the paper a few years back you'd bought the old Blackland Ranch, but last I heard, you were stayin' out of trouble."

Linc grinned. The old woman was a pistol. "I do my best, Miss Daisy." He turned. "This is Carly Drake, Joe Drake's granddaughter."

"Hello, Daisy," Carly said. "It's nice to meet you."

"You, too. Your granddaddy was a real good man."

"Thank you. Yes, he was."

"We need to talk to the sheriff about the Hernandez murder," Linc said.

Daisy's face wrinkled into a frown. "Bad business, that. I'll tell Sheriff Howler you're here."

The shuffle of boots drew their attention. "No need, Daisy—I got eyes." Howler ambled out of his office, tipped up his chin as a signal to Linc. "You want to talk, you and the little lady come on back."

Linc caught the stiffness that crept into Carly's shoulders. Looked like Joe's granddaughter was going to get along with the sheriff about as well as both Linc and her grandpa had. If they weren't there to find a killer, he might have smiled.

They followed Howler into his office and he sat down in the chair behind his desk. "What can I do for you?"

Carly spoke up. "I want to know what you're doing to find the men who murdered Miguel Hernandez."

Howler leaned forward across his desk. "Don't get yourself in a fret. We're gonna find 'em. Just takes time. This ain't San Francisco, little lady." He flashed Cain a sneer. "It ain't Dallas, neither. Our deputies have been out there asking questions, following up leads. But nobody saw nothin' and there ain't no sign of the truck."

"What about the crime scene?" Linc asked. "Surely some kind of forensic evidence turned up where the body was found."

Howler shook his head. "Just because you spent time behind bars, don't make you an expert on the law."

Linc ignored a shot of irritation. He and Howler had a history and it wasn't a good one. His gaze went to Carly. No surprise in those big blue eyes. Clearly she had done her homework before he'd shown up for yesterday's meeting. She knew he'd been in prison but instead of disapproval, she was glaring at the sheriff.

"There's no need for you to be rude, Sheriff Howler. Mr. Cain asked you a question that deserves an answer. I'd like to hear it myself."

Howler grunted. "Truth is, we didn't find much of anything. The morning Hernandez's body was discovered, it had rained off and on during the night. Any DNA evidence was washed away."

Linc thought of the detective he had hired. He wanted answers. He didn't figure he'd get them from Howler and so far he was right.

"Who found him?" Carly asked.

"Man and his wife driving back to Dallas from a visit to their folks in Texarkana. They'd pulled off to the side of the road to let their dog out to take a leak. Dog must have scented the body on the other side of the road. Hernandez had been dead a while by then."

Carly glanced away.

"What's the coroner give for time of death?" Linc asked.

"Between eleven P.M. and one A.M. You can talk to Doc Bradshaw yourself if you'd like."

"Conchita said she got a phone call from Miguel about eleven," Carly said. "He was fueling up at a truck stop a few miles south of Dallas. He told her he'd be home a little after midnight."

"Seventy miles to Iron Springs from Dallas," Linc said. "No traffic that time of night. Looks like the coroner got it right."

The sheriff picked up a pen on his desk and began to click it open and closed. "I know you want those bastards caught and so do I. But standing here jawing about it ain't gonna help. I need to get back to work."

Carly ignored him. "From the start, you've assumed there was more than one hijacker. Why is that?"

"Found traces of where a vehicle had been parked in front of the body. We think Hernandez pulled over to the side of the road behind the car, someone pretending to have engine trouble. He got out and walked up to the vehicle. Whoever it was, shot him, stole the truck, and drove away. Since the car was gone, too, someone else had to have been driving it."

"I'd like to take a look at the reports," Linc said. "Coroner's, deputies', any statements that were taken, everything you've got."

The sheriff came out of his chair. "That ain't gonna happen. You got no business in this and that's the way it's gonna stay."

Linc clenched his teeth to keep from saying something he'd regret.

Carly walked up to the desk, leaned over, and got

right in Howler's face. "Miguel Hernandez worked for me, Sheriff. That makes his death my business. I want to see those reports."

The sheriff's jaw went tight. "Now listen here, little lady—"

"My name is Carly or you can call me Ms. Drake." Those big blue eyes were spitting fire. Linc could almost see Joe's blood pumping through her veins.

"If you don't want more trouble than you've already got," she said, "you'll let me see those files."

Howler's face went beet red. "All right, fine. As a courtesy—and so you're satisfied there ain't nothing there—I'll let you see what's in the files."

"I can pick the information up or you can drop it off at my office whenever it's ready. Just call and let me know." Carly turned and started walking. "Have a good day, Sheriff."

They crossed the office together. Linc opened the door, then followed her out of the building, over to her truck.

"I know you want answers," he said. "So do I. But murder can be a dangerous business. Be better if you didn't get involved."

"I don't trust Howler to do the job."

"Neither do I. Which is why I've hired a private investigator to look into the case. His name's Ross Townsend. He's worked for me before so I know he's good."

"Has he found anything yet?"

"Not yet, but he's just getting started. Call me when you get those files. Look them over, then I'll take a look. Maybe one of us will see something the sheriff missed."

"All right. But in exchange I expect you to tell me what your investigator finds out."

Linc shook his head. "Like I said, Carly, you need to stay out of this."

She cocked a hand on her hip and looked up at him. "By now you must realize that isn't going to happen."

Irritation warred with amusement. Amusement won out. "Yeah, I guess I do." Another of Joe's traits—she was just as bullheaded. Joe wouldn't want her involved, but the determined set of her jaw said even Joe wouldn't have been able to stop her.

Linc jerked open her pickup door and Carly climbed in behind the wheel.

The engine started. He watched the pickup pull onto the road, heading back in the direction of Drake Trucking. He checked his watch. Forty-five minutes till his conference call on the tire rebuilding plant he was trying to open just east of Pleasant Hill. He didn't have time to think of Carly Drake and he didn't want to.

He couldn't deny he was attracted to her, all that sexy blond hair and a body that made a man want to strip her down and take her a dozen different ways.

He knew why Joe had never mentioned him to her over the years. He'd been a hell-raiser even after prison. Nothing illegal by then, but he'd liked to party and he'd liked beautiful women. And he'd had plenty of them. Still did.

Joe had wanted someone special for Carly. He hadn't wanted an ex-con taking advantage of his granddaughter.

But things were different now. Joe had trusted Linc with Carly's welfare and that meant keeping her safe.

Even from him.

He climbed into his truck. As soon as he had finished his conference call, he was taking the rest of the day off. He needed some time away, needed some space to breathe. He was meeting old friends and going for a ride.

Linc couldn't wait to get on the road.

Chapter Four

From the sheriff's department, Carly went home. She'd been at work earlier, planned to go back a little later, but she could use some lunch before she returned. And there was plenty to do at the house.

Little by little, she was cleaning out Joe's stuff, a difficult job even without all the memories and sorrow that went along with a lot of hard work.

She drove Joe's F-150 into the garage and went into the kitchen of the little beige two-bedroom, two-bath ranch-style house. She'd already cleaned everything out in here, arranged the dishes and pans the way she liked. After so many years, the walls had turned a dull robin's egg blue, but she'd painted them a nice pale yellow.

The whole house needed painting, but once she'd started working at the yard, she hadn't had time. She planned to fix the place up: new carpet and drapes, new furniture. She'd get around to it, but the company had to come first. Once Drake was making money again, she'd be able to afford it.

Carly sighed. If she didn't get things back on track at

Drake, she wouldn't have enough to pay the property taxes. Hell, the way she was going through her savings, she wouldn't have enough to buy groceries.

She fixed herself a bologna sandwich with real mayonnaise, a treat, and carried it and a glass of milk toward the living room.

The moment she stepped through the opening from the kitchen, a prickle of unease slipped down her spine. Something was out of place; she could feel it. She glanced at the worn beige sofa and chairs, at the brass lamps on the maple end tables that had been in the house since Grandpa Joe had brought her to live with him when she was ten years old.

Nothing seemed out of order, no sign that anything had been moved. Still, the feeling persisted.

Setting the sandwich and milk down on an end table, she walked quietly down the hallway and turned into the bedroom. When a noise sounded, her pulse leaped and she whirled toward the sound, sure someone was going to jump out at her. She relaxed when she realized the air conditioner had just kicked in.

Nothing to worry about. She just hadn't been living in the house long enough to get used to the everyday creaks and moans.

There was no one in the bedroom, nothing out of place. She returned to the living room, glanced down at the maple coffee table in front of the sofa. The latest copy of *Overdrive,* a trucker's magazine Joe had subscribed to, sat next to the *Iron Springs Gazette.*

Her unease returned, stronger now, making her palms go damp. She could have sworn she'd left the magazine on the other end of the table.

Her breath caught when she spotted the note, hand-written on half a sheet of yellow lined paper torn out of a legal pad. Her pulse accelerated. Her hand shook as she reached for it, started to read the message.

Sell Drake Trucking to Cain and you'll be as dead as Hernandez.

Carly started trembling. She needed to call the sheriff, but her cell was in her purse, which was in the kitchen, and after her encounter with Howler that morning, she didn't want another confrontation.

Telling herself not to panic, that she was fairly certain whoever had been in the house was gone, she hurried back to the bedroom, went over to the nightstand, and punched in the digital code that unlocked the metal gun safe sitting on top of it.

Lifting the lid, she took out Joe's semiautomatic pistol, a Glock nine millimeter he'd carried on long-haul runs. She'd fired the gun when she'd been in high school, gotten to be a pretty good shot. Joe had insisted she learn how to handle a pistol so that she could defend herself, but that had been years ago.

She studied the weapon, found the release button and dropped the clip, saw the magazine was full, and shoved it back in. The heavy metal click felt comforting as it vibrated up her arm.

She racked the slide, sending a cartridge into the chamber and cocking the weapon, then, just to be safe, carried it in to check the bathroom off the master bedroom. Finding it empty, she checked the closets and under the bed.

In the spare bedroom, she found the point of entry. One of the windows overlooking the backyard had been broken. She checked the room, then the bathroom at the end of the hall, reminding herself to call the glass company and have the broken window replaced.

In a small community like Iron Springs, there wasn't

much crime. Joe had never considered installing a security system, hadn't really needed one, and though that had clearly changed, at the moment she couldn't afford to have it done.

She thought again of the note, ridiculously thought of calling Lincoln Cain.

Sell Drake Trucking to Cain and you'll be as dead as Hernandez.

Since she wasn't selling to Cain or anyone else, she shouldn't need to worry.

But what did the note mean? Why had someone gone to so much trouble to deliver it? What did Miguel Hernandez's murder have to do with Cain? What did it have to do with Drake Trucking?

She went back to the master bedroom, found the clip holster for the pistol in one of the drawers in the nightstand, and shoved in the Glock. From now on, she was taking the pistol to work with her.

In the end, she called the sheriff's office, stayed till a deputy named Rollins arrived. The deputy bagged the note, dusted for fingerprints around the bedroom window, and took her statement.

"It's probably just some kid's idea of a joke," he said. "Everyone knows about the murder."

"A joke," Carly said darkly.

"Well, it's not very funny, but these days that's how some kids think."

"Why did the note mention Cain?"

The deputy just shrugged. In dark brown pants and a beige uniform shirt with a Texas state badge on the sleeve, he was beanpole thin, his ears sticking out beneath a tan felt cowboy hat.

"Cain's the richest guy around," he said. "Maybe the

kids just figured, Cain being in the trucking business and a friend of Joe's, he'd be making you an offer."

"That's crazy. No way would a kid think something like that."

The deputy just gave another shrug. "We might get prints. That could give us some answers. We'll let you know if anything turns up." The deputy helped her board up the window, then drove off in his white county sheriff's pickup as if nothing of any importance had occurred.

It seemed so anticlimactic, Carly wished she hadn't called.

By two o'clock she was back at the office. She told Donna about the break-in but asked her not to tell anyone else. The company was hanging on by a thread. She didn't want to give the employees anything more to worry about.

By seven-thirty, everyone had gone home and Carly was completely wrung-out. She'd made a few more marketing calls, but Saturdays weren't the best day to try to drum up business.

She was just packing up to leave when her cell phone rang.

"Hey, Carly, it's Row. How you doin', girl?" Rowena Drummond was another high school friend. They had reconnected since Carly's return and were rapidly rebuilding their relationship.

Carly sighed into her cell phone. "I've had better days if you want the truth. I feel as beat as a pounded steak."

Row laughed. "I've got a cure for that. My shift at the roadhouse ends in twenty minutes. Meet me there and I'll buy your first beer."

Besides her part-time job as a bookkeeper—the only

work in the area Rowena had been able to find—she bartended at Jubal's Roadhouse, a local joint a few miles out of town.

"I really shouldn't," Carly said. "I have to work tomorrow and I still haven't got the house sorted out." Which made her think of the break-in and the window that wouldn't be fixed until Monday. She ignored a little chill.

"Come on, Carly. You can't work all the time."

She took a deep breath, slowly released it. God, a night to relax sounded so good. "You're right. It's Saturday night. Make it a shot of tequila and you're on."

Rowena chuckled. "You sure about that? As I recall, tequila makes your clothes fall off."

Carly laughed. "It only happened once and it was a long time ago. I'll see you in twenty."

Jubal's Roadhouse was one of Joe's favorite hangouts. A lot of truckers went there after work for good cheap food and pitchers of beer.

She thought of the threatening note. The roadhouse could be a little rough sometimes and it was a ways out of town. But the Glock was under the driver's seat of the pickup. If she was really worried, she could take the required courses and get a concealed carry permit.

She slung her purse over her shoulder. Was she really thinking about it? What had happened to the first-class flight attendant who spent too much on clothes, wouldn't be caught dead without makeup, and had a standing appointment at the spa?

A lot had changed since she had come home, none of it good. Joe was gone. Miguel Hernandez was dead, her house had been broken into, and she was receiving threatening messages.

None of that mattered. She was back in Texas and she wasn't leaving. Carly took a deep breath, thought of the gun in the truck, and walked out the door.

The buzz of raucous laughter and conversation was revving up by the time Carly got to the roadhouse. She settled herself on the bar stool next to Rowena, a shapely, outspoken redhead just the opposite of shy, willowy Brittany, though all three of them were good friends.

After she'd left the yard, Carly had worked up her courage and stopped by the house to change. No intruder lurked inside as she pulled on a pair of dark blue skinny jeans with rhinestones on the back pockets, a red tank top that showed a little cleavage, then slid her feet into a pair of red cowboy boots.

Hey, it was Saturday night at the roadhouse. She might not have lived in Texas for the last few years, but nothing ever really changed.

She glanced at the bartender, a guy named Ricardo, a good-looking Latino with thick black hair and a sexy smile. He set the shot of Patrón that Row had ordered for her down on the bar, set a Jack and Coke down in front of Row.

"*Salud,*" he said with a grin, the Spanish version of *cheers.* He had to be at least five years younger than Carly, but the black eyes that measured the shape of her breasts said he didn't care.

Carly smiled and lifted the glass. "*Salud,*" she said, determined to enjoy her night off. She took a drink, not the whole shot—she didn't have a death wish— followed it with a lick of salt off the back of her hand,

and bit into the lime he'd set on a napkin next to the glass.

Always up for a good time, Rowena laughed at something the tall cowboy next to her said and took a sip of her drink.

The bar was about half full, with more people arriving all the time. Carly glanced around, enjoying the peanut-shells-on-the-floor atmosphere, the clack of pool balls, and the Willie Nelson song playing on the digital jukebox in the corner. She recognized her foreman, Gordy Mitchell, and another driver laughing in the corner with a couple of other truckers.

A lot of the regulars drove pickups and wore cowboy hats. There'd been a bunch of flashy motorcycles parked out in front, flames on the gas tank of one, a dragon on another, one glossy jet black with a black leather seat trimmed with silver conchos.

The roadhouse was the kind of place where cowboys and bikers mixed with the locals and everyone got along.

Mostly.

Carly had been back a few times over the years when she'd come home for a visit. One of those times she'd gotten a little drunk on tequila and started dancing on the table. The next thing she remembered was swimming naked in the pool at some guy's apartment. Fortunately Rowena had been with her, and even drunk they'd been smart enough to leave before they got in way over their heads.

She barely remembered the cab ride home, but she remembered how sick she'd been in the morning. She smiled as she took another sip of Patrón. *Never again.*

Laughter erupted from a table along the wall. From the corner of her eye, she caught a glimpse of black leather, guys in chaps and vests. The bikers. Four men, one with gleaming black hair, one dark-haired, tall, and brawny, one black with a shaved head, a blond guy with a horseshoe mustache and hair a little too long, all in great physical condition and sporting tattoos in various shapes and sizes.

Her gaze returned to the big guy, though she could only see his profile. Beneath a snug black T-shirt, a massive chest, and shoulders bulging with muscle. The tat of a single strand of barbed wire circled a huge left bicep. Two of the other men had colorful tattoo sleeves.

The big man laughed at something one of the others had said, a deep, husky sound. He turned a little and she caught a flash of white teeth in an amazingly handsome face. Carly blinked.

"What is it?" Row asked.

"Nothing." She shook her head. "For an instant I thought that big guy over there was Lincoln Cain. Crazy, huh?"

Row started nodding. "That's Cain. God, that man is gorgeous. A body like solid steel and a face that breaks hearts all over the country. And here he is, sitting in Jubal's Roadhouse just like your everyday Hell's Angel."

"No way."

"Well, not really. Those guys are all reformed. They used to ride with the Asphalt Demons, but one's a dental surgeon now and the other two are lawyers. They live in the area. They still get together to ride."

She couldn't stop shaking her head. "That . . . that can't be Cain." Her gaze slid back across the room. Just then he looked over at the bar, and before she could look away, he spotted her.

Brilliant green eyes locked on her face and she

couldn't stop staring. With supreme effort, she forced her attention back to Rowena.

"No man should look that good, right?" Row said.

Carly's face felt hot. Beneath her tank top, her nipples were hard. Dear God, Cain, the wealthy, expensively dressed entrepreneur, was one thing. Cain, the sexy tattooed biker, was completely amazing. She watched him shove up from his chair and start striding toward her and her pulse went through the roof.

Row smiled and waved. "Oh, good, he's coming over."

Her nerves rocketed skyward. *Not good, not good, not good.*

"Do you know him?" Row asked.

"We've . . . umm . . . met a couple of times. He was a friend of Grandpa Joe's."

"Yeah, I knew that." Row turned around on the bar stool, beamed as Cain walked up, the ultimate beefcake in black chaps over a pair of black jeans. The chaps outlined the bulge beneath his zipper, and suddenly she felt dizzy.

Row smiled. "Hey, Linc. Been a while. Good to see you."

"You, too, Row."

With her impressive cleavage and curvy figure, Rowena was a total man magnet, but Cain's gaze slid past her, moved over Carly's body as if he wanted to explore every inch. She forced herself to breathe.

"Can I buy you two a drink?" He looked up at the bartender. "Get the girls another round, Ricardo."

"Will do, Mr. C."

He didn't order anything for himself, just stood patiently waiting for them to be served. Several women were casting him glances, clearly liking what they saw. Carly had to admit, black leather suited him.

"So I guess one of those Harleys out front is yours," she said, working to make conversation.

"That's right. I like to ride. Gives me a chance to breathe."

She studied his face. "The black one, right? That one's yours."

The sexy way his mouth curved made the bottom drop out of her stomach. *Soo not good.*

"That's right. How'd you know?"

"That bike's all about power and control. That would be you."

His gaze remained on her face. "Or maybe I just like black." He turned to look at the three other men in his group, who were watching them as if they were performers on stage. "Old friends," he said. "Come on, I'll introduce you. Row already knows them."

Carly slipped off the bar stool, felt Cain's big hand at her waist as he walked her across the room. She tried not to notice the heat spreading out through her body.

He stopped in front of the battered wooden table. "The blond guy with the 'stache, that's Rick Dugan. You need your wisdom teeth pulled, he's your man." Dugan saluted, flashing a white grin that was a walking ad for his work.

"The black guy with the shaved head—that's Delroy Aimes. We call him Del." The black guy winked. "He's a criminal attorney. If you get in trouble, he's a good man to know."

Del chuckled.

"The guy with the pretty face and goofy grin is Johnnie Banducci."

"Hello, sweet thing," Johnnie said, clearly the ladies'

man of the group, though he wasn't much competition to Cain; at least Carly didn't think so.

"Guys, this is Carly Drake, Joe Drake's granddaughter."

Carly smiled. "Nice to meet you all. I live in Iron Springs now so I'm sure we'll be running into each other once in a while."

"Oh, I hope so, darlin'," Johnnie said.

Carly wished Cain would step back out of her space but instead he moved a little closer. The smile fell off Johnnie's face.

Carly looked up at Cain. "I need to get back to Row. I'll leave you to your friends. Thanks for the drink."

"My pleasure," he said.

Carly considered telling him about the note, but now wasn't a good time. Maybe she'd call him tomorrow. Or maybe not.

He walked her back to her seat at the bar, then sat back down with his friends.

"Wow," Row said as Carly climbed up on the bar stool. "That was interesting."

"What was interesting? You mean because he came over to say hello? He's helping the sheriff with the Hernandez case. We both wound up at the department this morning at the same time."

Row shook her head, shifting the dark red curls across her shoulders. "What was interesting was the way he was looking at you. Cain has a standing rule—no messing with the women in Howler County—or anywhere else around here. Blackland Ranch is his personal refuge. That's what he calls it. He doesn't want any hassles, and a pissed-off former bedmate can be a very big pain in the ass. Cain dates women in Dallas or pretty much anywhere he wants, but not here."

"Probably smart," she said, ignoring a stupid little pang.

"Yeah, that's his rule. But the way he was looking at you? Kind of seemed like he was thinking of breaking the rule."

Carly ignored a little jolt of something she refused to name. Cain had his choice of women. Even if he were interested in her, no way was she lining up in that queue. She reached for her tequila and finished the shot, took a sip from the fresh shot Cain had bought.

"We better order some food or we aren't going to be able to drive home," Row said. "Burgers sound good?"

She hadn't eaten much that day, and suddenly realized she was starving. "A burger sounds great." Then she was going home before the tequila kicked in, before the drink made her think of Cain and what might happen if her clothes fell off.

Chapter Five

It was time for Linc to go home. He didn't drink more than a beer or two when he was riding and he never stayed late. But Carly was still sitting at the bar, and with the trouble swirling around her, he wanted to be sure she got home safely.

Yesterday at the meeting in her office, she had dropped the bombshell that Drake Trucking was edging toward bankruptcy. Joe Drake had been a very successful businessman all his life. His health issues and medical bills could have been the source of his money problems, as Carly had suggested. Maybe it was the reason Joe had come to him for help.

But Joe hadn't mentioned money at all, and Linc had a feeling the old man didn't know how bad things had gotten. Linc wanted to know what had happened to take the company down so fast, and he intended to find out.

Be easier with Carly's cooperation, but that might take some convincing. She already saw him as powerful and controlling—which he was. But he was more than those things, or at least tried to be.

He needed to know what was happening at Drake Trucking, but first he'd do a little digging, ask around, see what he could turn up on his own.

He wondered if money problems were behind the hijacking and murder. Tomorrow he'd call Townsend, fill him in, and see if his P.I. had come up with anything.

In the meantime, his friends were still there. Johnnie was shuffling around the dance floor with Rowena to a slow country song on the jukebox. Carly had caught the eye of every man in the bar, though she seemed not to notice, or maybe she just didn't care.

She was polite, but not overly friendly, which for reasons he didn't want to consider, suited Linc just fine.

"You ridin' with us tomorrow?" Del asked.

Linc shook his head. One day off was manageable, two, not so much. "Gotta work. Maybe next weekend."

"I can't go, either," Rick grumbled. "I promised Ashley I'd take her on a picnic."

Johnnie sipped his beer. "If I had a girl as pretty as Ash, I wouldn't mind," he said.

"Yeah, just think what's gonna happen on that blanket after you're done with the food." Del wiggled his eyebrows, and Rick's fair complexion turned red.

The men returned to talking and Linc leaned back in his chair. Carly was packing up to leave. He'd give her a few minutes, then follow her outside. He'd stay in the shadows, just to make sure she got on the road okay. Linc leaned back and took a sip of his now-warm beer.

Carly slung her fringed leather bag over her shoulder. "It's been fun," she said to Rowena.

"Call me." Row waved as Carly headed for the door.

Cain was still there, she knew. She'd done her best to ignore him all evening, but it hadn't really worked. She could sense his presence like a big, looming shadow.

She didn't like it. She was determined to make Drake Trucking successful again. With the troubles she was facing, she needed to stay focused, be able to think clearly. Somehow that didn't happen when Cain was around.

She shoved through the old-fashioned swinging doors, out into the warm Texas night. Stepping down off the wooden boardwalk, she headed for her truck.

She was standing in front of the driver's door, digging her keys out of her purse, when a noise sounded behind her and a hand clamped her mouth. A man jerked her back against his chest and fear hit her. Carly twisted, tried to break free, slammed an elbow into his ribs and heard him grunt, then stomped her boot down on the arch of his foot. He swore but didn't let go.

Another man grabbed her, pinned her against the side of the truck. Her pulse raced when she spotted a third man, a big dark Latino with slicked back hair and a bushy mustache. A sharp click sounded and she saw the flash of silver as his switchblade popped open.

"Stop fighting, *chica,* before you get hurt."

She breathed through her nose and told herself not to move as the blade settled against the side of her neck, but her heart was hammering, trying to tear through her ribs.

"Did you get the message we delivered this morning?" the man with the mustache asked.

Had to be the scrap of paper she'd found in her living room. She managed to nod.

"We're here to make sure you understand. Do you see how easy it would be for us to kill you?"

When she didn't nod, the man holding her from behind tightened his hold, one of his hands sliding up to cup her breast. He squeezed lewdly and fresh fear rolled through her.

"Do you see?" the man with the knife repeated, the blade moving slightly as she swallowed.

She gave him a nod.

"El Jefe wishes to see you. Someone will call, let you know when and where. You will say nothing about tonight. No police, you understand?"

She nodded that she understood.

"Go home, *querida*." The mustached man ran a gloved hand over her cheek in an intimate caress, and nausea rolled in her stomach. "We will meet again soon."

"Hey, you! Get away from her!"

Carly's heart jerked. She knew that deep voice, knew it belonged to Lincoln Cain, and for once she was glad to see him.

The men started running toward the road, Cain hard on their heels. He grabbed the closest man by the collar at the back of his neck and jerked. The guy whirled and swung a punch Cain ducked. Cain's powerful arm shot out and buried itself in the middle of the guy's stomach, doubling him over. Another punch sent him careening backward. The man hit the ground, rolled, came up on his feet, and kept running, Cain close behind him.

A car burst out of nowhere, a big black SUV. Shots rang out from the driver's open window. Carly screamed when Cain went down. The car slowed long enough for her attackers to pile inside and Carly ran toward Cain.

He grabbed her wrist, jerked her down on top of him, and rolled her beneath him, shielding her with his body as the car sped off down the road, a couple of shots firing into the air, tires screeching on the asphalt as the vehicle disappeared.

Carly struggled to breathe, her heart beating frantically beneath the big body pinning her down. Cain lifted himself away and got to his feet, reached down, caught her hand, and hauled her up beside him.

"I thought . . . thought they'd shot you." She could still feel the imprint of his big, hard body, hear the slide of black leather as he had moved to protect her. "Are you okay?" Her voice was shaking, but so was everything else.

Cain swore foully. "I'm fine, smart enough to take cover, not run toward a guy who's shooting at me. You should have stayed back. You could have been killed."

She looked up at him. "So could you, but you came to help me anyway. I figured I owed you the same."

He just stared at her as if she'd lost her mind; then a faint smile touched his lips. "What the hell happened? Are you all right? Dammit, you're shaking." He pulled her into his arms, and though she told herself to push him away, she relaxed into that big broad chest and for the first time felt safe.

"Did they hurt you?" he asked, smoothing back her hair.

"No, but I thought . . . thought they were going to."

"You're safe now. Just take it easy."

His warmth seeped into her and her trembling began to ease. "I'd just reached the pickup. They seemed . . . seemed to come out of nowhere. I tried to fight, but one of them had a switchblade. He held the knife against my throat."

The F word whispered out beneath his breath. "Your legs are still shaking. Can you walk?"

She looked up at him. "I don't want to go back inside. I don't want any more trouble."

He glanced back toward the roadhouse. With all the noise, no one had heard the shots. "Give me your keys. We'll go someplace quiet where we can talk. There's a little café down the road. A friend of mine owns it. No one will bother us there."

She was too shaken up to argue, just dug her keys out of her purse and handed them over, let him help her into the passenger seat, buckle her in, and close the door. The adrenaline was wearing off. She felt completely drained.

Carly closed her eyes as Cain pulled the pickup out of the parking lot and drove off down the road.

It was eleven P.M. The sign for Loretta's Café glowed like a dull moon in the darkness. Linc parked Carly's pickup, walked around and helped her down, slid an arm around her waist as he led her inside.

"Two coffees, Loretta, and some privacy. Thanks, hon."

"No problem, Ace."

He gave her a slight smile, the best he could manage under the circumstances. He was supposed to be watching out for Carly. He had promised Joe. Tonight men had attacked her with a knife. When he'd seen her struggling, his protective instincts had kicked in and he'd wanted to tear them apart limb by limb.

In the old days he might have tried. He was a different man now. Smarter. More in control. He fought more with his head these days than his hands, though he still hit the heavy bag, even sparred with a partner once in a while.

They sat down at a table covered by a pink vinyl cloth. Loretta, a fifty-something blonde, set two china mugs of coffee in front of them and quietly walked away.

Cain turned to Carly, whose face was the same bone white as the mug. She hadn't told him everything. He'd made a fortune reading people. She hadn't lied but she was holding something back.

"Those guys weren't muggers," he said. "They wanted more than just your tempting little body. Something's going on. What is it?"

She hesitated several moments. Then a sigh whispered out. "Someone broke into my house this morning after I left. When I came home from the sheriff's office, I found a note on the coffee table. The message was a warning. 'Sell Drake Trucking to Cain and you'll be as dead as Hernandez.'"

Frustration tore through him. "Why didn't you call me? I gave you my card. I told you if you needed anything—"

"I called the sheriff. A deputy named Rollins came out and took my statement. He dusted for fingerprints around the broken window. They're also checking for fingerprints on the note."

He wanted to shake her, make her understand that he was there for her. He summoned his legendary control. "How did these guys know about the offer I made?"

"I don't know. People saw you at the yard. Donna asked me about it. I told her you wanted to buy the company. Since I didn't plan to sell, it wasn't really a secret."

"No, and word travels fast in Iron Springs. How's the note connected to what happened tonight?"

She wrapped her hands around the mug as if she needed something to hold on to. "The men in the parking lot . . . they asked if I'd gotten their message. They said they wanted me to understand how easy it would be to kill me. They said someone named El Jefe wanted a meeting. They said they'd let me know when and where."

Anger whipped through him, made his neck feel tight. "How'd they know you were at Jubal's?"

Her head came up. "I don't know. I hadn't thought about it until now, but . . . they must have been watching the yard, followed me after I left the office. Or they could have been watching my house. I stopped at home to change before I went out."

He shoved up from the table, paced away and back, trying to work off some steam. The place was empty except for an old man in a knit cap sipping coffee at the far end of the counter.

Linc took a couple of calming breaths, returned to the table, and sat back down. "I wish I'd punched that bastard harder."

Carly didn't quite smile. "What about El Jefe? Do you know who he is?"

"No, but by tomorrow I will."

Her mug trembled when she lifted it. She steadied her grip and took a drink, then set the mug back down on the table. He forced himself not to reach for her hand.

"They warned me not to call the police."

He sighed. "Howler's a worthless piece of . . . The sheriff's worthless anyway. Until we know what's going on, it might be better to leave him out of it."

She took a sip of coffee. It was black and old this time of night, but she didn't complain.

"I want you to know you can trust me, Carly. Your grandfather did. I went to see Joe at the hospital after his first heart attack. I promised him if anything happened to him, I'd look out for you. It's what Joe wanted."

She straightened in her chair, blue eyes zeroing in on his face. "Wait a minute. That's what your sudden interest in buying Drake was all about? You were doing it for Joe?"

"Drake's a viable company, worth my time. But the truth is I owe Joe, Carly. When I got out of prison, I was a pariah to everyone around. I had no money. No one would hire me. I couldn't get work as a dog catcher. I heard Drake Trucking was looking for a laborer. The day I interviewed for the job, I told Joe the truth, that I was an ex-con trying to turn my life around. Joe stepped up. He gave me work doing odd jobs in the yard. As soon as I turned twenty-one, he taught me to drive a truck. I learned the business, learned to be a man instead of a loser."

"Why don't I remember you?"

"I only worked for Joe a little over a year. You were just a kid back then, a sophomore in high school, I think. Probably more interested in clothes and teenage boys than your grandpa's business."

She nodded. "I was pretty much a girlie girl back then. I didn't hit my tomboy phase until a few years later."

His gaze flicked down to her pretty breasts. Tomboy? Not hardly. "By the time I came back to Iron Springs, you were all grown up and off on your own. But Joe and I stayed friends. Whenever things got tough, I thought of Joe. I knew he was the kind of guy who'd never give up, so I didn't either. I owe Joe Drake everything and the only thing he ever asked me in return was to watch out for you."

"I realize you're trying to help, but—"

"Think about the offer I made. We'll work out the details, come to an agreement on the price. Whatever's going on, I'll handle it and you'll be safe."

Carly shot up from her chair. Hands on her hips, she stood there glaring down at him. "I don't need someone to handle things for me, Cain. I'm twenty-nine years old. I've been on my own for years. I owe Joe, too. I'm going to make Drake successful again and I'm going to do it on my own. I don't want or need any help from you."

Linc couldn't believe it. For the first time he could recall, a woman didn't want something from him. Not his money, not his influence, not his protection.

"Please sit down," he said calmly, though he didn't feel calm at all. Carly Drake riled him up in a way no woman ever had. She pissed him off. She challenged him. She heated him up. And he liked it.

Carly sat back down. "I don't have any choice. You've got my car keys."

He managed not to smile. "I'll tell you what. Maybe we can call a truce. You owe Joe and so do I. Maybe we can work together to make things right."

She eyed him with suspicion. "How's that going to happen?"

"We're both trying to find Miguel's killer, right?"

"That's right."

"The note you got mentioned his death. What happened tonight connects the murder, the break-in, the note, and El Jefe."

"Yes, but what does it have to do with you and Drake Trucking?"

"I'm not sure yet, but I've got Ross Townsend working on it. If we share information, maybe we can figure out what's going on."

She seemed to ponder that. "You're talking to Townsend tomorrow, right? How about making it a conference call? I'll be working at the office. You could patch me in. I want to hear what the man has to say."

"I'll do better than that. I'll come down to the yard and we'll take the call there. That way we can brainstorm a little beforehand."

She didn't look excited about it, but she was nodding her head. "All right, that'll work."

"There's one last thing."

One blond eyebrow arched up. "Why am I not surprised?"

"Whatever happens, you can't meet El Jefe alone. I know you don't want anything from me and I assume that includes my protection, but—"

She reached across the table, rested her hand over his. A rush of heat went straight to his groin.

"Joe didn't raise a fool," she said, drawing her hand away as if maybe she'd felt it, too. "I'm grateful for what you did—I don't know many guys who would take on three dangerous men for a woman they barely knew. I'll let you know the minute I hear from El Jefe. I'll talk to you before I do anything, okay?"

He nodded. "Fair enough." Though he'd already decided to put security on her twenty-four/seven. He just couldn't let her know. He stood up from his chair. "Come on, let's get you home."

Carly just nodded.

She sat quietly in the pickup all the way back to the roadhouse. Linc wondered what she was thinking.

Chapter Six

Carly pulled the pickup into her garage, saw the single headlight of Linc's impressive black Harley coming down the street behind her. He'd insisted on following her home. She waved as she got out of the truck, hoping he would take the hint and leave, but instead he pulled his motorcycle into the driveway behind the truck and turned off the engine.

As she took the pistol out from under the seat, Linc walked up beside her.

He eased the gun out of her hand. "Stay here till I make sure it's safe."

She didn't argue. Now that she was home, the whole terrifying chain of events came rushing back with stark clarity. She followed Cain into the kitchen, thought of the Glock, and wished she'd had it in her hand when those men had attacked her.

She sank down in a kitchen chair to wait while Cain walked through the rest of the house. Tears welled. Dammit, she didn't want to cry. Joe had taught her to be tough. He'd known he wouldn't always be there for her.

But deep down inside, she was still the frightened ten-year-old who had walked into the bathroom and found her mother on the floor, dead of a drug overdose.

She closed her eyes, bit back a sob. She didn't realize she was crying till she felt Cain drawing her out of the chair and into his arms.

For several seconds she let him hold her, let the tears come, just wrapped her arms around his thick neck and hung on. Then she realized what she was doing and felt like a fool, eased back, and turned away.

"I'm sorry, I'm not . . . not a crier. Not usually. I'm sorry." She wiped her eyes, mortified that he had seen this side of her.

"Hey. It's been a helluva day." His mouth edged into a smile. "Maybe I'm the one who needed a hug, okay?"

She managed a smile in return. She wouldn't have thought he could be sweet. "Thanks for checking the house."

"No problem. You sure you'll be okay?"

Her smile returned, more real this time. "You're bigger than I am, but I've got the gun." Now resting on the kitchen table.

He chuckled. "All right, if you're sure, I'll see you in the morning."

He'd see her in the morning? Dammit, she'd forgotten he was coming to the office tomorrow for the call to his private investigator. "Good night."

Cain left the house through the garage, swung a long leg over the seat of his Harley, and fired up the engine. The biceps in his huge arms bulged as he grabbed the handlebars. Carly pushed the button on the garage door as he started backing away, turned the bike, and roared off down the block.

Exhaustion swamped her. Dragging herself into the bedroom, she stripped off her clothes, pulled on an XXL navy blue Drake Trucking T-shirt she liked to sleep in, and crawled beneath the covers. The pistol rested on the nightstand. She should have been able to sleep.

But she couldn't.

Linc got up Sunday morning at the crack of dawn, loaded his fishing gear onto the back of an ATV, and took off to one of the two lakes on Blackland Ranch. He'd called Townsend way too late last night and told him what had happened at the roadhouse. He'd instructed the investigator to set up security on Carly Drake twenty-four/seven and find out everything he could about a guy who called himself El Jefe.

Linc had slept a little after that, not much. He'd awoken early and decided he needed to clear his head. Tossing a line in the water, kicking back, and waiting to get a bite worked almost as well as morning sex.

Well, not quite. Hell, he hadn't been with a woman in nearly a month, too damned long as far as he was concerned. He needed to make a phone call, talk to Renee or maybe Melissa, see if one of his *friends with benefits* was up for a good time when he got back to Dallas.

Something stirred deep and hot inside him, made him begin to get hard. Unfortunately it wasn't an image of Renee or Melissa. It was Carly Drake who fired his blood.

As he leaned back against the trunk of a tree, the end of his line jerked. He waited for another tug, set the hook, and started reeling. Dammit to hell, whenever he thought of Carly, he felt like the fish on the end of that line. How had the little blonde managed to sink her hooks into him? How had she managed to snag his interest so quickly?

In fairness, she wasn't even trying. He knew women, knew she was attracted to him. He also knew she wasn't interested in climbing into bed for a couple of nights of fun.

And after his disastrous marriage to Holly, he sure as hell wasn't interested in anything more than that. If Joe Drake knew he was even thinking of taking Carly to bed, the old man would be spinning in his grave.

Linc reeled in his catch and swung the line toward shore. He grabbed the fish, unfastened the hook, and stuck the big silver bass in his creel.

"You're supper, buddy. Fried nice and golden brown." The real thing, not some fancy chef's version.

Not that he didn't like gourmet food. Over the years, he'd developed expensive tastes, but part of him still loved down-home Southern cooking and every once in a while, he indulged himself by cooking a meal for himself.

He checked his heavy stainless wristwatch. Just enough time to clean the fish, shower, and head for Drake Trucking and his meeting with Carly. As her image arose, heat sank low in his groin. He was famous for his self-control. In the next few days, he was going to need every ounce of it.

Carly leaned back in the chair behind her desk. The big white clock on the wall said nine forty-five. Lincoln Cain was due at ten for the conference call with his private investigator. Carly had spent all morning doing her best not to think of him, trying not to remember how Cain had looked charging across the parking lot to rescue her.

A big, tall, powerful figure in snug black leather, fists clenched, jaw iron hard. There'd been murder in those gold-flecked eyes, the threat of mortal danger. He'd been in prison. One thing she now knew. Cain was as tough as he looked.

She thought of the men who'd attacked her, remembered the feel of the blade against her throat, the rush of fear. In her mind, she could hear the shots, remember the terror when she'd thought Cain had been injured or killed.

God, she couldn't already have feelings for him. In a far different way, he posed as much danger to her as the men who'd attacked her.

She remembered the weight of his hard body on top of her, pressing her down, protecting her. Her breath quickened and her skin flushed with heat. She couldn't remember ever being so physically attracted to a man. And every time she was around him, it seemed to get worse.

Thank God tomorrow was Monday. Cain would be returning to Dallas. With any luck, he'd be too busy to come back to Iron Springs next weekend or anytime in the near future.

Donna knocked at the door, the signal he'd arrived. The door opened. "Mr. Cain is here."

"Thanks, Donna." She steeled herself for the impact of seeing him, watched him walk into the room with that confident swagger, saw the heat in those bold green eyes.

She pasted on a smile. "Good morning, Linc."

He took one look at her and frowned. "You've got a bruise on your cheek. Did I do that?"

Unconsciously she reached up and touched the spot. "Probably. It's okay, considering you were trying to save my life."

"What?" Donna gasped.

Damn, the moment Cain had walked in, she'd forgotten Donna was there. "It's nothing. A couple of guys gave me some trouble at the roadhouse last night. Linc happened to be there. He . . . umm . . . handled things."

Donna flashed Cain a look of admiration. "Wow, Carly's lucky you were around." She glanced at Carly. "You'll tell me later, right?"

She smiled, liking Donna more and more. "Sure." She'd give her a modified version, skipping over El Jefe until they figured things out. Donna grinned, backed out, and closed the door.

Linc's gaze returned to the bruise on her cheek. "You okay?"

Self-conscious now, she reached up and tightened the ponytail she'd pulled her hair into that morning. "I had a little trouble falling asleep, but I'm okay."

His eyes gleamed. *I've got the perfect sleeping pill,* those green eyes said. She blocked the image of black leather chaps framing the bulge beneath his zipper.

"I hated leaving you alone last night," he said. "I should have slept on the sofa."

No way! "I was fine. I had Joe's gun, remember? I need to get in some practice at the range, but I know how to use it if I have to."

"Half the women in Texas carry. I should have figured Joe's granddaughter would be one of them."

God, he looked good today, in a pair of faded jeans

that hugged his long legs and a forest green T-shirt that
outlined the muscles in his massive chest. Every time
he moved, she caught a glimpse of the barbed wire
tattoo around his amazing bicep.

She glanced down at the worn cowboy boots he was
wearing. Big feet. Big hands. Big . . . everything.

Don't go there. Do not go there!

"What time is the conference call coming in?" She
needed to get him out of there, the sooner, the better.

"We've got about twenty minutes. I figured if you're
up to it, we'd go back over what happened last night,
see if you can remember something more that could
help us."

She nodded. "I've thought about it a lot. I could
probably pick out the one with the knife in a lineup."

"We'll call Howler as soon as we talk to Townsend,
bring the sheriff up to speed."

"So what's the deal with you and him? It's pretty
clear you two don't like each other."

A muscle jumped in his cheek. "Howler's been sheriff since I was a kid. He's the guy who arrested me the
night I tried to rob that convenience store."

"You and two other boys."

"That's right."

There was more to the story. She'd really like to
know. On the other hand, the less she knew about
Cain, the better off she'd be.

Donna's familiar knock sounded. Carly walked over
and pulled open the door. "What is it?"

"We've got a problem. Pete Sanchez, one of the new
guys, was trying to park a double and screwed up. The
rig is jackknifed and he's freaking out. I'm afraid he's
going to do some damage. We can unhook it and move
it by hand, but—"

"Let me take a look, see if we can do it the easy way first." She turned to Cain. "I'll be right back."

She hurried out behind Donna, her mind on the problem in the yard. Two weeks after Joe's death, as soon as the blinding grief had cleared enough for her to realize she wanted to keep the business, she'd enrolled in the All-Trucking driver's school in Dallas, an intense two-week training course.

Until she'd returned to Texas, she hadn't considered actually getting her Class B license, but Joe had taught her the basics, and as the classes progressed, she realized she knew more than she'd thought.

She had no plans to actually drive for the company, but she worked with tough men and women and she wanted their respect. And if a problem came up, like today, she wanted to be able to step in if necessary.

She opened the driver's door. Pete Sanchez's face was red, his black hair standing on end. "Take a break, Pete. Let me give it a try." Pete climbed down with a sigh of relief, and Carly climbed into the cab.

Linc walked out of the inner office, out of the metal building, into the asphalt yard. The big rig double trailer was jackknifed pretty good, wedged in tight between the dock and the wash rack.

He was only a little surprised when he saw Carly's blond ponytail bobbing behind the wheel. The truck was moving. She was giving it her best shot, but getting the mess undone wasn't going to be easy.

He watched her work the gears, pulling forward, spinning the wheel, moving back, moving forward, trying to straighten out the trailer without tearing up the dock or damaging the rig. It was helping, but it wouldn't be enough to solve the problem.

He started walking. He could get the job done. He still knew how to drive. Hell, he owned one of the biggest trucking companies in the country. He paused as he sensed her frustration mounting.

He could do it for her, but . . . He was beginning to understand her a little, know how much she valued her independence. Solving the problem for her was exactly the wrong thing to do.

He walked up to the open driver's window. "Pull forward about three feet, then crank it hard to the right."

She looked down at him, weighing his instructions, whether he knew what he was doing or if he'd just make things worse. He heard the gears drop into place. She pulled forward, then cranked the wheel as far as she could.

"Now back up a couple of feet and crank it left all the way."

She did what he said and the trailer freed up a little.

"Do it again," he said.

She pulled forward, turned the wheel, backed up, and stopped.

"You've almost got it. A couple more times ought to do it."

The trailer rolled back farther this time, missing the dock by just a few inches. He stood where she could see him, held up his hands to let her know how much clearance she had. She idled the truck forward, then back, then pulled farther ahead.

"You got it. Nice job."

The trailer straightened out as she drove it across the yard into a pull-through parking spot and turned off the big diesel engine.

Carly jumped down and hurried back to him, flashing a smile brighter than anything he'd seen from her before. He felt it like a kick in the stomach.

"That was great," she said. "Thanks. Pete and I are both still learning. I really appreciate the help."

"No problem."

They walked together back into the building, into her office, and closed the door. He'd vowed to leave her alone, but it was getting harder all the time. He smiled at the unintended pun.

She grabbed one of the two chairs positioned in front of her desk and pulled it up next to where she was sitting, then sat down in her chair. Linc forced his mind back to the reason he was there, Miguel Hernandez's murder, the threatening note, and the attack on Carly last night.

He made the phone call to Ross Townsend on the landline, put it on speaker.

"Ross, it's Lincoln Cain. I have Carly Drake here with me. What have you got?"

"First off, I took care of that security concern we discussed."

"That's good. E-mail me the details."

"Will do. Regarding El Jefe, from what I could find in a short amount of time, the guy came out of nowhere, grew himself into a mid- to upper-level drug dealer. His territory covers the entire East Texas region, all the way down to Houston."

"Why isn't he in jail?"

"So far no one's been able to link him to anything illegal. Plus no one knows who the hell he is. No known photos of him; no one knows where to find him. Or at least, no one's been willing to come forward. The ones who do wind up dead."

Considering the guy wanted a meeting with Carly, Linc didn't like the sound of that. "Or he's paying them for their silence."

"That's right. Probably got some law enforcement on his payroll so you need to be careful who you trust."

Linc thought of Howler. He was the local law in the county. Linc didn't know whether or not the sheriff was corrupt, but with the bad blood between them, he couldn't trust his usually reliable instincts where Howler was concerned.

"Anything else?" he asked.

"Not yet, but I'm heading for Iron Springs. I want to do some digging, see what some of the locals have to say about the hijacking, see what they say about Miguel Hernandez."

An alarm went off in Linc's head. "What are you thinking?"

"I'm wondering if there's a chance Hernandez wasn't as lily white as everyone thought he was. Maybe he was working for El Jefe and something went wrong. Hernandez got axed and the hijacking was just a cover."

Carly spoke up. "I don't believe it. Miguel was a family man. My grandfather trusted him completely. No way was he working for some drug lord."

"Your loyalty is commendable, Ms. Drake," Ross said, "but it's my job to find out the truth, no matter what it turns out to be."

"But—"

"You can stay at the house while you're in town," Linc said. "I'll tell the housekeeper to expect you."

"Sounds good. I'll be there tomorrow. If you haven't left for Dallas, we can talk then."

"I'll be here. I've got a project in front of the county

commissioners' court tomorrow afternoon." Linc looked at Carly. "Anything you want to add?"

Her mouth looked tight. She just shook her head. She was still fighting the notion that her employee might have been involved in some kind of criminal activity. But the things people did rarely surprised Linc anymore.

"I'll see you in the morning," he said to Townsend and ended the phone call. "You okay?" he asked Carly.

"Miguel had a wife and three kids. I don't believe he'd get involved with a drug lord."

"For his family's sake, I hope you're right, but it's Ross's job to find out. Now that El Jefe is pressing you for a meeting, it's even more important. In that regard, I think we should hold off on talking to the sheriff. Let's see what Townsend comes up with first."

"You don't trust Howler?"

"I don't like him and he doesn't like me. I don't know if he's on the take; I'm just not sure of him. If he's on El Jefe's payroll—"

"You're right. We need to wait." She looked up at him. "I thought you'd be heading back to Dallas tonight. I mean, you do run a big corporation and Monday's the beginning of the workweek."

The hopeful look in those big blue eyes irritated the hell out of him. With his money, women fell all over themselves trying to get his attention. Carly had spent most of her time trying to get rid of him.

"Sorry, sweet pea, I'm not going back till tomorrow. Tex/Am is opening a tire rebuilding plant a couple of miles outside Pleasant Hill, the first of a chain. The plant's good for the community, creates jobs, brings money into the area. But a bunch of environmentalists from out of town are fighting the project."

"Sometimes they do good things," she said. "Sometimes they just don't have enough to do."

"Sad thing is, what we're planning is actually recycling, re-using old tires instead of just throwing them into a land fill or burning them up and sending toxic waste into the atmosphere. So far, they aren't convinced. You want to go to supper tonight?" he asked, just to see her scramble. "We can talk about the case."

She squirmed in her chair, fiddled with her ponytail, glanced away, then back at him. "Thanks, but I . . . umm . . . already have plans."

"Too bad," he said, not the least surprised she'd refused him. The lady was no fool. Staying away from him was exactly the right thing to do. Unfortunately.

He came up out of the chair. "I've got to get going. I'll call you if Townsend comes up with anything new."

"Thank you." She walked over and opened the door. "And thanks again for what you did last night."

Linc turned to face her. "Remember what we talked about—you don't meet with El Jefe. You call me the minute you hear from him. Give me your phone." She hesitated a moment, then grabbed it off the desk and handed it over. Linc plugged in his private number.

"You call me—you understand? I don't care what time it is."

She gave him a reluctant nod. "Okay."

He leaned down and brushed a light kiss on her cheek, heard her sharp intake of breath. "Stay safe, Carly."

Unconsciously she touched the place where they'd made contact. "Good-bye, Linc."

He left her there in the office. But he had to make himself walk out the door.

Chapter Seven

"We need a loan." Carly said the words aloud even though she was the only one in her office. Over the past few weeks, she'd spent hours scanning page after page of bills and invoices on the computer, looking for a solution, but a loan seemed the only way out.

It was Monday morning. Earlier she'd made sales calls, managed to bring in another client, but the shipment of drilling parts wouldn't be ready for delivery for two more weeks. She was convinced she could make Drake profitable, but she needed time. She needed enough money to stay afloat until the checks started coming in.

This afternoon she was going to Joe's bank. He'd been a customer with the Iron Springs Credit Union for years. She'd apply for the money and she'd get it.

Donna's quick knock preceded the door swinging open. "A Deputy Rollins just stopped by. He left these for you."

Carly stood up behind the desk. "It's the Hernandez case files. I really didn't think the sheriff would let me see them. He wasn't too happy about it."

"That's our beloved Sheriff Howler." Donna set the files down on the desk. "He thinks he knows everything."

"If he knows so much, why hasn't he caught Miguel's killers?"

"Good question."

Actually it was. Maybe the sheriff really was on El Jefe's payroll. It didn't seem likely, but still . . .

Donna left the office and Carly opened the file folder, which contained copies of documents: Texas Highway Patrol reports, a Howler County deputy's statement, the coroner's report, statements from the couple who'd found the body.

Carly thought of Cain. He wanted to see the reports. As soon as she finished going over them, she'd call him. By then he'd probably be back in Dallas. *She hoped.*

The man was a walking, talking sexual temptation. After he'd left yesterday, she'd gone back and Googled him again, read up on his exploits, the beautiful models and starlets he dated. He'd been married to a former Miss America beauty pageant finalist, Miss Colorado. A marriage that had ended after just three years.

No serious relationships since then, at least according to the tabloids. Obviously he'd learned his lesson and was no longer a marrying kind of guy. But then she wasn't really interested in marriage, either.

She had too much going on in her life. Too much to accomplish, too many promises to keep, debts to repay. Add to that, she wasn't really a believer in happily ever after. Her mother had gotten pregnant when she was a teen. Carly didn't even know her father's name.

Joe had been married twice and had two kids. Both marriages had ended in divorce. Besides her mother, he'd had another daughter with his second wife, but there had been some kind of rift. Joe and the daughter had lost touch years before she'd been killed by a drunk driver.

It occurred to Carly that maybe she should just sleep with Cain and get him out of her system. She was a grown woman and wildly attracted to him. After years of dealing with men, she had no doubt Cain wanted her, too.

Maybe a couple of nights would be enough to satisfy her curiosity as well as the fierce lust she felt for him. Enough for Cain, too.

But what if it wasn't? What if the attraction only grew stronger—at least for her?

She wasn't ready to take that kind of chance.

Carly opened the file. There was a message pinned on top. *No fingerprints on the note in your house or around the windowsill in the bedroom.*

She turned to the stack of documents, began to shuffle through the pages. Maybe she would find a clue that had been missed.

An hour later, she hadn't found a thing. The gruesome details of the shooting, execution-style to the back of Miguel's head, turned her stomach. Just looking at copies of the crime scene photos was enough to make her nauseous.

It looked as if Miguel had struggled some with his attackers, but according to the report, it hadn't been much of a fight. Why hadn't he tried to escape? Could he have known them? She didn't want to think so, but as Ross Townsend had said, they needed to find out the truth.

More likely, Miguel hadn't realized the hijackers were actually going to kill him. Maybe he'd thought if he went along with them, they would just take the truck and leave.

The couple, a man named Andy Granger and his wife, Maria, had both given brief statements. They'd pulled over to let their puppy out. The animal had caught the scent and darted across the road to where Miguel's body lay just off the pavement. The couple had seen the bullet hole in his skull and all the congealed blood and immediately called 9-1-1.

Carly felt a stab of pain for Miguel's wife and hoped she hadn't been told the terrible details. She wondered if someone should follow up with the Grangers in case they had remembered something later. Cain would be in Dallas. Maybe he'd want to talk to them.

She closed the file, pulled Cain's card out of the top desk drawer, walked out, and spoke to Donna. "Make a copy of these, will you, then send them to Tex/Am in Dallas. His information is on the card. It's kind of expensive but I guess we'd better overnight them."

"I'll make sure he gets them right away," Donna said.

Now that she'd reviewed the file, Carly could drive into Iron Springs for her meeting with the banker. She had mostly been in jeans since she had returned to Iron Springs, but until last year when she'd moved to San Francisco, she had been living in New York City, had been flying the New York-Paris route.

She'd spent every extra dime on fabulous designer outfits, some forward in fashion, some classic, like this one. Hey, it was Paris, okay? And she'd learned to ferret out every possible bargain.

Today she was wearing a russet skirt suit with a cream silk blouse, a bright Givenchy silk scarf she had splurged on and bought on the Rue du Faubourg

Saint-Honoré in Paris, and a pair of Jimmy Choo high heels.

Since classic clothes stayed in style for years and she was good at mixing and matching, she was set, at least for a while.

Grabbing her taupe Chanel bag and the information she'd put together, she headed out the door to apply for a loan.

Linc strode out of his meeting, summoning all his control to clamp down on his temper. Making his way outside the big red and gray stone building, he pushed his way through the throng of protesters, heading for his truck. The sky had closed up, turned dark and sullen. Looked like it would rain later in the day.

He wished the clouds would open up right now, release a downpour, and send these idiots running.

"Keep Pleasant Hill green!" someone shouted, a thin man with big, horn-rimmed glasses.

"Take your filthy rubber and go back to Dallas!" A tiny black-haired woman jabbed a sign in the air that read SAVE MOTHER EARTH. STOP POLLUTION NOW!

Linc clenched his back teeth together and kept walking. He didn't recognize any faces. He'd been told almost none of the people who were protesting lived in the area. Instead, they were out-of-towners who didn't know squat about the needs of the people in the community, all of them swarming around like angry bees.

He'd learned at the meeting that they were concerned about the tire retreading process, the rubber dust it created, the storage of the tires themselves, the solvent, the cement vapors, the extra workload the plant might create for the Pleasant Hill volunteer fire department.

None of them could see the good the plant would do for the locals, the jobs it would create, the money that would flow into town in the form of taxes and spending. And the plant would be run as cleanly and efficiently as modern technology allowed.

Hell, he might have joined their cause if they had been right. He donated to a number of environmental organizations. In this case they were wrong.

If he'd known it was going to be such a hard sell, he'd have sent a team down to present the facts, guys trained to handle the concerns of the environmentalists—unlike Linc, who barely resisted the urge to throw a punch at one or two of the most obnoxious members of the group.

Once he reached his truck, he climbed in and cranked the engine. He was just backing out of the parking lot when his cell phone buzzed. The main Drake Trucking number appeared on the screen.

"Mr. Cain? Hi, this is Donna from Carly's office. Are you still in Iron Springs?"

"I'm here for a couple more hours. What is it?"

"I just wanted to let you know the sheriff sent those case files over. Carly's already gone through them. She asked me to overnight them to you, but I thought if you were still in town, you might want to pick them up."

"I'm not far away. I'll be there in ten minutes." He ended the call and checked the time. The helicopter was due at the ranch in two hours. Plenty of time to look at the files before he went back to Dallas. While he was at the yard, he could check on Carly.

He thought how happy she'd be to see him and smiled at his own sarcasm.

He drove through town and out the highway, pulled into the trucking yard a few minutes later, and parked in the lot. Unfortunately when he walked into the building, Carly wasn't there.

"I'm afraid she had an appointment with the bank," Donna said. "I thought she'd be back by now. I'll get you that file."

"Thanks." He knew Joe's office manager, Donna Melendez. She'd be a big help to Carly—unless he could convince her to sell. He still hadn't completely given up on that idea, though the prospect of her handing over the reins seemed dimmer by the hour.

Donna handed him the file. "Here you go."

"I think I'll take a look at it while I'm here. Okay if I use the office?"

She smiled. In her fifties now, she was still attractive, and she had completely worshipped Joe. "Well, sure."

Linc carried the file inside and sat down at the desk, put up with the seat being set wrong for a guy his height, and went to work.

An hour later, he hadn't been able to pick out anything useful. Though it might be worthwhile talking to the couple who'd found the body. And he wanted to go over the crime scene report one more time.

He was just closing the folder when the door swung open and Carly walked in. Surprise widened those big blue eyes. "What are you doing here?" Apparently Donna hadn't warned her.

Linc stood up from the chair, let himself take a good long look, appreciate the expensive russet suit and high heels—along with the pretty legs and soft curves of the woman beneath the clothes. "You clean up good, Ms. Drake. You'd never know you were a lady trucker."

She glanced down at herself as if she'd forgotten what she had on. "Thanks. I think."

"Donna called. She said you'd gotten the case file. I figured it'd be faster if I just took a look before I left town."

"Oh. Did you find anything?"

"No, but Ross Townsend's due out at the ranch. I'll take it out to him, see if he can pick up anything."

She nodded. "Those are your copies. I didn't see anything, either."

He gave her a lingering glance. "So what's the occasion? Hot date?" It was supposed to be funny, but as the words spilled out, he discovered it wasn't.

She laughed. "Hot date with a banker and he wasn't impressed." She plunked down in her chair and slipped off her heels. "Neither were the other four bankers I talked to in various locations."

"What's the problem?"

She looked up at him. "Money. Something you wouldn't understand."

"There was a time I understood it plenty. I haven't forgotten. I take it you were trying to get a loan."

"That's right."

"How much do you need?"

She bent over and massaged a sore foot. It took a strong shot of will not to offer to do it for her.

"If you want the truth, I barely made payroll last week. If I don't get a loan right away, I can't come up with enough to write the next round of paychecks." She straightened. "I thought getting the money would be easy, you know? Joe was never late on a bill in his life. He always repaid his debts. I figured the bank would give me the same opportunity."

"Unfortunately you aren't Joe."

She sighed. "The thing is I know I can rebuild the business. I've been making marketing calls. I've already picked up one of Joe's old accounts and signed up a new company we've never dealt with before. I just need some time."

Time was something he could give her. "I'll tell you what. I'll make you the loan. I'll need to see the numbers, but I'll get you what you need."

She started shaking her head. "No way. I'm not taking money from you."

"I'm not offering you money. I'm offering you a loan. I'll have the necessary papers drawn up and secure the money with a lien against the business, just like the bank would have done."

She eyed him with a mixture of suspicion and interest. "This would be strictly business, right? Nothing personal. Just a loan backed by Drake Trucking."

"That's right."

"What happens if I can't repay the money?"

He took his time answering. He wanted her to say yes and she wouldn't if she thought he wasn't playing it straight with her. "You don't pay when the note is due, I take controlling interest in the business."

Her eyebrows narrowed. She didn't like that. "If I don't pay when the note's due, you take forty percent of the business."

He shook his head. "Sorry. That's a deal breaker. You don't cut it, I take over. You'd still own forty-nine percent, but you wouldn't run things. You want the money or not?"

She sighed. He had her; he could see it. "I don't

have any choice. I'll have Donna make you a copy of the P&L I took to the bank, along with a list of assets."

He thought about the company's financial problems. "I'd also like to have my people look at your accounting records, make sure there aren't any unforeseen problems." Now was his chance to figure out how Joe had gotten the company into so much debt.

She cast him a suspicious glance. "I'm trusting you with a lot of company information. How do I know you aren't just trying to find a way to force me to sell?"

It was a good question, a smart question to ask. "If I was a different man, you'd have every right to question my motives. But Joe was my friend. By extension that makes his granddaughter my friend. I want to help you. That's all I want."

She sat back in her chair. Studied him for several long moments. "Okay. It's a deal."

He smiled and nodded. He stretched out a hand and she slid her smaller hand in his. A feeling of protectiveness went through him. She was trusting him. He wouldn't let her down.

Linc picked up the case file. "I've got to go. I want to talk to Townsend before I leave." He held up the file. "I'll show him this."

"Let me know if he sees something."

"I presume you haven't had a call from El Jefe."

"No. Maybe he changed his mind."

He cocked an eyebrow. "You really think so?"

"No."

"Neither do I. Stay in touch and keep that gun of yours handy."

Linc left the office. But the more he thought about the note and the attack on Carly at the roadhouse, the more it bothered him to be leaving Iron Springs.

Chapter Eight

Carly changed out of her suit and heels into jeans and a pretty ruffled blouse she'd brought with her from home. It was almost closing time when she heard a polite knock on the door. Not Donna this time.

"Come in."

The door swung open and Rowena walked into the office. She was in skinny jeans and a tube top, her dark red hair curling around her shoulders.

"I was just driving by and I realized it was almost time to close. I thought I'd stop and see if you wanted to go somewhere for a drink on your way home."

She sighed. "I'd love to, but I can't. I'll be here at least a couple more hours before I can leave. But I'm really glad you stopped in. Anything interesting happen after I left the roadhouse Saturday night? You and Johnnie Banducci seemed to be having fun."

Row sat down in the chair next to the desk. "Johnnie's a good guy, but not really my type. What about you and Cain? He walked out just a few minutes after you left. I figured maybe the two of you hooked up."

The thought of being in bed with him unleashed a

curl of heat low in her belly. She remembered his heavy weight on top of her, the way his breath warmed the side of her neck.

"I . . . ummm . . . had a run-in with some guys in the parking lot that night. Linc came to my rescue."

"Wow. No kidding! Are you okay?"

"I'm all right now, but at the time, I was pretty shook up."

"I'd be shook up, too. So what about Cain? He saved you. Did you spend the night with him?"

"Of course not. He bought me a cup of coffee and we talked about what happened. He was great."

One of Row's russet eyebrows went up. "He seemed really interested in you. Did he ask you out?"

Carly studied her friend, couldn't help wondering if Rowena had been one of Cain's conquests. "I thought you said he didn't mess with the local women."

Row caught her look. "He doesn't—and that includes me if you're wondering." Row gave her an all-knowing smile. "On the other hand, where you're concerned, my guess—Cain's the kind of guy who thinks rules are made to be broken."

She shouldn't have felt so relieved. "I won't deny I'm attracted to him. God, he's the most masculine man I've ever met."

"And that body. I saw him outside the roadhouse with his shirt off once and I almost had an orgasm. The man is sex personified. If you get a chance to sample some of that, you have to do it. You have to come back and tell Britt and me about it so we can live vicariously."

Carly laughed. "He's gorgeous, but he's clearly a heartbreaker. I don't need that."

"Are you kidding? You don't have to fall in love with the guy just because you have sex with him. You're a woman. You have needs. You'd just be letting Cain take care of them."

And dear God, she had no doubt the man could handle the job. "It's a moot point at the moment. He didn't ask me out and I don't think he will."

Rowena sighed. "Too bad. At least one of us ought to have a go at him."

Carly chuckled and just shook her head.

Row stood up from her chair. "I gotta go. Call me if anything exciting happens—and you know what I mean." Heading for the door, Row pulled it open, wriggled her fingers over her shoulder, walked out, and closed the door.

Row was gone, but her words still rang in Carly's head. *You're a woman. You have needs. You'd just be letting Cain take care of them.*

Carly slammed a mental door on the notion and went determinedly back to work.

By the time she was finished, the office was empty. Some of the drivers were still there, hanging around the truckers' lounge after their runs, drinking Coke or cups of coffee. No smoking allowed anywhere on the grounds. Too much fuel and other flammable material. Some of the men grumbled, not many. Better safe than sorry.

She waved to Pete and Gordy as she climbed into her pickup and started the engine. A few drops of rain had begun to fall. She needed to get home before the storm hit in earnest.

She sat there a moment, idling the truck and thinking. When she'd gone to the roadhouse Saturday night, she'd been followed. Someone had been watching either the yard or her house. It was already late and with the heavy cloud cover, it was dark.

She glanced around the parking area, surrounded by a high chain-link fence, but didn't see anyone. Dropping the pickup into gear, she drove out of the lot onto the road, keeping an eye out for anyone pulling in behind her.

Pete drove out and turned in the opposite direction. No cars in front of her, no one behind. She relaxed as she headed down the highway.

She'd only gone a couple of miles when she noticed a pair of headlights in the rearview mirror. She told herself it was just somebody who happened to be traveling in the same direction, going home, maybe, just as she was, but her pulse kicked up a notch.

It was probably nothing. She didn't want to be totally paranoid, but just to be sure, she slowed. The headlights stayed the same distance away. She slowed even more, forcing the driver to come up behind her. The headlights brightened as the car grew nearer.

Finally the vehicle pulled around her and continued down the highway. The dark brown Chevy Malibu didn't look much like a drug dealer's car and there was only one person inside.

Relieved, she headed on home. Some soup sounded good. Maybe she'd make a batch of potato and onion, her favorite; then she remembered she was out of milk.

The Stop and Shop, a small local market, was on the way. She pulled in and parked, went inside, and bought a quart of milk and a package of Ding Dongs. Not the usual healthy fare she'd gotten used to eating after she'd left Texas, but she'd worked a long day and she deserved a treat once in a while.

She paid for the food and started for the door, suddenly thought about the dark brown Chevy. It wouldn't take a minute to look out back, see if the car was anywhere around. Making her way down the cereal aisle, she shoved open the rear door, grateful no alarm sounded.

The sky was overcast but the rain was intermittent, slashing down, then changing to a light patter. A car turned down the side street and for a moment its headlights illuminated the flat, grassy landscape around the store. A chill slipped down her spine when she spotted the brown Malibu parked on the street, the headlights turned off, the driver sitting behind the wheel, waiting for her to get back on the road.

She wasn't sure if she was more scared or mad; both, she figured. The driver was the only person in the car, not the three thugs who had attacked her before, so she felt a little better.

She thought about calling 9-1-1, but as soon as the guy spotted the flashing lights, he'd be gone; then sooner or later, he'd be back.

Instead, she returned to her truck, left the bag of groceries on the floor, pulled her Glock out from under the seat, and stuck it in her purse.

A few moments later, she was back in the store, making her way toward the rear door. The guy behind the register was busy with a customer and didn't pay her any attention.

Pulling the pistol, the barrel pointed down at her side, she eased the door open and slipped into the darkness, started quietly making her way around behind the Malibu. The rain was coming down a little harder, making it easier for her to stay out of sight.

She finally got close enough to the car to read the plate number on the back: BVX 72W.

Crouching low, she rounded the back bumper, came up on the side, and noticed the driver's window was rolled down. The man was leaning back, his head on the headrest, hands relaxed around the steering wheel. Keeping low, she made her way along the side of the car and stuck the barrel of the gun into the man's face as she popped up beside him.

"Don't move or I'll pull the trigger!"

The guy jumped six inches. "Jesus Christ!" His gaze shot to her face and recognition flashed in his eyes. "What the hell are you doing?"

"What the hell are *you* doing? Why are you following me?"

He sighed. "Take it easy, okay? You scared the piss out of me. Put the gun down. I'm not gonna hurt you."

"I asked you a question. Why are you following me?"

"Christ, you're gonna get me fired." He scrubbed a hand over his face. "Name's Frank Marino. Ross Townsend hired me and a couple of other guys to provide 'round-the-clock protection, follow you, and make sure you stay safe."

Anger rolled through her as the pieces all clicked into place. "And Townsend works for Cain." She put the Glock back in her purse, hauled out her cell phone, and punched in Cain's number. It only rang one time.

"This is Cain."

"Are you crazy? You could have gotten someone killed!"

"Calm down, Carly. What are you talking about?"

"I'm talking about the guy named Frank you hired to follow me. A few minutes ago, I had my Glock nine mil shoved into his face."

Cain sighed. "Okay, look, I should have told you, all right? I knew you'd pitch a fit. I was hoping he'd be good enough you wouldn't see him. Tell him he's fired, by the way. If you could sneak up on him, so could the bad guys."

She couldn't argue with his logic. She turned to the guy in the car, noting his red hair and freckled pale complexion, his slightly crooked nose. "Cain says you're fired."

Frank released a long sigh.

"I don't need someone guarding me," she said to Cain. "I've already applied for my concealed carry permit. I'm taking the class this weekend."

"Dammit, Carly. Remember what happened at Jubal's? Those guys weren't kidding around."

A shiver crawled over her skin. She remembered the hand repulsively cupping her breast. Since she didn't want to think about it, she changed the subject.

"You talked to Townsend, right? Did your detective come up with anything?"

"We talked on the phone. He's working a couple of angles, nothing yet."

Carly waved good-bye to Frank and started walking back to the pickup, her cell phone against her ear. "I don't know what else we can do. I'm going home. Good night, Linc."

"Listen, Carly, let Townsend's men do their job, at least until we get a little more information. It wouldn't hurt for one of them to be parked in front of your house. It might discourage someone thinking of giving you trouble."

"The men said they'd call. I think they will. When they do I'll let you know. Good night." Carly clicked off and headed back to her truck. Her life was complicated enough without having human guard dogs to worry about.

Lincoln Cain was a major pain in the ass. Still, it felt

kind of good to know he was worried about her. Over the years, very few people besides Joe had cared anything about her.

She was smiling as she drove off toward home. When she spotted the taillights behind her a couple of miles down the road, she just shook her head. Good ol' Frank wasn't giving up. What the heck? Let him sit outside the house if that's what he wanted.

Then the car speeded up, rushing up on her way too fast. Another car roared up beside her, a big black SUV. Fear shot through her. She knew who it was, knew it was the same men who had attacked her at the roadhouse. Her heart was racing, pounding in her ears. Adrenaline pumped through her veins.

She pressed down hard on the accelerator and the pickup shot forward, fishtailed on the slippery pavement, then picked up speed. The car behind stayed right on her bumper and the SUV continued to box her in.

All three of them roared down the road. Her wipers were useless. A pothole at this speed could kill her. There was a curve up ahead. No way to make the turn at ninety miles an hour, especially not in the rain.

She had two choices: careen off the road at breakneck speed and die in a blaze of glory, or slow down and let them force her over to the side of the two-lane highway.

Carly thought of the gun in her purse, slowed, and pulled onto the side of the road.

Chapter Nine

Linc paced the floor of the huge, two-story, wood-paneled, book-lined study in the big stone mansion at the ranch. He was still in Iron Springs. When he'd left Drake Trucking, he'd called his chopper pilot and put the return trip to Dallas off until tomorrow morning. A bad feeling had been nagging him all day. Over the years, he'd learned to listen to his instincts.

Instead of leaving, he'd gone back to the ranch and called his assistant, had Millie reschedule his late-afternoon meetings. He'd have to go back tomorrow; there were things he absolutely had to do. But once he was finished, he was clearing his calendar for the rest of the week, working from the ranch instead of the office.

Townsend hadn't been at the house when he'd arrived. They had talked briefly on the phone but Ross hadn't shown up until a few minutes ago. The housekeeper had settled the detective in a suite upstairs, then shown him down to the study.

Linc glanced up as Ross walked in, a good-looking guy in his thirties with brown hair and a short-cropped beard around his mouth.

"Sorry I couldn't get here sooner," Ross said. "I had some leads I wanted to follow. Figured that'd be the best use of my time."

Linc agreed. He wanted the P.I. out doing his job. He rose from behind his big mahogany desk as Townsend approached, walked around, and the men shook hands.

"Anything new happening on this end?" Ross asked.

"Yeah, you might as well cancel that protection detail you arranged. Carly spotted the guy on her way home from work and sent him packing. The little witch thinks she can take care of herself. Considering she was able to shove a Glock in his face and hold him at gunpoint, I'd say she might be right."

"Crap. So I guess he's fired."

"Maybe. On the other hand, the men who went after her at Jubal's are a different breed. They won't hesitate to take her out if she gives them any trouble."

"Not good."

He tipped his head toward the carved mahogany table in the corner where the case file sat open, and they both walked in that direction.

"You spot anything in the file?" Townsend asked as they each pulled out a chair and sat down.

"One thing kind of bothered me. The cops at the scene didn't spend much time with the couple who found the body and didn't do any follow-up."

Ross started nodding. "It's possible they saw something, didn't remember it till later. Worth a check for sure."

"What about you? You come up with anything?"

Ross told him he'd been talking to people in the area, digging around, trying to find out if Miguel Hernandez could have been working for El Jefe. Trying to find out as much as he could about the drug lord and his minions without stirring up too much gossip.

"At this point, we can't be sure Hernandez's death and El Jefe are connected," Ross said, "but we can't rule it out, either. Which means the hijacking may be part of a bigger operation. Good chance by now the truck has been repainted and driven across the border into Mexico."

"If El Jefe is involved, it has to be more than just stealing a truck. A guy who rakes in millions in drug money can afford to pay for a semi if he wants one."

Ross's phone rang just then. "Sorry, I should have silenced it." He pulled it out of his pocket to turn it off, checked the number on the screen. "It's Marino. He probably wants to beg for his job back. I'll call him later."

"Take it," Linc said, his instincts kicking in again. Marino had been with Carly less than an hour ago.

"I'm busy," Ross said into the phone. "I heard about your little run-in with the client so unless it's important—"

Linc couldn't hear the conversation on the other end of the line, but he caught the flash of eye contact Ross made with him, saw the pulse beginning to pound in the detective's neck. Something was going on, something to do with Carly.

"Put it on speaker," he said.

"Cain's here," Ross said to Marino as he set the phone down on the table. "Start from the beginning."

"Okay, so after I got the message from Mr. Cain that I was fired—"

"We'll talk about that later," Ross said. "Go on."

"I started driving back to Iron Springs, then I thought maybe it wouldn't hurt to check on the lady before I packed it in. I didn't want anything to happen to her because of me, you know."

"Get to the point, Frank."

"I went to her house, figuring she would be home by the time I got there, but she hadn't made it home yet. I waited a few minutes, then decided to go back and trace the route she'd taken from the Stop and Shop, which was different from the way I'd gone. A few miles away from the store, I found her pickup. It was parked at the side of the road, but Ms. Drake wasn't in it."

Linc leaned over the table. "Where are you now?"

"I'm parked behind the truck. The doors are locked, no keys inside."

"Maybe she had car trouble," Ross suggested, "left the truck, and hitched to town."

Linc dragged out his cell and hit the contact button. Carly's phone went straight to voice mail. "She's not picking up."

"You think it's El Jefe?" Ross asked.

Every instinct in Linc's body was screaming. "Yeah, I do."

"Shall I call nine-one-one?" Frank asked.

The call would be dispatched to the sheriff. Linc didn't trust Howler. At best the man was a fool. If the sheriff got involved, Carly might wind up dead.

"Just hold tight. We're on our way." Linc disconnected, tossed the phone back to Ross, grabbed his windbreaker off the back of a chair, and headed out the study door.

On the way to the garage, he tried Carly again. Nothing. As Linc punched in the code and the garage door slid open, Ross stuck a hand under his jacket, checking the pistol in his shoulder holster.

After prison, aside from owning a gun for protection

in his home, Linc wasn't allowed to carry. He was glad Ross was armed.

They jumped in the truck. His Mercedes, parked in another garage, was faster, but if they found Carly's trail, they might need to traverse rough country and the pickup had four-wheel drive.

They belted themselves in good and tight. It had been raining off and on all day so the roads were slick. Linc shot backward out of the garage, spun the truck around, and hit the accelerator. The wipers went on as he headed down the long driveway toward the highway, Ross using his GPS tracking app to locate Frank, who waited for them at the abduction site.

Linc didn't doubt that's what had happened. El Jefe wanted to talk to Carly. He'd been waiting for his chance and tonight he'd found it.

Anger at Frank Marino swept through him. He didn't like incompetence. He liked it even less when it could wind up getting someone he cared about hurt or even killed.

He forced the thought away and increased his speed, traveling the dark two-lane road at the maximum he could push the truck without ending up in a ditch. When the rain lessened, then stopped altogether, he pushed even harder.

"We're almost there," Ross said. "Just around that curve."

Linc slowed the truck, took the curve, and spotted the white pickup with the Drake logo parked on the shoulder on the opposite side of the road. Frank's dark brown Chevy Malibu sat on the shoulder behind it.

Linc slammed the big GMC to a halt and turned off the engine, got out, and strode across the pavement to Carly's abandoned pickup. When Frank Marino walked up, Linc's hand unconsciously fisted. His fighting days were over, he reminded himself.

"I'm really sorry, Mr. Cain."

Linc held up a hand. He didn't want to hear Marino's excuses.

"Okay," Frank said. "I get it. The thing is I found evidence of tire tracks in the mud, a vehicle behind the pickup, one in the other lane. I think they boxed her in. She was probably trying to outrun them." He almost smiled. "After meeting her, I'd say no way did she just pull over."

Some of Linc's anger eased. No, she would have tried to get away. So far Marino's theory seemed spot on. "Go on."

"She sees the curve, knows she can't make it at the speed she's traveling, so she slows and pulls over."

"That sounds about right. We need to figure out what happened next."

"She had a gun," Frank said. "She didn't just get into their vehicle and let them drive away."

Ross spoke up. "Or maybe she did. Maybe she stuck the gun in her purse. Maybe they didn't search her. Maybe she's still armed."

"Possible," Linc said, "but I'm guessing she wouldn't have gone with them without a fight."

He searched the area around where the vehicle behind her had been parked, found nothing, crossed the road, and searched the other side. Linc knelt and picked up a small wet piece of cotton fabric.

He turned to Frank. "You remember what she was wearing?"

Frank nodded. "Yeah, this pretty little ruffled blouse, kind of a soft pink with some pale blue flowers. I remember the way it kind of hugged her br—"

Linc's hard glance cut off the words. He held up the piece of fabric. "This it?"

Frank nodded. "Pink and blue. That looks like part of a ruffle."

"So she tried to get away, but they forced her into their vehicle. Probably that big SUV that showed up at Jubal's." He looked down the road, followed the tire tracks melting into the mud, saw where the vehicle had pulled back into the right lane and continued toward Iron Springs.

"Maybe she left that piece of cloth on purpose," Linc said. "If she did, maybe she left a trail. Let's go."

Blindfolded, her wrists bound behind her with a plastic tie, Carly sat in a straight-back wooden chair, her feet resting on a rough concrete floor. She had no idea where she had been taken. Her cheek still stung where one of the men who had run her off the road had slapped her.

She bit back a grim smile. It had taken four of them to wrestle her gun away from her. She'd pulled the trigger three times, had them leaping around and swearing, but they'd pinned her as they'd fought for control of the weapon, and the shots had gone wild.

Before they'd blindfolded her, she'd recognized one of them, the jerk at the roadhouse who had fondled her breast. One of them had called him Lopez. The big guy with the mustache was also there. She heard him called Cuchillo, which meant "knife" in Spanish. But he and the others were on their good behavior tonight, since their boss, El Jefe, had been waiting for them when they got to wherever the hell she'd been taken.

She heard heavy footfalls as their leader walked

forward. She knew he wanted something from her or she would already be dead. It gave her the courage to put up a brave front even if she was actually scared to death.

"We meet at last, *Señorita* Drake," the man said.

"So . . . you must be El Jefe."

"*Sí*, that is correct."

She ignored the too-rapid beat of her heart. "You had me brought here. They said you wanted to talk. What do you want?"

He reached out and caught her chin, tipped her head back. She couldn't see him, but she could feel the calluses on his fingers.

"I only wish for us to become friends. You see, the two of us, we are about to become business partners."

Carly shook her head. "No way. Not a chance in hell." Beneath the bottom of the blindfold, she saw a pair of black leather sneakers with white rubber soles. The Ferragamo label on the side said they had to have cost somewhere close to a thousand dollars. They were a fairly big size. El Jefe wasn't a small man.

"You are not listening to me." He slapped her, not hard, not too easy. With enough force to definitely get her attention. "One way or another, we are going to be working together. You can make it hard on yourself or easy." He gave her another stinging slap, this one harder. "*Comprende, chica?* Which will it be?"

Her heart was racing. She was starting to hyperventilate. She needed to calm down, get control of herself and start thinking clearly before he really hurt her.

"I don't understand what you want me to do."

"The same thing you do every day. You will provide trucks when they are needed, send them to a particular location. The trucks will be loaded and you will deliver the goods to whatever location you are told. In return, you will be very well rewarded. No more money problems, eh? You will make more in three months than your company could earn in a year."

She reined in the urge to tell him to shove his demands where the sun didn't shine. She wanted to stay alive and clearly El Jefe was a dangerous man. "That kind of money sounds intriguing. What's the catch?"

"The catch? The *catch* is you will do what I say. You will ask no questions. You will follow instructions. You will do exactly as you are told. That is the catch, *chica*. And you will keep your pretty mouth shut. You will not discuss this conversation or our business arrangement with anyone."

Carly made no reply. She thought of Linc, hated to admit that he had been right, that she should have accepted his protection.

"What is your decision?"

She bit her lip, pretended to consider the deal. "How long do I have to think it over?"

He slapped her hard enough to split her bottom lip. "Your time has already run out."

She felt a trickle of blood at the corner of her mouth. "Then I guess my answer is yes."

"A very wise choice." He spoke to the other men, five of them in all, probably the same bunch who had attacked her at Jubal's or been in the car, Lopez being one of them.

"Take the *señorita* back to her pickup." El Jefe wiped the blood off her chin, his touch repulsively intimate, and a shiver ran through her. "We will be in touch very soon." She heard the squeak of his footsteps on the concrete floor as he turned and walked away.

Two of his men grabbed her arms and jerked her out of the chair. "Time to go home, *chica*," Lopez said.

Carly didn't protest as they dragged her out of the building and loaded her back into the SUV. No way were these men going to hurt her. At the moment, she was under El Jefe's protection. Unfortunately, once he found out she wasn't going along with his plans, that would be coming to a very abrupt and dangerous end.

The driver started the engine and the SUV began to bump over the muddy dirt road, back in the direction they had come. At least it looked as if she would survive the night.

She trembled, tried not to imagine what would happen when her reprieve was over.

Chapter Ten

Linc continued to drive the road, searching for any sign of where the vehicle holding Carly might have pulled off the highway. But the rain had returned, become a steady downpour, and any tracks that might have shown up had been washed away.

"We aren't going to find her," Ross said. "We need to call the sheriff, get some deputies out to help with the search."

Linc's insides tightened. Deep down, his gut was telling him that getting the cops involved was exactly the wrong thing to do. But Ross was right. He couldn't just leave her out there. He had to do something and he had to do it soon.

He slowed, turned the truck around, and headed back toward Carly's pickup. Frank was there in case she returned. Linc wanted to take a last look around before he called Howler—before he put Carly's life in the hands of a man he didn't trust.

He pushed down on the accelerator, worry gnawing at his insides. He should have handled things differently, found a way to convince her of the danger. She was his responsibility. He'd given Joe his word.

"Slow down," Ross said. "There's someone walking on the road up ahead."

He braked a little, spotted the lone figure moving along the edge of the pavement in the direction of the pickup, head down against the rain, hands jammed into the pockets of a pair of rain-soaked jeans. The headlights outlined a woman he recognized immediately. Linc slid to a halt behind her, jammed the truck into PARK, jumped down, and started running.

"Carly!"

She turned at the sound of her name, realized who had called out to her, and started running toward him. "Linc!" She reached him, collided with his chest, and his arms went hard around her.

"Carly. Honey, are you okay?" He was shaking. He didn't know if it was relief or fear.

A sob escaped. Her fingers curled into the nylon jacket he was wearing over his T-shirt. She buried her face in his chest and just hung on.

He cradled the back of her head. "It's okay, honey. Everything's okay."

Carly looked up, stared into his face, and for the first time seemed to realize what was going on. "I'm . . . I'm wet and . . . and muddy. I'll ruin your clothes."

He pulled her closer. "I don't care about my damned clothes. Just tell me you're okay."

She swallowed and nodded. "I'm . . . I'm all right."

He didn't let go, just scooped her up in his arms, and started striding back to his truck. Her body softened against him and he prayed she was telling the truth, that whoever had taken her hadn't hurt her.

Ross slid over behind the steering wheel. Linc climbed

in on the passenger side, settled Carly in his lap and turned up the heater, hoping it would stop the shivers running through her body.

"That's Ross Townsend," he said, working to stay calm. "He's the P.I. you talked to on the phone."

Ross flicked her a glance. "Glad you're okay, Ms. Drake."

"It's . . . it's just Carly." She returned her attention to Linc. "It was El Jefe. You were right. I should have listened to you."

"I don't want to be right. I just want you safe."

For several moments, she let herself rest against his chest. As the shaking began to ease, she sat up and slid off his lap, onto the seat beside him. "I need to tell you what happened, but first I . . . I've got to get my truck. It's just . . . it's only a little ways down the road."

"We'll pick it up tomorrow," he said.

"Please, I just . . . I want to go home, Linc, please."

He looked down at her, saw that her bottom lip was puffy in one corner, and a wave of fury hit him. He wanted to know what the hell had happened, what the hell was going on. He wanted to make sure nothing like this happened to her again.

"You heard the lady," he said to Ross. "Take her back to her pickup. You can drive it back to her house and Frank can follow you." He didn't mention that once he got there, he'd be staying with Carly while Frank drove Ross back to the ranch.

Ross put the GMC in gear and headed down the road.

A few minutes later, after only a minor protest, Carly was belted into the passenger seat of his truck, Linc back behind the wheel. Ross and Frank followed in the F-150 and Frank's Chevy Malibu.

The rain picked up again, battering the windshield as he drove back toward Iron Springs. The slap, slap of the wipers filled the quiet inside the cab.

Carly remained silent.

Worried, Linc started talking, telling her how they had found her, hoping his words would somehow make things easier.

"After you left Frank at the market, he decided to stop by your house, make sure you'd gotten home okay. When you didn't show up, he went back to the Stop and Shop and tracked you from there. He found your pickup on the side of the road, but you weren't in it so he called Townsend, who's staying at the ranch. Ross and I went back to your truck and started trying to track you from there."

She looked up at him. "I'm glad you didn't call the sheriff. If the cops had shown up . . ." She let the sentence trail off, went back to staring out the window.

"That's the reason I didn't call. I was afraid it would only make things worse for you."

She leaned back in the seat, kept her eyes fixed on the beads of rain rolling down the glass.

"They took my gun," she said softly. "I got off a few shots, but there were four of them. They pinned me down and the shots went wild."

He clamped down on his temper. If she realized how upset he really was, it would only make things worse. "Where did they take you?"

"I don't know. I was blindfolded. The only thing I know about El Jefe is he wears thousand-dollar high-top sneakers and they were at least a size twelve."

"So you never got a look at him."

"No. But the guy has kind of a deep raspy voice and

he speaks with a Spanish accent. I remember his feet pointed in like he was slightly pigeon-toed."

"He hit you?" he asked, making the question sound casual when he was feeling exactly the opposite.

"He slapped me a few times to make his point."

His hands tightened around the wheel. "Which was?"

"He wants Drake Trucking to start working for him. We're supposed to haul his goods—whatever they are—take them wherever he wants them taken. No questions asked. In return, he pays me a boatload of money."

"And if you don't do it?"

"He didn't say exactly, but I'm guessing he kills me."

Carly let Linc help her out of the truck and walk her into the house. He checked the place over while Ross Townsend parked her pickup in the garage and drove off with Frank.

"Nobody here," Linc said. "Doesn't look like there has been."

"I think they'll leave me alone for a while." She crossed the living room to the front door. She needed him to leave. She needed to get herself together. "I really appreciate everything you did tonight. You've been a good friend, Linc. Grandpa Joe would be very grateful."

She started to open the door, but Linc pushed it closed.

"Why don't you go in and take a shower? Get cleaned up and go to bed? I'll sleep out here on the sofa."

She started shaking her head. "You don't have to do that. Those guys aren't coming back tonight. El Jefe delivered his message loud and clear. You can go home. I'll be fine."

"I'm not leaving, Carly. Not tonight. I need to be here. I need to be sure you're okay."

There was something in those green eyes she couldn't read. Worry, perhaps? Regret that he hadn't been able to protect her?

She reached toward him, set her palm against his cheek, felt the roughness of his late-night beard. "I appreciate what you're trying to do, Linc, I really do, but—"

"I'm staying," he said, and all the soft feelings those green eyes summoned flew right out the window.

"You're leaving and that's the end of it." She took a couple of steps and jerked open the door.

Linc slammed it closed. "I'm staying. I have to be back in Dallas in the morning. Tonight I'm staying right here."

She jammed her hands on her hips. "Damn you, I can't do this! Not tonight!" Her eyes welled. "Don't you understand? I can't have you here, not after what happened!"

He reached out and caught her shoulders. "You said he didn't hurt you. You said—"

"He didn't hurt me! He just scared the hell out of me! I'm still scared! That's why I need you to leave!"

"You aren't making any sense."

A sob escaped. She turned away from him and walked into the kitchen, her eyes glazed with tears. She felt him come up behind her, ease her back against his chest. She wanted to turn around and just burrow into him, feel those big hard arms go around her, hear him tell her she was safe.

"What is it?" Linc asked softly. "Tell me."

She turned and looked up at him, wiped tears from her cheeks. "You're so strong, so damned big and capable. Whenever you're around, I turn into a helpless, crying female. I just want to hand all my troubles over to you and let you take care of them, take care of me. I hate myself for it. I won't be that person. I've worked too hard learning to take care of myself."

"I've got broad shoulders, Carly. Taking a little of the weight off yours doesn't bother me."

"It bothers me, Linc! I don't want to be dependent on you or anyone else!"

His jaw hardened. "Unless you're willing to call the sheriff and have me thrown out, I'm staying. Tomorrow I'm setting up a protection detail—a real one this time. You'll have a bodyguard twenty-four/seven. I promised your grandfather. I won't break my word."

Frustration rolled through her, along with a shot of temper. Her hand flew back. She took a swing at his too-handsome face, but it never connected. Instead, he caught her wrist and didn't let go. The heat of his fingers, the calluses she didn't expect to feel, made her nipples tighten. He was so close, she could see the gold around the pupils in his eyes.

His nostrils flared. His eyes locked with hers and her breathing went ragged. She wanted to kiss him even more than she wanted to hit him.

He drew her closer, until their bodies were touching full length. Her breath caught at the feel of the hard ridge beneath his zipper, the knowledge that he was as fiercely aroused as she.

"We . . . we can't do this," she whispered.

For several long moments they just stood there staring at each other, both of them breathing too fast.

Then Linc let her go and stepped back out of her space.

"Go take your shower," he said softly. "Get out of those wet clothes and get warmed up. Tonight I'll sleep on the sofa. Tomorrow we'll work this out, find a way to compromise, okay?"

She swallowed. Her lip throbbed; her body hurt all over. She felt like crying again.

He reached up and touched her cheek. "We'll talk things over, come up with a solution. You can trust me to make this right, Carly."

She finally nodded. Turning away, she started down the hall. He was Lincoln Cain. He'd made a fortune at the bargaining table. He knew how to handle people, knew how to get whatever he wanted. He knew she was attracted to him. He could use that attraction to manipulate her, bend her to his will.

And yet she trusted him. Aside from Grandpa Joe, more than any man she had ever known.

Carly thought of him in her living room, six-foot-five-inches, two hundred plus pounds of pure male muscle watching over her.

No matter what she'd told him, it was good to feel that at least for tonight she was safe.

Linc punched the uncomfortable pillow he'd found in the hall closet and stuffed it beneath his head. He was too long for the sofa, which was old and lumpy at best. Sometime during the night, he'd heard soft footsteps, realized it was Carly bringing him a blanket, draping it over him while she thought he was asleep.

He'd caught a few hours off and on, not enough. At least there hadn't been any more trouble.

He thought about what she'd said, that she refused to be the person who needed someone to take care of her, that she'd worked too hard learning to take care of herself.

He knew her story, that her mother had been a junkie who had died of an overdose when Carly was ten. Joe had taken her in and raised her. Both his daughters had been fragile women, unable to cope with life, Joe had said. According to Joe, both were now dead.

Joe had taught Carly to be self-reliant, to make her way in the world without him—or anyone else.

Linc smiled darkly. When it came to El Jefe, Joe's careful planning had backfired. Carly needed help but she was determined not to take it.

The rain had stopped hours ago. Gray light filtered in through the living room curtains, brightening the dingy room. Linc rolled off the sofa, pulled his jeans on over his briefs, and padded down the hall to the bathroom at the end.

Returning to the kitchen a few minutes later, he spotted the coffeemaker on the counter and went to work brewing a pot.

He had to get going. His pilot would be picking him up at the ranch in a little over an hour. The coffee began to brew, dripping into the carafe, giving off that robust, first-cup aroma.

He found a couple of mugs and set them on the counter, glanced up to see Carly walking down the hall in a pair of boxer brief pajama bottoms that showed off her long, sexy legs. A tank top shifted softly over the fullness of her breasts while a tangle of long blond waves cascaded around her shoulders.

He thought of what had almost happened last night and desire flared hot and thick in his blood.

As she neared the kitchen, Carly spotted him in front of the counter and jerked as if she'd awakened from a trance. Her big blue eyes ran over his bare chest, over the tat on his bicep, down to the bulge in his jeans. He felt the contact like a cattle prod, making him even harder.

"I-I need a shower," she said, then turned and started back down the hall in the opposite direction.

He needed a shower himself, a long, ice-cold one, but he didn't have time right now. "Give me a minute before you go. I've got to get back to Dallas. I'd appreciate if we could talk for a minute before I leave."

She took a deep breath, turned around, and walked into the living room, plunked down in a chair. "What is it?"

When he grabbed his T-shirt and dragged it on, Carly seemed to relax. Linc sat down across from her. "How long has it been since you've had a day off?"

A smile touched her lips. "You mean since I've been back in Texas? Let me see . . . if you count Granddad's funeral—one."

"That's what I thought. I have to go back to Dallas, but I don't have to stay. I was thinking maybe you could come with me. I chopper in and out so it only takes a few minutes to get there. As soon as I wrap up my business, we can come back here."

"What am I supposed to do while you're working? I can't go shopping—I don't have any money. Even if I did, I don't need any clothes. Besides, I have a lot of work to do at the office."

"You could take some of it with you. We'd set you up

at a desk somewhere. You'd get a little break from Iron Springs and I'd feel better knowing you're safe."

She sat forward in the chair and he forced himself not to stare at the soft mounds beneath the tank top. He clenched his hands into fists to keep from reaching out to cup them.

"What about tomorrow, Linc, and the day after that? You can't protect me every minute."

"Maybe not completely, but if . . ." He paused when she narrowed her eyes as if she saw the blow coming.

"If what?" she asked.

"If you stayed out at the ranch, you'd be a helluva lot safer than you are here."

Her eyes widened. "Are you crazy? I can't just move in with you."

"The house is fifteen thousand square feet, Carly. It wouldn't be like we were living together. All the bedrooms are suites. We wouldn't even have to see each other. The thing is, the property's gated and there's security twenty-four/seven."

She started shaking her head.

"A lot of people stay there. Ross Townsend stayed at the house last night." He reached over and caught her hand. The contact speared heat into his groin. A flush rose in Carly's face and spread across her chest.

Linc let go of her hand but kept talking. "I'm asking this as a favor. I made a promise. I need you to help me keep it."

He glanced around the dingy, worn-out living room. Back in the day, Joe could have afforded to remodel if he'd wanted, but after Carly left, he was comfortable with the place the way it was.

"There's a swimming pool," he said, hoping to tempt her. "And a couple of smaller heated pools. There's a

Jacuzzi tub in every guest suite. I'll have the chef come in and take care of meals. You could think of it as a mini vacation."

She eyed him across the space between them. She'd cleared a lot of stuff out of the house and painted the kitchen, but even fixed up, it was no Blackland Ranch. What woman wouldn't enjoy a few days of living in undeniable luxury?

"You'd still be working in Dallas, right?" she said.

"Not this week, but next week, yes." Unless he needed to be closer, but he didn't say that.

"And I could still go to work every day?"

"I'd want you to have some kind of personal protection, but yes, you could definitely go to work or anywhere else you wanted to go."

She sighed. "Even if I agree, it doesn't solve the problem. What am I going to do about El Jefe? The man expects me to join his criminal empire. God only knows what he wants me to do. Whatever it is, if I do it, I could go to prison. If I don't, I could end up dead."

"Come to Dallas. I've got a couple of ideas, but we need to talk them over, and right now I have to leave. Will you come with me?"

Carly hesitated too long to suit him, then sighed and slowly stood up from the chair. "All right, but I need a few minutes to get ready. Once you're back in Dallas, you'll be Lincoln Cain, hotshot millionaire. I don't want to look like one of your poor relations."

Linc chuckled. "Take your time." He needed to get to the office, but he'd find a way to make it work. He didn't tell her his meeting this morning was with the governor.

He didn't want her to change her mind.

Chapter Eleven

Out her front window, Carly watched the big black helicopter with the red and black Tex/Am logo, an image of the state, hover then set down in the vacant field next to the house. Since they were running a little late, Linc had phoned his pilot and changed the pickup spot.

"I've got a meeting I can't miss," he said to her. "We need to go." Grabbing the handle of the overnight bag she had packed so they could go straight to the ranch when the chopper returned to Iron Springs, he headed for the door.

Carly slung the strap of her laptop over her shoulder and picked up the quilted beige Chanel bag she carried with the apricot skirt suit and patterned navy and apricot silk blouse she was wearing. Hurrying, she walked out the door in front of him.

She hadn't lied about not needing clothes. She'd been a real fashion diva when she'd flown the JFK-Paris route. For the first time, the expenditures seemed worthwhile.

She stepped off the porch and kept going. It wasn't

easy running across the muddy, uneven ground in a pair of Gucci high heels. When she stumbled, Linc steadied her.

"Wait here. I'll be right back."

He took the computer off her shoulder, carried it and her bag over to the chopper, then strode back and scooped her up against his chest—a big, powerful chest that she now knew was as gorgeous as Rowena had said.

Carrying her beneath the rotating blades, he set her down inside the helicopter, then climbed in behind her, settling his big body into the leather seat next to hers.

The pilot pulled off his headset. "You ready, Mr. C?"

"Dillon, this is Ms. Drake." Linc strapped himself in and Carly did the same.

"Nice meetin' ya, Ms. Drake," Dillon drawled; he was an attractive dark-haired man somewhere in his late twenties.

She started to tell him she'd rather he just called her Carly, opened her mouth, shot a glance at Linc, and figured it was a bad idea.

Linc just smiled. "She'd rather you called her Carly," he said.

Dressed in a crisp white shirt and black slacks, Dillon touched the brim of his Tex/Am baseball cap, flashed her a grin, and went back to working the controls.

Linc pointed to the headset next to her seat and she put it over her ears as the helicopter lifted away. The swooping sensation had her stomach floating up, but she didn't think the ride would bother her, not after all the flights she'd been on, some in pretty rough weather.

They made minor conversation on the way, but as Linc had said, the slightly over seventy-mile trip to his office didn't take long. Below her, the fields made a quilted pattern along the roads. Dark green vegetation contrasted with rich black soil and clusters of houses.

"A lot less traffic this way," Linc said as the chopper reached the city, hovered, then settled on the roof of a multistoried mirrored glass building on the north side of Dallas.

When they got out, one of the guys who was waiting on the roof took her computer while Linc grabbed her hand and tugged her toward a brushed chrome door that turned out to be an elevator. She noticed one just like it on the opposite side of the roof.

"One goes to my office. One goes to Beau's."

The elevator dropped down and opened into an impressive office with big glass windows. She didn't have time to notice much more than the wide teakwood desk and tables and the caramel-colored leather chairs.

He tugged her toward a paneled door in the wall, hesitated an instant, then pulled it open and led her inside.

"Where are we?"

"Suite off my private office. Living room, bedroom, and bath. If I'm pressed for time, I can shower and dress right here, or catch a few hours' sleep. Since we left directly from your house, I need to change. Give me a few minutes and I'll be right with you."

She nodded and Linc disappeared into the bedroom, which gave her a chance to prowl the compact living area. A leather sofa and chairs matched the furniture in Linc's office; the tables and built-in bookshelves were also made of teak.

Leather-bound books: Twain's *Huckleberry Finn* pressed against Ayn Rand's *Atlas Shrugged,* Aldous Huxley's

Brave New World, and a book of poems by Lord Byron. She wondered if he'd actually read them, had a hunch he had.

There were photos on the shelves, not many. A good-looking man with slightly longish black hair and high cheekbones wearing a driver's racing suit stood next to Linc, their arms draped over each other's shoulders, both of them grinning.

Had to be Linc with his partner, Beau Reese.

Reese was broad-shouldered, but leaner than Linc, not as muscular, and a few inches shorter, still a very tall man, and extremely good-looking.

Her gaze wandered to a different photo, this one of a younger man wearing military camouflage. She had no idea who he was, but . . . She studied his amazingly handsome face, picked up on the small cleft in his chin.

She didn't know who he was, but she was sure he and Linc were related.

"That's my brother," Linc said as he walked up beside her, smelling faintly of cologne. "Josh is a Marine serving in Afghanistan."

"I didn't know you had a brother."

"Half brother," he said. In a navy Armani suit with very fine pinstripes and a snow-white, French-cuffed shirt, he looked amazing, and completely remote, no longer the biker or the virile half-naked man she'd seen in her living room that morning.

"I didn't know it either until five years ago," he said. "Josh dropped me a note. He said he'd known about me for a while, but he wasn't sure how I'd feel about a younger brother showing up out of nowhere. I'm pretty sure Josh believed I'd think he was after my money."

"Did you?"

"I had him thoroughly vetted, of course. Josh is one of the good guys. He's a special operations sniper who's been serving his country for years. Our old man was a drunk. He treated my mother like a punching bag until I got big enough to stop him. She got cancer and died and my old man took off. Apparently he conned some other woman into taking him in and got her pregnant. At least he had the balls to marry her before he took off again."

"Oh, Linc."

"Giving me a brother was the only good thing my old man ever did for me."

Her heart went out to him. He had so much now, but he'd grown up with so little.

He glanced down at the heavy gold Rolex he was wearing on one thick wrist. "Listen, I've got to go. Millie knows you're in here. She's my assistant. She'll set you up at one of the desks or you can work right here. I've got meetings for the next couple of hours. We'll take a late lunch, work a little longer, then head back. If that's okay with you."

"That's fine." As he turned and walked away, disappearing back into his office space, a heavy weight settled on her chest. She was out of her depths here. As if she'd tumbled down a rabbit hole and couldn't wake up.

It wasn't the wealth that intimidated her. She'd met a lot of wealthy men while working in Delta first class, had gone out with more than a few.

It was Linc himself, the confident businessman she had only caught a glimpse of at the funeral. The man who ran a billion-dollar corporation. The man who was as comfortable in a two-thousand-dollar suit as he was in a pair of jeans.

She had never been more grateful to be wearing an expensive designer suit.

A soft knock sounded at a door she hadn't noticed across the living room. When she walked over and opened it, a petite brunette stood outside.

"I'm Millie," the woman said. "Welcome to Tex/Am Enterprises."

"I'm Carly Drake. Nice to meet you."

Millie smiled. "Linc doesn't usually bring anyone into his private suite. You must be special."

"Special circumstances, more like."

"Okay. Let's get you settled. Linc has meetings going on in his office. We set your laptop up at one of the desks, or you can work in here if you'd rather."

She'd rather see what went on in a company this size. She might even learn something. "The desk is fine."

It was actually a cubicle, large and fairly open. She could watch the comings and goings and still get some work done.

The place hummed with activity, nicely dressed men and women moving around, all walking briskly, relaying information, going in and out of the conference room. No one entered Linc's domain.

An hour or so after she'd arrived, his office door opened and a man walked out. Carly blinked, focused, blinked again. Holy crap, it was the governor!

Apparently Lincoln Cain had some very powerful friends.

She went back to work, sent some e-mails to Donna at the office. Her office manager was getting together some of the info Linc had requested so that he would make the loan she so desperately needed.

The thought didn't sit well. She didn't like being obligated to him in any way. She also didn't like the idea he might wind up owning the controlling half of Drake Trucking.

Since she desperately needed the loan, she had no choice. She pulled up Drake's accounting records for the last five years and sent them as an attachment to the address she'd been given in Tex/Am's accounting division, then went back to work.

She tried not to dwell on the problems she faced at Drake. She tried not to think of El Jefe and the threat looming over her head, but she was less successful at that.

At half past one, Linc came out of his office. A town car was waiting to drive them the short distance to a restaurant called Piero's not far away.

A black-haired maître d' beamed as Linc walked in. "Mr. Cain, it's good to see you. We have your usual table ready. Please . . . if you will follow me." He led them to a private booth near the back, where she found white tablecloths and a nice wine list. Neither of them ordered a glass.

The food was Italian and tasted delicious, but with so much on her mind, she wasn't really hungry. Since she didn't feel much like talking, Linc carried most of the conversation, telling her about his meeting with the governor, then a road construction project in New Mexico one of his companies was involved in.

"It's a big job," he said. "Rebuilding and widening the highway north of Santa Fe. Tex/Am Construction just broke ground last week. Of course we're doing the whole project with mules and wagons, so it may take us a little longer."

She nodded, forced a smile. "That's interesting."

"You know, I actually think building a freeway with mules and wagons would be interesting—if it was possible, which it isn't. You aren't listening. What going on?"

She flushed. She'd been thinking about the loan she needed, but it wasn't the most important thing on her mind.

"I keep thinking about El Jefe, trying to figure out what I'm going to do."

"I was hoping to have this conversation later, but Ross Townsend called. A deposit was made into Miguel Hernandez's bank account the month before he was murdered. All cash, twenty thousand dollars. Looks like he was involved with El Jefe after all."

Carly started shaking her head. "That can't be right. He worked for Joe for years. My grandfather trusted him completely."

"Then how do you account for the deposit? Surely the man didn't earn that kind of money."

"No, but . . . How did Townsend find out?"

"I didn't ask. Finding things out is what I pay him to do."

"Okay, I'll talk to Conchita. Maybe she can explain it."

"We'll both talk to her. In case you haven't figured it out, we're in this together."

She hesitated. "All right." But she could tell he was convinced Miguel was guilty. After her terrifying experience with El Jefe, Carly thought Miguel might have had no other choice.

Chapter Twelve

"You finished?" Linc asked as their lunch came to an end.

Seated across from him, Carly tossed her white linen napkin down on the table. "I'm done."

This late in the afternoon, the restaurant was nearly empty, just a few waiters moving around picking up and resetting the tables for the supper crowd.

Linc stood up and pulled out her chair. "I need to get back to the office. I've still got a couple more hours of work before I'm finished."

"I've got plenty to do," Carly said.

"I pulled the address of the couple who found Miguel's body out of the case files."

"The Grangers," she said. "I remember seeing their name."

"I thought we could pay them a visit before we head home. Sometimes people remember something later that doesn't seem important at the time."

"I had that thought myself."

"Ross could do it, but I'd rather he keep digging around in Iron Springs." Linc ushered her out of the restaurant, into the back of the town car. She'd seemed preoccupied all day, but so had he. He figured she was thinking of El Jefe and what had happened last night, worrying about how to handle things from here.

Linc wished she'd sold him the company, let him deal with the threat, but that wasn't going to happen.

At the office, both of them went back to work. By six o'clock he was finished and guiding her toward the elevator up to the roof.

"What about the Grangers?" she asked. "I thought that's where we were going."

"Millie called to set up a time. They're out of town until tomorrow. We've got a one o'clock appointment tomorrow afternoon. I thought we'd come in and talk to them, then catch an early dinner before we head home."

Carly didn't jump at the idea but eventually she nodded. "Okay."

The chopper took them back to the ranch. From the helipad, Linc grabbed Carly's overnight bag out of the helicopter while she shouldered her laptop.

Walking beside her, he carried her suitcase up the wide stone steps into the massive entry and set the bag down on the floor.

"You want a tour first or shall I take you up to your suite?"

She didn't answer. She was too busy staring at the twin sweeping staircases leading up to the second story, the huge crystal chandelier suspended above the inlaid Italian marble floors, the black and sienna sunburst pattern beneath her feet.

Her gaze went left, to a living room done in white

and gold with heavy gold draperies and gilded French antiques.

"So what do you think?" he asked, watching her closely.

"It's . . . umm . . . It isn't exactly . . . It's just . . ."

"It's just what?"

"It's just that it . . . It just . . . it doesn't seem to fit you."

He frowned. "You don't like it?" He had never brought a woman to the house who didn't gush over the opulent interior, who wasn't impressed by the sheer spectacle of the place, the millions it had cost to build.

"It's fine. It's just . . . it's a surprise, is all."

"It's a surprise because you don't think it fits me."

"Well, I don't know, I didn't expect—"

Linc reached down and grabbed her bag, turned, and started striding back toward the door.

Carly adjusted the strap of her laptop on her shoulder and ran after him. "Wait a minute! I didn't mean to insult you. It's a very nice house. It's just—"

He stopped so fast as he turned, she collided with his chest. "It just doesn't fit me—that's what you said." He started walking again, heading for the garage.

"Where are you going?" She trailed after him as he punched in the code and one of the garage doors began sliding open.

He walked over to the black Jeep Wrangler sitting in the bay, tossed her suitcase into the back, slid in behind the wheel, and fired it up.

He backed out of the garage, turned and pulled up next to her. "Get in." The Jeep idled like a big black cat. One of his favorite toys, it was fully tricked out: chrome rims, wide off-road tires, a heavy duty roll bar. A top covered the front seats, but the rest of the vehicle was completely open. It was rugged, perfect for the ranch.

In her slim skirt, Carly struggled to climb into the passenger seat. Linc grabbed her hand and pulled her aboard. He took her laptop and settled it behind her. Carly buckled her seat belt and Linc hit the gas. The vehicle lurched forward, speeding off down the dirt road that headed toward the back of the ranch.

"So . . . umm . . . where are we going?"

"Someplace else."

She leaned back against the seat as he drove the Jeep along the dirt road. He was taking her someplace he had never taken a woman. It was the second time it had happened that day.

He'd told himself to stay away from Carly, that it was what Joe would have wanted.

But it wasn't what Linc wanted. Linc wanted Carly in his bed. He wanted her with a need he had never felt for another woman. He wanted her for more than a night, though how much longer he couldn't say.

He thought of Joe and the promise he had made. But Joe Drake was a very smart man. He knew Linc and he knew his granddaughter. He must have considered what could happen. Carly wasn't a fool, and Linc wasn't the same wild kid he had once been.

A few minutes later he pulled up in front of the single-story red brick ranch house. Outbuildings dotted the open fields around it: a barn, and what he called his toy garage where he kept a pair of ATVs, a Prowler UTV, and other miscellaneous recreational gear.

Carly followed his lead and jumped down from the seat. He grabbed her overnight bag out of the back while she retrieved her laptop. Setting a hand at her waist, he guided her into the house. In the living room, he set down her bag.

Carly set her laptop down on a side table. "What is this place?"

"This is where I live. I stay in the big house when I'm entertaining, but when I'm at the ranch by myself, I stay here. This is my home."

Carly just stared. Linc had brought her into his home. His inner sanctuary. When he said nothing more, she slipped off her heels and began to wander the living room, trailing a hand over the burgundy leather sofa that had to be at least nine feet long. There were brass studs around the rolled arms, the arms of both matching chairs, and the legs of the ottoman.

The furniture sat on a throw rug done in an Indian design in front of a big rock fireplace. The coffee table and end tables were very dark oak and they looked as if they carried some kind of brand.

"This is the original ranch house," Linc said. "That's our brand. Rocking BR—for Blackland Ranch." Which explained the burn marks in the wood.

She studied the paintings on the walls, very Western, with herds of cattle being driven to market, one of a cowboy catching a nap on his horse. A colorful painting of a run-down roadhouse hung a few feet away, a group of men sitting on their motorcycles out in front.

She kept walking, spotted a wall of photos. Pictures of Beau Reese with his race car, photos of Linc sitting on his motorcycle in his leathers with the guys she had met at Jubal's.

She looked up at him. Everything about him appealed to her: his size, his strength, his intelligence.

"I've never brought a woman here before," he said. Carly went still.

"I don't know where this is going," he continued. "Neither of us can know that. I can pick up that bag and drive you back to the big house. You'll have your own private suite. I'll play the gentleman and we can take our time, get to know each other, play the game."

She moistened her lips. She couldn't manage a single word.

"Or you can stay here. There are two other bedrooms besides mine, but aside from the powder room, the only spare bathroom is down the hall. There's no chef to cook for you, just me. No housekeeper to chaperone us. What's it to be, Carly? You want to stay with the man who lives up at the big house? Or you want to stay with the man who lives here?"

Her throat felt tight. Her heart was beating, thumping inside her chest. Tension seemed to scorch the air between them. There were so many problems, so much she had to deal with. She couldn't get involved with Lincoln Cain.

She took in a slow breath of air, her mind battling the desire pulsing through her body. Just looking at him made heat throb between her legs. She had never wanted a man the way she wanted Cain. Never felt this kind of need.

She picked up the suitcase and started down the hall, paused in front of the master suite. "Your room or the one next door?"

"Mine," he said, his hot gaze like a fire burning into her flesh.

She dropped the bag just inside the door, turned, and walked back to him.

She slid her arms around his neck. "I want you to kiss me. You can't imagine how much."

His eyes moved over her face, fixed on her mouth. "I can't make you any promises." His big hands spanned her waist. "I don't know how this is going to work."

"I don't need any promises."

He dragged her hard against him and his mouth crushed down over hers. She could taste his hunger, his desire. His tongue was in her mouth and hers was in his. The kiss went on and on, deep and plundering, as if he couldn't get enough. As if she couldn't.

She wanted him out of his clothes, wanted him naked, wanted to be skin to skin, nothing but heat between them. She wanted him to touch her all over.

Carly shoved his suit coat off his broad shoulders and it fell to the floor. She loosened his tie, pulled it off, started unbuttoning his shirt, dragged it open, ran her fingers over the beautiful muscles across his chest.

Linc kissed her again. "Too many clothes," he said, and began peeling them off. He toed off his shoes and unfastened his cuff links, stripped off his shirt. He was down to his slacks, bare-chested, biceps bulging and amazing.

An instant later, her suit jacket was gone. He unfastened the clasp in front of her apricot demi-bra and tossed it away, unfastened her skirt, and it dropped to the floor.

She was wearing an apricot lace thong, her lingerie as expensive as the rest of the clothes she'd splurged on in Paris. When Linc stepped back to look at her, when she saw the glitter of heat in his eyes, she knew the cost was worth it.

Linc kissed her, long and deep, kissed her until her

legs felt weak and her skin burned. All the while, he caressed her breasts, cupped them, plucked her nipples.

Carly moaned. She reached for the button on the waistband of his slacks. "Too many clothes," she said.

Linc caught her hand. His fingers were big and strong, as powerful as the rest of him. "We can go into the bedroom, take this nice and slow. Or I can take you right here, take you as deep and hard as I want to. The choice is yours."

The words sent need pounding through her. Her breasts were aching, her body throbbing. Carly went up on her toes, slid her fingers into the hair at the nape of his neck, and pulled his head down for a kiss.

"Right here," she whispered. "Right now."

His erection leaped against her. His mouth claimed hers as he backed her up against the wall. She heard the jangle of his belt buckle, then the glide of his zipper as he freed himself.

She was wet and trembling as he slid the thong down over her hips, let it fall to the floor, found her sex, and began to stroke her.

"I knew it would be this way," he said. "I could feel the heat from across the room."

She whimpered.

A condom came out of his wallet. He sheathed himself, lifted her, and wrapped her legs around his waist. Carly gasped at the feel of him, even bigger than she had imagined.

"It's all right," he said, pressing his mouth against the side of her neck. "I won't hurt you. We'll just take it slow."

He slid in a little deeper and her body relaxed around him. He felt so good. Unbelievably good. She wanted more. She wanted all of him. She began to squirm, pressing herself down on him. "Please, Linc."

"Dammit, I don't want to hurt you."

"Please . . ."

Linc caught her mouth in a savage kiss and thrust home. Carly cried out. She had waited so long for this, wanted him so badly. The instant he moved, she started coming. The world expanded, colors exploded behind her eyes. He was driving hard and deep and she just kept coming. Clinging to his powerful shoulders, she hung on tight as her body spun out of control.

The moment seemed to go on forever. She was beginning to spiral down when Linc finally let himself go, reaching his own powerful climax, which set her off again.

For long moments she floated back to earth. Linc just held her, the clock on the shelf ticking softly. Kissing the top of her head, he slowly lowered her to her feet, kissed her, and left to dispense with the condom.

When he returned to the living room, he scooped her up and carried her into his bedroom, settled her in his big king-size bed.

She watched him moving around the room, all hard muscle, long legs, broad back, and narrow hips. He rummaged around in the closet, took a carryon bag down from the shelf, unzipped it, and pulled out a string of condoms.

"We're going to need these," he said, and tossed them onto a nightstand. None next to his bed. He had told her the truth. He didn't bring women into his home.

As he settled himself on the mattress, she realized he was already hard again. She took a shaky breath, was aroused once more just looking at him, wanting to touch him all over.

Linc followed her gaze to his heavy erection, and a corner of his mouth edged up. He came up over her and very thoroughly kissed her. Sliding himself deep inside, he slowly began to move.

Linc's cell phone buzzed, vibrating softly next to the bed. Instantly awake, he turned onto his side and plucked the phone off the nightstand. The number on the screen belonged to his foreman, Joaquin Santos. Santos didn't call if it wasn't important.

Linc answered before the phone could ring again. As he rolled out of bed, he flicked a glance at Carly, who still slept soundly, a tangle of heavy blond hair spread out on the pillow next to his.

Even though he'd had her three times last night and again this morning, arousal slid through him. With a resigned sigh, he ignored the urge to climb back into bed with her and padded out of the room into the hall.

"Joaquin, what is it?"

"There is trouble at the gate, *Señor* Cain. The security guard called me. I am there now. People with signs are marching around. Some of them are giving speeches, some are singing songs."

"Songs," he repeated, his mellow mood darkening. Had to be the same bunch who had hassled him outside the courthouse.

"*Sí, señor.* I tried to get them to leave, but they will not go. Do you want me to call the sheriff?"

"Not yet. Let me see if I can talk to them. I'll be right there." Ending the call he went back into the bedroom to grab a pair of jeans and a T-shirt, found Carly sitting up in bed.

Though his mood had turned foul, he smiled when he saw her. "Morning, sweetness."

She shoved back her thick blond hair. "What's going on?"

"Long story short? Those protestors I mentioned are out at the gate trying to stop Tex/Am from opening that tire rebuilding plant I told you about."

"We use those rebuilt tires all the time," Carly said. "Saves money and recycles the rubber instead of having to find some way to dispose of it."

"Exactly." The shower would have to wait . . . which might not be bad if he could talk Carly into joining him. "I've got to go. I'll be back as soon as I can."

"Give me a minute and I'll go with you. Maybe I can add something that will help."

It wasn't a bad idea. Drake Trucking had been a fixture in Iron Springs for years. "All right, but you better be quick. If we don't get out there soon, they'll probably tear down the gate."

Five minutes later, he and Carly walked out the door. They climbed in the Jeep and he drove past the stone house to the big iron gates out on the highway.

Joaquin was right. Twenty some people paraded up and down the roadway carrying the same damn signs he recognized from the courthouse. SAVE MOTHER EARTH. PROTECT PLEASANT HILL. STOP POLLUTION NOW! Linc took one look at the group, felt the hostile vibes pouring off of them, and knew any sort of confrontation would only make matters worse.

"Call the sheriff," he told Joaquin. "Let Howler

handle this. Rousting a bunch of loonies might actually be something he can handle."

"*Sí, señor.*"

They got back in the Jeep, turned around, and drove off to the sound of jeers and a fresh chorus of singing. One guy was playing a harmonica, a self-styled Bob Dylan.

"People can really be idiots," Linc said as he pulled up in front of the ranch house.

"Maybe they aren't idiots. Maybe they're doing this because they want something. Someone could be stirring up trouble because he's got some kind of agenda."

Linc paused at the front door and gave her a look. She had Joe's brains, too. "You could be right. I'll have my people look into it, see if they can find out who their cheerleader is and what his motives are."

"The plant would be good for Pleasant Hill and also Iron Springs. I hope you get it approved."

He smiled. "So do I."

They walked into the house and Carly headed for the bedroom. "I really need a shower," she said as he walked down the hall behind her.

His eyes ran over her sweet little ass in the snug-fitting jeans. "Yeah, so do I."

Carly turned and grinned up at him. "I've seen the size of your . . . shower. I suppose there's room for two."

Linc chuckled and followed her into the bathroom. For now, he'd leave the protestors to the sheriff. The trouble at the front gate could wait a little while longer.

Chapter Thirteen

An hour later Carly was dressed and ready to accompany Linc to Dallas. Last night had been a respite, hours of amazing sex and worry-free slumber.

Lincoln Cain was everything a man could be—at least in bed. The rest remained to be seen.

The sex had been fantastic, but today reality was setting back in. Whoever had murdered Miguel Hernandez was still on the loose, and El Jefe, who might have been responsible, still expected her and Drake Trucking to join his organization.

"You ready?" Dressed more casually today in dark blue Levi's, a white western shirt rolled up to the elbows, and a pair of black cowboy boots, Linc walked out of his home office down the hall.

The residence, apparently over a hundred years old, had been completely remodeled. It was simple and masculine, yet everything inside was modern and entirely first-class, including the stainless kitchen, the bathrooms, powder room, Linc's office, and home gym.

And everything about the place fit him perfectly.

"Let me grab my purse."

In a pair of jeans and a sleeveless blue print blouse, she joined him in the slate-floored entry. She'd only brought an overnight bag. Aside from what she'd worn yesterday, she hadn't packed the kind of clothes she would need for the city. Since Linc wanted to go to his office after they talked to the Grangers, then later they were going out to supper, he'd agreed to stop by her house so she could change into something more appropriate.

And now that it appeared she was staying at the ranch—she flushed at the memory of last night—she needed to bring more of her clothes back to his place.

With the strap of her laptop slung over Linc's shoulder, she walked beside him out of the house. He helped her into the Jeep and they headed for the helipad, where the chopper was waiting when they arrived. It swooped up, crossed the short distance between their two homes in minutes, and set down again in the field across from Joe's little house.

Carly went around to the back door and unlocked it, but Linc caught her before she had time to get inside.

"Let me take a look first."

It seemed a little over the top. She didn't think El Jefe would be lying in wait in her small rundown house, but under the circumstances, caution wasn't a bad idea.

When Linc returned a few minutes later with a grim look on his face, a shot of fear slid through her.

"What is it?" She pushed past him into the kitchen and he didn't try to stop her. First she noticed the broken window over the kitchen sink, then the awful destruction around her. Her legs refused to move. She couldn't believe what she was seeing. She heard the crunch of broken glass as Linc came up behind her, drew her back against his chest.

"It's only stuff," he said softly. "It's easily replaced."

She glanced around the room, at the shattered coffee cups on the floor, the pictures smashed against the walls, and her eyes filled. "It's not just stuff. It's my stuff . . . and Joe's."

She felt his muscles tighten.

Carly started walking through the debris, seeing dishes dragged out of the cupboard and broken into pieces, the stuffing from the sofa tossed onto the living room floor.

Linc opened the door to the garage and flipped on the light. Walked out then walked back in. "Your pickup's okay. They must not have gone into the garage."

Her legs shook as she headed down the hall to her bedroom. The bedding had been pulled off, the perfume bottles and photos on the dressers had been shoved off onto the floor.

"Why?" she asked. "I told him I'd do what he wanted. Why would he destroy my home?"

"We don't know it was him. Not for sure. I didn't see any kind of note. If it was El Jefe, he didn't leave a message like before."

Her legs felt wobbly as she crossed the carpet to her closet and slid open the doors. Some of her clothes had been ripped off the hangers, but most still hung on the bar.

"He was wearing down by the time he got to the bedroom," Linc said, "his anger mostly spent."

She brushed a tear from her cheek, sank down on

the foot of the bed. She glanced up at Linc, whose features looked as grim as she felt.

"You sure you didn't do this just so I'd have to stay out at the ranch?" she teased, trying for a lighter note.

His eyes met hers and his lips twitched. He sat down beside her and pulled her onto his lap. "I'm glad you've still got your sense of humor."

Her gaze lit on a broken framed photo of her and Joe. It was her graduation from high school. Joe had been so proud of her that day. Her throat tightened and a fresh rush of sadness swept through her. "Yeah."

"I'll put some people on this, have the place put back together."

"You don't have to do that."

"I know." His eyes crinkled at the corners. "I promise I won't make it so nice you'll want to move back in."

She sliced him a look.

"At least not too soon."

Carly managed a smile.

"I'm going to have your bedroom packed up and moved to the ranch house. We'll put your stuff in a spare bedroom until your place is cleaned up and you're ready to move back in. I'll get one of the hands to drive your pickup out to the ranch, okay?"

She didn't want to do it. She didn't want to be completely under Linc's control. But she didn't dare stay in the house alone—not until they figured out what was going on.

"There's a set of pickup keys on the hook next to the door."

He nodded. "We've got to call the sheriff. They'll need to dust for prints."

"You think they'll find any?" she asked.

"I don't know. Probably not if it's El Jefe."

She just nodded. She felt numb all over as she went to the closet and picked out a sleeveless black linen dress with a matching short-sleeve pink and black jacket, a garment that could easily transition from day to evening. The bathroom wasn't as bad as the bedroom. She changed, found a pair of strappy, mid-heeled Ferragamos in the closet, and slid them on her feet.

When she walked up to Linc, he caught her chin, bent, and softly kissed her.

"So far I'm doing a pretty rotten job of taking care of you," he said.

Carly's lips curved in a smile. "Oh, I don't know . . . you did a great job last night." Turning, she walked in front of him out of the bedroom.

Linc waited impatiently for a sheriff's deputy to arrive. Deputy Rollins finally showed up, the guy Carly had talked to after the original break-in.

As the deputy walked into the house and saw the destruction, he lifted his cowboy hat and scratched his head. "Looks like those kids came back. Damn, they sure made a mess. My dad would have licked me good for doing something like this."

"I don't think this was done by kids," Carly said.

"Maybe not. We got a fella in the office does the fingerprinting. He's real professional. He's on his way over now. Meantime, I need to get a statement from you."

Linc sat next to Carly at the kitchen table while she told the deputy how she'd been away all night and had just returned home that morning. How they had found the house vandalized.

Rollins shifted his gaze to Linc. "So you two were together all night?"

"That's right," Linc said.

"But you didn't stay here."

"No," Linc said, tamping down his irritation. "We stayed at my place."

The deputy eyed him with suspicion. "You sure this wasn't just some lovers' spat that got out of hand? Insurance won't pay if it was. But I guess you wouldn't know about that."

Anger snapped in Carly's eyes. "The man you're accusing of lying is Lincoln Cain. He probably owns the damn insurance company. No, we didn't have a lovers' spat. Someone broke in and destroyed my house. It's your job to arrest whoever did it."

Beneath the brim of his tan cowboy hat, the deputy's face turned red. "Sorry, Mr. Cain. I should have known it was you when I saw that helicopter. I hope you understand it's my job to get the truth."

"I understand. In return for that understanding, I expect you and your department to do everything in your power to find the man or men responsible."

"Oh, we will. You can count on that."

"Good. Now if you don't mind, Ms. Drake and I have business in Dallas. I hope you'll expedite the results on any prints you find."

"Yes, sir, I sure will."

Linc handed the deputy his business card, not the personal one he had given to Carly. "If there's anything else you need, call my office." He turned to Carly. "You ready?"

She nodded. He could tell she didn't like the conclusion the deputy had drawn—that they had spent the night together in bed. It would be all over Iron Springs by the end of the day. Couldn't be helped, and though Linc worked hard to keep his private life private, he actually liked the idea.

Carly was his, at least for now. Less trouble if people understood that.

Out in the field, Dillon waited patiently in the chopper. In minutes they were belted in and airborne, then setting down on the Tex/Am rooftop, there to speak to the couple who had found Miguel Hernandez's body.

From the roof, they took the elevator all the way down to the underground garage. The parking attendant waved at Linc and ran to get his black Mercedes. He owned a pair of S550s: a two-door coupe he kept in the city, a four-door sedan out at the ranch.

"Wow, sexy ride," Carly said as she slid into the deep leather passenger seat and the attendant closed the door.

"It's comfortable, nice, and safe on the freeways." He leaned over and punched the Grangers' street address into the GPS on the dash. The navigator's soft female voice pointed him in the right direction.

"Gretchen," he said, his nickname for the faceless travel guide.

Carly made no reply. He could see worry weighing her down like a heavy shroud.

"We'll talk to the Grangers," he said matter-of-factly as the car rolled along the busy streets toward the freeway. "If nothing comes of it, we'll try something else. I'll talk to a friend of mine, guy I know in the FBI."

"What!" Carly shot forward so fast her seat belt snapped her back against the seat. "You can't do that!

El Jefe warned me not to say anything. If he found out I talked to the FBI, he might kill me!"

"Take it easy. This would be strictly off the record, not an official conversation. I've known Quinn Taggart for years. He's a good man. Quinn might be able to help us."

Carly shook her head. "You weren't there. You can't know the kind of man El Jefe is. He liked hitting me. He liked controlling me, having me at his mercy. I have to find a way to stop him, but it can't involve the police."

Linc's gaze went to the bruise at the corner of her mouth and his hands tightened around the wheel. "It's all right, honey, I'm not going to do anything we don't both agree on." *At least not yet.*

But sooner or later, El Jefe was going to have to be dealt with. Carly couldn't do it by herself. Linc had connections, people he could trust, but it might not be enough.

They arrived at the Grangers' apartment building and Linc found a parking spot on the street. He helped Carly out of the Mercedes and they walked into the building together, took the elevator to the third floor, and headed down the hall.

A sharp knock and the door swung open. Andy Granger, with curly blond hair, slightly crooked front teeth, and a friendly smile, stood in the opening. "Mr. Cain?"

"That's right. And this is Carly Drake. She was Miguel Hernandez's boss as well as his friend."

"Please come in. This is my wife, Maria." Olive skin and big brown eyes, only a few inches shorter than her husband. The Grangers were in their late twenties.

"It's nice to meet you both," Carly said as Linc guided her into the apartment, which was simply furnished, neat and clean, with a tweed sofa and chair, and old-fashioned shag carpet in the living room.

A little beagle puppy came racing out of the back hallway, dashing straight to Maria, who scooped the small dog up in her arms.

"This is Waldo," she said. "He found your friend. Andy and I are both very sorry."

"Thank you," Carly said.

"I'm glad you called," Andy said. "Yesterday, when Maria was picking up Waldo's toys, she found this." Andy handed Linc a folded-up piece of paper. It was water-spotted and smeared with dried mud.

"At first Maria couldn't figure out where it had come from. Then she thought, with the mud and water stains, maybe the puppy had carried it off that day on the highway. We considered phoning the sheriff, but then you called. We thought we'd give it to you."

Linc unfolded the piece of paper, wrinkled from the rain and mud. A rusty spot on the corner looked like it could be blood. He held it out for Carly to see.

"It looks like a work order," she said. "A cargo manifest."

Part of the top was torn away, along with part of the printed words. The rest were almost unreadable but he could clearly make out the last five letters, *CKING.*

"I think it's ours," Carly said. "It looks like it said DRAKE TRUCKING."

"I think you're right. That makes it part of the crime scene." He turned to the Grangers. "We'll follow up on this, see if it has anything to do with the murder. Thanks for giving it to us."

"I hope it helps," Maria said.

They talked to the couple a while longer, but there was nothing more to add to their original statement. Still, the paper might prove interesting. He'd get the brown spot tested, see if it was blood. If so, maybe they could find out whose.

They left the Grangers and Linc drove back to the office. He had a quick meeting, some calls to make; then he was done for the day. They could go out to dinner, then chopper home.

Linc flicked a glance at Carly and desire slipped through him. He had plans for her tonight and sleep wasn't high on the list.

As the car rolled down the North Central Expressway, the mirrored windows of the Tex/Am building glinted in the sunlight ahead. He pulled the Mercedes into the underground lot and got out. The attendant opened Carly's door, then hurried around and slid in behind the wheel.

Linc grabbed Carly's laptop out of the car and they rode the private elevator up to his office. He should probably give the paper to the sheriff for DNA testing, but he still wasn't sure Howler wasn't involved.

Instead he would send it to the City DNA Lab here in Dallas, see what turned up. Tomorrow he'd talk to Conchita, see what she had to say about the twenty-thousand-dollar bank deposit.

It should be an interesting conversation.

Chapter Fourteen

It was Thursday morning. Carly sat across from Linc at the round oak breakfast table in his sunny kitchen, both of them drinking coffee as if they were just a normal couple on any normal morning.

As if time weren't ticking away, danger pressing in from all sides, getting closer by the minute.

Through the window, beyond a small courtyard with a fountain in the middle, she could see horses playfully running through a grassy pasture. It was so peaceful here. No wonder Linc loved it.

After their conversation with the Grangers yesterday, they'd had supper at an elegant but quiet Dallas restaurant called the Abbey, then they'd returned to the ranch, and Linc had taken her straight to bed. The man was practically insatiable and when she was with him, so was she.

Now it was morning and they both had things to do. She needed to go into her office. She'd been working on her laptop, getting a few things done, but she needed to pay bills and appease creditors, which meant she needed the loan Linc had promised her.

Damn, she hated to bring it up. Having just climbed out of his bed, it felt a little like selling herself.

"What's troubling that mind of yours this morning?" he asked. "I can almost see your brain spinning around."

Carly sighed. "I've got to go into work. I've missed too much time this week already. You said my pickup's in one of the garages. You wouldn't have to drive me."

Linc took a sip of the rich, freshly brewed dark coffee, and set his mug back down on the table. An empty plate that had held a toasted bagel, bacon, and some scrambled eggs sat next to it, along with an empty glass of orange juice.

"I had a feeling you were thinking about that loan I promised you," he said. "You'll find the paperwork at your office when you get there. Sign the documents, and the check will be deposited into whatever account you want this afternoon."

How did he do that? Practically read her mind. Or maybe it was her face. She'd bet he was great at poker.

"You'll pay it back," he said, still tuned in to her thoughts. "Just keep doing what you have been and it'll all come together."

"I hope you're right." Dressed in stretch jeans and a crisp white cotton blouse, she grabbed her purse off the counter. "I've got to get going. If you could just open the garage door so I could get my—"

"Your truck should show up out front any minute."

Carly flicked him a glance. Slinging the strap of her purse over her shoulder, she started walking. Linc came up behind her as she stepped into the entry and pulled open the door.

"There's someone in the passenger seat," she said. "What's going on?"

"That's good ol' Frank. Ross says he's very good at

his job. Says he was having an off night the evening of your little run-in at the Stop and Shop. I don't think he'll let his guard down again."

"What, he's my bodyguard?"

"You haven't forgotten our deal? I told you I'd insist on personal protection. I wasn't talking about condoms."

If she wasn't semi-pissed, she would have laughed. "What's he going to do all day while I'm working?"

"His job. Which is making sure no one tries to abduct you again or shoot you."

Her shoulders slumped. Hard to argue with that. "All right, fine. I'll take good ol' Frank with me." She started for the door.

"There's one more thing."

She turned back. "What's that?"

"You forgot to kiss me good-bye."

Her eyes widened. "Seriously?"

His sexy mouth edged up. "Seriously."

Something melted inside her. She walked back to him, went up on her toes, and pressed a soft kiss on his lips. "Bye, Linc."

When she started to turn and leave, he hauled her back into his arms and took the kiss to a whole different level. "I'll pick you up around lunchtime and we'll go see Conchita."

Ignoring a flare of heat, Carly headed for the truck. "Sounds good," she called over her shoulder, then climbed in behind the wheel and slammed the door.

"I want to apologize for the other night," Frank said from the other side of the vehicle. "To tell you the truth, I underestimated you and the situation. It won't happen again."

"Good to know."

She drove down the dirt road toward the main house, noticed a pair of men wearing camouflage and tactical vests riding ATVs.

Carly slowed. "What's going on?"

"Mr. Cain isn't taking any chances. Until we know more about the situation, he's got security set up around the main house and the ranch house."

"The situation with El Jefe?" Ross Townsend knew about the drug lord. He and Frank Marino had been there the night she'd been abducted.

"Him, or that bunch of fanatics lined up at the gate yesterday morning."

She blew out a breath. It seemed as if trouble was all around them. "I guess it's better to be safe than sorry."

"Exactly," Frank said. He was wearing a shoulder holster under a lightweight jacket, letting her drive so he could be ready for trouble if it came.

Any day she expected to hear from El Jefe. They needed to figure things out and they needed to do it soon.

Linc arrived to pick up Carly at eleven-thirty that morning. She looked frustrated and frazzled, the phone stuck to her ear as she talked to customers and tried to sort out problems.

She shoved the signed loan papers toward him. Linc picked them up, stuffed them into his briefcase, and flipped the latches. He phoned his people and had the money transferred into the Drake Trucking account at the Iron Springs Credit Union.

Carly hung up the phone and leaned back in her

chair. "I told him the check was going in the mail today. I don't think he believed me."

"He'll believe you when he gets the check. Money's being transferred as we speak. You ready to go?"

She stood up from behind her desk, grabbed her purse, and slung the strap over her shoulder. Linc held the door for her and she walked out into the main office, where she paused to speak to Donna.

"Everything's set," Carly said. "I'll need those checks ready for my signature when I get back."

"No problem," Donna said with a smile. "I'll put them on your desk."

Linc escorted Carly out of the building, passing Frank as he led her to his truck. "Take a break and get some lunch," Linc said. "We'll be back in a couple of hours."

"Yes, sir."

They climbed into the GMC and left Drake Trucking, drove down the highway to the address at the other end of town where Conchita Hernandez lived with her three kids.

"She has to know about the deposits," Carly said. "Twenty thousand dollars shows up in your checking account, you're bound to notice."

"Yeah, and you're probably going to ask your husband where the hell the money came from."

Linc pulled up in front of a small yellow house with a clapboard front and brown metal roof. Both of them got out and started up the front walk. Linc rapped lightly on the door. The kids would be at school this time of day, but he'd called ahead, so Conchita was expecting them.

The woman opened the door and stepped back, inviting them into the living room. "Please come in."

She was petite, late twenties, with glossy black hair pulled into a single long braid. Linc figured under different circumstances, Carly would have hugged her, but too much intrigue swirled around them. No way to know whom to trust.

"How are the boys and your little girl?" Carly asked.

"They miss their father." Conchita led them farther into the living room, which looked very Latin, with a colorful serape draped over the sofa and a statue of the Virgin Mary in an alcove at the end of the hall.

"Please sit down," Conchita said. "Would you like something to drink? Some coffee or a soda?"

"Nothing, thank you." Linc urged Carly toward the sofa and both of them sat down.

Conchita sat in a chair across from them. "You said you wished to see me. What is this about?"

"The sheriff's still trying to find the man or men who killed your husband," Linc said. "We're trying to help him. A couple of days ago, something turned up we need to ask you about."

"*Sí*, what is it?"

"Apparently you and your husband recently came into a good sum of money. Twenty thousand dollars. The deposit into your bank account was made in cash. In order to clear things up, we need to know where that money came from."

Eyes wide, Conchita straightened. The hands she gripped in her lap began to tremble. She moistened her lips. "I-I told him not to take it. I told Miguel it was wrong, but he wouldn't listen." A sob slipped from her throat.

"Just take your time," Linc said.

"Miguel, he was afraid for our daughter. Our . . . our little Angelina . . . she is sick with the asthma. There was a doctor who could help but he wanted money. Miguel was frantic. He knew it was wrong, but he couldn't . . . couldn't stand to see his little girl suffer."

Conchita bent her head and sobbed against the arm of the chair. Carly walked over and crouched beside her. "We all do things we regret," she said, reminding Linc of words he'd once said. "Miguel was trying to do what was best for his family."

Conchita raised her head. "I will find a way to pay the money back. My children need me. I cannot go to prison. Please, I am begging you. Tell the sheriff I will find a way."

Linc was good at reading people. No way was this woman involved. "It's all right, Conchita. You don't have to worry about the money. We just need to know who gave it to Miguel and what they expected him to do in return."

Conchita wiped tears from her cheeks. "I do not know, *Señor* Cain." She swallowed. "Miguel would not tell me. He said it was better if I did not know."

Linc sat back on the sofa. He figured it was the truth. Latino males didn't like to involve their wives in business.

"So you don't have any idea what he was being paid to do?" Carly asked.

Conchita just shook her head. She glanced up. "Do you think that was the reason he was murdered? Maybe he was paid to do something but he changed his mind. Maybe that is why they killed him."

Linc glanced over at Carly, whose eyes met his. "It's possible," he said. "Joe Drake trusted your husband. If

Miguel had agreed to help the hijackers in exchange for the money, he might have had second thoughts."

Fresh tears rolled down Conchita's face. "He was a good man. A good husband and father. He never did anything bad, not until this."

Linc stood up and Carly joined him. "I know some people who might be able to help your daughter," Linc said. Pulling a business card out of his wallet, he jotted down a number.

"Tell the woman who answers I told you to call. She'll make sure Angelina gets whatever treatment she needs."

"You are not calling the sheriff?"

"No. Just take care of your family."

Conchita grabbed his hand and kissed the back, knelt on the floor at his feet. "God bless you, *Señor* Cain. I will never forget your kindness."

Linc just nodded. Uncomfortable, he withdrew his hand and turned to Carly. "Let's go."

A few minutes later, they were back in the truck and heading down the highway toward the office.

"That was a nice thing you did back there."

He shrugged. "Probably drug money. No need for her to pay it back."

"You're helping her daughter. You didn't have to do that."

"I support a lot of different charities. They owe me a favor or two."

Carly just smiled. "You know, I'm actually starting to like you—besides just in bed."

Linc laughed. He liked her, too. Probably too much.

"We didn't get any new information," she said, her saucy smile fading.

"No, we didn't. The cargo manifest might give us something. Or maybe Townsend's come up with a lead. I'll call him when we get back to the yard."

"Maybe the sheriff will find fingerprints in my house."

"Could be. At the moment, anything would be useful." He glanced over, tried not to let his gaze slide down to the soft mounds barely visible at the top of her white cotton blouse. "How about some lunch? I'm starving."

She gave him a look.

"What?" he said.

"From the fit of your jeans, I know what you're hungry for."

No point in denying it. He chuckled. "Too bad we both have to work. Which reminds me I have to make a quick trip to my office late this afternoon. I'm taking you with me."

"I'm not dressed for a trip to the city."

"They've seen you all dressed up. I'm not changing, and those sexy jeans look just fine."

She smiled but shook her head. "I really have too much to do."

"Humor me."

Carly sighed. "I take it back. I really don't like you at all—except in bed."

Linc laughed, signaled, and pulled the truck into the drive-thru at Burger King.

Chapter Fifteen

It was late afternoon in Dallas when Carly settled herself in front of her laptop, seated at the same desk on the executive floor she had used the last time she'd been in Tex/Am's headquarters building.

After the visit to Conchita, Linc had driven her back to the yard. She'd gotten a good deal of work done before he'd returned to pick her up for the quick chopper ride to the city, but there always seemed to be more to do.

For the past hour, he'd been locked away behind closed doors. Carly had busied herself with her customer list, checking what needed to be done to make sure the clients were all satisfied, making a list of potential new customers.

It surprised her to realize how good it felt to bring in a new account. Wherever Joe was, he'd be pleased.

Since Linc was still working and she needed a break, she decided to do a little more digging. He was an interesting man, but not particularly forthcoming about himself. She typed in his name and started clicking up Web links with information about him.

The executive floor was humming away, people moving around at a rapid pace. The pace was brisk and efficient at Texas American Enterprises.

After a particularly interesting article, she looked up at the sound of voices close by and saw a tall, slender, raven-haired woman talking to Millie, pointing toward Linc's office. She was wearing a sleeveless dove gray dress with white trim, a slim skirt that fell midcalf, with a wide self-belt, definitely a designer brand. The garment curved perfectly over her hips, and sky-high heels pushed her to over six feet.

The woman had a fabulous figure and she was stunningly beautiful.

"I'm sorry, Ms. Aiello," Millie said. "Linc is tied up all day. There's no way you can get in to see him."

"That is ridiculous. Please tell him Sophia is here. We must discuss the gala coming up next week. We need to talk, finalize our plans for next Saturday night. I must have time to choose the right gown to wear."

Millie shook her head. "I'm sorry. Mr. Cain gave me strict instructions he isn't to be disturbed. You might try calling him later. Or perhaps tomorrow."

The woman's plump lips turned down in a pout. "Linc will be very angry when he finds out Sophia was here and you would not let her see him."

"I'm sorry," Millie firmly repeated.

"Fine." The woman spun around and swanned elegantly across the carpet to the elevator. The doors slid open with a *ding*. She stepped inside, pushed the button, the doors closed, and the woman disappeared.

Carly just sat there. Her stomach was churning as if she'd swallowed a handful of rocks. Her breath seemed to be stuck in her chest. It was insane. She had no claim on Lincoln Cain. So they'd slept together. So what?

They were both adults. She'd wanted him and he'd wanted her.

Aside from that he was just trying to help her, doing her grandfather a favor.

She leaned back in her chair and closed her eyes, suddenly weary. Surely she hadn't thought it was more than just sex. Linc was a normal, red-blooded male, and sex was always on a man's mind. At the moment, he was enamored of her because she was someone new.

She thought of him with the gorgeous raven-haired woman. He'd be spending next Saturday night with her. Carly wondered what excuse he would come up with. Or maybe he would just tell her the truth. He'd never said their relationship would be exclusive.

Her eyes burned. Why did it always turn out this way?

Because men were jerks and that wasn't going to change. Surely she had learned that lesson by now.

At the sound of footsteps, she looked up to see Millie standing in front of her. "It's not what you think."

Carly sat up a little straighter, embarrassed the woman had caught her eavesdropping. "I-I don't know what you mean."

"That was Sophia Aiello. She's a *Vogue* cover model. She and Linc are slated to attend a charity event together a week from Saturday. It's just a publicity stunt to help raise money. Linc has no interest in Sophia . . . though I won't deny she might have considerable interest in him."

Carly didn't doubt that. She shrugged as if it didn't matter, tried to will the ache in her chest to ease. "It's none of my business."

"Maybe not. But Linc's never invited a woman into his private suite. Special circumstances or not, he took you in there. Whatever is or isn't going on between the two of you, I don't want that catty, spoiled little . . . *Italian* to give you a false impression."

Carly forced herself to smile. "Thank you."

But in truth, it was exactly the right impression. Somehow, with all the trouble swirling around her, she had let down her guard, let Lincoln Cain slip beneath her defenses.

She'd started to trust him. To believe he was somehow different. She'd slept with him. More than that. She'd given herself more freely than she had ever done before.

Just thinking of what they had done in bed made her red with embarrassment. It made her want to drag him back to the bedroom and have mindless, scorching, totally amazing sex with him again.

Stupid. Stupid. Stupid.

Millie turned and went back to her desk and Carly looked back at her computer screen. She tried to immerse herself in Drake Trucking business and not think about Cain, but it was impossible to do.

She made it through the next two hours, but when Linc appeared in the cubicle and asked if she wanted to go to supper before they went back home, she told him she had a headache—which by then was true—and she didn't feel up to going.

He cast her a glance. "All right. The helicopter is waiting whenever we're ready."

She just nodded. She packed up her computer and they headed for the roof. She hoped the headache excuse would be enough to get him to let her sleep in one of the other bedrooms. Tomorrow she would tell him she had changed her mind, that she wanted to return to her own home, that she appreciated his help, but from now on, she could take care of herself.

The flight back was quick and uneventful. All the way there, Linc watched her. By the time they reached the ranch house, her heart hurt and despair had her mouth so dry she could barely speak. As soon as they walked through the door, she headed for the kitchen to get a drink of water and distance herself from Linc.

As if he had some kind of Carly radar, he followed her into the room and just stood watching her. She worked to keep her hand steady as she finished the water and set the glass down in the sink.

"What happened today?" he asked, the unnatural calmness in his tone putting her on alert. "Something happened that changed things between us. What was it?"

He was amazingly perceptive. She thought about lying, but it wasn't worth the effort. She might as well end things now.

"Sophia happened. She reminded me of the way things really are."

"Sophia Aiello?" He frowned. "What does Sophia have to do with anything?"

"She came to see you. You didn't have time for her, but I'm sure she'll forgive you."

"I've never slept with Sophia."

"You have a date with her next week. Were you going to tell me the truth or make something up?"

A knot of anger appeared in his jaw. "It's just a PR stunt to raise money. I have no interest in a woman like that."

"No? You were married to a beauty queen."

"That's right. Three years of misery and that god-awful house was the result. One thing you can be sure of—I'm a man who learns from his mistakes."

She looked up at him. She wished she'd never met

him. Wished Joe had never asked him to watch out for her.

"I want to go home. I'll sleep in one of the other bedrooms tonight, but tomorrow I'm going home."

His jaw went harder. "You're not leaving. I'm not letting you put yourself in that kind of danger."

"You can't tell me what to do."

"You don't think so? I'll tell you this—I'm not letting some spoiled, self-absorbed female I don't give a fuck about ruin what's happening between us."

Her head came up. "Nothing's happening. It's just sex."

"Is it?" He stalked toward her, caught her shoulders. He was mad, furious. She didn't understand why he was so angry.

Linc hauled her closer. "I don't know where this is going. But if Sophia upset you that badly, I mean more to you than just sex. We're going to see where this leads. We're not going to let other people decide the outcome."

He fisted a hand in her hair to hold her in place and his mouth crushed down over hers. Heat speared through her, and wild, uncontrollable lust. She told herself to stop him, that he was just saying the things every woman wanted to hear, that he would get tired of her and leave, just like Garth and Carter, men who had professed to love her.

But what if she was wrong? What if Linc was the one man she could trust? The one man who was everything he seemed? She wanted to believe it so badly.

Carly struggled against him, but the heat was too much, the yearning too strong. Her body went primal, demanding she give in to him, let him take what he wanted. Carly kissed him back with all the need she felt for him, all the hunger, slid her fingers into the hair at the nape of his neck and her tongue into his mouth. Linc kissed her until her legs felt weak, until she couldn't think of anything but him. She whimpered when he broke away.

"Another thing you should know. I'm not above using sex to get what I want. Since I know how much you like sex with me, I'm going to remind you why you decided to stay with me in the first place."

Carly gasped as his big hands circled her waist, lifted her up, and set her down hard on the kitchen counter. He found the button on the waistband of her jeans, popped it open, then buzzed down her zipper. Her shoes landed on the floor. He lifted her and jerked down her skinny jeans, her panties along with them.

Carly couldn't breathe. Heat roared through her. Every part of her body was sizzling. Linc pulled her to the edge of the counter, kissed her long and deep, parted her knees, and moved between them. Her blouse vanished and he was feasting on her breasts, turning her nipples diamond hard. Kissing his way past her navel, he suckled and tasted, used his hands and his mouth to bring her to a screaming climax. Her head fell back as pleasure spilled through her; the world tilted sideways, into a wash of color and sweet sensation.

Limp and sated, she lay back on the counter, too boneless and numb to protest when he unzipped his Levi's and freed himself. Linc leaned over and kissed her. She whimpered as his hard length began to fill her.

"You like this?" he asked.

"Oh, yes . . ." she whispered. She loved the way he touched her, loved everything he did to her body.

"I'm glad you do because we're only getting started."

Pinning both wrists together above her head, he took her right there on the counter, took her hard, claiming her in some way.

For a moment, fear gripped her. She was getting in deep with Lincoln Cain. Risking her emotions, setting herself up for heartbreak. The thought slid away as Linc moved above her, surging deep, driving her toward another searing climax.

Carly closed her eyes and let the storm of passion roll over her.

Chapter Sixteen

Dawn filtered in through the windows, a soft purple glow in the darkness. Linc sat in a chair across the bedroom watching Carly sleep.

He'd scared her a little last night. Hell, he'd scared himself. He hadn't realized he could be so possessive of a woman, that he could demand so much from her. And yet she'd taken everything he'd tossed at her and hadn't for a moment backed down.

They were good together. Better than good. He wanted to know if the things he was feeling were real. If whatever was happening was more than just an affair.

In the years since his failed marriage, he'd told himself he wasn't interested in getting involved with a woman on more than a superficial level. He could do just fine, the way he always had.

Over the years, he'd dated any number of women and enjoyed them. But this was different, at least for him.

Linc was the kind of man who went after what he wanted. Trouble was, in this case, he didn't exactly know what that was. If things went wrong, Carly could get hurt. He didn't want that. And there was always a chance it could end up the other way around.

He studied the woman asleep in his bed, smiled at the tangle of heavy blond hair spread over his pillow. She was important to him. He'd do his best not to hurt her. But he wasn't letting her back away from him, not when she clearly had feelings for him, too.

Not until they had time to figure things out.

Beyond that, she needed his protection.

Yesterday in Dallas, he'd had the Drake cargo manifest from the crime scene messengered over to the City DNA Lab. He'd paid extra to have them put a rush on it, asked Townsend to keep an eye out for it, but it would still take a few days.

If the spot turned out to be blood, and he had a hunch it was, he needed to know if it was Miguel's. If it belonged to someone else, they might have a suspect. If the lab could come up with a DNA sample, Townsend could get it run through the Combined DNA Index System (CODIS), look for a match.

Tightening the sash on his terry-cloth robe, he rose from the chair and padded barefoot down the hall for a quick workout in the weight room adjoining his home office. Changing into a T-shirt and a pair of navy blue gym shorts, he pushed the weights around for a while, hit the heavy bag, then jogged for half an hour on the treadmill.

Since Carly still wasn't up and he didn't want to wake her, he went into the bathroom at the end of the hall and took a quick shower. Wearing the robe again till he could get something out of his closet, he sat down behind the desk and forced himself to focus on work, starting with the notes he'd made on the tire rebuilding plant.

When he looked up, Carly stood in the doorway, looking rumpled and pretty, reminding him of last night and making him start to get hard.

She walked toward him in one of his T-shirts, which hung on her like a sack but did nothing to cool his ardor. She sat down in a chair on the other side of the desk.

"You okay?" he asked. "I was pretty rough on you last night."

A slow smile spread over her face. "Sometimes rough is good."

His mouth edged up. No question last night had been great.

She toyed with a lock of gold hair. "So . . . umm . . . how many times have you used sex to get what you want?"

Amusement slid through him. "Counting last night? One."

She smiled, relaxed back in the chair.

"It's early," he said. "Why aren't you still asleep?"

"I've been doing some thinking."

"Yeah, what about?"

"About you . . . about El Jefe. About the sheriff."

"Sounds intriguing."

"We could use the sheriff's help to stop whatever's going on, but you don't trust him. I know it has something to do with the night you were arrested. You know a lot about me. Except for what I've read, I don't know much about you."

He tilted back in the black leather executive chair. "What do you want to know?"

"I'd like to know what happened the night of the robbery."

"Attempted robbery," he corrected. He didn't talk

about it. Not ever. It had happened to a different man, happened in the past, and he wanted it to stay there.

But he had pushed her last night. He hoped they had turned some kind of corner. "There were three of us. Me and two friends. One of them came up with the idea. I didn't want to do it. I was afraid we'd end up in jail—which we did."

"What happened?"

"We were always trying to find ways to prove ourselves, prove how tough we were. Our home lives sucked. All we had was each other. The guys wanted to rob the convenience store. I didn't want to let them down, so I went along with it. Two of us went inside; the third guy, the driver, waited in the car. We were wearing ski masks and carrying pistols. We walked in, went up to the register, and demanded money. That's when the owner pulled a shotgun out from under the counter. We had three choices. Kill him. Try to get his gun and maybe he'd kill one of us. Or surrender. We were kids. We didn't want to kill poor old Mr. Lafferty and we didn't want to die, so we laid down our weapons. Lafferty called the sheriff and he hauled us off to jail."

"That doesn't sound like enough to hold a grudge for all these years. Who were the other two boys?"

He just shook his head.

Carly eyed him with speculation. "Those trips to Dallas where I was trying to keep busy while you were working? I decided to do a little more research, read more about you on the Net. I think I can guess who was with you that night."

He went still, his heart slowing to a dull thud. "You think so?"

"Maybe. In high school, Beau Reese was one of your

best friends. I saw that in an article I read. Beau's hobby is driving race cars, a love he developed in his teens. I think Beau was driving the car that night."

He didn't say a word, which was an answer in itself.

"I wondered what the connection was between you and Sheriff Howler; while I was online, I read up on him, too. He's been county sheriff for a long time so there's a lot written about him and his family. Turns out he has a son almost the same age as you. I Googled his son. Your birthday's in May. Kyle's isn't until July. That makes Howler's kid a few months younger, same as Beau."

He just sat there. Never in a million years would he have believed she would figure it out. "Don't stop now. It's just getting interesting."

"It turns out Howler's son went to Pleasant Hill High, graduated the same year you would have if you hadn't been in prison. You and Beau, you both turned your lives around and became extremely successful, but Kyle became a drug addict. He's been in and out of rehab for years. I think Kyle went into the convenience store with you the night of the robbery. I think the sheriff blames you for the way his son turned out."

He leaned back, tried to pretend nonchalance. The information was out there for anyone to read. No one else had cared enough to put it all together. "Why ask me if you've already figured it out?"

"I know you've always kept silent about it. But Miguel is dead. I might be next. I guess I was hoping you'd trust me enough to explain what's going on."

He rose from his chair and walked around the desk. She seemed surprised when he pulled her up and into his arms.

"I'm glad you know," he said. "I probably should be

mad as hell that you've been digging around in my past, but all I feel is relief."

She smiled at him softly. "Your secret is safe with me."

He believed her. It occurred to him that he trusted her. He wasn't exactly sure when that had happened, but it was a feeling he'd never had with a woman he was involved with before. They always wanted something from him. All of them but Carly.

"Howler blames me, but the truth is, it was Kyle's idea. I think he wanted to show up his old man. Kyle never did anything good enough to please his dad. Beau and I felt sorry for him. Robbing the store was supposed to be some kind of payback, kind of a secret jab at the sheriff, a guy none of us liked."

"You and Beau came out okay. If Kyle had been stronger, he could have learned from his mistakes, too."

"I suppose that's true." Linc bent his head and softly kissed her. "I'm glad we talked, cleared the air. Secrets can be dangerous, especially with what's been going on. Now go get dressed before I haul you back to bed. I've got a lot of things to do."

Carly smiled. "So do I." She hurried for the door and he watched her bottom moving sweetly beneath the soft cotton fabric of his T-shirt.

"Thanks for being honest," Carly said over her shoulder as she ducked out and headed down the hall.

Linc's body stirred as he watched her go. He was in trouble here. Big damn trouble. He just hoped it was a two-way street.

Carly sat at the desk in her office that Friday morning, while Frank Marino was on duty outside in the main room. Every so often, he went outside and prowled the yard, checking for any sign of trouble.

Carly didn't think El Jefe or his men would show up at Drake Trucking, not when half a dozen burly truckers milled around, to say nothing of the mechanics and people who worked inside. Still, Linc had insisted Marino accompany her, which she didn't really mind as long as the man stayed out of her hair.

Linc had reluctantly gone to Dallas, though he had promised to be back in Iron Springs before she closed the office for the night.

"I'll pick you up," he'd said when he'd phoned her at work. "If it looks like I'm going to be late, I'll call."

"Okay. I was . . . umm . . . thinking . . ."

"About what? More ways to cause trouble?"

She smiled. "I was hoping we could stop at the road-house after work. Rowena's bartending and it'd be nice to see some friends."

"I don't see why not. A beer sounds good. I'll see you late afternoon."

Surprised her request hadn't turned into some kind of confrontation, she'd gone back to work, kept at it till noon. Donna went out for sandwiches and brought them back for lunch and they ate in the break room. Afterward she started making cold calls.

She'd just hung up, proud of herself for the meeting she'd set up with Ajax Furniture to discuss the company's shipping needs, when the second line rang. Joe's private number.

Carly picked up the phone. "Drake Trucking."

"*Señorita* Drake. It is good to hear your voice."

Her stomach clenched. El Jefe's words made her blood run cold. "What do you want?"

"It is time to schedule a pickup. Very soon you will

receive a text giving you the location and the time your truck is to arrive."

She moistened her lips, steeled herself. "I've changed my mind. I've decided I'm not interested in your deal. You need to find someone else."

A grating chuckle rasped over the line, zipping along her nerves. "You will do what you are told. You will make the pickup and you will tell no one—not even the rich gringo you are whoring for."

Her fingers tightened around the receiver. "What I do is none of your business."

"Sleep with Cain—I do not care—as long as you do what you are told. Fight me and you and Cain will both be dead. You understand?"

Oh, God. "Yes."

"As I said, word will arrive very soon." The line went dead.

Carly's hand shook as she hung up the receiver and leaned back in her chair. She'd known this was coming and yet some part of her had refused to believe it.

A familiar knock sounded and she glanced up. When the door opened and Linc walked in, a wave of relief hit her so hard, she felt dizzy.

He took one look at her face and the scowl he was wearing went even darker. "What is it? What's happened?"

Her voice shook. "El Jefe just called. He's got a load he wants picked up."

"Christ."

"He didn't say what it was, where he wants it delivered or when. He says I'll get a text with the information."

Linc ran a hand through his thick dark brown hair. "What else?"

"He knows we're together. He says he'll kill both of

us if I don't do what he says." Her eyes burned. "I never should have gotten you involved."

He caught her shoulders, drew her out of her chair. "You didn't have any choice. I was involved from the moment Joe asked me to look out for you."

Carly closed her eyes. She told herself everything would be okay; Linc was going to help. She took a steadying breath, worked to slow her pounding heart. "What are we going to do?"

"We're going to consider our options, figure the best way to handle this. One of the reasons I went to Dallas was to talk to Quinn Taggart."

Alarm slammed through her. "Taggart? You said Taggart was FBI!"

"That's right."

"You said you wouldn't do anything we didn't both agree on. That's what you said!"

"Take it easy. I just talked to him, nothing more. I mentioned El Jefe, outlined, theoretically, what might become a problem. I didn't give him any names, nothing specific."

"You shouldn't have done it—not until we talked."

"We have to do something. You know it as well as I do."

She took another deep breath, steadied herself. "What did Taggart say?"

"He knows about El Jefe. He says the guy started out fairly small potatoes, running drugs, extortion, that kind of thing. In the last year or so, he's grown more and more powerful. He's amassed a sizable fortune, and according to word on the street, he's just getting started. The FBI wants him—bad."

Hope swelled inside her. "Maybe they'll arrest him before I get the call."

Linc shook his head. "The feds haven't got jack on this guy. They don't even know what he looks like. They're desperate for information."

"I don't know anything! I know the size of his shoes—that's it!"

Linc's mouth edged up. "I know."

She tried to hold on to her irritation, but it slowly slipped away. In jeans and a chest-hugging T-shirt, he was so hot, for a moment she forgot El Jefe's phone call and just enjoyed the view. Then her brain began to function and worry swept back in.

"At least we've made contact," Linc was saying. "We know the feds are interested. If El Jefe calls you with a pickup location—"

"You aren't suggesting I give them that information? If I do and they don't catch him, we could both end up dead."

"I told you we'd consider our options. At least we know the FBI will be more than willing to step in when the time comes."

He was right. The only way out of this was to catch the man who threatened them. They needed help to do that. But it didn't make her feel any better.

She pulled out her cell phone. No texts from El Jefe. She wondered how long it would be before he sent word of his demands? How long before the drug lord sent her down the road to ruin?

Or to hell.

Chapter Seventeen

It was closing time, though the yard was never completely empty. Drivers were in and out around the clock and there was a night watchman on duty.

Linc waited for Carly to pack up then guided her out of the office. "I think we both need that beer," he said. "Frank can drive your pickup, follow us out to the roadhouse. Won't hurt to have a pair of eyes outside."

Some of the tension seemed to drain from Carly's shoulders. "I was afraid you'd change your mind."

"Much as I'd like to keep you chained to my bed where I know you'll be safe, it's probably a bad idea."

Carly flashed him a naughty grin filled with possibilities. "Could make for an interesting evening, though."

Linc chuckled, trying to block the image he had stupidly created. "We won't stay too long," he said.

As they walked out of the building, Carly dug her keys out of her purse and handed them to Frank; then Linc walked over to his big GMC and they climbed inside. A few minutes later, he was driving down the highway, pulling into the parking lot at Jubal's, really looking forward to that beer.

He'd had the same crap day Carly had. He'd met Quinn Taggart at a small café instead of FBI head-quarters, just to be safe. He hadn't told Carly how hard Quinn had pressed him to get his unidentified *friend* to help the FBI catch El Jefe.

"This could be just the break we've been hoping for," Taggart had said. "Your guy could set up some kind of meet. We'd be there holding his hand the whole time—metaphorically speaking, of course."

"Of course," Linc said sarcastically.

Taggart shifted on the opposite side of the booth they were sitting in, a good-sized blond guy with a buzz cut in a typical FBI dark suit.

"Look, he'd be wearing a wire," Quinn continued. "We'd be listening to every word. If he got in trouble, we'd be there to protect him."

Linc just shook his head. "Not going to happen, Quinn. But if something turns up that'll help you, I'll see that you get the information."

Taggart sighed, clearly unhappy. "You might be making the wrong move here, Linc."

It was possible, but no way was he putting Carly in that kind of danger. He and the FBI agent had parted ways and Linc had returned to his office for the chop-per ride back to Blackland Ranch.

It was ten to seven when he walked Carly across the roadhouse parking lot, Frank discreetly covering their progress.

Linc's cell signaled as he reached the swinging double doors leading inside. Frank moved casually into position out front and Carly paused next to Linc as he pulled out his phone and checked the caller I.D.

It was Millie. Since his assistant usually texted, he figured it was important. "What's up?"

"Glen Barker called." Glen was the CPA going over the Drake accounting records. "He says it's urgent he speak to you. I've got him on the other line."

He flicked a glance at Carly. "Patch him through."

Glen's familiar voice floated over the line. "Mr. Cain, I'm sorry to bother you this late, but I'm calling in regard to those records you asked me to review."

"What about them?"

"Someone's stealing, and it's been going on for quite a while."

Anger sifted through him, making his jaw feel tight. No wonder Joe's company was going broke. "How long?"

"Nearly two years. Whoever's doing it is logging the payee into the digital record as if the account is legitimate, but when you pull the actual checks, the recipient doesn't match what's in the records. It's a simple but effective technique if the person doing it is a trusted employee. No one is physically going back to make sure the checks and the records match."

"Who's the money actually being paid to?"

"The payee is a bank routing number. The money's sent directly into the account."

"How much are we talking about?"

"In the last two years, nearly two hundred thousand dollars."

Linc clamped down on a fresh shot of temper. Jesus, more trouble Carly didn't need. At least it explained what had been happening, why Drake was edging toward bankruptcy.

"Thanks, Glen. I appreciate your work on this." Linc hung up the phone.

"What is it?" Carly asked.

He settled a hand at her waist and guided her through the swinging doors into the roadhouse, needing that beer more than ever. This early, the place wasn't packed, but there were plenty of people sitting at tables.

From behind the bar, Rowena waved and smiled at Carly, and Linc urged her in that direction, not looking forward to the conversation they were about to have.

Row tossed back her long dark red curls and grinned. "Hey, Linc, hey, Carly. Good to see you guys."

Carly climbed up on a bar stool. "You, too, Row."

When Linc settled himself next to Carly at the bar, Row's gaze shot back and forth between them.

"So . . . I didn't expect to see the two of you in here . . . together." Row flicked a what-kind-of-friend-are-you glance at Carly, whose cheeks turned a little pink. Sometimes she could really be cute.

"Linc's been helping me with some problems," Carly said.

"I'll just bet he has," Row said with a grin.

Fighting not to smile, Linc studied the row of taps behind the bar: Buffalo Bayou, Alamo, New Republic, Texian. "How about a couple of beers?" he asked. "A Shiner Bock sounds good. Carly?"

"I'll have a Lone Star."

"You got it." Row glanced at Linc. "On your tab?"

He nodded. Row popped the tops and set two icy bottles down in front of them. "Here you go."

A customer walked up to the other end of the bar, a lanky young guy in jeans and a battered straw cowboy hat. He sat down on a stool and Row headed in his direction. Linc could hear the guy laughing, saw the way his eyes strayed to Row's full breasts.

Linc felt a tug of amusement. He knew Rowena fairly well. He doubted the cowboy would get lucky, but he'd have a good time trying.

"Let's get a table." Linc grabbed Carly's beer and his own, slid off the stool, and headed for a quiet spot along the wall. Both of them sat down at a battered wooden table that had years of initials carved into the top.

"What's up?" Carly asked, picking up her beer and taking a drink.

"The call I got outside? That was Glen Barker, the CPA I asked to look at your account books."

The color drained out of her face. "Did he find a problem? I swear, Linc, I wasn't trying to hide something so you'd give me the loan."

He reached across the table and caught her hand. "Hey, I know that. Someone's been stealing from you. Actually from Joe before you took over."

"What?"

"That's right. Been going on for nearly two years, about the time Joe first started having serious heart trouble."

"I can't believe it. How much?"

"Pushing two hundred thousand dollars."

"Oh, my God!"

"Who writes the checks, Carly?"

"Joe did, but . . ." She took a deep breath. "Until a couple of years ago, Joe personally oversaw the checking account. When he started having health problems, he delegated the task." She looked up at him. "Until I started working there, Donna was paying the bills."

* * *

They didn't leave Jubal's right away. Carly was too stunned to get out of her chair. Donna Melendez had been stealing money from Drake for nearly two years.

"You'll need to call the sheriff," Linc said. "The woman is a thief and the money she embezzled wasn't small change. This isn't something you can handle on your own."

Carly nodded, feeling a mixture of anger, resentment, and sadness. "I want to talk to her first. I'll call her in the morning. She isn't scheduled to work, but I'll tell her I need some help in the office, see if I can get her to come in."

"I want to be there. I'll have Glen send whatever he's found. If she tries to deny it, you'll have the proof you need."

"It's hard to believe. Joe considered her a friend. When I took over, her help was invaluable. I don't know if I could have done it without her."

"Yeah, and all the while she was helping herself to your money."

The anger returned, stronger this time. Footsteps sounded, coming toward the table from behind her.

"Hey, look who's here!" Delroy Aimes, Linc's beefy black biker friend, walked up, earring glinting in his ear. Johnnie Banducci sauntered up beside him, smoothing back his hair as if he wanted to be sure not a glossy black strand was out of place.

Instead of leathers, the men were in jeans and T-shirts and both of them looked hot.

"Good to see you guys," Linc said.

"You gonna ask us to join you or what?" Johnnie asked.

Linc looked over at Carly.

"I could use another beer," she said. *Or five. Followed by a couple of tequila shooters.*

Linc relaxed. Carly could read his thoughts: he'd given her the bad news but she hadn't panicked. She wasn't happy, but she hadn't fallen apart. And he was about right. She'd handled the information—barely.

"This round's on me," Johnnie said. Turning, he headed over to the bar while Del sat down at the table.

"I heard you ran into a little trouble when you left here last time," Del said to Linc.

"Carly ran into some trouble. I was in the right place at the right time. I'm glad I was able to help."

Del leaned back in his chair, his weight making it creak. "I heard it was a little more serious than that. Heard it was some of El Jefe's boys."

Johnnie returned to the table, Rowena beside him. She unloaded the tray she balanced on the flat of her hand, setting a bottle of beer down in front of each of them.

"Enjoy," Row said with a smile. As she walked back to the bar, hips swaying, Carly had a flash of brilliance. She tucked the idea away and returned her attention to the men.

Johnnie spun a chair around and sat down facing the table, zeroing in on the conversation as if he hadn't missed a word. "El Jefe. That guy's a bad dude, Linc."

"Yeah, I figured that out when the bullets started flying."

Del grunted. "Word is El Jefe's on the march, trying to expand his empire. You need to stay as far away from that hombre as you can get."

"I wish it was that easy," Linc said. He took a swallow of beer. "What can you tell me about him? I was under the impression the guy stays way off the grid."

"He does," Del said. "But some of his boys like to throw their weight around, brag about their exploits. Your name came up. One of the Demons got wind of it. He came to me, thought you might want to know."

Linc just nodded. He'd been a fringe member of the club since he was a kid.

Johnnie tipped up his beer and took a swallow, set it back down on the table. "The guys said to tell you, you need some help, just let them know."

"Appreciate that," Linc said. Steering the conversation in a lighter direction, he and Carly finished their beers. They said good-bye to Del, Johnnie, and Row and left the roadhouse, Frank following the truck in Carly's pickup.

"Row mentioned you used to ride with the Demons," Carly said as the headlights lit the strip of pavement in front of them.

"I was never an official member of the club, but when I was younger, I rode with some of them."

"Del, Johnnie, and Rick."

"That's right. And some of the other guys in the group. The Demons aren't one-percenters, not like the Bandidos or Hell's Angels, MCs involved in drugs and other criminal activities. But the guys can be plenty tough when push comes to shove."

As the truck rolled along, Carly's mind went over the evening. Del, Johnnie, and Rick were former members of the Asphalt Demons. She knew their reputation, knew the members of the club were tough. Though on the surface Linc's friends seemed jovial and easygoing, they had an underlying aura of strength.

In the faint light inside the cab, she studied Linc's

profile. As handsome as he was, there was a hard edge to his features that said his life hadn't always been easy. The beard shadow along his jaw hinted at the toughness inside him, the obstacles he had conquered to make him the man he had become.

Her gaze dipped to the powerful arm gripping the steering wheel. "Was that when you got the tattoo? When you were riding with the Demons?"

He glanced down at the single strand of barbed wire wrapped around his bicep. "I got that after I got out of prison. To remind myself what it feels like to be fenced in."

Carly fell silent. Linc had committed a crime, but he had served his sentence and turned his life around. It was a shame more people weren't willing or able to do that.

"I need to replace Donna," she said. "I'm going to ask Rowena to take the job."

Linc's gaze swung to hers. "I know Row works part-time as a bookkeeper. You really think she can manage your office?"

"Row's good at just about everything. I think she'll be a tremendous asset."

"It's not always good business to work with your friends."

"And yet you and Beau seem to be doing just fine."

"Good point," Linc said. "Beau and I make a great team. I'll introduce you at the benefit."

She frowned. "What benefit?"

Linc flicked her a sideways glance. "Oh, did I forget to mention? Sophia found another date for the charity event next Saturday night."

"She did?"

"That's right. Turns out she'll be going with Beau.

I'm going to owe him big-time for the favor, but that can't be helped."

"I don't understand."

One of his dark eyebrows arched up. "You don't?"

"No."

"Then let me spell it out for you. I'm not interested in Sophia Aiello—I told you that before. My date is sitting in the passenger seat. That night she'll be sleeping in my bed, same as she will be tonight."

Carly's heart made a funny little kick. Linc had changed his plans to be with her. He wasn't interested in stunningly beautiful Sophia Aiello. He was interested in Joe Drake's granddaughter, the owner of a nearly bankrupt trucking company. She opened her mouth, but nothing came out.

"I presume that's a 'Yes, I'd be thrilled to go with you, Linc.'"

"Umm . . . okay. I'd love to go to the benefit with you, Linc."

"That's better. It's black tie. If you need something to wear—"

"I've got something. Several somethings. They're packed in those boxes you had brought over to the ranch house."

"Good."

"The benefit isn't till the end of next week. I guess that means you don't think the problem with El Jefe will be solved and I'll be back in my own house by then."

"Or maybe it means that even if it's solved, you're still the woman I want to take to the benefit."

Something shifted inside her. It made her want to smile. Then her worry kicked in and the feeling changed, morphed into something closer to fear. Every day she was getting in deeper with Linc. Every night she gave him more of herself. When it was over, she was going to be very badly hurt.

Linc's green eyes came to rest on her face and there was a gentleness there she hadn't expected. "It's just an evening in the city, okay? That's all it is. We'll go to the gala, spend the night at my apartment, and come back here the next morning."

She nodded, felt a little better. It was a date, an evening with a wealthy, handsome, incredibly sexy man. She could handle a date with a man like that. She'd done it more than once over the years. Well, none of those other guys were even close to Linc, but still . . .

She began to relax.

Then the tall, wrought-iron gates of Blackland Ranch appeared up ahead. There was a guard on each side of the entrance. In the distance, several sets of headlights illuminated the fields, moving in indiscernible patterns, armed men riding four-wheeled ATVs.

Tomorrow she would have her grandfather's most trusted employee arrested for embezzling.

For the first time since she'd decided not to sell Drake Trucking, Carly wasn't sure she had done the right thing.

Chapter Eighteen

The weather was warm, the humidity high, a typical late-September day in East Texas. Linc drove Carly to the truck yard that Saturday morning for her meeting with Donna Melendez. Earlier, Carly had phoned her office manager and asked her to come in. Then they were calling the sheriff.

Embezzling was a crime. Like the robbery Linc had attempted when he was a kid, there was no excuse.

Carly was sitting at her desk, Linc standing a few feet away, when Donna arrived. The door to the inner office stood open.

"Come on back," Carly called out to her.

Silver-streaked black hair clipped at the nape of her neck, Donna smiled as she hurried into the private office. "Sorry I'm late. One of my grandkids has chicken pox. Her mother is frantic. I stopped to bring her some calamine lotion."

She paused when she spotted Linc, leaning casually against the wall a few feet away. His height and build intimidated people. It was one of the reasons he was there.

"Oh, I didn't see you, Mr. Cain. Good morning." She glanced back and forth between him and Carly, took in their serious expressions. "What's going on?"

Carly stayed seated, spoke to Donna across the desk. "I think that's a question you need to answer, Donna. Why don't you take a seat?"

The woman's black eyebrows pulled into a frown as she sat down in one of the metal chairs on the other side of the desk. "How am I supposed to know what's going on when I just got here? You aren't making sense." Her gaze shot to Linc. "Tell me what's wrong."

"You know about the loan I made Drake Trucking," he said.

"Of course. That was very kind of you."

"It was a business transaction. You gave me the profit and loss statement, but I also asked Carly for Drake's account records. I had my CPA go over the books for the last five years, examine the records in detail."

The color drained from Donna's face.

"I bet you can guess what we found," Carly said.

"I don't . . . don't know what you're talking about."

Linc pushed away from the wall. "I think you do. I think you know exactly what we found in those books."

Donna shook her head, shifting her long dark hair across her back. Her eyes filled with tears. "You don't understand."

"I understand you're a thief," Carly said. "That you pretended to be Joe's friend—my friend—then stole two hundred thousand dollars and nearly bankrupted the company."

"You worked for Joe for years," Linc said. "He trusted you completely. Two years ago you started stealing from him. What happened? Or did you just get greedy?"

Donna leaned forward, her arms wrapped around her middle, hugging herself. She straightened, took a shaky breath. "I didn't do it for me—I did it for Joe. I did it to protect him." Donna burst into tears.

When Carly started to rise, Linc shot her a glance that warned her to stay in her seat. Now wasn't the time for her to be softhearted.

"Stealing is stealing," he said. "You took the money. Now you're going to jail."

Donna swallowed a sob. "I didn't know what else to do. He wanted money. I knew Joe wouldn't pay him. I had to do something. You don't know what that man is like."

"Who?" Linc pressed.

"El Jefe. Three of his men came . . . came to my house." Donna inhaled a shaky breath. "They knew Joe was sick. They said El Jefe would take care of the people who worked here. He would ensure their loads would arrive safely. The drivers would not . . . not be harmed. He would provide protection, but it would cost money. Joe was a man of principle—I knew he wouldn't pay."

Carly leaned across the desk. "So you made the decision yourself—using Joe's money."

Donna wiped tears from her cheeks. "I didn't know what else to do. One of El Jefe's men gave me instructions. I was to open a bank account. Every month, I was to transfer money into the account."

"Which added up to a couple hundred thousand dollars," Carly said.

"Almost."

"How did El Jefe get the money?" Linc asked. "I doubt he was writing checks."

She swallowed. "The bank account was a way to keep the transfer secret. A few days after I transferred the money, I went into the bank and took it out in cash. I put the money in a paper bag, then set it beside a trash can in the city park, and someone picked it up."

"You saw them?" Carly asked.

"No. They told me to put the bag down and leave, so that's what I did."

"And you never saw anyone," Linc pressed. "You gave El Jefe two hundred thousand dollars and never saw a thing."

She glanced up, her eyes wet and glistening. "It didn't all go to him. Part of the money went . . . went to me." She pressed her trembling lips together. "They insisted I take it so I would keep quiet. I would be part of it whether I liked it or not. Ten percent of what I stole."

Linc should have been surprised but he wasn't. "So you aren't completely innocent in all this, are you?"

"I kept it. I didn't know what else to do. I meant to give it back to Joe when he got well. But then Joe died and Miguel's little girl got sick, so I gave it to him."

Linc just shook his head. "Jesus . . ." Unbelievable. He sure as hell hadn't seen that one coming.

Carly stood up behind her desk. "I don't know what to say. I don't know how much of what you're telling me is true. I know twenty thousand dollars showed up in Miguel's bank account. Apparently it went to a doctor for Angelina so some good came out of this. If I'd come home earlier, maybe I could have done something. Joe and I could have found a way to deal with the problem and maybe none of this would have happened."

Linc's anger began to build. "You're not taking the blame for this," he said to Carly. He focused his attention on Donna. "Whatever your reasons, it wasn't your decision to make. Joe was a smart man. Over the years, he'd faced men as tough as El Jefe. He would have figured a way to handle things."

It took every ounce of his willpower to keep from overstepping and firing the woman on the spot. Tossing her in jail? That was another matter. There was a good chance she'd actually thought she was helping Joe.

"Carly?" he said, hoping she would make the right decision.

"Whatever your reasons, you can't work here anymore, Donna. I don't trust you now, and in your job as office manager, that's crucial."

Donna started crying again. "I don't want to go to jail. Maybe I can find a way to pay you back."

Carly glanced over at Linc, but he stayed silent. The decision was hers.

"You have to leave Drake, but I don't think you should go to jail. You were doing what you thought was best. You didn't spend the money you got from El Jefe. You gave it to a sick little girl. Joe might have done the same thing."

Donna made a sound in her throat. Tears rolled down her cheeks. "Thank you."

"One last thing," Linc said, regaining Donna's attention. "After Carly took over, no more payments were made to El Jefe. Is that the reason Miguel Hernandez was murdered?"

Donna crossed herself. "*Dios mío*, I pray that's not the reason, but I don't know."

"Pack your things," Carly said. "I don't want to see you when I come in here Monday morning."

Donna just nodded. Tears in her eyes, she rose from the chair and left the office, closing the door quietly behind her.

Linc walked over to Carly and eased her into his arms. He could feel her trembling. "You did exactly the right thing. I'm proud of you."

Carly buried her face in his chest and started crying.

Carly sat in Linc's truck as he drove back to the ranch. It was only eleven o'clock in the morning and already she'd had one hellacious day.

Her gaze went to Linc where he sat behind the wheel. "When we were talking to Donna, I remembered something El Jefe had said."

His eyes met hers. "What was it?"

"Something about money—that after I started working for him I wouldn't have any more financial problems. He knew the company was in trouble, Linc. He knew because he was draining the profits, putting Joe in a financial bind."

"He was trying to push your grandfather into a corner, leave him no choice but to cooperate. At least that was the plan."

"Grandpa Joe would never have agreed. He'd have lost the business before he'd do anything illegal."

"So you believe Donna's story. You think most of the money she embezzled went to El Jefe and not to her."

Carly glanced over. "I'm sure your investigator can find out, but I know what El Jefe's like, how vicious he can be. I think Donna's telling the truth. I think she believed El Jefe would kill Joe."

"Miguel is dead, so maybe she was right."

Carly thought of the crime scene photos, the pool of blood beneath Miguel's head, and a shudder rippled through her.

"Donna cost you a couple hundred thousand dollars," Linc said. "That's not chump change."

"I know. You may not believe it, but it's partly my fault. If I'd come back when I should have, it might not have happened."

"Carly—"

"It's done. I'm here now and I'm starting where Joe left off. As far as I'm concerned, that's the end of it."

"Except for El Jefe."

With a sigh, she slumped back in the seat. "Yes."

Linc reached over and squeezed her hand. "We'll deal with him together. You aren't alone anymore."

She didn't argue, though it wasn't really true. For now Linc was her ally. Once he fulfilled what he considered his obligation to Joe, he would be out of her life and she would again be on her own.

She felt tired just thinking about it.

She jumped when her cell phone rang, hurriedly dug it out of her purse. The phone was playing her ring tone, not signaling a text, so it wasn't El Jefe, or at least she hoped not. She checked the screen but didn't recognize the number.

"This is Carly."

"Sheriff Howler here. Got some news for you on that break-in at your place. You need to come down to the department."

She covered the phone. "It's Howler. He's got information on the break-in. He wants me to come in to his office."

Linc slowed and pulled the truck over to the side of the road. "Tell him we're on our way."

"We'll be right there," she said to Howler as Linc started turning the truck around.

"You and Cain?" the sheriff asked.

Carly's mind flashed back to Deputy Rollins's report, which mentioned the night they had spent together. "That's right."

"You bein' Joe's granddaughter, I figured you had more sense. I'll see you when you get here." The sheriff hung up the phone.

Carly tried to ignore what felt like embarrassment mixed with uncertainty. Was she making a fool of herself with Linc? Was half of Iron Springs laughing at her behind her back or maybe feeling sorry for her?

She didn't want to be another of Lincoln Cain's women and yet here she was, sleeping with him while the whole town speculated on how long the affair would last.

There wasn't nearly enough time to compose herself before Linc pulled the GMC into a parking space in front of the Iron Springs Sheriff's Department. With a sigh, Carly climbed down from the truck and the two of them walked into the building. Silver-haired Daisy Johnson was at work behind the counter.

"Sheriff's been expecting you," Daisy said, dragging a pair of reading glasses off her nose as she rose from the chair at her desk. "I'll let him know you're here."

"Send 'em in," the sheriff called out from his office, mostly out of sight behind the open door.

Howler kicked his boots from the top of the desk to the floor and sat up a little straighter as they walked in. "Take a seat," he said.

They sat down in straight-backed wooden chairs across from him. "You told me you had information on the break-in," Carly said. "What did you find out?"

"We got prints," the sheriff said. "Plenty of 'em. Guy wasn't trying to hide his identity."

"Who is he?" Linc asked.

"Fella's name is Raymond Jackson Archer. White male, thirty-six years old, arrested in Austin six days ago on a domestic violence charge. Beat the hell out of some woman he was living with. Got out on bail and took off. The break-in at your place is the first sign of him the law's come across since he skipped town."

"I don't understand," Carly said. "Why would Raymond Archer vandalize my house?"

"Good question," the sheriff said. "We're looking into it, getting all the facts lined up. I was hoping you might have something to add that would be useful."

"Such as?"

He studied her down the length of his nose. "Maybe Archer was an old boyfriend. Or someone else who had a grudge against you."

"No. I've never heard of him."

"The thing is, destruction like that looks to be personal. You gotta figure there's some kinda connection."

"I'm telling you I don't know him."

The sheriff turned to Linc. "What about you? Appears you're in the picture now. Whole town's talkin' about Carly staying with you out at your place. This guy got some kind of beef with you? Maybe he's taking it out on the little lady?"

Carly's mind slid past the irritating phrase to the news that the whole town was talking about her. But then she had known that already.

"I've got enemies," Linc admitted. "None by the name of Ray Archer."

"Well, I guess we'll see." The sheriff lumbered to his feet, hitching his pants up so they fit better over his belly. "Anything new turns up, I'll let you know. In the meantime, till we find this guy and bring him in, you best keep your eyes open."

Linc made no reply.

It wasn't surprising that a man as successful as Linc had enemies, but obviously so did she.

Carly felt as if the weight of the world had settled on her shoulders. Who the hell was Ray Archer? Was the trashing of her house really personal? If so, why was his anger directed at her?

Chapter Nineteen

Linc pulled the truck out onto the road and started back to the ranch house. As the GMC picked up speed, he hit the command button on his steering wheel.

"Dial Ross Townsend," he said into the mic. The call went through and the phone began to ring.

"Townsend." Ross's voice came over the speaker.

"The guy who trashed Carly's house? Name is Raymond Jackson Archer. He's out of Austin, arrested six days ago on a domestic violence charge, and skipped bail. I want everything you can find on him."

"I'm on it," Townsend said.

"You still at the house?"

"I was planning to drive back to Dallas this afternoon, but I can work from here if you think I need to stay."

"Plan on it. I want that info ASAP. I'll talk to you when I get there." He disconnected the line.

On the seat next to him, Carly rode in silence. She'd had a rough day and it was just early afternoon.

In the distance, the big iron gates of Blackland Ranch appeared, guards posted at the entrance. Linc groaned as he spotted the group in front of the wrought-iron fence. The protestors were back, milling and marching and singing, waving their signs in the air.

"I really don't need this today," he growled. He already had more than enough on his plate without this bunch of crazies. "There's a dirt road into the back of the ranch, but it's pretty rough and it's miles out of the way. Might be worth the trouble."

"We're already here," Carly said, stating the obvious.

Linc pulled up and the gates slowly swung open. A couple of protestors tried to push their way onto the property but two guys on ATVs rode up and blocked their way.

Linc drove through the gate to the sound of shouts and jeers and the gates closed behind them.

"I'm liking your helicopter better all the time," Carly said.

Linc felt the pull of a smile. "It does have its advantages."

Passing the main house, he drove on down the dirt road toward home. Once they were settled inside, he walked over to the wet bar built into a wall in the living room and opened the dark oak cabinet.

"You want a drink? I'm pouring myself three fingers of whiskey. You're welcome to join me."

"Sounds perfect," she said. "I'll take mine neat."

He was only a little surprised. He poured them each a Stagg Kentucky Bourbon, an expensive brand he'd grown fond of, and carried Carly's glass over to where she'd collapsed bonelessly on the sofa.

Linc handed her the heavy crystal tumbler and sat down beside her. "Rough day," he said.

"Seems like they've all been pretty rough lately."

He took a sip of his drink, savored the taste and the burn. "Yeah."

Carly sipped her whiskey. "I don't know anyone named Raymond Archer. I have no idea why he would destroy my home."

"Sometimes we have enemies we don't know we have. Maybe you crossed paths with this guy and don't remember. Hell, maybe he was just some drunk on a plane you pissed off because you wouldn't serve him another round."

She tilted her head against the back of the sofa. "Maybe."

"Townsend will find the link if there is one. In the meantime, I'm glad you're staying here."

She sat up and her eyes found his. "Why, because you want to protect me? Or because you need a woman in your bed and I happen to be handy?"

Irritation trickled through him. "Where's that coming from? I thought we'd already settled this particular issue." He set his heavy crystal glass down on the coffee table. "Wait a minute. It's what Howler said, isn't it? That the whole town was talking about us."

She shrugged, pretending it didn't bother her, but clearly it had. "I knew they would." She took a sip of her drink. "I'm being stupid, I guess."

He took the drink from her hand and set it down on the table next to his. Reaching over, he caught her chin, bent his head, and very softly kissed her.

"You're the woman I want, Carly. The way we are in bed together, I've got to figure I'm the man you want. We're doing what's right for us and the hell with the rest of them."

She looked at him and some of the clouds in her eyes seemed to fade. "You're right. I'm being a coward.

Granddad didn't raise me to be a coward. To hell with the rest of them." She stood up and reached down to him. "Take me to bed, Lincoln Cain. Remind me again why I'm staying with you."

Linc laughed. Standing, he took hold of her hand and she led him down the hall. It didn't take him long to remind her. It didn't stop him from worrying about her.

At the ranch house Sunday morning, Carly worked on her laptop. It sat on a desk in the spare bedroom she was using as an office. Figuring Rowena had probably worked at Jubal's last night, she waited till nine o'clock to call her. With Donna gone, she was desperate for someone to take the job as office manager, but she wanted someone reliable, someone she could trust. She prayed Rowena would accept the position.

"Row, it's me. Did I wake you?"

"No, I had the early shift last night."

"Good. Have you got a minute to talk?"

"Sure. If you're going to dish on Cain, I've got all the time in the world."

Carly laughed. "Sorry, no. All I'm willing to say about Linc is the man is smokin' hot."

Row chuckled. "You'll get no argument from me. So what's up?"

"You know that full-time job you've been looking for? Something interesting that pays well and provides benefits?"

"How could I forget? I've been pounding the pavement for nearly a year."

"What would you think about a job at Drake Trucking? Office manager. Donna just quit."

"What, are you kidding me?"

"Completely serious. I think you'd be a real asset. If you wouldn't mind taking orders from me."

"I'd take orders from the devil himself if the job was right."

"Then you're hired. But before you say yes, there are a couple of things you need to know. I'd rather not discuss them over the phone."

"Now you've got my attention."

Carly flicked a glance at the bedroom doorway, wondering if Linc would mind her going in for a while this morning. "I don't suppose you'd have any time today? We could talk things over. If you're still interested, we could spend a couple of hours getting you acquainted with the way we've been doing things, maybe throw some ideas around about changes you might want to make."

"Sure, I could do that. Say half an hour?"

"That'd be great. I'll see you there." She hung up the phone.

"I gather Row accepted the job." Linc stood in the open doorway. Six-foot-five inches of glorious male that could grace the cover of any muscle jock magazine.

She forced her eyes to his face. "I have to tell Row about El Jefe. It wouldn't be fair to keep her in the dark about something that could be seriously dangerous."

"You sure you can trust her?"

"We've known each other since I was ten years old. I'm absolutely sure."

"All right. You know you're risking your friendship if the job doesn't work out."

"It's a risk I'm willing to take." If it worked the way she hoped, Carly would have an ally in the company and also someone she believed would do a very competent job.

"I know it's Sunday," she said, "but Row's agreed to meet me at the office for a couple of hours. It won't be busy today and I need to get this settled. I hope you don't mind. I can be back by noon or a little after."

"It's cooler today. I thought we might go for a ride on my Harley. If we went out the back road, no one would know we were gone. But I realize hiring someone is a problem you need to solve."

"Rats. I'd really like to go. Maybe we could go riding this afternoon."

Linc started nodding. "All right, I can make that work. We'll go after you're finished. Frank's off today. I'll drive you in, take some work with me. I've always got plenty to do."

"Are you sure you need to go? It's daylight. I should be safe enough."

He cast her a look more eloquent than words.

"Okay, I get it." She thought of El Jefe and figured Linc was right. She wondered about the text the drug lord was planning to send her. She wondered what she would do when it came. "I'll finish getting ready and be right with you."

They arrived at the yard a few minutes before the scheduled meeting, but Rowena's older-model red Chevy Camaro was already parked in the yard and Rowena was sitting inside it. Sunlight gleamed on her dark red curls as she got out of the car and walked over to join them in the hip-swaying gait that hadn't changed since high school.

"So you brought the big man with you," Rowe said as she approached, flashing Linc a grin.

"He's playing bodyguard," Carly said. "Long story and one I'm about to tell you."

Rowena's russet eyebrows went up.

"Let's go inside," Linc said.

Carly unlocked the door and they went into the main office. The employee lounge was next door, with a separate entrance so the drivers could use it whenever they came in from a run.

A couple of trucks were parked in the yard. They'd be pulling out soon, off to pick up and deliver their loads.

As soon as the door closed, Rowena turned to Linc. "So I guess you heard the news—I'm about to become a Drake Trucking employee."

He smiled. "Better than that—office manager. Congratulations."

"Thanks. I'll do my very best to fill Donna's more than capable shoes."

Carly shared a glance with Linc.

"Why'd she quit, anyway?" Row asked. "She worked for Joe for years."

"Maybe now that he's gone, she was ready for a change," Carly said, sticking to the story they'd agreed on. After all the woman's years of loyalty, Carly believed Joe would have wanted Donna to have the benefit of the doubt. Besides, Townsend had verified that a total of twenty thousand had gone in and out of Donna's personal account, given to Miguel, she had to assume. The rest had apparently gone to El Jefe as Donna had said.

While Linc set up his computer and went to work at one of the desks in the main part of the office, Carly led Row into the inner office and they sat down at the small round table in the corner.

"Okay, so what's going on?" Row asked.

"As I said, there are some things you need to know before you accept the job." Taking a deep, steadying breath, Carly told her friend about the night she'd been abducted, about El Jefe's threats, and that he might be the man behind Miguel Hernandez's murder.

"I don't want you going into this job blind," she said. "That wouldn't be fair. I don't think you'd be in any danger working as office manager but there's always a chance."

Row leaned back in her chair. "Wow. I can't believe this is happening to you. You've only been here a couple of months and you're dealing with death threats and murder. It must seem like the weight of the world is crashing down on your head." She straightened. "You can trust me not to say anything to anyone. You know that, right?"

"I know. Linc and I are trying to figure a way out. He's hired a private investigator, and he's got some very influential friends, but there's always a chance something bad could happen."

"I trust Linc and I trust you even more. I really want this job and I'd really like to help. So yes, I accept your offer."

Carly felt a wave of relief. It was going to work out. She had someone capable and trustworthy to help her. All she had to do was find a way to deal with El Jefe. *Yeah, right.*

"When can you start?"

"How soon do you need me?"

"Tomorrow if you can swing it. If not, we'll manage until you're ready."

"I'd have to give notice to my part-time employer and cut my hours at the roadhouse, but I can juggle things for a while. I can start tomorrow if you need me."

Carly grinned. "Terrific."

While the women were talking, Linc sat in front of his laptop in the main part of the office, reviewing plans for the tire rebuilding plant, the first in a chain— he hoped. Dammit, everything was in order. All they needed was the county permit. It should have been a done deal.

Instead, he'd be sending in a team next week to discuss concessions Tex/Am would be willing to make to get the permit they needed to break ground. He hoped to hell it would work.

He glanced up at the sound of Carly's office door swinging open. "Gotta run," Row said, waving at Linc as she hurried through the main room toward the front door. "See you tomorrow, Carly."

"See you then," Carly said.

Linc smiled. Looked like Row had accepted the job. Carly needed someone she could trust, and from what Linc knew of Rowena, she was trustworthy, as well as smart and capable.

"Glad it worked out," he said.

Carly smiled. "Me, too." The door had just clicked shut when the knob turned and one of the drivers pushed it back open. He walked in holding onto a kid by the collar at the nape of his neck. Linc recognized Pete Sanchez from the day Carly had freed up the jackknifed big rig—a slender man in his late twenties, at least part Latino.

"What's going on, Pete?" Carly asked.

"I found this kid hiding in the break room. Looks like he's been there all night. He won't talk, just keeps asking for Joe."

The boy was around ten years old, too thin, blue-eyed, and nearly towheaded. Linc noticed a bruise on his cheek, turning from purple to an ugly greenish yellow. The boy jerked free of Pete's hold and stood up a little straighter.

"I want to see Joe Drake. I'm not leaving till I talk to him."

Carly looked at Sanchez. "You didn't tell him?"

Pete shook his head. "Figured that was your business."

Linc studied the boy, wondered at his connection to Joe, and a pang of sympathy tightened his chest. He remembered the way he'd felt when he'd gotten the phone call from Johnnie Banducci telling him Joe was dead.

"How do you know Joe?" Carly asked gently as Pete backed out of the office and closed the door.

The boy ignored the question. "I gotta see him. I need to talk to him. It's important."

"What's your name?" Few people ignored a question Linc asked; the kid took one look at him and answered.

"Zach Archer. I wasn't doing nothin' wrong. I was just waiting for him. I'm . . . I'm his grandson."

Linc's gaze shot to Carly, whose shoulders stiffened at the news.

"Zach Archer. Your father wouldn't be Ray Archer?" Linc saw Carly putting the pieces together same as he was. Archer, the guy who had vandalized her house.

"He's my dad. I need to see Joe." The boy reached into the pocket of his dirty jeans and pulled out an envelope, tightly folded and yellow with age. Carly took the envelope from his small unsteady hand, carefully unfolded it, and pulled out a wrinkled sheet of paper.

The boy looked up at her. "My mom said if I ever got in trouble, I should come to Iron Springs. I should ask for Joe Drake. The letter has directions how to get here."

"Keep going," Linc encouraged when the kid hesitated, but seemed to have something else to say.

"Joe was my mom's dad. She died but she left me the letter. She said Joe would help me."

Carly glanced down at the note. When she finished reading it, she turned to the boy. "Zach, I'm really sorry, but your grandpa died almost two months ago."

The kid's face went bone white, making the bruise on his cheek stand out. He stumbled backward, caught hold of the desk to steady himself. "Joe can't be dead. He can't be."

Linc set his hands on the boy's narrow shoulders. Beneath his plaid shirt, he was trembling. Linc squeezed gently, commanding his attention.

"Joe isn't here, Zach, but I am. Joe was my friend. That makes you my friend, too. That means if you need help, I'll help you. You understand?"

"I can't believe he's dead."

"Listen to me, son. Joe can't help you, but I can."

The kid blinked as if he was only now hearing the words. Then his eyes teared up. "You mean it?"

"I mean it. We're both going to help you. How did you get here?"

Zach sniffed, wiped his nose with the back of his hand. "I hitched."

"When was the last time you ate?"

"I don't know . . . yesterday, maybe. I took the money out of my savings bank, but I ran out a couple days ago."

"How long have you been traveling?"

"Five or six days, I guess. I didn't leave town right away. One of my friends hid me out for a couple of days and I got stranded a few times on the road."

Probably left Austin the night his father went on a rampage, Linc figured as the puzzle became clearer. The night Archer beat the hell out of the woman he was living with and apparently his son, as well.

Linc's gaze remained steady on the boy. "All right, Zach, here's what we're going to do. First we're going to get you fed, then we're taking you home. We'll talk and we'll figure this out."

"Who are you?"

"Like I said, I'm a friend of Joe's. My name is Lincoln Cain." Linc managed to smile even as he was thinking of putting his hands around Ray Archer's throat and squeezing some sense into him. "You can call me Linc. The lady is Carly Drake—she's Joe's granddaughter."

The boy's gaze swung to Carly, who managed to summon a smile. "I think your mom and my mom were half sisters. I know Joe had two wives and they each had a daughter. One of them must have been your mom. That makes us cousins."

Hope washed away some of the worry in the kid's blue eyes. "Really?"

Carly's smile went from forced to sincere. "Yes. It's nice to meet you, Zach."

"It's nice to meet you, too. Are you really gonna help me?"

"You're family. Of course we're going to help you."

"If you're ready," Linc said. "Why don't we go get that food?"

Carly rested a hand on the boy's back to urge him toward the door and he winced. Linc lifted his shirt, saw the angry red stripes, and silently cursed.

"Everything's going to be okay, son," he said. "I promise."

The boy swallowed. Linc could tell he was fighting to hold back tears. Wrapping an arm around the kid's bony shoulders, he pulled him into his side and hung on. Zach took a shuddering breath and for a moment leaned against him.

Over the boy's head he saw Carly wiping moisture from her cheeks.

Chapter Twenty

Why was it when you thought things couldn't get any worse, they always seemed to do just that?

Carly sat in the front seat of the truck, parked in the Burger King lot. In back, Zach Archer, apparently a cousin she hadn't known she had, sat wolfing down a Whopper, double fries, and a super-size chocolate shake.

Behind the wheel, Linc cast her a glance. "You okay?"

"Just trying to piece it all together." She took a last bite of her chicken sandwich and stuffed the wrapper into the paper bag. Linc had already finished.

"I remember Joe mentioning his second wife," she said. "I know she was way younger than he was. Joe said they had a daughter named Caroline and I know she died in a car accident, but according to Joe, he and Caroline had lost contact years before it happened. Apparently she married Ray Archer and had a child."

"I don't think Joe knew Caroline had a son," Linc said. "If he'd known, he would have mentioned him."

"No, I'm sure he didn't," Carly said.

"So Archer was at your house looking for his kid."

"What?" The small voice came from the backseat.

Carly turned to look at Zach. "You know your father was arrested, right?"

Pain flashed in his face. He was a good-looking kid, with fine features and blue eyes a little lighter than her own.

"He was beating Suzy up real bad," he said. "I tried to stop him, but then he got mad at me, too. I didn't know what to do. Suzy was bleeding and crying. I called nine-one-one, then I got my stuff and took off while he and Suzy were still fighting."

"Calling the police was the right thing to do," Carly said.

"Running away from the cops, however, was a good way for you to get hurt," Linc added.

"But you're here now and safe," Carly finished. "That's what's important." She caught the amusement in Linc's eyes. *What?* she silently mouthed. *He's just a little boy.*

"I thought my father was in jail," Zach said, his features dark with worry. "You said he came here. You said he was looking for me."

"Your dad got out on bail," Linc said. "You know what that means?"

He nodded. "I saw it on TV. Where you put up money to prove you won't run away."

Carly reached across the seat and caught hold of his hand. "I'm sorry, Zach, but your dad did run away. He came here looking for you."

The boy's face went pale and he started breathing too fast.

"He's not going to find you, Zach," Linc promised. "We're going to make sure you're safe."

"You don't know him. My dad can be real mean. He might have a gun. He might shoot you."

"We have guards at the ranch," Linc said calmly. "He won't be able to get to you there."

"Are you sure?"

"You can see for yourself when we get to the ranch."

The stiffness in Zach's small shoulders eased. "Okay."

Carly made sure the boy put his seat belt back on; then Linc pulled the truck out of the Burger King parking lot and headed back toward the ranch.

Luckily the protestors had decided to take Sunday off. The guards stood at the gate and the men on ATVs were patrolling the grounds. Carly felt a rush of relief when Linc continued past the big stone mansion to the sprawling redbrick house down the dirt road.

She'd been afraid Linc would want to leave Zach with the housekeeper. That he was bringing the boy into his own home sent a wave of gratitude through her.

Linc parked the GMC out front and they went inside. Carly gave Zach a quick tour of the ranch house, then settled him in the empty bedroom and showed him the bathroom he could use at the end of the hall.

"Why don't you take a nice hot shower, Zach? You've been on the road for a while."

"You sure it's okay with Linc?" Zach asked. "He's real big. I wouldn't want to make him mad."

Carly thought of the welts on the boy's back and her heart squeezed. She tried for a reassuring smile. "I know Linc's big, but he'd never hurt you. He's going to help you, Zach. Both of us are."

Zach seemed relieved. While the shower was running, Carly took one of Linc's XXL T-shirts into the bathroom, and grabbed Zach's dirty clothes. Carrying them into the laundry room, she tossed them into the washer. A spare pair of holey jeans and a second faded shirt were all he'd taken with him when he'd left his house. She washed those, too. At least now his clothes would be clean.

Linc was waiting for her in the kitchen when she walked out of the laundry room. When he saw her, he opened his arms and Carly walked straight into them.

She rested her head against his chest. "I can't believe this is happening."

Linc's hold tightened. "We'll figure it out."

We. It was a word she rarely used herself. Except for Joe, there had never been a *we* in her life. Guilt slid through her. Zach wasn't Linc's problem; he was hers.

"I can't ask you for any more help, Linc. It isn't fair."

He kissed the top of her head and eased her a little away. "You aren't asking me for anything. Even if Zach wasn't Joe's grandson, I'd do what I could to help him. I know what it is to have a father like Archer. I know what it's like to have the hell beat out of you for no reason at all. No kid deserves that."

Carly turned away and walked over to the window, wrapped her arms around herself as if she felt a chill. The horses were visible in the fields behind the house but she barely noticed them.

She couldn't take more help from Linc. She didn't want to be more indebted to him than she was already, couldn't allow herself to continue to rely on him. It was only going to hurt more when they parted.

And she knew they would. All men left, sooner or later. Joe's first wife had died before he had time to get tired of her, but he had divorced his second wife and left her with a baby girl. Joe had provided for them financially, of course, but what about the heartbreak his wife had suffered when he had thrown his family away?

Linc walked up behind her, slid his arms around her waist, and eased her back against his chest. She wanted to turn around and just hang on, let him take all her problems away.

She knew better. Joe had made sure she understood the only person she could depend on was herself.

Linc turned her around to face him. "Everything's going to be okay, all right?"

She just nodded. She could hardly remember the last time everything was okay.

"While you were getting Zach settled," Linc said, "Townsend called. He had info on Archer, including the fact he has a son. The police are looking for the boy. We'll have to call them, tell them Zach's safe."

She jerked as if he'd hit her. "We can't do that. They'll call child protective services. They'll put Zach in the system. I know what that feels like. I know how scared he'll be."

"Carly . . ."

"I was Zach's age when my mother died. I remember the police coming to the house and taking me away. I remember how scared I was, how alone I felt. I don't want that to happen to Zach."

Pity flashed in Linc's eyes. "It isn't the same, Carly. You didn't have anyone. Zach has us. He might have to go in for a while, but"

"He's just a kid, Linc—he's already suffered enough."

Linc tipped up her chin, forcing her to look at him. "Listen to me, honey. It won't be for long. Just a few days until I can get him out. I'll have my attorney do whatever's necessary to see you get temporary custody. I'll take custody myself if that's what needs to be done."

Her heart was pounding. Worry for Zach made her chest ache. Linc had a reasonable answer for everything. But the more he took over, the more afraid she became.

"You don't understand," she said, turning away from him. "You can't keep doing this. You can't keep solving my problems."

"Why not?"

Because sooner or later you'll be gone. Sooner or later I'll be back on my own. Because if I get in any deeper, I'm going to fall in love with you and you're going to break my heart.

Watching Linc with Zach, seeing the man he was, made her want things she could never have. Dear God, he was Lincoln Cain! She didn't dare fall in love with him.

"Why not?" she repeated. "Because I need to take care of myself. I always have and that isn't going to change."

His features darkened. He didn't like the sound of that. He was used to being in charge.

"Fine, if that's the way you want it. But whatever you do, the boy needs our help. Surely you can at least agree to that."

She sighed. She had to agree. She had to do what was best for Zach.

Carly wished she could just run away, get as far from Lincoln Cain as she possibly could. She wished she could find a way to protect herself, to distance herself from all that appealing, self-assured masculinity, from all the things he made her feel.

But she had to think of the boy who was now her responsibility.

"You're right," she said softly. "Zach has to come first." She moved a few steps away from Linc, then mourned the distance she had put between them. "I'd better check on him, make sure he's okay."

Linc said nothing as she headed down the hall. When she reached Zach's bedroom, she found him curled up on top of the covers, sound asleep. He looked so innocent, so vulnerable, her heart clutched. There was a time she had wanted children, a family. She tried not to wonder what Linc would want. He had never had children. Would he want them?

The thought sent a shockwave through her. After two failed engagements and years of dating men whose actions had convinced her *happily ever after* wasn't for her, she had given up dreams of home and family.

But there had never been a man who made her feel the way Linc did, one she trusted the way she trusted him. No matter what happened, she wasn't ready to give him up.

Summoning her courage, Carly turned and walked back down the hall. Hands clasped behind his back, Linc stood staring out the kitchen window.

"I'm sorry," she said softly. Linc turned. "I've never let anyone in before, no one except Joe. I've always relied on myself. It's hard for me to accept help from you or anyone else. Please forgive me."

His handsome features softened. Linc strode toward her, pulled her into his arms. "You're the strongest woman I know. I wouldn't change that for anything."

A hard lump rose in her throat. No man had ever accepted her for the person she was inside. Maybe Linc was different. Maybe she should let things play out.

Carly trembled. She had never been a risk taker, but she was taking a big risk now.

Linc lowered his head and kissed her—just as her phone chimed a text coming in.

Carly jerked away. "What if it's him?"

"Let's find out." Linc crossed to the breakfast table, grabbed Carly's purse, and handed it over. He watched as she nervously ransacked the bag, fished out her smart phone, and read the text at the bottom of the screen.

"Oh, God."

Linc took the phone from her hand and read the message out loud. "Tuesday night, one A.M. Pickup site to follow."

"It's him. What . . . what am I going to do?"

Linc caught her shoulders. "I know you don't want my help, but these people are deadly and they're not going to stop until someone stops them. Miguel Hernandez was murdered and El Jefe is likely the man responsible. There's a chance you could be next."

A shaky breath whispered out. "I know."

"I'm going to call Quinn Taggart and set up a meeting. We'll talk to him, but we won't give the FBI details until we've got some kind of plan that won't end up getting you killed. All right?"

For once Carly didn't argue. "Okay."

Linc pulled out his cell phone and hit Taggart's contact number. The FBI agent picked up on the second ring.

"Quinn, it's Cain. We need to talk about that problem we discussed."

"What's going on?" Taggart asked.

"Things are heating up. El Jefe's been in contact. Trouble's coming and we need your help."

"Where do you want to meet? I can get there tomorrow or you can come here."

"The guy's got eyes and ears all over. We'll meet in Dallas, same place as before if that works for you."

"I've got a few things to deal with in the morning. Eleven A.M. okay?"

Linc turned to Carly. "Eleven A.M. in Dallas?"

She nodded.

"We'll be there," Linc said.

"*We?*" Taggart asked.

"I'm bringing that friend I mentioned. See you tomorrow." Linc hung up and turned to Carly. She wasn't a fragile woman, but she looked ready to break right now. He wanted to pull her into his arms and just hold her, tell her everything would be okay. He was afraid it would only make things worse.

"I know you're not ready for this," he said, thinking of Zach, another problem she had to face. "There's a second call we need to make." Her gaze shot toward the bedroom where Zach lay sleeping. "It has to be done, honey." When her eyes glistened, his chest clamped down.

"Zach's been hurt so much already," she said. "Can't we wait another day, give him a chance to sort all this out? We need to talk to him, explain what we're going to do."

He didn't want to wait. The cops were looking for the boy, spending their time and energy on a wild-goose chase when the kid was here and safe. But one look at the tears Carly was fighting so hard to hold back and his decision was made.

"All right, dammit, he stays until tomorrow. He gets a good night's sleep and plenty to eat and tomorrow when we come back, we'll talk to him, make sure he understands we aren't abandoning him. While we're in Dallas, I'll call my lawyer, set things in motion. Okay?"

Relief eased the worry in her face. "Thank you."

"Everything's going to be okay, baby. We just have to take things one at a time."

She relaxed a little more. "I'm going to call Brittany. She's a teacher. She's really great with kids. If she isn't substituting, maybe she can come out and stay with Zach while we go to Dallas."

"Good idea."

She walked away with the phone against her ear, came back smiling. She was the most resilient woman he had ever known.

"Britt's off tomorrow. I told her the guards at the gate would know she was coming and let her in."

Linc nodded, felt a little better. Things were beginning to line up. He didn't like chaos. He always felt better when he had a plan. Tomorrow he'd talk to Taggart, work things out with the FBI, find a way to bring El Jefe down.

He glanced at the woman weaving her spell around him. Whatever happened, he'd find a way to keep Carly safe.

Chapter Twenty-One

Carly awoke Monday morning beneath a dark cloud of dread. A nightmare that included a knife-wielding El Jefe had jolted her awake sometime after midnight with a scream locked in her throat. Linc had drawn her into his arms and held her, put her back to sleep with some of his magnificent lovemaking.

Today she had a meeting with the FBI. Tomorrow she was supposed to pick up El Jefe's shipment of God-only-knew-what. She had no idea how either of those things was going to turn out.

Tired and out of sorts, she wandered into the kitchen to the smell of frying bacon, found Linc cooking breakfast for Zach. Ignoring a shot of guilt that she hadn't gotten up earlier and done the cooking herself, she gave Linc a grateful smile. "Smells great," she said.

He smiled back. "I hope you're hungry."

As soon as the eggs were scrambled, the three of them sat down around the dark oak breakfast table and dug into the delicious eggs accompanied by bacon, juice, toast, and coffee, and a big glass of milk for Zach.

"You're a really good cook, Linc," the boy said. Carly

wondered if he had any idea how few people were privileged to call Lincoln Cain by his first name.

"Thanks, Zach. Breakfast is about all I've got. Pizza is my go-to food for supper."

"I love pizza," Zach said. Whatever had been going on between Linc and Zach this morning, the boy seemed a lot less tense.

The hearty food and cheerful conversation bolstered her spirits and a thread of optimism surfaced. She could handle this. So a little boy needed her help. If Joe were alive he would take care of Zach. Carly could do the same.

She took a sip of coffee, savored the rich dark flavor of freshly ground beans, eased into a change of subject.

"Linc and I have to go into Dallas for a couple of hours today, Zach. It's no big deal, just some business that can't wait." She hated to leave when he needed her support so badly, but there wasn't any choice.

The boy's head swiveled toward her. Sunlight streaming in through the window turned his wheat-blond hair to silver. "You have to leave?"

There wasn't a scrap left on his plate or a drop of milk in his glass. She wondered if he was storing up in case he needed to run again. The thought sent a pang into her heart.

"We won't be gone long," Linc told him. "We'll be back this afternoon. You'll be safe here till we get home."

Carly managed to smile. "I've got a friend coming over to keep you company. Brittany's an elementary school teacher so she knows lots of kids your age."

Zach sat up straighter in his chair, his chin jutting out. "I don't need a babysitter."

Linc casually sipped his coffee. "You're right. A kid

who could make it from Austin to Iron Springs on his own can clearly take care of himself. We just didn't want you to get lonely. Britt's going to take you swimming. That is, if you know how to swim."

Swimming hadn't been part of the plan, but the excitement in Zach's face said it was a fine idea.

"I'm a good swimmer," Zach said. "I learned in summer school." His expression turned wary. "I didn't see any pool."

"Linc has a big pool up at the main house," Carly said. "You and Britt can swim up there."

The boy's blue eyes rounded. He turned to Linc. "That big house is yours? I thought it belonged to someone else."

"It's mine. I use it for entertaining, but I prefer to stay here."

Zach looked at him as if he'd lost his mind. "Could I go inside sometime? I've never seen a house so big."

"You can go in with Britt," Linc said. "You'll find swimsuits in the cabana. There's bound to be something close to your size. There are towels and soft drinks so you won't need to take anything with you."

"What's a cabana?"

"It's a place to get out of the sun," Linc explained. "It has toilets and showers, pool toys, air mattresses, stuff like that."

"Wow."

Linc started smiling. He looked at Carly. "I'd forgotten what it was like to be a kid."

"You and Britt are going to have a great time," Carly said, suddenly wishing she could join them. "I'd better call her. She'll probably want to bring her own swimsuit."

She had already filled her friend in on the basics,

told her about Zach and his abusive father, shared some of what was happening with El Jefe, revealed as much as she dared. Britt and Row were her two best friends. She trusted them completely and she desperately needed their support.

Twenty minutes later, they drove up to the main house to meet Brittany, who looked pretty in a soft pink ruffled top and a pair of khaki crop pants, her long dark hair pulled into a ponytail. A bright orange canvas beach bag dangled from her fingers.

"Zach, this is my good friend, Brittany Haworth. Britt, this is my cousin, Zach Archer."

Around children, Britt wasn't shy. "Hey, Zach. Nice to meet you. The kids at school call me Miss Haworth, but you can call me Britt, okay?"

He just nodded.

"I hear we get to go swimming." Britt flashed him a wide smile. "I love to swim. How about you?"

Zach gazed down at the toe of his worn sneaker. Britt was really pretty and suddenly it was Zach who was shy. "I gotta find a swimsuit out in the cabana."

"Okay, we can do that."

"Zach wants to see the house," Linc said. "Mrs. Delinski, my housekeeper, is expecting you. She can show you around before you go out to the pool."

"Perfect," Britt said, and Zach beamed.

And they would be safe. Frank Marino would be at the house, keeping an eye out for trouble, along with the guards at the gate and the armed men patrolling the property. If Ray Archer showed up, he would find himself on his way back to jail.

"You ready, Zach?" Brittany asked.

Zach's gaze shot to the big stone mansion. He was up on the balls of his feet, practically jumping up and down. "I'm ready. Let's go!" The boy dashed toward the front door, so excited he forgot all about their leaving.

Carly could only imagine the expression on the ten-year-old's face when he got a look at the sweeping double staircases and massive crystal chandelier.

"I haven't gone swimming in ages," she said wistfully. "It really sounds like fun."

"Yes, it does." His gaze swept over the dark blue skinny jeans, navy blazer, and white lace blouse she was wearing for her meeting with the FBI. As if she wore only a skimpy bikini, the gold in his eyes gleamed. "We'll take a nice private swim the first chance we get."

A private swim? Carly's stomach floated up. The image of Linc in a swimsuit made her pulse race. "Okay," she said a little breathlessly.

From the ranch, the chopper made a stop at the truck yard so Carly could get Rowena settled in for her first day. She told Row about Zach showing up just as she'd left yesterday, about his dad being responsible for the vandalism at Joe's house, and warned there was a possibility Ray Archer might show up at the yard.

"He's a wanted man, Row," Linc said. "Don't take any chances."

"You can bet I won't. I've handled my share of crazies out at the roadhouse. I'll be okay."

"There are always truckers around," Carly said. "Tell the men to keep an eye out for him."

"Okay, I will."

Carly waved good-bye to Row and they left the office. She didn't mention the FBI or the latest threat from El Jefe. There was only so much a normal person could take.

* * *

At eleven in the morning, before the lunch crowd started to arrive, the Tex-Mex Café wasn't too busy. Linc escorted Carly inside and guided her between the tables to one of the booths at the rear where FBI Agent Quinn Taggart sat bent over his iPad.

Taggart glanced up as Linc approached, didn't quite mask his surprise that the *friend* Linc had mentioned was a woman.

"Have a seat," Quinn said, but didn't stand up. The less attention they drew the better.

"Special Agent Quinn Taggart, meet Carly Drake," Linc said as they sat down. "She owns Drake Trucking— that's the company with the problem we discussed."

Assessing hazel eyes swung toward Carly and lit with interest. Linc had met Taggart a few years back when Quinn had been investigating a string of murders in the Dallas area, one of which involved a female employee at Tex/Am Transport.

Linc liked the way Taggart had handled the investigation and Quinn had appreciated the access Linc had given him to company records. The FBI man was smart and capable and more than passably attractive. Fortunately he was happily married with a couple of kids.

"Linc and I discussed your situation in a very general way," Quinn said to Carly, "but we didn't talk specifics. I'm glad you decided to come forward."

"I'm hoping you can help me, Agent Taggart."

Linc cast her a glance. Carly still didn't understand that they were in this together. The way Taggart was looking the two of them over, Linc had a feeling Quinn understood exactly what was going on.

A gray-haired waitress arrived to refill Quinn's coffee cup. "You having lunch or breakfast?" the broad-hipped woman asked Linc.

"Just coffee." He turned over the heavy china mug in front of him and Carly did the same. The older woman filled both cups and sauntered away, bringing them back to the conversation.

"Why don't you start from the beginning?" Taggart suggested. "Then we'll go forward from there."

For the next few minutes, Carly explained the situation with El Jefe, beginning with the murder of Miguel Hernandez, the money that had been embezzled from Drake Trucking to force her grandfather into joining the man's criminal activities, her run-in with the drug lord's men, and meeting the man himself.

"Unfortunately I was blindfolded. I have no idea what he looks like, except he has big feet and he's a little pigeon-toed."

Taggart sighed. "You're not alone. No one seems to know who he is, or if they do, they're afraid to get involved."

"I would probably recognize some of his men."

Taggart nodded. "That would be useful. We can have you look at mug shots on your computer. We don't want to bring you in to headquarters because we don't want anyone to know you're working with us."

"Hold it," Linc said. "She's not working with you. She's giving you information. We need you to arrest this guy and put him out of business."

"That's exactly what we're trying to do. But we won't be able to do it without Carly's help."

"What kind of help are you talking about?" Carly asked.

Taggart eyed her shrewdly. "You've filled me in on what's been happening, but I have a feeling you're leaving something out." Which was true, since neither of them had mentioned the load Drake Trucking was supposed to pick up and deliver on Tuesday night.

"Before this goes any further," Quinn continued, "I need you to tell me what brought you here today. Last week, Linc was very circumspect about how much he told me. Today both of you are here. Obviously something has changed. If you want the help of the FBI, I need to know what that something is."

Carly looked at Linc, clearly uncertain.

"We need your help, Quinn," Linc said. "But before we tell you anything more, we need to know exactly what you expect in return."

Quinn's focus centered on Carly. "You've actually met this guy who calls himself El Jefe—*the boss*. Under the right circumstances, he might want to meet with you again. If that happens, we'd have the chance to go in and arrest him. Until that point, we need you to play along, do exactly what he tells you. In the meantime, we'll be putting a case together. There's a chance you'll even be able to provide us with evidence. In exchange for your help, we'll provide you with protection."

"No." The single word had both their heads snapping toward him. "She's not getting near that bastard again."

Quinn looked at him with a trace of pity. "She needs to do this, Linc. Whatever threats this guy has made, he isn't afraid to carry them out. Carly's best bet is to help us catch him before he kills her or someone else."

Silence settled over the table. There had to be another way, a plan that would keep Carly out of danger.

"Drake is supposed to pick up a load for El Jefe on Tuesday night," Carly said, and Linc softly cursed. "I have no idea what's going to be in it. The text I received said they would text us the pickup location. I'm guessing they'll tell us where to take the load once we get the cargo loaded."

Quinn's satisfied smile made Linc's jaw feel tight. He didn't want her involved with this. For the first time, he questioned whether he should have brought her here.

"Now we're getting somewhere," Taggart said.

"What do you want me to do?" Carly asked.

"No way is the guy going to be there," Linc interrupted before Taggart could reply. "If the FBI shows up, it'll be a minor bust that'll get you nowhere and Carly will become a target."

"I'm not suggesting that." Taggart turned back to Carly. "I want your truck to pick up and deliver the load just as you're instructed. From now on, you'll do whatever it takes to win El Jefe's trust. Once that happens, you'll be able to set up a meet and that's when we'll step in."

"Who do you suggest makes the pickup?" Linc asked. "The last driver who butted heads with El Jefe wound up dead."

"We'll supply the driver. He can take over after the truck leaves the yard."

"Too risky," Linc said. "What if someone's watching? What if one of El Jefe's men sees the driver exchange?"

"I'll drive the truck," Carly said.

Linc felt a cold stab of fear. "No way. That isn't happening. It's too dangerous. I won't have it."

Carly bristled. "It isn't your decision, Linc."

"Take it easy, both of you," Taggart said. "We'll figure it out. Maybe we can put an agent undercover as a driver, someone who's presumably on your payroll. If anyone's watching the yard, they'll see an employee driving the truck in and out, smooth and easy, no problem."

"He'd be someone new," Linc said. "A new guy doing the first pickup might arouse suspicion."

"If I can make it happen, he'll be a new hire starting today," Quinn said. "A new hire shouldn't necessarily be suspicious, right? In a company that size, employees change every once in a while."

Carly looked at Linc. "It could work. At least we'd have a plan."

It was a plan. But his instincts were screaming it wasn't a good one. Unfortunately at the moment, he didn't have a better idea.

"All right. I just hope to Christ the guy you send actually knows how to drive an eighteen-wheeler."

Chapter Twenty-Two

Horns blew and brake lights went in front of them as Linc's sexy black Mercedes S550 coupe wove through the Dallas traffic.

"Where are we going?" Carly asked, noticing the route back to the Tex/Am building wasn't the direction they were heading.

"You lost your gun. We're getting you a new one."

She started to tell him she couldn't afford a new pistol, but the look he sliced her way kept the words from spilling out. With everything that had been going on, she missed the comfort of having a weapon, but guns didn't come cheap.

"I feel like I should start keeping a list of the money I owe you," she said.

"You don't owe me anything." Wrapped around the expensive wood-grained steering wheel, his big hands made handling the powerful car in this heavy traffic look easy. "Joe paid your debt a long time ago."

Carly leaned back in the deep black leather seat. She missed Joe every day. It was a wound that wouldn't heal. Even though she'd rarely come back to Iron

Springs, she had talked to him at least twice a week, nothing important on either side, just the kind of call that warmed you on the inside and made you feel loved.

"Tell me something about him," she said, "something about you and Joe."

Linc flicked her a sideways glance. "He kept me from going back to prison."

"What?"

"That's right. I'd served my time, but Howler was always trying to find a way to send me back to jail. I probably should have moved somewhere else but Beau still lived in Pleasant Hill. So did Del, Rick, and Johnnie. And I had a job with your grandfather I really liked."

"What happened?"

"One night Beau and a couple of his friends got drunk. I had an early run so Beau knew I wouldn't be drinking. He called me, asked me to pick him and the other guys up and drive them home. Unfortunately Howler was working that night. He was in the middle of a traffic stop when I drove past. The sheriff spotted Beau's fancy red Mustang convertible, realized I was behind the wheel, and followed us. Pulled me over just outside of town."

"How did my grandfather get involved?"

"Joe had a police scanner. He heard the call come in over the radio, heard an arrest was being made, and my name was mentioned. Joe showed up at the jail. I told him I hadn't been drinking—I was just making sure the guys got home safe. Joe told Howler he would have his badge if he tried to press charges."

Carly thought of her grandfather and felt another

soft pang. He'd been the only constant in her life and now he was gone.

"Joe knew the sheriff would let me go," Linc said. "Your grandfather was one of the few people who knew Howler's son was with me and Beau the night we got arrested."

Carly smiled, not surprised that Joe would stand up for someone he believed was being treated unfairly. "Okay, so I guess you can buy me a gun."

Linc laughed.

With no waiting period in Texas, Carly walked out of Drury's Gun Shop two hours later with a sweet little Glock 19 that fit her hand perfectly. There was a gun range behind the store, which she used to get comfortable firing the weapon. She'd never gotten her concealed carry permit, but she could keep the gun with her in her vehicle, at home, or at work, and she planned to do just that.

They grabbed a bite to eat, then went to Macy's to buy Zach some new clothes and a pair of sneakers she hoped would fit him.

After their shopping spree, Linc drove back to his office. He spent half an hour on the phone with his attorney, instructing the man to make arrangements for Carly to get temporary custody of Zach.

She felt sick about the little boy having to go into protective services, but she couldn't hide him from the police, and it would only be a few days. At least he'd know he had someone waiting for him, someone who wouldn't let him down.

While Linc held a brief staff meeting, Carly spent time on the phone with Rowena, going over office procedures. It was late afternoon when they left the Tex/Am

building and climbed aboard the chopper for the short
flight home.

Home. The thought shocked her. Dear God, she was
beginning to think of Linc's house as home and she
couldn't let that happen. She needed to move back to
her own house as soon as possible, but with Archer
still on the loose and the danger from El Jefe, it just
wasn't safe.

As much as she hated to admit it, she needed Linc's
protection. Aside from that, she wanted to be with him.
Both sides of the argument chased around in her head.
In the end, she decided to enjoy the time they had
together and worry about the consequences once all of
this was over.

Carly leaned back in her seat, feeling the vibration
of the helicopter blades beating the air over her head
as the chopper flew east. They had almost reached
Blackland Ranch when Linc's phone signaled. She
saw him reach into his pocket, pull it out, and read
the text.

Speaking through the headphones, he told her
the text was from Taggart. An FBI agent using the
name Mark McKinley would be waiting for them at
Drake Trucking, there to start his "new job."

Linc's pilot made a course adjustment, hovered,
then set down in the grassy field across from the truck
yard. Carly and Linc jumped out, made their way to the
entrance, then across the asphalt inside the chain-link
fence to the big metal building.

"Your new hire is here," Rowena said as they walked
through the front door. "Mark McKinley? I didn't know
you'd hired a new driver."

Carly hated secrets. And yet she didn't want to burden

her friend with more of her problems. "Sorry, with so much going on, I must have forgotten to mention him."

"He's drinking a Coke in the truckers' lounge. He said you knew he was coming. He figured you'd be here fairly soon."

"I'll go get him." Linc strode off in that direction.

Seated behind her metal desk, Row looked up at Carly. "I can't believe you didn't mention this guy. I mean, the man is hot."

Coming from Row, who had her choice of men and rarely got involved with any of them, that was a rare compliment. "You think so?"

"He looks more like a movie star than a trucker." As if to prove the point, the door swung open and Mark McKinley walked in. Row was right. The undercover FBI agent was handsome, no more than late twenties, with slightly overlong black hair and intense brown eyes. The beard stubble along his jaw made him look like he should be riding Linc's Harley instead of working for the FBI.

Rowena smiled at him, but his return smile was anything but friendly. The man was clearly all business. Or maybe he was married. Men rarely ignored a smile from Row.

When Linc followed him into the room, an alpha male as hot or hotter than Mark, there was so much testosterone in the air, Carly felt a little dizzy.

"Let's go into my office," she said.

Linc and McKinley followed her in and Linc closed the door.

"I assume you have a class B license," Carly said.

"I'm fully licensed," McKinley said. "I drove trucks for three months on a previous assignment before we had enough evidence to make an arrest."

"Good to know," Linc said.

"How's this going to work?" Carly asked.

"Simple. I take a load out tonight, which makes working for you look official to the rest of the drivers and anyone who might be getting information. Tomorrow night I make the pickup and delivery. If El Jefe's men give me any trouble, I'll tell them you're paying me double not to ask questions. Hopefully that'll be enough to satisfy them."

"Sounds good," Linc said.

"I called and got the truck lined up for tomorrow night's run," Carly said. "It's a Peterbilt like the rest of our rigs, but it's one of the newer models. I don't want any engine trouble, no breakdowns, nothing like that."

"Any reason he can't take the same rig out on his run tonight?" Linc asked. "Make a trip somewhere and come back, get familiar with the equipment?"

"No reason at all," Carly said.

"He could head down to Tex/Am Transport in Dallas. They've got cots in the truckers' lounge. He could get some sleep, then drive back here, be ready for the run tomorrow night."

"Works for me," Mark said.

Linc pulled out his cell phone. "I'll call ahead, let them know you're coming."

"Gordy should still be around," Carly said. "I'll ask him to give Mark the tour, get him familiar with the rig."

She led Mark out to the lounge, found the older man drinking a bottle of water, filled him in on what she wanted Mark to do, and left the agent in her foreman's very capable hands.

When she returned to the office, Linc was waiting. "You finished here?" he asked.

She nodded. "I need to get back. I want to check on Zach, make sure he's okay."

"Then let's go home."

It sounded good, except that when they got there, they would have to turn Zach over to the authorities.

Weariness settled over her like thick oil sludge. She heard Linc's heavy footfalls coming to a halt in front of her, felt his fingers beneath her chin, forcing her eyes to his face.

"We aren't going to let that boy down," he said. "We're going to make sure he understands that."

Her heart squeezed. Linc wouldn't let Zach down; she knew that soul deep. Some of her exhaustion fell away. Linc wouldn't let Zach down, and no matter what happened, neither would she.

They were back at the mansion, the helicopter lifting off the asphalt pad as Linc led Carly up the front steps to the big stone house. Using his key, he let her into the entry, walked her past the sweeping staircases, down the main hall. For a moment, he stopped in the kitchen to introduce her to his housekeeper, Betty Delinski, then guided her into his study, the only room in the house he actually liked.

It was the one room he'd had designed to his taste, a beautiful space, two stories high, with skylights in the upper part of the ceiling, polished rosewood furniture, and dark jewel-tone upholstery on the sofas and chairs.

The wood-paneled walls were filled with leather-bound books, and a huge fireplace dominated the far end of the room.

According to the phone calls Carly had made to her friend Brittany during the day, Britt and Zach were still out by the pool. The weather was warm and slightly humid, but the exhausting heat of the summer was beginning to wane.

Seated behind his massive desk, Linc phoned his attorney, Graham Steiner, for an update on Zach's situation, while Carly waited impatiently for him to finish. He could tell she was eager to see the boy, but they needed to know where they stood before they talked to him.

"We're going at this full tilt," Steiner told him. "As per your instructions, my staff is making this a top priority. I spoke directly to the Department of Family and Protective Services. By now the DFPS has informed the authorities, let them know the boy is safe. But with Archer still on the loose and fresh charges filed in the vandalism case, they want the child under their protection."

"You pressed them to leave the boy with his cousin or me until we can get things worked out, right?"

"I did, but that isn't going to happen right away. You know how these things work."

Linc knew from personal experience exactly how they worked. He thought of the armed guards patrolling the ranch. Blackland was the safest place he knew. Wouldn't matter to the bureaucrats who ran social services.

"Will you be bringing him in or do you want them to pick him up?" Steiner asked.

Linc looked at Carly, read the anxiety on her face. "We'll bring him in."

"They'll have people in Iron Springs waiting to transport him to the facility in Hunt County," Steiner said. "What time should they expect you?"

"We need to talk to the boy first. We'll be there in an

hour." Linc ended the call and rose from his chair. He
looked at Carly, knew how worried she was. "Come
here," he said softly.

With a shuddering breath, she walked into his arms
and he tightened them around her. He tried not to
think how good she felt, how perfectly she suited him.
He remembered the day he had taken her to the ranch
house, how she'd said the place fit him. He remembered the wild, hard-driving sex they'd had that day.
Since now wasn't the time for erotic memories, no
matter how pleasant, he eased her a little away.

"Come on. Let's go get him. We'll explain things,
make sure he understands."

Carly nodded. They walked arm in arm through the
house, out the French doors that led to the wide ex-
panse of pool decking, the huge kidney-shaped swimming pool, twin hot tubs set at different degrees, cabana,
and landscaping that stretched for nearly two acres.

They found Britt sunbathing on a chaise lounge,
Zach sitting in front of her as she slathered sunscreen
over the boy's still-healing back, careful not to hurt him.

"Hey, you two!" Carly called out with a wave. "How's
the swimming?"

Zach jumped up and raced to meet them. "The
water's great! Why don't you guys grab your suits and
come in with us?"

"We'll do that next time for sure." Carly smiled, but
her lips barely curved. "I need you to go get dressed,
Zach. There's something we have to discuss."

The kid's big smile faded. "Is it my dad?" He glanced
from her to Linc.

"In a way," he said.

Carly gave him a playful shove. "Go get dressed and
we'll talk."

Zach grabbed his towel and reluctantly padded off to the cabana.

Wearing a white one-piece swimsuit printed with big pink flowers, her dark hair wet and slicked back from her face, Britt wrapped a towel around her hips and walked up to them.

"Thanks for coming over," Carly said.

Britt smiled. "We had a great day. Thanks for letting us use your pool, Linc."

"The pool doesn't get much use. I'm glad you two had fun."

"You ought to see Zach swim. He's a regular fish in the water. He ought to go out for the swim team."

"That's a great idea," Carly said. "Once we get things worked out and I enroll him in school, maybe he could do that."

"So you're planning for him to live with you?"

Carly glanced toward the cabana where Zach had disappeared. "I don't know. This has all happened so quickly. I'll do whatever's best for Zach."

Linc thought of the bachelor life he'd been living since his divorce. Could he handle a ready-made family? Would Carly even be interested in making a life with him and the boy?

It was a thought that should have sent him running. If Beau found out the notion had even crossed his mind, his best friend would make an appointment for him with a shrink. And yet when he looked at Carly, when he thought of having a son, maybe children of his own, something seemed to settle deep inside him.

"Zach's the sweetest kid," Britt was saying. "I can't believe his father beat him the way he did."

Anger snapped in Carly's eyes. "He won't get another chance. I can promise you that."

Linc flicked a glance toward the cabana. "No, that's never going to happen to Zach again. Ever."

Brittany said her farewells and headed for the car she'd parked out front while Carly sat across from Linc and Zach at a table in the shade next to the pool. Mrs. Delinski brought a tray with a pitcher of lemonade and they sipped quietly as she walked away.

"What's going on?" Zach asked as soon as the woman disappeared back inside the house.

"Since the night you left Austin," Carly said, "the police have been looking for you. People are worried something bad will happen to you."

"I'm safe here. This place looks like an army base."

"Yes, but the police don't know that," Linc said. "They've been expending a lot of manpower searching for you. It wasn't fair to let them keep doing that."

Zach's head jerked up. "You called them? You called the cops and told them I was here?"

Carly pushed back damp strands of his wheat-colored hair. She wanted to hug him, but she didn't think he'd let her. "We had to, Zach. We didn't have any other choice."

The boy shot to his feet so fast, his chair tipped over and crashed onto the pool decking. "You said you'd help me. You said I could trust you. You said you'd keep me safe."

"You are safe, Zach," Linc said. "But staying here is only a temporary solution. We need a permanent solution. That's what we're trying to get."

Zach glanced wildly around. "Are they coming here? Are the cops coming to get me?" He looked ready to bolt, and Carly's heart went out to him.

"They aren't coming here, Zach," she said. "Linc's lawyers are working to get me temporary custody while we figure things out. Until that happens, you'll be in protective care."

"You mean jail! I'm not going to jail! I can take care of myself!"

He turned to run, but Linc caught him in two long strides, pulled him back, and trapped him in his arms. The kid struggled, but Linc didn't let go.

"Take it easy, son. We aren't going to let anyone hurt you. We're going to do everything we can to help you, just like we promised."

"You have to believe us, Zach," Carly said, desperate to make the boy understand. "My mom died when I was ten. They took me away the night I found her, so I know what it's like. I know how alone you feel. And Linc had a father who beat him. Neither of us is going to let that happen to you again."

Zach stopped struggling. His shoulders drooped and he looked up at her with tears in his eyes. "What . . . what will they do to me?"

Linc let him go but kept a hand on his shoulder. "They'll transport you to a facility in Hunt County. You have to be somewhere your dad won't be able to get to you."

"Your father isn't stable," Carly said. "He's dangerous and that's the reason the police want you somewhere they can protect you."

"You could protect me here."

"I know," she said, "but the authorities have rules and they won't break them."

The boy stared down at his feet. "My dad isn't as mean when he isn't drunk. When he drinks, he sort of goes crazy."

Carly felt a rush of anger. Ray Archer was never getting his hands on his son again. "We bought you some clothes when we were in Dallas. At least you'll have something to wear."

Zach's eyes widened. "You bought me clothes?"

Carly smiled. "I hope I picked things you'll like. I saw the size when I washed your stuff yesterday. We got you some sneakers, too. They're Nikes. LeBrons. Linc picked them out."

"LeBrons? Are you kidding me? They cost a fortune. Where are they? I wanna see 'em."

"They're in Linc's study." Before she could stop him, Zach raced toward the French doors and disappeared inside the house. Carly prayed he wouldn't just keep running.

Instead, he returned carrying two shopping bags filled with jeans, shirts, and underwear. Zach pulled out the shoe box and popped the lid, stared down at the white-and-red, hundred-sixty-dollar pair of sneakers as if they were the most precious gift he had ever received.

He pulled out a shoe with great care and examined it closely. "They're exactly my size." He turned the shoe over and over in his hands. "Wow, these are great." He looked up at Linc and she caught a hint of moisture in his eyes. "Thank you."

"You're welcome," Linc said.

Zach grabbed one of the bags and pulled it open, saw the jeans and shirts. "Cool!" He fished through the bags. "I'm gonna change into the new stuff. At least I'll look good when they put me in jail."

Carly's heart constricted. She turned away so Zach wouldn't know she was crying.

Chapter Twenty-Three

Leaving Zach with child services had been even harder on Carly than Linc had expected. She and Zach both carried Joe's blood. Maybe that was the reason the bond had formed so quickly. Or maybe it was because Carly understood what the kid was going through.

Linc had promised again it would only be a matter of days until Zach was released into their care, but with Archer still on the loose and the problems with El Jefe, Linc was glad the boy was out of harm's way.

Tuesday rolled around, the day of the cargo run El Jefe expected Drake Trucking to make. That morning, Agent Taggart had e-mailed an attachment to both Linc's and Carly's laptops, containing files of mug shots. They went over them, but couldn't find a photo of the big mustached Latino called Cuchillo or any of the men who had attacked Carly at Jubal's. Nor did she recognize any of the men who had abducted her and taken her to El Jefe.

Then Ross Townsend phoned. The results from the cargo manifest found at the crime scene had come back from the lab in Dallas.

"You were right," Ross said. "The rust-colored spot was blood and it didn't belong to Hernandez."

"Did they get DNA?" Linc asked.

"They got it. The bad news is, they ran it through CODIS but didn't get a match."

Linc swore softly. He'd had high hopes for that bit of evidence.

As soon as breakfast was over, Frank Marino drove Carly in to work while Linc worked out of his home office. Things appeared to be moving forward with the tire rebuilding plant, or at least the county commissioners were starting to listen to the team of environmental experts he had sent in to convince them.

A call to his project manager brought him up to speed on the highway construction going on in New Mexico, which appeared to be progressing without too much trouble.

Late in the morning, an e-mail from Millie reminded him of the charity ball coming up at the end of the week. With everything going on, he considered canceling, but the auction proceeds went to cancer research, a charity he heavily supported. It was important for him to be there and he refused to live his life around El Jefe's demands.

At the end of the day, he picked Carly up at the yard and they drove to Greenville to the Hunt County Juvenile Detention Center to see how Zach was settling in.

Since the boy was only there for protection, he'd been separated from the main population, put in a special housing unit with children waiting to be placed in foster homes.

Zach looked pale and even thinner than when he'd arrived. Linc knew how the kid was feeling. He'd been in juvie for truancy in middle school, in again in high school for fighting, and once for underage drinking.

Though the detention officers were doing their best to keep Zach away from the general population, he ate in the cafeteria with the other kids and was occasionally exposed to them in the play yard. The boy was clearly unhappy and a little afraid.

"I hate it here," Zach said glumly. "I never should have let you take me in. I should have run away." They were sitting at a white plastic table and chairs in a small, private visiting room. Carly reached over and caught hold of Zach's hand.

"You aren't going to be here long, Zach. Just till we can get things worked out."

"Listen to me, Zach," Linc said. "Sometimes things happen we can't control. That's just life. But if you know it's only temporary, if you believe it's going to get better, you can get through it. You need to make the best of this place until we can get you out of here."

Carly squeezed the boy's hand. "Can you do what Linc says?"

Zach sat up a little straighter, looked Linc right in the face. "I can do it."

"Good boy," Linc said.

Zach seemed a little better by the time they left. Linc didn't think Carly was doing nearly as well. She was extremely softhearted and she already loved the boy. He was her family, all she really had.

"He'll be okay," Linc said as they drove home. "He's a tough kid or he wouldn't have made it all the way to Iron Springs in the first place."

"I know."

Linc's phone rang just then, interrupting the conversation. Earlier, he had phoned his attorney but hadn't been able to reach him. This was Steiner calling him back.

"We've got a problem, Linc." The attorney's voice came over the hands-free speaker.

"I must be on a roll. What's going on?"

"Turns out the boy has other family besides Carly. Protective Services contacted them and told them what happened and they want custody of the boy."

"Who are they?" Linc asked.

"His grandmother, Amanda Weller, and her husband, Tom."

"Amanda must be Joe's second wife," Carly said. "Joe never talked about her. I wasn't even sure she was still alive."

"I did some digging," Steiner said. "Amanda Weller is fifty-five years old. Tom is fifty-six. They live in San Antonio. Tom's a doctor, a G.P. with a very good reputation. Still has his own practice."

"I remember she was a lot younger than Joe," Carly said.

"Why are they just now coming forward?" Linc asked. "They must have known Zach's circumstances. Seems to me it's too little, too late."

"Apparently her daughter married Ray against her wishes. According to Mrs. Weller, they were close to her and Zach until she died, but then Archer moved to Austin and wouldn't let them see the boy. They didn't realize how bad Zach was being treated until this happened. They're making arrangements to see him."

"I wonder why Zach didn't mention them," Carly said.

"They've filed a petition for custody," Steiner continued. "At best it's going to slow things down."

"I want the boy out of there," Linc said. "Do everything you can to make that happen."

"You know I will."

Linc ended the call.

"I want to meet them," Carly said.

"Absolutely." He liked that she was so protective of the boy. Zach needed someone in his life like Carly. "We'll get this resolved, honey. In the meantime, at least we know Zach's somewhere safe." Or as safe as he could be in a place filled with the occasional pedophile and some very bad-ass kids.

By the time they reached the ranch, the purple glow of evening had begun to settle over the vast stretches of prairie. Cooler air whispered through the dense foliage along the creeks at the bottom of the ravines.

He checked his watch as he drove toward the house at the back of the ranch. El Jefe's cargo pickup was scheduled for one A.M. Figuring they were going to be up late, on the way home from Greenville, Linc had stopped at the grocery store and stocked up a little on food. He had bought a cook-at-home pizza.

As evening settled in, Carly made a salad and they ate the pizza for supper. Linc was hungry and pepperoni was his favorite, but Carly picked at the meal and barely finished a single slice.

The purple of evening slid into full darkness. A fingernail moon rose over the harsh Texas landscape. Nine o'clock approached and still no call from El Jefe. Agent McKinley was back in the yard and ready to make the run, but he couldn't leave until the text came in with the pick-up location.

Time passed with agonizing slowness. After trying and failing to catch up on some reading, Linc started pacing, wishing he had something to do besides worry.

Carly had gone in to use his home gym, anything to tire herself out. She was in great physical condition, which he'd noticed even before he'd taken her to bed, her body strong and nicely toned. She liked to stay in shape, used his gym whenever she had time, which there seemed to be plenty of tonight.

At five to ten, she walked back into the living room fresh out of the shower, smelling sweetly feminine and making him want her. Linc forced his mind in another direction and willed El Jefe to call.

At exactly ten-thirty, Carly's cell phone chimed a text. Linc read the message over her shoulder.

"Take 154 through Harleton. North on Baker. Stay right . . . 7.2 miles to red barn on N side."

She looked up at him. "Harleton. That's less than two hours away."

"You call McKinley and give him the location. I'll call Taggart, bring him up to speed."

They hurriedly made the calls, then settled back down in the living room. The plan was, after the cargo was picked up and McKinley was on the road to whatever delivery location he was given, he would call Quinn Taggart and fill him in. Taggart would phone Linc's cell with an update.

McKinley didn't plan to confront El Jefe's men, but there wasn't the slightest doubt the agent was putting himself in grave danger. McKinley wasn't wearing a wire. It was too dangerous. If he was searched at the loading site or later at the drop site and El Jefe's men found the recording device, there was every chance he'd be killed.

The FBI would be monitoring his cell phone's GPS location and the feds would be somewhere in the area,

but if things got dicey, they might not get there in time
to help him.

And any interference from the FBI would put Carly
in even greater danger.

The hands on the clock seemed to move with excru-
ciating slowness. Linc tried to watch a late-late comedy
show but in his dark mood, nothing seemed funny.
One A.M. finally arrived. Since neither of them would
be sleeping until this was over, Carly went into the
kitchen and brewed a pot of coffee.

Two A.M. No call from Taggart. Three. Three-thirty
and still no phone call.

Fighting a battle with exhaustion, Carly took a sip
of coffee from the mug she had just refilled. "Agent
Taggart said McKinley would contact him as soon as
the cargo was loaded and the truck was back on the
road. That should have happened by now."

"Depends on how much cargo they had to load, how
soon they actually got started—could be anything."

"You think it's drugs?"

"Probably."

Carly leaned back and closed her eyes, though
Linc doubted she'd be able to fall asleep. Restless, he
headed down the hall to his office, sat down, and went
through his e-mail, but it was tough to concentrate.
Eventually he gave up and padded back into the living
room, was pleased to see Carly had actually fallen
asleep.

At four-thirty in the morning Linc's cell started ringing. He grabbed the phone off the coffee table. Carly's
eyes snapped open and she jerked upright on the sofa.

"It's Taggart." Linc hit the speaker and set the phone
back down on the table in front of them.

"El Jefe's men never showed," Quinn said. "McKinley

waited two hours before he finally gave up, turned the truck around, and started back to the yard."

Not good. "Any idea what happened?" Linc asked.

"Not the slightest. Maybe it was a test to see if the truck would actually show up."

"Or maybe they know we talked to the FBI," Carly said glumly.

"At this point, there's no reason to make that assumption," Taggart said. "We had to bring in the local authorities, but that's protocol for an operation like this. We didn't want some cop stumbling onto the scene and getting himself killed."

"You brought Howler into this?" Linc asked, his voice rising along with his temper.

"Your names weren't mentioned, nothing about Drake Trucking. We've got very little authority here, Linc. My boss was adamant we keep Howler in the loop about our presence, as well as the Harrison County sheriff, since that's where the pickup was supposed to be made. Any reason they shouldn't have been informed?"

A dozen reasons but they were mostly personal. The bad blood between him and Howler didn't prove the man was dishonest. He didn't know the Harrison County sheriff but there was no reason to suspect him.

"Whatever happened," Quinn said, "odds are El Jefe or one of his men is going to be in touch. Let me know the minute that happens."

Linc worked a muscle in his jaw. "We'll let you know." But he was no longer sure bringing the feds in had been the right decision. He hadn't wanted Carly involved in the first place. After tonight, she might be in even more danger.

"What do you think?" she asked after he'd hung up the phone.

"I think we'll find out what happened when El Jefe is ready for us to know."

"I'm worried," Carly said. "I wish I hadn't told the FBI about the pick-up."

Linc stood up from the sofa, drew her up beside him. Knowing the stress she was under, he had ignored the desire pulsing in his groin all evening. But the tension for both of them had just ratcheted up another notch.

"It's almost morning," he said. "I'm taking you to bed." Tipping up her chin, he settled his mouth very softly over hers. The kiss was brief and gentle, a promise of things to come. "You need to get your mind off El Jefe and with any luck, I'm the man who can make that happen."

Carly smiled for the first time that night. Sliding her arms around his neck, she went up on her toes and kissed him. Just a brush of lips, a tasting that heated into something more. When her soft mouth parted in invitation, his tongue swept in. His body tightened, his erection throbbed, and an ache rolled through him. He wanted this woman, had almost from the moment he had met her.

The bedroom seemed miles away. He carried a condom in the pocket of his jeans. When she pulled his T-shirt over his head and pressed her mouth against the muscles across his chest, his decision was made. Stripping her out of her clothes, he sat down on the sofa and pulled her down to straddle his lap.

Her pretty breasts bobbed forward, tempting him. He palmed them, caressed them, bent his head, and drew each one into his mouth. The rose tips hardened into tight little buds he nipped with his teeth and soothed with his tongue.

Carly whimpered. Cupping her face between his hands, he kissed her, sank into those soft lips. Trailing kisses along her throat, he returned to her breasts, nibbling and tasting until she was panting and squirming on his lap, begging for exactly what he intended to give her.

His erection throbbed. He unzipped his jeans, retrieved the condom, and sheathed himself. Carly lifted, took him deep inside, and Linc groaned.

"I love the way you make me feel," she whispered. "I need you, Linc."

Sweet Jesus, he needed her, too. The woman drove him crazy.

Bracing her hands on his shoulders, her thick blond hair forming a curtain around them, she rose up and sank down, rose and sank down, taking him deeper, gloving his heavy arousal, up and then down, riding him, turning his erection to steel.

He let her take charge, gritted his teeth to stay in control until he couldn't wait a moment more. With a growl of possession, he gripped her hips to hold her in place and drove upward, taking what he so desperately needed, giving her what she needed in return.

A moan escaped as her body tightened around him and she reached her peak, but Linc didn't stop, not until she cried his name and came again. His own release struck hard, a wild, untamed response to a woman who was becoming as necessary to him as breathing.

He held her as they spiraled down, their bodies, still joined, slick with perspiration, her arms locked around his neck, her head on his shoulder.

A deep breath whispered out. Seconds passed. With

a last soft kiss, he eased her off his lap, rose, and headed for the bathroom to dispose of the condom.

When he returned, he smiled at the sight of Carly curled up on the sofa, still naked, her eyes closed, a soft smile on her face, so damn sexy he wanted her all over again. Then her phone started ringing.

Linc growled low in his throat, wishing he could ignore it, knowing he couldn't.

Carly grabbed her T-shirt and pulled it on while Linc slid into his jeans and sat down on the sofa beside her. Her hand trembled as she plucked her cell off the coffee table and checked the screen, saw the number was blocked.

Biting the plump bottom lip he loved to taste, she held the phone to her ear, tilted a little so Linc could hear the conversation. "This is Carly."

"You've been a very naughty girl, *Señorita* Drake." The familiar male voice, touched with Spanish, sent a shot of dread down his spine. "Perhaps I should punish you," El Jefe said. "Yes, I think I would like that."

Linc's hand unconsciously fisted.

The voice hardened. "I told you no police."

"I don't know what you're talking about," Carly said.

"Do not make the mistake of thinking I am a fool."

Carly looked at Linc, who nodded. There was no use denying it.

"You wanted me to do something illegal," she said. "I didn't know what else to do."

"I will tell you what you are going to do. You are going to tell the FBI you no longer wish to cooperate. That it was a misunderstanding. You will get rid of them and do exactly what I tell you. If you do not, you know that pretty little blond boy you are so fond of? Disobey my orders again and one of the older boys in detention will use him as a *puta*. Do you understand what I am telling you?"

Carly's face went as pale as glass.

"Do you hear me, *señorita*?"

"I-I hear you."

"What about you, *Señor* Cain? I know you are there. You are a wealthy man. You understand the price of doing business, no?"

He wanted to tell the bastard if he didn't leave Carly and the boy alone, he was going to pay a far bigger price than he could begin to imagine. Instead, he said, "I understand."

"Get rid of the FBI. I will give you some time to make that happen. Then you may expect to hear from me. Oh, and one more thing, *señorita*. You are Joe Drake's granddaughter. Next time you are the one who will be driving the truck." The line went dead and Linc softly cursed.

Even if the police had been able to trace the call, he didn't think they would have had enough time to get a location. Probably a disposable phone anyway. The guy was no fool.

Worry darkened Carly's eyes to a deep crystalline blue. "None of us are safe," she said softly. "Not Zach, not me, not you. What are we going to do?"

Anger filtered through him. He latched on to it, used it to clear his head as he had taught himself, used it to focus on the problem he needed to solve.

"We're going to do what El Jefe wants us to do. We're going to stop cooperating with the FBI. Without us the feds have nothing. They haven't even been able to find a connection between El Jefe and Miguel Hernandez's murder. The FBI doesn't expend resources on dead ends and that's what this is about to become."

"So that's it? We just do whatever that bastard wants?"

"No. We let him think that's what we're going to do. The FBI has rules to follow, procedures." Determination rolled through him, honing into a single, solitary purpose. "I don't have to follow anybody's rules but my own."

Chapter Twenty-Four

Even with as little sleep as she'd had, Carly went to work the next day. Frank Marino accompanied her to the yard, while Linc choppered into Dallas. They both had things to do if they were going to deal with El Jefe.

When Linc returned from the city, he picked her up and drove her to Greenville to see Zach, stopping along the way to buy some children's books from a local bookstore. Zach's face lit up so brightly when she and Linc walked into the visitor's room, it broke her heart.

"How are you doing?" she asked.

Zach shrugged his thin shoulders. "Okay, I guess." He looked up at Linc, who sat down across the table. "When I get scared, I remember what you said, how if you know it's gonna get better, you can get through it. I just gotta make it a little while longer."

"That's exactly right," Linc said. "I'm proud of you, Zach."

Carly ran a hand over the boy's pale hair. "Your grandmother wants to see you." She wasn't sure what Zach would say. She was still trying to deal with the news the boy had someone else in his life. Though she was happy for him, she wasn't exactly sure what it meant for her.

Zach's interest sharpened. "She does?"

Carly nodded. "Why didn't you tell me about her?"

Zach toyed with the book on top of the stack, *The Strange Case of Origami Yoda*, recommended as a great book for kids. "I haven't seen her in a long time. I figured she forgot about me."

"She said your dad refused to let her visit you. She didn't know you were being mistreated until child services called."

He opened the book cover and thumbed through the pages. "Sometimes when things got real bad I thought about finding her. But I was worried what might happen. Grandma Weller's a real nice lady and I didn't want my dad to hurt her."

Carly's heart squeezed. She wished the police would find Ray Archer and get him off the street.

"What about your grandmother's husband?" Linc asked. "You like Tom, too?"

"I remember he bought me a model airplane for Christmas. He was gonna help me put it together, but then my mom died and everything sort of got mixed up."

"They'd like to see you," Carly said. "If it's okay with you."

Zach's face lit up. "Really?"

Carly smiled and nodded. "I'm not sure when, but soon."

"Maybe they can get me out of here."

"Maybe," Carly said.

"We all want that, Zach," Linc said.

Zach studied the book in front of him. "My dad never liked them. He used to get mad at my mom when we went over to see them. I wouldn't want him to hurt them."

"The police won't let that happen," Carly said.

Zach's eyes came up to her face. "What if they never catch him?"

Carly thought about the man who had beaten his son and the woman who lived with him, a man so filled with rage, he had destroyed her home.

She looked at Linc and said the words she knew were true. "Then Linc will keep you safe."

With a few more hours of work left to do, Carly went back to the truck yard while Linc drove on to the ranch, leaving Frank to accompany her home.

At the end of the day, she sat at the wheel of the F-150, with Frank in the passenger seat, ready for trouble. Under a short-sleeved flowered shirt, his shoulder holster held a big black semiautomatic pistol. The red-haired, freckle-faced Magnum wasn't nearly as handsome as Tom Selleck, but he was definitely taking his job seriously. Carly had actually come to like him.

Currently she didn't believe she was in too much danger. After the phone call last night, she didn't expect to hear from El Jefe for at least a few more days, maybe not until next week, which gave them some time.

She wondered how he'd known about the FBI's involvement, but the man seemed to have spies everywhere so there was no real way to know.

Carly prayed the drug lord wouldn't call at all, but she was a realist. El Jefe was determined to force her cooperation, though she had no idea why he was so fixated on Drake Trucking. Why not coerce some other company into helping him?

But with the embezzling scheme, the murder, and her abduction, he had already invested a great deal of effort in bringing her to heel. With a man like El Jefe, it might be no more than exerting his power. She continued to thwart him, which wouldn't go over well with him.

Nor would it look good for El Jefe to back down in front of his men.

Whatever the reason, she couldn't suspend her life waiting to hear from him. She had a business to run and so did Linc.

She thought of the conversation they'd had at breakfast that morning and the plan they had come up with.

"El Jefe's going to call you sooner or later," Linc had said. "When he does, he's going to demand you make the pickup and delivery he wanted you to make Tuesday night."

"I know," Carly said darkly.

"McKinley couldn't wear a wire, but what if the truck itself were wired? What if there were cameras and listening devices hidden inside and out? We could record everything that happens."

She brightened. "Oh, wow, I like that."

"Good, then while I'm in Dallas, I'll get everything set up. I know who to call to get it done."

No surprise there. Though fitting a truck out with fancy surveillance gear was bound to cost a fortune, Carly didn't argue. There was no way she could win a battle with Linc over money. He could afford it, and lives were at stake.

She took a sip of her coffee. "We'd have the installation done in Dallas, right?"

"That's right. We'll make it look like an ordinary run, but instead of picking up a load, the truck will go to Tex/Am Transport. We can get the job done there."

"How do we know which driver we can trust?"

"Easy. I'm going to drive. I'll take the truck out late tomorrow night. You work the schedule around so all the drivers are back before midnight. I'll go in after that, take the rig to our yard, and have the installation done while I'm at work the next day. I'll bring the truck back here that night."

"That sounds good. Once it's back, I'll keep the rig off the schedule till we get the call from El Jefe." She ran the idea around in her head. "I think it could work."

"It's going to work. We might have to make a few deliveries before we get the evidence we need, but eventually we're going to have enough to take to the FBI."

Her worry returned. El Jefe expected her to drive the truck that would make those deliveries. Linc would never agree. Inwardly she sighed. She would argue with him when the time came.

"We might get some kind of evidence of the smuggling," she said, "but how do we catch El Jefe? He won't be there and we have no idea who he is."

"We will. Those payoffs he makes to his informers can work both ways. For enough money, sooner or later someone who knows who he is will come forward."

"Are you saying what I think you are? You want to put a bounty on his head? If El Jefe found out—"

"It's a risk, I'll admit. But I've got friends willing to help. They don't like this guy anymore than we do."

"Who?" Carly asked.

Linc's mouth curved into a hard-edged smile. "The Asphalt Demons. We're going to the roadhouse tonight. You never know who you might run into."

Just before dark, Linc called the head of the ranch's security team, Deke Logan. He was in his mid-forties, former special ops, part-time bodyguard, and all-around good guy. He told Logan he'd be leaving with Carly, taking his Harley on the back road out of the property. He didn't want any of Logan's armed, hand-picked guards mistaking him for a trespasser, shooting them as they roared off into the night.

For the meeting ahead, he dressed in his black leather vest and chaps, pulled on a pair of motorcycle boots, and headed down the hall to where Carly waited for him in the living room. Her head came up when she saw him, her big blue eyes running over him, head to foot.

He was no stranger to the heat in a woman's eyes when she wanted a man. When this woman looked at him that way, it was all he could do not to drag her back to bed and forget all about Jubal's.

"Wow," was all she said, but her hot look never wavered.

Lust slammed into him, and beneath the fly of his jeans, he went rock hard. "Any chance you can hold that thought until we get home?"

Her cheeks flushed prettily. "I don't know what you're talking about."

He laughed, clearly reading her correctly. He loved her sensuality, appreciated that she had a need that stood up to his own. "You ready for this?"

The grin that spread over her face made him smile. "I am sooo ready."

Linc tossed her the spare helmet he kept in the weight room. Carly caught it and tucked it under her arm.

"I'm excited," she said. "I haven't been on a motorcycle since college and it was a rice burner, not a Harley."

He grinned. *Rice burner,* slang for a Japanese model, probably thought up by a Harley man.

"The road's pretty bad going out the back way so we'll have to take it slow till we get to the highway. I'm not as stupid as I was as a kid so if you're looking for a wild ride, it isn't going to happen."

"I'm not that stupid anymore, either. I'd prefer to get there and back in one piece." She looked cute with her golden hair plaited into a single long braid, her stretchy jeans tucked into the same red leather cowboy boots she'd had on at the roadhouse the first night he'd seen her there.

Arousal burned through him, the same as it had when he'd seen her in those boots that night. Linc managed to tamp it down and glanced at the watch in the leather band on his wrist.

"Time to go." He'd retrieved his Harley earlier, parked it in front of the house, a customized black and silver CVO Street Glide that was everything he loved in a bike.

He swung a leg over the seat and waited for Carly to swing on behind him. He could feel her soft breasts pressing into his back as her arms went around his waist, feel her thighs cradling his, and his hard-on returned, which didn't make for comfortable riding.

He sighed. As much as he was looking forward to

getting out on the road, it was going to be a damn long night.

"You ready?" he asked, pulling on his black and silver helmet.

"You bet." Carly pulled on her helmet and fastened the chin strap. He made a mental note to buy her one that fit her better. While he was at it, he might as well get her a set of riding leathers, an image that made him hot all over again. Inwardly he groaned.

Linc shoved the kickstand up with his boot and fired the engine, revved the motor, and rolled off down the dirt road.

The breeze kicked up. The wind whistled past his visor as the headlight cut through the darkness in front of him. He loved the throb of the powerful engine between his thighs almost as much as the soft female body pressing into his back.

Even with the bumps in the dark stretch of dirt winding along the creek, it didn't take much time to reach the paved road running parallel to the back of the property. He pulled onto the asphalt and headed east, turned south once they reached the highway leading to the roadhouse.

The ride wasn't nearly long enough. He wished he could just keep going, pull over somewhere and spread the blanket he kept in his saddlebags, spend the next few hours looking up at the stars and making love to the lady behind him.

Instead, he slowed as he spotted the illuminated sign for Jubal's. Though it was the middle of the week, the parking lot was more than half full. He didn't miss the row of bikes, their front wheels turned and aligned, parked to the right of the entrance.

He recognized Rick Dugan's Harley and the bikes

belonging to Del Aimes and Johnnie Banducci, all parked together. His friends were here, as well as what appeared to be half a dozen Demons. "Once a member, always a member" seemed to be their motto, along with any friendlies, which had always included him.

Linc set a hand at Carly's waist as they climbed the wooden stairs, crossed the old board floors of the porch, and pushed through the swinging doors. As they stepped inside, he eased her closer. These guys were friends, but they were still men. He didn't want anyone to doubt she belonged to him.

The jukebox was playing Willie Nelson. Guiding her toward the bar, he wasn't surprised to see Rowena pouring drinks. Along with her new job at Drake, she planned to bartend a few nights a week just for fun.

"Hey, Row." Carly waved as they approached.

Rowena smiled. "Hey, boss."

Carly grinned at the name and Row grinned back.

"Your friends are waiting," Row said to Linc, tipping her head toward the group at the back of the bar, a cluster of rough-looking, tattooed men in motorcycle leathers. Silver glittered in studs and piercings.

"Give me a Shiner Bock and Carly a Lone Star and put it on my tab," Linc said.

"Will do." Row popped the caps off a pair of ice-cold bottles and set them down on the counter. They picked up their beers and began to weave their way toward the rear of the bar.

"Hey, Cain, over here!" Del Aimes shoved a chair out from the table with his boot. "Have a seat, girl."

"Hi, Del." Carly sat down and Linc spun a chair around and sat down next to her. "You know these three troublemakers," he said, referring to his friends, then turned to the other men. "Guys, this is Carly Drake. She owns Drake Trucking. Carly meet Tag, Baldy, Wolf, Lenny, Spaceman, and Bat."

"Good to meet you," she said.

The men tipped their chins up in greeting. In the pecking order, Tag was the leader, six-two, beefy and darkly tanned, with shaggy brown hair to his shoulders. "We hear you got trouble," Tag said. "What can we do?"

For the next half hour, Linc told them about El Jefe, about the threats he'd made, their need to find him and put an end to him and his organization.

"So what do you need from us?" Baldy asked, his bare head gleaming.

"I need you to put the word out," Linc said. "Twenty five thousand to the man who can give me a name. Fifty if he gives me a name and a location. It needs to be real. If it is, he gets paid."

Lenny whistled, a blond guy with long hair pulled back in a ponytail. "Fifty grand," he said. "That ought to stir things up."

Linc tipped back his beer, took a long swallow. "The trick is no one can know either of us is involved. That comes out, one or both of us is likely to wind up dead."

Tag blew out a breath. "Man, you got that right. Word on the street, the guy's a bad motherfucker."

"Dude's into some heavy shit," Baldy said, "but nobody seems to know what it is."

"You do this," Linc said, "you need to be careful. I don't want any of you getting dead, either."

Tag picked up his glass and threw back a shot of tequila. "We'll talk it over, work out a plan. We ain't forgot the favors you've done us over the years."

"Yeah, like the time you put up the money for Wolf's

hospital bills when he took that bad spill out on the interstate."

"Or the time you helped us repair the clubhouse when that motherfuckin' tornado took it to the ground," Lenny said.

"Would have taken years to raise enough to rebuild," Wolf agreed, "even with part of it covered by insurance."

"It hasn't all been one-sided," Linc said. "You guys have been good friends over the years. I appreciate that and I appreciate what you're doing to help me now."

A murmur of acknowledgment rolled around the table. Linc tipped up his beer and finished it off, saw Carly doing the same; then both of them stood up.

"Keep me posted," he said. "Tag, you got my number?"

"I got it," Tag said. The number of a disposable phone no one could trace back to him. Rick, Del, and Johnnie also knew where to call.

"Don't do anything too risky," Linc said.

Tag chuckled. "We take a risk every time we get on our bikes. Some risks are worth it."

Linc just nodded. Riding was these men's lives. They craved freedom like other people craved air. He understood it, in a way envied it, occasionally got to enjoy a brief taste of that freedom when he took his Harley out on the road.

When they reached the door, Linc checked the parking lot but didn't see any sign of trouble. Only a few people knew where he'd gone tonight and they were people he trusted with his life.

He got back on the bike and Carly swung on behind him. Things were progressing. Tomorrow night he'd take the truck in and have it fitted with surveillance gear. Then they'd wait for El Jefe to call.

Until then, he'd keep his friends close and Carly closer. He felt her arms slide around his waist as he shoved the kickstand up with his boot. Linc smiled as he imagined what he'd do when he got her in bed, revved the engine, and roared off down the road.

Chapter Twenty-Five

Carly rescheduled pickups and deliveries the next day, changing the times so all the returning drivers would be back in the yard before midnight. She had to delay a load from a furniture manufacturer in Texarkana, but she didn't think the one daytime shift would cause a problem for the company.

That left only the night watchman to worry about and with any luck, he wouldn't be a problem.

In the afternoon, she and Frank Marino drove over to Greenville to see Zach. His grandparents, Amanda and Tom Weller, had called to set up a meeting. If they seemed anything less than perfect for Zach, or if Zach would rather live with her than the Wellers, she would fight them for custody all the way.

Deep down, she had already begun to think of a life that included the boy. Sooner or later, her affair with Linc would be over. The sad truth was, no matter how much he desired her, she was only a passing fancy. She had never deluded herself about that.

It was different for her. She was crazy about Linc and it was going to break her heart when he was gone.

Once it was over, having a child in her life would help ease the pain. Add to that, Iron Springs was a good place to raise a kid, and she believed she could give Zach the loving home he deserved.

Carly met the older couple in front of the single-story redbrick building that housed the Hunt County Detention Center. On the flagpole next to the sidewalk, the Stars and Stripes and Texas state flags gently whipped in the breeze. Linc had gone to Dallas, giving her the chance to handle things on her own.

"It's so good to meet you," Amanda Weller said. At fifty-five, she was an attractive woman with silver-blond hair who looked years younger, while Tom Weller was handsome, with a trim, athletic build. "We'll never forget what you've done for Zach."

Amanda leaned over and hugged her. "Anything could have happened to him if you hadn't taken him in."

"Zach's family," Carly said. "All I really have left. I'm happy to help him any way I can."

"We've been Skyping quite a lot lately," Amanda said. "He's growing up so fast. He seems to be a very level-headed young man."

"Yes, I think he is," Carly said. "Considering the life he's been living with his father, he's a pretty amazing kid."

"He talks incessantly about you and Mr. Cain," Tom said. "I was hoping we'd get to meet him."

"I think he wanted us to have a chance to get to know each other. Linc is . . . well, he tends to be a little overwhelming at first. He's just so . . ." Powerful? Dynamic? "Linc's an incredible man," she finished, unable to come up with a better word.

Waving to Frank, who stood a few feet away, Carly

followed the Wellers inside the building. They found
Zach in the small private visitors' room they had been
meeting in all week. Amanda took one look at him,
bit back a sob, hurried over, and pulled him into a hug.

When Zach hugged her back, then turned and
hugged Tom, Carly relaxed. Giving them a moment
alone, she walked a few feet away. A sound in her purse
alerted her to a call coming in. Carly dug out her
phone, saw it was Linc, and walked to the far side of the
room to answer the call.

"How's it going?" Linc asked.

"The Wellers seem like really nice people."

"That's good, because Graham Steiner called. Ray
Archer was spotted in Dallas. He's been staying with a
buddy from high school. Cops have the place staked
out. He's facing assault and vandalism charges. Steiner
thinks the police will have him in custody by tonight."

Carly's eyes closed on a wave of relief. "That's great
news."

"Archer's going to jail, hopefully long enough for
him to get his head on straight. Of course, he hasn't
been arrested yet, but it shouldn't be long now."

"I'll tell the Wellers. I know they'll be relieved."

"There's something else."

She caught the note of uncertainty in his voice.
"What is it?"

"Protective Services is willing to release Zach into his
grandparents' care. We can push for custody if that's
what you want, but according to Steiner, the authorities
refuse to place the boy in the hands of a twenty-nine-
year-old single female who has no previous relationship
with Zach. Not when they can release him into the care
of a highly regarded doctor and his wife who are the

boy's grandparents. I'm willing to go for custody myself if you think that's best for Zach, but—"

"No . . ." She glanced across the room to where Zach sat next to his grandparents, laughing at something one of them said, his grandmother holding tightly to his hand. "I think he's found a good home."

And the bitter truth was, Zach was better off with the Wellers than with her. Carly was struggling to keep Drake Trucking afloat, working long hours for very little pay, and that wasn't going to change anytime soon. Add to that the trouble she was facing with El Jefe. Zach wouldn't be safe with her, at least not right now.

"I hope he'll visit me as often as he can," she said, "but I think he's going to the right home."

"All right. I'll tell Steiner your decision. With any luck, Archer will be in jail maybe as early as tomorrow and Zach will be able to go home with his grandparents."

She smiled into the phone, happy for Zach but sad at the loss she was suddenly feeling. "I'll tell them the news. Thanks for everything, Linc," she said softly.

"Honey, you don't need to thank me. That's just what friends do." The call ended. Carly held on to the phone for several more seconds before she turned and walked back to the table.

A storm blew in that night. A sullen black sky loomed overhead while the wind tore foot-thick branches from the trees. Great sheets of rain sliced into the walls of the ranch house.

"I don't think you should go," Carly said. "I think we should reschedule."

It was one o'clock in the morning. Linc was heading to the yard, picking up one of Drake's big Peterbilt tractor trailers and driving it down to Tex/Am Transport, where tomorrow the rig would be completely fitted with state-of-the-art surveillance equipment.

"Everything's set," he said. "Plenty of other drivers on the road tonight. I'll be fine."

"Even the weatherman didn't realize we were going to be hit this hard," Carly argued. "Some of the other counties have already had tornado watches."

"Watches, not warnings, and none around here. It's less than two hours to Dallas even in this weather. I'll be there before the storm gets any worse. Tonight I'll stay in the city, work tomorrow while the equipment's being installed, then bring the rig back late tomorrow night."

"I wish you'd wait."

"Yeah, well, I wish you'd stay up at the main house, but apparently that isn't going to happen either."

Her chin went up. She hated the gaudy house and the reminder of the beauty queen Linc had married. "I'm fine right here."

He rubbed a hand over his face. "So I guess we're both going to do exactly what we want."

Carly just smiled.

"If anything happens, we've got armed men all over the property. The guy who heads the security team is Deke Logan. He knows you're here and so does Frank Marino. I put Deke's number in your phone and Frank's is already in there. I can have Frank stay here if you'd feel safer—"

"I've got a brand-new Glock, thanks to you, and I know how to shoot it. You're the one who's going to be in danger out in that storm."

He smiled faintly. "Can't be helped, sweetheart. And I've driven in far worse than this." He dragged her into his arms and kissed her so thoroughly, her stomach melted. "I'll see you tomorrow night."

Carly followed him to the door. "You know which truck and where it's parked, right?"

"You've only told me half a dozen times so yes, I know."

"The night watchman knows one of the drivers is taking the rig out, so he won't be a problem."

"I know that, too. Now go to bed and get some sleep." Determined to get his plan up and running, he headed out into the rain. His GMC sat rim-deep in mud as he climbed inside, started the engine, and drove off down the road. Rain pelted the windshield, making it hard to see, but it wasn't anything he hadn't dealt with before.

Thirty minutes later, he was behind the wheel of a Drake tractor-trailer, heading for the Tex/Am truck yard off I-635 east of Dallas. This late and without any traffic, he could make the run in an hour and a half, but with the wind howling, the road wet and slick as glass, he planned to take it slow.

The wipers set up a rhythm, slapping rain off the windshield as the semi rolled along. He slowed to avoid a low spot full of water, dodged the branches of a downed tree, and speeded up again, a little surprised at how good it felt to be sitting behind the wheel.

But then he'd always enjoyed the growl of a powerful engine, enjoyed making the big monster truck respond to his commands.

He was moving right along, getting close to Dallas, nearing the turnoff onto the road leading to the Tex/Am yard when he heard the news broadcast. A tornado watch for Howler County had just gone into effect for the next four hours. Lots of power outages. All of Iron Springs was down.

His nerves started humming. *A watch isn't a warning,* he reminded himself. Still, he didn't like to think Carly might have to face a tornado alone.

He should have insisted she stay at the big house, where the basement had been fitted out as a storm shelter, with food, water, beds, blankets, and medical supplies. Out at the ranch house, there was nothing but an old root cellar that hadn't been used in years.

He spotted the turn into the truck yard before he had time to call her, convince her to make the drive before the storm got any worse. He turned the rig and drove through the front gates across the asphalt to a row of service bays.

He'd called ahead, had everything set up. One of the guys ran out as he pulled up. Linc rolled down his window and a sharp gust of rain blasted into the cab.

"I can take it from here, Mr. Cain."

Linc put the truck in NEUTRAL, set the brakes, and swung down from the seat. "It's all yours, Monty. There'll be a crew here in the morning to work on it."

"Yes, sir."

Linc pulled out his cell and hit Carly's number. The phone didn't ring, just went straight to voice mail. He tried again, got the same result. He'd insisted she charge the battery, so he knew it wasn't low. He tried Frank's number, got nothing. Cell tower had probably gone down.

He phoned the land line at the ranch house, then the main house—still nothing. The power in the area was out, phone lines could be down.

His worry went up another notch. His gaze went to

the pair of black Tex/Am Chevy pickups parked in front of the office, the company's red-and-black logo on the doors. He'd planned to drive one of the trucks to his apartment and spend the night. The keys would be under the front seat.

He thought of Carly, wondered if she had driven up to the main house. Frank was staying there. If the storm got bad enough, the guards would take shelter inside as well.

But his gut said Carly wouldn't go. She'd never felt comfortable in the mansion. She'd hole up in the ranch house, figure she would be safe inside.

Head down into the stinging wind and rain, he started walking. Despite the weather, he could be back in Iron Springs in less than two hours. Linc opened the pickup door and climbed in behind the wheel.

Carly had forgotten how fierce an East Texas storm could get. The power had gone out over an hour ago. Frank Marino had come to check on her shortly after it happened, but she'd told him she'd be okay and sent him back to the mansion.

The ranch house was sturdy, solidly constructed of brick. It had survived on this piece of ground for decades before Linc had bought the property. It was in far better shape now than it had been then.

Unable to sleep with the wind whistling and rain battering the walls, Carly settled herself on the living room sofa, spread a quilt over her legs, and curled up to read.

Before he'd left, Linc had set his battery-operated radio on the kitchen counter. She'd turned it on when the power had gone out so she could hear any weather updates.

She turned the page of the romantic suspense novel she was reading by the light of an old-fashioned glass kerosene lamp she'd set on the end table. Combined with the glow of an antique brass lamp on the coffee table, the shadowy light formed eerie patterns on the walls.

It was after four in the morning. Linc should have reached Dallas by three. She'd expected him to call, let her know he'd arrived safely. Then she'd discovered her cell wasn't working. With the power out, there was no way to reach anyone on the land lines, either. Linc would be worried, but hopefully he'd been following the weather reports and knew what was going on.

Currently Howler County was under a tornado watch, not uncommon in this area. Usually a storm like this passed without a funnel cloud being spotted or the weatherman updating the watch to a warning.

Instead of being frightened, Carly found herself enjoying the fierce beating rain and the sound of the wind whistling through the branches of the trees. An occasional flash of lightning bit through the inky blackness, followed by the roll of thunder.

She must have dozed off for a while. She wasn't sure what awoke her, perhaps the roar of the storm. As her grogginess faded, she realized how much stronger the wind had become, how the house seemed to shake with each furious gust.

Tossing aside the quilt, she hurried into the kitchen to listen to the radio. At the weather report, worry hit her. The watch was now a full-blown tornado warning. She was supposed to take shelter immediately.

Fighting down a wave of panic, she forced herself to

think. Frank had told her there was a basement up at the mansion. Both he and Linc had urged her to spend the night up there in case the storm got worse, but she had refused to leave.

Now she realized the mistake she had made. Her pulse began to thrum. Blowing out the glass kerosene lamp, she picked up the brass lamp and hurried toward the bedroom to change out of her nightgown and grab her raincoat.

Her pickup sat out front. The road would be bad but the truck had four-wheel drive and there was still time to reach safety.

The howl of the wind grew louder. As she walked down the darkened hall, the flickering light of the lamp set her nerves on edge. She told herself there was no need to panic, had almost convinced herself when she stepped into the bedroom. As lamplight illuminated the interior, she froze.

A man stood in the shadows, medium height, thick dark hair a little too long. As he moved toward the light, she recognized his face—the heavy brows, the eyes a little too close together—though she'd only seen his photo once before.

She forced herself to breathe, tried to calm her speeding heart and stay in control.

"How did you get in?" When her hand shook, making the light flicker and betraying her nerves, she set the lamp down on the dresser.

"It wasn't hard," Ray Archer said. "Not on a night like this. Power's out. Alarm's down. You didn't even hear me bust the glass out of the window. Where's my boy?"

Her gaze went to the jagged edges of the broken

window, where gusts of rain blew in. A bolt of lightning
lit the sky outside and thunder rattled the house.

"Your son isn't here," she said. "Is that why you came?
You thought Zach was here?"

He took a step toward her, his hand balling into a
fist. "I knew the boy'd come here. I been keepin' track
of you. Not hard to find out you was shacking up with
the rich guy who owns the place. Where's Zach? What
have you done with him?"

She refused to let him see her fear, managed to
stand her ground. "He's in Greenville, under protective custody." Anger filtered through her, giving her a
jolt of courage. "Maybe you remember the last time
you were with him—the night you beat him and he ran
away?"

"Boy shouldn't have interfered in his daddy's business."

"That business being you using your fists on the
woman you were living with?"

"Bitch deserved it."

She wanted to argue, tell him what a rotten bastard
she thought he was, but she was alone with him. She
needed to stay calm, talk him down.

"There's a tornado warning," she said. "We need to
take shelter. There's a basement up at the big house. My
truck's out in front. We can drive up there together."

He laughed maniacally, sending a chill down her
spine. "You think I'm a fool? We'll ride it out here.
Tomorrow we'll go get my son."

She felt vulnerable in her nightgown. She wished
she'd been wearing the robe lying at the foot of the
bed. "They aren't going to let you take him, Ray. Surely
you know that."

When he moved, something glinted in the lamplight,

the barrel of the pistol he held in his hand. Her gaze went to the bedside table. She'd left her gun in the drawer when she went into the living room. Ray stood between her and her weapon.

He raised the pistol, waved it around. "If they won't give him to me, I'll take him. I'll trade you for Zach." When he started toward her, Carly bit back a scream.

At the evil grin that split Ray's face, she turned and bolted out of the bedroom, her heart hammering as she raced down the hall, Archer right behind her. Grabbing a pottery jar off a side table, she spun and hurled it at Ray's head. It slammed into the hand he put up to block it, and she heard him curse.

Carly kept running, spotted the broom she'd used that morning to sweep up, grabbed it, turned, and rammed the handle into Ray Archer's stomach hard enough to send him flying backward, landing on his back in the hall.

"You bitch! You'll be sorry for that!"

Desperately fighting her fear, Carly worked the dead bolt and jerked open the front door, ignored the stinging rain battering her face, the jagged flash of lightning, as she bolted into the raging storm.

Chapter Twenty-Six

The deep mud had the pickup sliding sideways before Linc could get it righted and back on the road, but he was almost there. He could see the roof of the ranch house up ahead. He'd grab Carly and head back to the big house, where they would be safe.

Knowing her as he had come to, he hadn't bothered to stop at the mansion, just blew past, and headed straight for the ranch house.

She was there; he could feel it.

He could see the front door now, knew a moment of relief that he had made it on the slick, muddy road. The feeling disappeared as the front door flew open and Carly rushed out of the house, bare feet flinging mud, rain plastering her thin cotton nightgown against her body, the wind whipping her hair.

A man ran out of the house behind her, running hard to catch her as she raced toward the trees. Linc saw a muzzle flash, heard the echo of a shot barely audible in the roar of the storm, and a wave of fury hit him like a jolt of electricity.

His foot jammed down on the gas pedal, jolting the

pickup forward, the vehicle fishtailing in the mud. The truck bore down on the man, closing the distance, getting nearer and nearer. When the guy burst into the trees where the pickup couldn't follow, Linc slammed on the brakes, jumped out, and ran hard into the pouring rain.

The storm had cranked up, driving branches and leaves into him with gale force winds. Lightning clawed the sky, and ear-shattering thunder followed. Linc kept running.

"Carly!" No way could she hear him, and the man chasing her didn't seem to care. Linc's mind spun. His gut told him this wasn't El Jefe or one of his men. His jaw clenched. *Ray Archer.* Had to be.

The thought congealed an instant before Linc spotted him up ahead through the trees. He increased his speed, his boots sliding in the mud as he closed the distance between them. With a leaping tackle, he slammed Archer to the ground.

"He's got a gun!" Carly shouted as the two men rolled in the boggy earth, fighting for control of the weapon.

Linc heard the shot Archer fired, heard Carly scream, and felt a jolt of pain in his ribs. He grappled for the pistol, snagged Archer's wrist, and managed to pry the gun free and send it into the air, but it landed just inches from Archer's head.

Linc drew back and punched him, but Archer's hand snaked out and wrapped around the handle of the pistol. The barrel swung toward him, Linc knocked it aside and the shot went wild.

For an instant, Archer rolled on top of him as they fought over the weapon, Linc's hand clamped around Archer's wrist. From the corner of his eye, he saw Carly running toward them, wielding a tree limb, swinging it toward Ray Archer with all her strength. The limb crashed into Archer's head, knocking him sideways. The gun went flying, and so did Ray, landing hard against the trunk of a tree and not moving.

Gritting his teeth against a stab of pain, Linc pushed to his feet, saw Carly running toward him, and caught her against his chest. The jolt sent a fresh shot of pain roaring through him.

She looked down, must have seen the blood. "Oh, God, he shot you!" She tried to pull back, but he wouldn't let her go.

"I'm okay," he said, hoping it was true.

"Where . . . where are you hit? How bad are you hurt?"

"It's not deep, just a graze, I think." A branch flew past, the wind blowing so hard he had to lean into it to keep his balance. "We've got to get out of here. Get somewhere safe."

"What about Archer?"

"We'll have to take him with us." He turned, saw that the man was no longer sprawled on the ground, but up and running, heading toward the woods. A ragged streak of lightning flashed. Linc heard the vicious crack of a huge tree splintering, saw the great tree crash to earth—right on top of Ray Archer.

Carly couldn't get her feet to move. Her heart felt as if it might explode through her chest while needles of rain slashed into her face. Twigs and leaves felt like steel slivers cutting into her skin.

"Stay here!" Linc shouted, holding his side as he moved off toward the man on the ground. Inside her chest, her lungs were burning with the effort to breathe as she waited for the words she was sure she would hear. The tree was massive. All she could see were Ray Archer's legs.

Her throat closed as she pictured his bones crushed or his legs severed from his body.

Linc strode back to her, shouting to be heard. "He's dead! There's nothing we can do! We need to go now!"

She just stood there. Trees were coming down around them. The wind seemed to singe her skin. She felt Linc's hand wrap around hers, felt the tug that jerked her forward, pulling her along behind him. They ran through the woods back toward the pickup, but when they got there, the road was completely impassable, the mud in puddles bumper-deep.

She looked up at the dark, looming clouds, the flashes of lightning coming closer and closer. They would never make it to the big house.

"The root cellar!" Linc shouted. Gripping her hand, he pulled her along in his wake as he ran toward the barn. There was a wooden door in the ground on one side she'd never noticed. Linc struggled to pull it open, fighting the wind and the rain. The door flew back and he led her down a set of wooden stairs, fought to close the door behind them, finally slammed it shut, then slid a heavy wooden bar into place to hold it.

Images filled her head and she started trembling. Ray Archer's lifeless body crushed beneath the tree. The tornado bearing down on them. Visions of snakes and bugs in the underground cellar.

She could hear Linc moving around in the darkness, then the sound of a match being struck. She caught a whiff of sulphur and a candle began to glow, illuminating the inside of a chamber that reminded her of an underground tomb. Linc lit another candle, brightening the small space a little more.

"It's not as bad in here as you're thinking," he said. "It's cement, not dirt. The last owners had that done for safety before I bought the ranch. It smells like mildew, but it's clean. There's a cot and some blankets, plenty of water. As soon as the worst is over, we'll get out of here."

Linc drew her into his arms and held her, and though the storm seemed worse by the minute, her trembling began to ease. He had been right to come here. They never would have made it to the big house.

She looked at Linc and her muddled brain suddenly began to clear. "Oh, God, Linc—let me see how badly you're hurt." She didn't wait for his permission, just dragged the black T-shirt he was wearing off over his head and saw the bloody gash across his ribs. "Oh, God."

"I was right," he said, examining the wound himself. "It's just a graze. No broken ribs. I'll be fine."

She swallowed past the lump in her throat. Dear God, he could have been killed! Nausea rolled through her as she remembered the instant she had believed he might be dead, the violent surge of grief that had nearly overwhelmed her. He was so vital, so strong. She couldn't imagine a world without him.

Clamping down on her emotions, she forced herself to remain under control. "I need to clean the wound, get it bandaged."

Linc glanced over at a stack of metal shelves against the wall. "I think there's a medical kit there some-where."

She hurried over, found a metal box with a red cross

on the front on one of the shelves, opened it, and took out bandages, tape, alcohol, and a clean roll of gauze.

Linc grabbed a blanket, stripped out of his wet, muddy clothes, wrapped the blanket around his hips, and sat down on the cot.

Ignoring his glorious chest with all its intriguing muscles, fascinating valleys and shadows, his lovely curved pecs, and smooth tanned skin, she used the gauze to wipe away the blood oozing from the gash across his ribs.

Cleaning the wound as best she could, she applied some antiseptic cream she found in the kit and taped on a thick gauze bandage. Satisfied it would hold until Linc could get medical attention, she stripped off her own wet clothes, wrapped herself in another blanket, tucked it in beneath her arms, and sat down beside him to wait out the storm.

Linc ran a finger down her cheek. "You scared me tonight. When I saw that bastard chasing you, shooting at you, I wanted to kill him with my bare hands."

Carly thought again how close Linc had come to dying and emotion washed through her. "I thought he'd killed you." She took a deep breath, fighting not to cry.

Linc pulled her against his uninjured side, his arm gently wrapping around her. "I'm hard to kill, baby. I learned that about myself in prison. Ray Archer didn't stand a chance."

She just leaned into him, breathed in his scent. She tried not to think how much he meant to her, how deeply she had come to care for him.

She thought of the ranch house Linc loved and hoped it would survive the storm. She thought of the horses out in the fields, safer perhaps than in the barn, and prayed they would find shelter.

She thought of Zach losing his father and her heart went out to him. No matter how bad Ray Archer was, the man was still Zach's dad.

Linc's husky voice rolled over her. "We're gonna be all right, you know."

"I know."

His gaze moved over the blanket, all that covered her nakedness, and his mouth edged up. "I don't suppose now is a good time to be thinking about sex."

In spite of the exhaustion that enveloped her, Carly laughed. She looked like a drowned rat and felt even worse, felt as if every muscle in her body had been battered into submission by the storm.

Linc kissed the top of her head. "Why don't you lie down, honey, and try to get some sleep."

No way was she letting go of him, not after he had come so close to dying. Not after she had come so close to losing him. "I'm okay right here."

His arm tightened around her.

Carly wouldn't have believed she could fall asleep nestled against Linc's shoulder. But when she awakened, they were both still alive—and the storm was over.

Linc stirred at the pounding he thought was in his head. Sitting on the cot, his back against the cement wall, with Carly nestled against him, he realized it was morning and someone was beating on the cellar door. A sharp pain in his side reminded him of last night as he eased Carly over, rose from the cot, and made his way to the wooden stairs.

Sliding the bar out, he shoved open the door and

bright light hit him. His foreman, Joaquin Santos, stood next to Frank Marino, Deke Logan, and three other men, their backs to the early-morning sun.

"Is Carly in there with you?" Frank asked, his face clouded with worry. A thick white bandage was wrapped around his head, making his russet hair stand up.

"She's here. We're both okay."

"Thank God."

"What happened to you?" Linc asked.

"When the tornado warning went out, I drove back to the ranch house to bring Carly to the shelter. Halfway back to the main house, my car got stuck in the mud. When I got out, a piece of flying debris hit me in the head. One of the guys found me early this morning and got me patched up. We went back to the ranch house but Carly wasn't there."

"When we got there," Deke said, "one of my guys spotted the Tex/Am truck so we figured the two of you were together. We started a search, weren't having much luck till your man Santos showed up and brought us here, said you knew about the shelter."

"Damn good thing I did," Linc said. Carly came up beside him, tugging on her blanket to keep it in place. Linc slid an arm around her shoulders, keeping her close.

Every time he looked at her, he remembered the terror he'd felt when he'd seen her running out of the house into the deadly storm, seen Ray Archer shooting at her.

Carly turned to Frank. "I should have gone with you. I'm really sorry, Frank."

"I'm just glad you're okay."

"Unfortunately not everybody made it." The short, barrel-chested guy next to Frank was one of the guards patrolling the property. Like the others, he was still wearing his sidearm. "Tree took him out."

"The dead man's Ray Archer," Linc said. The men knew who Archer was, had been warned to keep an eye out for him.

"He shot Linc," Carly said. "Linc needs to get to the hospital."

"It's just a graze." But concern crept back into the men's faces. "The first thing we need to do is call the sheriff."

"Cell tower's back up," Frank said. "I'll call the sheriff and get an ambulance out here ASAP." Frank walked away to use his phone.

After one look at Carly's worried face, Linc knew telling her he'd be okay wouldn't work. Besides, they needed the ambulance to transport Archer's body, and with the damned wound in his side throbbing like a sonofabitch, he could use a pain pill or two.

Now that the search group had found them safe and plans had been made, the men departed.

Half an hour later, Linc and Carly were back in the ranch house, which had suffered mostly rain damage from the open door and broken window, but survived the storm. Linc showered and pulled on jeans and a T-shirt and Carly did the same.

She re-dressed the gash across his ribs, then they sat in the living room, waiting to talk to the sheriff. The tornado had touched down in one of the distant fields, but jumped over the ranch house before continuing its path of destruction, which had luckily detoured around town.

The entry was full of water, the bedding and carpet wet and soggy in the master bedroom. The barn roof was gone, but according to Santos, the horses had sheltered in a ravine and were grazing again this morning as if nothing important had occurred. The main house had come through unscathed.

For everyone but Ray and Zach Archer, life would go on little changed. Now that Ray was dead, the boy would be leaving detention with his grandparents. Linc knew Carly had hoped to see him before he left, but the Wellers wanted to be back at home in San Antonio before they told Zach about the death of his father.

The grandparents were handling the funeral arrangements, which would include a memorial service a few weeks after the cremation. Linc wondered how many people would bother to attend.

With the Wellers so anxious to get home, Carly was forced to settle for talking to Zach on the phone.

"We're family," Linc heard her say. "That means we stick together no matter what."

He couldn't hear the boy's reply but Carly told him she loved him and was going to miss him, and wiped away a tear.

Linc took the phone. "You remember what I told you, Zach. Whatever happens, we're friends. That means if you need anything, you call me. Okay?"

"Do you think I could come and visit you sometime?"

Emotion expanded in his chest. "You'd better come see us. Carly just found out she has a cousin. You're the only family she has. She needs you as much as you need her."

Linc could hear the relief in the kid's voice.

"I'll watch out for her," he said, "I promise."

"Good boy." They talked a little longer; then it was

time for Zach to leave with his grandparents for the ride back to San Antonio.

When the call came to an end, Linc turned to Carly. "First chance we get, we'll go see him."

Her eyes swung to his and something shifted in her features. After he'd been shot last night, she had stuck to him like glue. But after they'd left the shelter, he'd noticed the shift, the subtle attempt to distance herself. The storm had been a nightmare. Ray Archer's violent death had made the horror even worse. Linc told himself she was bound to be upset.

"You don't have to feel obligated," Carly said. "You've been great to Zach, but—"

"Wait a minute. I thought we agreed we'd do what was best for the boy."

She took a deep breath. "I'm trying to be practical."

"Are you?"

"Yes. I was thinking . . . now that Archer's no longer a threat, maybe I should move back home."

Irritation trickled through him, along with a feeling he didn't want to examine too closely. "What about El Jefe?"

"I can't hide from him forever. Sooner or later I will have to deal with him."

He started to remind her they would be dealing with the drug lord together, but after almost losing her last night, an argument was the last thing he wanted.

"Why don't we table this discussion for a day or two? The truck will be finished late this afternoon. I made a call, changed things around so one of my drivers will be bringing it back tonight. That means I won't have to make another trip to Dallas."

She started nodding. "That's good. He can drive the Tex/Am pickup back to the city."

"That's right. That takes care of the immediate problem. Then unless you aren't feeling up to it, tomorrow night we'll attend that benefit the way we planned."

She bit her lip, but didn't say no, which he took as a good sign. Since they had only dozed a few minutes off and on in the shelter, as soon as the sheriff took their statements, he would insist they get some rest.

He knew exactly how to make her forget the events of the night, and afterward they could curl up spoon-fashion and both get some badly needed sleep.

Since he was getting hard just thinking about it, he forced his mind back to the benefit. "Sound okay?"

"I promised I'd go with you," Carly said. "I won't break my word."

A faint smile touched his lips. "You know, there's a chance you might even enjoy yourself."

She relaxed and her expression softened. "You know what? I'm going to an exclusive black-tie ball with a gorgeous, amazingly sexy man. Maybe I just will."

Linc smiled. He intended to see to it personally. Except for work, Carly had practically been a prisoner on the ranch. He'd made plans for tomorrow evening, big plans, and despite everything that had happened, he was really looking forward to giving her a special night.

Linc bent his head and very softly kissed her, felt her response, tentative at first, but then she melted against him. Desire pulsed through him. They were good together. Surely she could see that.

Reluctantly he pulled away. "We need to get going. The sheriff's meeting us up at the big house."

Carly sighed, which made him smile, and they headed for the door. Though the road was mired in mud, with four-wheel drive, they managed to make it up to the mansion. When they got there, the ambulance was waiting, and so was Emmett Howler.

Linc steeled himself for the inevitable confrontation he was sure the sheriff would enjoy.

Chapter Twenty-Seven

While the medics tended the groove Archer's bullet had sliced across Linc's ribs, Carly waited for the sheriff in Linc's impressive study, one of the few places she felt comfortable in the huge stone mansion.

The room was clearly his, and she felt close to him there, while the house itself reminded her of his ex-wife, of the money he had spent to build it for her, of the enormous power he wielded. It reminded her of the Lincoln Cain he was when he wasn't at the ranch.

And reinforced all the reasons she couldn't afford to get more deeply involved with him.

The realization of just how close she was to falling in love with him had hit her in the lightning bolt moment she had heard Ray Archer's gun go off, when she realized Linc had been shot.

In that instant, her fear had been so overwhelming that for several seconds, she had been nearly blinded by it. It was a glimpse of what it would feel like to lose him if she didn't do something to protect herself.

She remembered losing her first love, Garth Hunter,

the college quarterback who had sworn he loved her and asked her to marry him, only to dump her a month later for one of the cheerleaders.

Or even more painful, Carter Benson's abrupt departure years later, a reality check that had taken her to disturbing lows from which she hadn't been sure she would recover.

Or at least she had felt that way at the time.

Her feelings for Linc were already far deeper than any emotion she'd ever felt for Garth or Carter. If she allowed herself to believe she could be part of Linc's future, if she let herself fall in love with him, when he left it would destroy her.

She had to pull back, find a way to be with him for as long as it lasted yet keep her heart intact.

The door swung open and Sheriff Howler walked in, Stetson in hand, belly hanging slightly over his leather belt. He could have been a character out of *Smoky and the Bandit*.

"Hello there, litt—Ms. Carly. I hear you had yourself quite an excitin' night. Got a dead man out there to prove it. You want to start from the beginnin', tell me what happened?"

"Of course." Very succinctly she told the sheriff about Ray Archer showing up after the guards had been forced to take shelter, breaking into the house during the worst of the storm, and threatening her with a gun.

"He thought he could use me as a bargaining chip to get to his son."

"Where was Cain? I thought you two were staying out there together."

She and Linc had talked about this. Linc didn't trust

the sheriff. No way was she telling Howler their plan to equip a Drake truck with surveillance gear.

"Linc went to Dallas on business. He heard about the storm and decided to drive back in case it got worse, which it did. I just thank God he showed up before it was too late."

They talked for another twenty minutes, Howler asking the same questions in different ways, getting the same answers, since she was telling him the truth—at least about what had happened during the storm.

Then Howler asked her to leave while he interviewed Linc, who gave him the same story.

When the sheriff called her back into the study, Linc sat at the table with a scowl on his face.

"We're done here," the sheriff said to her. "Guess you might as well move back home since Archer won't be givin' you any more trouble."

Howler's attention swung back to Linc. "I know Ms. Drake filed for custody of the boy. Real convenient his dad showin' up on your property like that, then a tree fallin' on him, killin' him dead."

Linc's jaw tightened. "I assure you, Sheriff, no matter how much money I have, I can't command God to crash a tree down on someone I don't happen to like."

Howler just grunted. The heavyset sheriff picked up his paperwork. "A few more questions may come up. Be somewhere we can find you." He ambled out of the study, and Carly felt a wave of relief.

"I'm glad that's over," she said.

Linc's gaze remained on the study door the sheriff had just closed behind him. "Archer's no longer a problem." Linc's attention returned to her. "Now we need to deal with El Jefe."

Any relief Carly was feeling slipped away.

* * *

It was Saturday morning. Linc was packed and ready to leave for his trip with Carly into Dallas for the charity ball. Crews were at work on the ranch, cleaning up the mess left by the storm, rebuilding the roof of the barn. The good news was, the storm had caused enough mayhem that the protestors were too busy taking care of their own problems to hassle him.

And the truck, completely fitted with surveillance equipment, now sat once more in the Drake truck yard. Things were moving forward, but until they heard from El Jefe, or the Demons came up with his identity, there was nothing more he could do.

"It'll be good to get away for a while," Linc said. Carly walked beside him as he carried her overnight bag and hanging garment bag from the bedroom out to the living room. "We can relax a little once we're there, get ready for tonight."

"I guess so . . ." Pausing in the entry, Carly glanced around as if she might never see the house again, and alarms went off in his head.

"What are you thinking? We're only going to be in Dallas one night. Are you nervous about the benefit?"

She shrugged. "Not really. It's just . . . you'll be different there. You won't just be Linc. You'll be Lincoln Cain."

He set the luggage down and strode toward her, caught her shoulders in his hands. "I'll be the same man you slept with last night. The same man you'll be sleeping with in Dallas." Bending his head, he very soundly kissed her. "The same man I am right now."

She swallowed, seemed to collect herself. "You're

right. I'm being silly." She glanced away. "Just so much going on, I guess."

He wanted to shake her, make her understand it didn't matter which man he was, she was still the woman he wanted. Instead his cell phone rang and he let her go.

Linc pulled the phone out of his pocket. "Cain."

"FBI Agent Quinn Taggart. We need to talk, Cain. It's important." The formal tone of Quinn's voice relayed the man's irritation.

Linc should have phoned, as Taggart had expected, given him something, even if it wasn't completely the truth. No choice now. "We'll be in Dallas within the hour. Where would you like to meet?"

"Maybe you and Ms. Drake should come in to FBI headquarters. Maybe we'll be able to communicate better there."

Unease filtered through him. "You don't really think that's a good idea?"

"What I think is, we need to discuss your situation. We expected to hear from you. If you come in, maybe you'll understand how serious this is."

Never good to piss off the FBI. He should have found a way to stall them. Once they had evidence of a crime, they could bring the feds on board.

"Why don't we meet at my apartment?" Linc suggested, a place Taggart had been before. "If you park in the underground garage and take my private elevator, no one will see you."

"All right. I'll give you an hour and a half to get into town and get settled."

"Fine. We'll see you there." He turned to Carly, hating that they weren't going to be able to escape their problems even for a day.

"Taggart?" Carly asked.

Linc nodded. "We're meeting him at my place." He sighed. "I should have phoned him, given him enough to keep him hanging until we have what we need."

"It's not too late. We can do that when we see him. We'll tell him something, just not what we're planning to do. He doesn't have to know anything we don't want him to."

He smiled. He loved her toughness, a vivid contrast to the sexy, feminine side of her. "You're right. We can talk about it on the way."

The high-rise condominium apartment building on Pearl Street in Uptown Dallas was near the art district and close to the park. Carly had been to Linc's office on a number of occasions, but never to his condo. Standing next to him in his private elevator, she felt her curiosity ramp up as the conveyance rose, lifting her stomach along with it. The place a person lived could be a mirror into his soul.

Though definitely not in her case. After she'd left Iron Springs, she had never really put down roots. The longest she'd lived in one place had been the Park Slope district of Brooklyn when she had flown the New York-Paris route out of JFK.

With rent in the district high, she had shared an apartment with three other flight attendants, all of them in and out on different schedules.

She'd met Carter Benson in a small, local café, the son of a renowned architect. His family was wealthy. Carter had gone to the best private schools, then on to a top architectural college. He worked for Benson and Associates, his father's prestigious firm, and had already begun to build a name for himself by the time she met him.

She had fallen hard for Carter, who had promised her the moon and given her the boot instead. At the time, the pain and insecurity of losing him had been devastating.

As she looked back on it now, she saw it was Carter's good looks and charm, the bright lights of his success that had attracted her, rather than anything of actual substance, or anything they had in common.

The elevator doors slid open with a soft *ding* and Carly walked out into a slate-floored entry, while Linc carted her bags into the room behind her. Through an impressive wall of windows in the living room, views of the city stretched endlessly below.

"Go ahead, take a look around," Linc said. "I'll put your stuff in the bedroom."

"Okay." She wandered, pleased he was inviting her into his personal space so completely, strolled into the open living/dining space, comfortably modern, done in shades of dark brown and cream, with lots of dark wood tables and accent pieces. A beautiful dark walnut dining table that easily seated eight, could probably stretch to ten.

She wandered into the kitchen: granite countertops and state-of-the-art stainless steel appliances, including a Sub-Zero fridge. As she continued her journey, she passed another living space, more of a den, with brown leather sofas and chairs and a big-screen TV. Clearly this was Linc's man cave.

She wanted to prowl, see what she could discover about him in that room, but the rest of the apartment beckoned. Down the hall, she passed his wood-paneled study, where a black granite fireplace was built into one wall. A high-tech computer sat on his desk and a big projection screen hung on the wall.

She found him in the master suite, hanging up the bag that held the gown she planned to wear to the gala. A king-size bed covered by an elegant brown silk comforter and a stack of cream and brown throw pillows made her think of what would happen later, and warmth settled low in her belly.

Through an open door, she caught a glimpse of a huge marble bathroom, wandered past the dresser, where framed photos of Linc with Beau sat beside a photo of Linc with his brother, Josh. She picked up a picture of Linc with Joe, Linc's arm around Joe's shoulders, and her throat closed up. The photo told her how important her grandfather had been to Linc, which somehow made her feel closer to him.

Footsteps warned of Linc's approach. He bent his head and kissed her, took her hand, and tugged her toward the door of the suite.

"I'm getting hard just watching you walk around in here," he said with a grin. "Since the FBI will be here any minute, I think we're safer in the living room."

Carly laughed. Linc led her out the door and back down the hall. "I bought this place after my divorce. Four bedrooms, each with a private bath, great views from every room. But the selling feature was this. . . ." He led her through a set of sliding doors off the dining room, onto a lovely landscaped terrace.

"Sixteen hundred feet of outdoor living space. I can actually breathe out here."

She glanced around the terrace. "And it still has beautiful views."

"Plus a gazebo with a hot tub. It's great when I need to relax."

"Your place is wonderful, Linc."

One of his dark eyebrows arched up. "You think it fits me?"

She thought of the masculine furnishings, the fireplaces, the dark wood used throughout, the lovely terrace with its potted trees and blooming flowers. "Yes. It definitely fits you."

He pulled her into his arms. "That's what I've been trying to tell you, Carly. A man can enjoy different things and still be the same man." Lowering his head, he kissed her, softly at first, then deeper, more thoroughly. He was a big, powerful man and yet when he held her, she felt more cherished than threatened.

Emotion rose inside her, feelings that went far past desire. Carly pulled away.

"Taggart will be here any minute," she reminded him.

Linc sighed. "You're right. With any luck he won't stay long."

She didn't miss the heat in his eyes, the promise of what would happen when they were alone. He was so incredibly sexy. Just looking at him turned her on. "No, if we're lucky he won't stay."

Linc kissed her one last time, then set her away as if she were too much temptation. An instant later the intercom buzzed, indicating their visitor had arrived.

Linc walked over and hit the speaker button. "Agent Taggart, I presume."

"That's right."

"I'll key in the code so you can come up."

They had strategized during the helicopter ride into the city. Both of them knew what to say. Carly hoped it would be enough to satisfy the FBI until they could get the evidence they needed against El Jefe.

As the elevator arrived in the entry and the elegant

dark wood doors slid open, she took a deep breath and
slowly released it.

Showtime, she thought. Flicking Linc a conspirator-
ial glance, she smiled as Agent Quinn Taggart walked
into the room.

Linc led the agent with the buzz-cut blond hair into
the den. The tightness around Taggart's mouth said he
wasn't happy. Linc needed the man to relax, feel comfortable, and let down his guard.

Moving to the built-in bar, Linc filled three highball
glasses with ice, popped the top on a can of Coke, and
poured the bubbling liquid into the glasses, opened
another can and filled them to the top. Taggart was on
duty. No way was he drinking anything alcoholic.

"Let's sit down so we can talk," Linc suggested.

Each of them carried a glass of soda over to the seating area in front of the huge flat-screen TV. He and
Carly sat down on the sofa while Taggart sat in a deep
leather chair.

Without taking a drink, Taggart set his glass down
on a leather coaster on the coffee table. "We might as
well get down to business, and don't even think of
telling me El Jefe never called."

Linc leaned back on the sofa. "You're right. He called
not long after we talked to you Tuesday night . . . or
should I say Wednesday morning?"

Fortunately the drug lord had been polite enough
to wait until after they'd had a round of steamy, very
satisfying sex.

"You should have phoned," Taggart said, "brought
us up to speed. What the hell were you thinking?"

"Maybe we would have called if we were sure we

could trust you." Linc leaned forward and set down his drink, ice clinking against the sides of his glass. "El Jefe knew we'd been in contact with the FBI. He knew he was being set up—that's the reason his men didn't show. How the hell did he know, Taggart? You got a leak? Or were you just careless? Because either way, we're out. That's what we told El Jefe and that's what we're telling you."

Taggart leaned forward so they were face to face. "You don't get it, do you? You aren't out as long as El Jefe's in business. You think he's just going to let you walk away?"

"Yeah, I do. You see, we made a deal. He leaves Carly and Drake Trucking the hell alone, takes his business elsewhere, and we tell you guys to go fuck yourselves."

Taggart's mouth thinned. He just stared. So did Linc.

"You're the one who screwed up, Agent Taggart," Carly said, breaking the pissing contest he and Taggart were having. "If you hadn't told half of two counties what was going on, this might have turned out differently. As it is, we're out, just like Linc says."

Taggart swore softly. "You need to think this over."

"We've thought it over," Carly said.

"And you're sure this is the way you want it?"

"Damn sure," Linc said.

Taggart rose from the sofa. "You're making a mistake. Surely you can see that. Let me know when you come to your senses. I just hope it happens before someone else gets killed."

Linc rose and so did Carly. They walked the agent back to the elevator, waited till he stepped inside and the doors closed, blocking him from view.   ▾

"Looks like our strategy might actually have worked," Carly said, clearly relieved.

"We just bought some time. We'll bring the feds back in as soon as we've got what we need." Or at least that was the plan. But plans had to stay fluid. He had learned that a long time ago.

Most important was keeping Carly safe. That had been his priority from the start and it hadn't changed.

But he was no longer doing it for Joe.

Linc was doing it for himself.

Chapter Twenty-Eight

The morning slid past. They ate on the terrace, enjoying the meal and the sunshine as they looked out over the city. It felt wonderful to have nothing to do but relax and enjoy each other.

As the time for the ball grew closer, Linc surprised her with a team of beauticians from a nearby salon. A woman named Heidi gave her an exquisite massage, a gray-haired lady named Betty did her nails and gave her a pedi.

Twenty minutes later, a makeup artist named Jonathan arrived to apply her makeup, followed by a petite hairstylist named Mandy who shampooed and arranged her hair, curling, then sweeping her blond locks up on one side.

Carly hadn't felt so totally feminine since the days of her monthly spa appointments in San Francisco, which seemed to be a completely different lifetime.

Mandy helped her into her gown, a rich dark blue chiffon floor-length Oscar de la Renta with indigo beading on the narrow straps and across the bodice.

The dress hugged her curves before falling to the floor in a simple but elegant line.

She would cut out her tongue before she'd admit she had bought the dress at a discreet little pre-owned clothing shop off the Rue Saint-Honoré in Paris. The dress, which originally cost six thousand dollars, had sold in the shop for three hundred Euro.

"Now the finishing touch." Mandy presented her with a selection of perfumes in lovely crystal bottles, each of which had to cost a small fortune.

Carly dabbed on a Chanel fragrance called Misia that hinted at violets, then handed the bottle back to Mandy.

The woman just smiled and shook her head. "It's a gift from Mr. Cain."

Carly's eyes burned. She clutched the expensive crystal bottle against her heart. It was a wonderful gift, one that would remind her of Linc and their elegant evening, and she would always treasure it.

Mandy took the rest of the bottles and quietly left the condo. Carly was slipping her feet into a pair of strappy dark blue satin heels when she heard a light knock and Linc walked in.

He looked gorgeous in black Armani, a white shirt with tiny tucks down the front. Just looking at him turned her on as she admired the way his towering height and perfect vee-shaped body showed the tuxedo off to best advantage.

"My God, you're beautiful." He began striding toward her as if he had just awoken from a trance. When he reached her, he lifted her hand to his lips. "Thank you for agreeing to come with me this evening. I couldn't be more proud to have you by my side."

Her heart was beating too fast. She tried to tell herself

it was just a date, that he was her lover didn't change things.

"Thank you for the perfume."

Linc leaned over and inhaled the fragrance next to her ear. "I'm the one who gets to enjoy it. You smell as delicious as you look."

Her face warmed into a blush, though she wasn't a blushing sort of woman.

"I have something else for you." He held a square blue velvet box up in front of her and opened the lid. A glittering marquis-cut diamond that had to be at least four carats hung from a thin white-gold chain. A pair of earrings, each a strand of smaller matching diamonds, sat next to it.

He took the necklace and walked behind her, draped the chain around her neck, and fastened the clasp. "I took a look at your dress so I knew these would work. I hope you like them."

She touched the diamond pendant nestled in the hollow of her throat. "They're gorgeous."

"I knew what I wanted," Linc said as she put on the earrings. "I phoned Cartier and had them sent over."

Cartier. Unease filtered through her. "The diamonds are magnificent, but . . . You aren't saying these are for me?" She had thought he'd borrowed them the way movie stars did. With his connections it would have been easy.

"Of course they're yours. They're a gift, just like the perfume."

Her shoulders stiffened. "I'm not accepting these, Linc. How could you think I would? If you want me to wear them tonight, I will, but there's no way I'm keeping them."

"What are you talking about? I can afford to give you these and I want you to have them."

"It doesn't matter what you can afford. Don't you understand? This makes me feel like a kept woman. I'm already living with you—at least for the time being. You've made me a loan for the business. Expensive gifts turn this into something it isn't."

His temper was heating, she could see it.

"If I kept these," she doggedly continued, "I'd just have to sell them to help repay the money I owe you."

His features tightened. "Dammit, woman, you are the most . . ." Linc took in a calming breath. "Since I want this evening to be special, I'm not going to argue. Wear the diamonds tonight and I'll return them tomorrow."

Relief trickled through her. "Thank you."

A slow smile curved his lips. "You're amazing. If I haven't already told you, I'm telling you now. You're also stubborn to a fault and way too damned independent."

"And you're domineering, controlling, and too used to getting your way." Moving closer, she slid her arm through his. "Now that we've got that settled, let's go to the ball, Prince Charming."

Linc laughed.

They took the elevator down to the underground garage. Carly wasn't surprised to see a big black stretch limo waiting to whisk them off to the charity ball.

Aside from their unsettling encounter with Agent Taggart, Carly had enjoyed every moment of the day. But as they neared the hotel where the gala was to be held, her nerves began to build.

This was clearly an important night for Linc. She was going to meet his business partner and best friend, Beau Reese. For Linc's sake, Carly wanted Beau to like her. The Dallas Art Gala, a benefit for cancer research, was the most prestigious ball in the city. The elite of the elite would be there. She wanted everything to go smoothly, wanted Linc to be proud of her.

When the limo reached the front of the hotel, a white jacketed valet opened the door and helped her out, and Linc followed. Cameras flashed as she took his arm and they started up the red carpet to the door.

Her stomach fluttered, tightened. Her fiancé, Carter Benson, had earned an extremely high salary. She had dated wealthy men, but she had never attended an affair as prestigious as this. She had never been with a man as rich as Linc or so well-known.

Members of the media called his name as they walked past. Linc waved and stopped a couple of times so the press could get a shot. Carly's chest clamped down as she realized how much of a celebrity he actually was, and suddenly it was hard to breathe. Brittany had mentioned his appearances in the tabloids, but Carly hadn't completely understood until tonight.

This was the real Lincoln Cain, she realized, not the man in black leather who rode a Harley. This man wore a tuxedo with the ease of a pair of jeans.

As they walked into the marble-floored entry, her anxiety ratcheted up another notch. The Adolphus was old Dallas, done in an opulent French décor with rich dark woods, gilded ironwork, a sweeping staircase, and Renaissance paintings on the walls.

As they moved toward the Grand Ballroom, Linc paused several times to introduce her to people he knew. Carly smiled and struggled to remember their names, something she had always prided herself on when she had been a flight attendant.

Tonight she couldn't seem to focus, couldn't calm

her raging nerves, and if she didn't get herself under control, the evening was going to be a disaster.

They reached the entrance to the ballroom, where a line of elegantly dressed men and women waited to go in. She clutched Linc's arm and hoped he couldn't feel her trembling.

He looked down at her, an assessing look on his face. Carly managed to smile. Suddenly he turned and started striding back down the hall, forcing her along beside him.

"Where are we going?"

He didn't answer, just kept walking. At the corner, he turned into another corridor, strode past the ladies' room, the men's room, paused in front of a door just beyond, reached down, and turned the knob.

Carly gasped as he swept her inside what appeared to be a linen closet filled with stacks of white tablecloths, napkins, and kitchen towels. The clean smell of soap and starch filled the cramped interior as the door closed softly, leaving them cocooned in darkness. She trembled as she felt Linc's arm slide around her waist, pulling her back against his front. He lifted her hair aside, and his lips brushed the nape of her neck.

"What . . . what are you doing?"

"I'm going to help you relax."

"In . . . in here?"

"Right here." His warm mouth pressed against her bare shoulder, sending a wash of heat across her skin.

"What about your ribs?"

"I'll be fine." He nipped the side of her neck.

"How . . . how did you even know this room was here?"

He slid one of the beaded straps of the gown off her shoulder. "I've been in the building before." His hand slid inside the fabric to cup her breast and heat washed into her stomach. "Have I brought a woman in here I wanted to fuck? No."

Oh, my God. He lightly pinched her nipple and desire spilled through her.

"I promise I won't ruin your makeup." He kissed the side of her neck as he slid the other strap off and tended to the other breast, massaging, palming, sending pleasure out through her limbs.

Carly moaned.

"Brace your hands on that stack of linens in front of you," he softly commanded, all the while toying with her breasts, making her wet and hot.

In the darkness, she found the pile of linens and bent forward, felt his big hands sliding her dress up around her waist. Linc moved aside the tiny silver thong she was wearing. She heard the glide of his zipper, heard the tear of a foil packet, felt his hardness nudging against her, then he was inside.

Need burned through her. Her mind shut down. She was blind in the darkness, able only to feel. Linc gripped her hips to hold her in place and started moving, slowly at first, then increasing the rhythm, driving her toward climax. The distant chords of the orchestra melted through the walls and nothing existed but the two of them in their small private world.

Faster, deeper, harder. Pleasure rolled through her in thick, saturating waves. Her breath came in short, sharp gasps.

She heard Linc's deep voice in the darkness. "You're close. Let yourself go."

His words pushed her over the edge and sweet oblivion engulfed her, dragged her into bliss. Linc followed, his body tightening, his low growl rumbling through the pitch darkness.

As she began to spiral down, he drew her up against him and for a moment just held her. Then he pulled her straps back up, let her gown fall back into place over her hips, and she heard the buzz of his zipper. A crack of light appeared as he checked their surroundings. Linc opened the door and led her back out into the corridor.

Dazed, her body limp and her mind ridiculously at ease, she looked up at him. Linc pressed a soft kiss on her lips.

"We'll take a moment to freshen up, then we'll go inside."

She glanced toward the ladies' room. "'Kay." Turning away, she disappeared into the bathroom.

By the time she took Linc's arm a few minutes later and he started leading her back toward the ballroom, she was no longer shaking. Her entire body felt energized and at the same time completely relaxed.

Ready to face the evening ahead, she managed to ignore the faintly smug expression on Linc's handsome face as they walked along the corridor.

A secret smile tugged at her lips. Maybe he was the man in black leathers after all.

Chapter Twenty-Nine

Six hundred people sat at linen draped tables in the elegant Grand Ballroom. White and silver floral centerpieces rested on mirrored bases in the middle of each table.

Linc guided Carly through the crowd, not surprised by the number of heads she turned. He'd known she was more than pretty. He hadn't realized she could hold her own with some of the most beautiful women in Dallas.

Oddly enough, it was the Carly she was out at the ranch who appealed to him most, the strong, spirited woman determined to make it in a man's world.

The social hour hadn't ended. Lifting a glass of champagne off a passing waiter's tray, he handed it to Carly, then took one for himself.

"I see Beau over by our table. I want you to meet him."

"I'd love to," Carly said. A faint blush still colored her cheeks from their interlude in the linen closet. He felt a sweep of possessiveness that was highly unusual for him and mildly unsettling.

He spotted Beau standing next to the table he had purchased, ten seats for a mere thirty-two thousand dollars. He reminded himself it was for charity, and urged Carly toward Beau.

His best friend was outrageously handsome, tall and lean, with thick black hair and blue eyes. If it weren't for the thin scar running along his jaw from a fistfight with the school bully when they were in junior high, he might have looked a little too pretty. As it was, women loved him, always had.

He'd come from a wealthy family that was completely dysfunctional, a society mother who totally ignored him, a dad whose biggest concern was making more money and was never around. Beau had rebelled, and to spite them, become friends with the local bad boys, which included Linc.

After the robbery, Beau had reformed. He'd just graduated college when his grandfather died, leaving him a minor fortune but not the foggiest idea what to do with it.

He'd come to Linc because he felt guilty, felt he owed Linc for taking the fall for the robbery. Linc, being no fool, had accepted Beau's offer to work for him. Their boss-employee relationship had become a partnership. Together they had built the company into the vastly successful corporation it was today.

"Carly, this is my partner, Beau Reese. Beau, this is Carly Drake."

"Nice to meet you," Carly said with a smile.

"Linc's told me a lot about you," Beau said.

Linc didn't miss the surprise on her face. What? She didn't think he'd mention the woman he was living with to his best friend? Irritation trickled through him.

Beau flashed one of his signature smiles. "Don't

worry, it was all good. He says you've been having some problems with the company but you're getting things worked out."

"I have some great employees. We're going to make it work." She looked up at Linc and her features softened. "Linc's been really great."

His irritation faded. She thought he was great? She'd sure never said anything like that to him.

Beau's gaze went over Carly's head and Linc realized the moment he'd been dreading had arrived as Sophia Aiello walked up to Beau. She gave Linc a disdainful look down the length of her nose, which tilted even higher when she spotted Carly.

"Sophia, this is Carly Drake," Beau said. "Carly, Sophia Aiello."

A perfect black eyebrow arched up. "So you are the one. You were working in his office. What are you, some kind of secretary? If you think you can sleep your way to the top, you are a fool."

Carly's mouth thinned.

"Ms. Drake is a businesswoman," Linc said, hoping to defuse the situation before the vicious little witch sank her fangs any further into Carly. "She owns Drake Trucking. We've been friends for some years." *More or less.*

"I see."

Beau cast Linc a long-suffering glance and took Sophia's arm. "Why don't we take a walk around, see what auction items will be up for bid?"

Sophia sniffed petulantly. "Perhaps you will buy something for Sophia, yes?"

"Maybe I will." Beau cast Linc a look that said *and Lincoln Cain is going to pay for it.*

Linc just smiled.

Carly seemed to relax as they walked away. "There's some wonderful art up for sale," she said, glancing at the artwork on display around the room.

"The theme this year is Latin Legends. Some of the art that's going to be auctioned was donated by collectors. There's a Diego Rivera, a piece by a Chilean artist named Roberto Matta, a number of other important South American artists." There was also pottery, sculpture, and handmade jewelry.

"According to the catalog," Linc said, "the prize of the evening is a Botero, a gift from the Weldsburg Foundation. It's valued at over a million dollars."

"Will you be bidding?"

"Not on that. This is a charity auction, so I'll buy something." He smiled down at her. "Maybe you can help me choose."

Carly smiled back. "That sounds like fun."

The two of them wandered, greeting people he knew, sipping champagne. Linc introduced her to Randall Conners and his wife, Andrea, two of the people seated at his table.

Carly said something about traveling, Andrea mentioned Paris, and the next thing he knew they were chatting away in French, rolling their eyes and laughing.

Linc never would have guessed she spoke French and he had to admit he was impressed.

"I flew New York to Paris, remember?" she explained when he asked. "Being able to speak the language was one of the reasons I was assigned the route."

Andrea, a slender brunette, said something else in the elegant language, then turned to the men. "If you gentlemen will excuse us, we need to powder our noses. We'll be right back."

Linc smiled. Seemed like Carly had just been to

the ladies' room, but typical women, they had to go together. He was glad Carly was fitting in so well. He hadn't really expected it and the truth was he really didn't care. It was nice just the same.

He wandered a little, but stayed close to the table so she could find her way back to him. Since it was almost time to sit down, he made sure their place cards were on the opposite side of the table from Beau and Sophia Aiello.

Linc thought of the turn of fortune that had allowed him to come here with Carly instead of the spoiled Italian model, and said a silent *thank you* to his best friend.

It was only a few minutes later that Carly and Andrea walked out of the ladies' room, heading back toward their table. Andrea Conners was a few years older than she but didn't look it, and her gold satin, off-the-shoulder gown showed off a terrific figure. She was fun and the two of them just seemed to click.

They were almost back to their men when Andy—as Andrea preferred to be called—spotted someone she knew.

"Go say hello," Carly said. "I'll see you back at the table."

Continuing her journey, she wove her way through the glittering throng, paused for a moment to get her bearings and locate Linc's table, then heard a familiar voice. She paused, trying to place it, deep, slightly rough, tinged with a Spanish accent.

She glanced toward the speaker, trying to recall the person the voice belonged to, caught the profile of a tall, black-haired man she didn't know. Then her brain started working and her heart slammed hard, set up a terrified clatter against her ribs.

She knew that voice. The threats that voice had made were burned into her brain. Careful to stay out of sight behind a cluster of guests, she looked down at the man's shiny black patent leather shoes. Big shoes. And the toes turned slightly inward.

Fighting not to panic, Carly swallowed back her fear and started walking, trying not to run. She needed to get a better look at him, but if he spotted her, he would know she had recognized him and the knowledge might get her killed.

People were beginning to take their seats. Carly spotted Linc, taller than the other men standing next to the table. Scanning the crowd in search of her, he must have read her distress because his features went tense. He strode toward her, caught her hands just as she reached the table.

"What is it? What's happened?"

Her legs were shaking. "He's here. El Jefe."

His broad shoulders stiffened. "You're sure?"

"Yes."

Linc walked her to her chair, pulled it out, and eased her down into it, which was good since she was afraid her legs were going to buckle. He took the chair beside her, reached for her hand beneath the cloth. With ten people at the table, they were seated close together. The noise in the room drowned out their conversation.

"Did he see you?" Linc asked.

"No. I don't think so. I was careful." She took a deep breath and tried to stay calm. "I need to get a better look at him so we can figure out who he is."

Linc shook his head. "Too dangerous. Don't worry,

we'll get a better look. There are cameras all over the ballroom. We'll run the video back, see where you were when you spotted him, figure out who he is."

Relief trickled through her. "Great."

"We can't leave right now. If we do, he might get suspicious."

"I know." She sighed. "This is going to be the longest dinner of my life."

Beneath the table, Linc squeezed her hand. "We'll leave as soon as we can do it without being noticed. Maybe at the end of dinner before the auction starts. In the meantime, I'll introduce you to the rest of the guests."

Carly just nodded. Pasting a smile on her face, she turned toward the other people seated at the table and hoped she'd be able to remember their names.

After supper, during the break before the auction started, Linc made their excuses and was able to slip away. As soon as they were seated in the limo and heading back to his apartment, he pulled out his cell, brought up his contacts, and called Ross Townsend.

While the phone began to ring, he flicked a glance at Carly, who still looked a little pale.

"What's up?" Ross answered, probably still working since it was before midnight.

"Carly spotted El Jefe at the Dallas Art Gala tonight. We need to look at what's on the video cameras, figure out who the hell he is."

"Great, we're finally catching a break. I'll talk to the hotel security people first thing in the morning, make up some story they might actually believe, see if I can get you in to take a look sometime tomorrow."

"That'll work. We're staying in Dallas. We'll wait to hear from you." Linc ended the call and turned to Carly. "Ross is going to make arrangements for us to view the video recordings. We'll find you in the images, locate El Jefe, see which chair was his, and find out his name."

Carly sighed. She let her head fall back against the deep leather seat. "God, I'm sick of all the intrigue. One night without it wouldn't have been too much to ask."

"No, it wouldn't." He slid an arm around her waist and drew her closer. "On the other hand, if you hadn't gone with me to the gala, you would have missed out on the linen closet."

Carly laughed, the sound rolling over him, easing some of the adrenaline still running through his blood. When she'd told him El Jefe was there, it had been all he could do not to confront him, grab the man by his satin lapels, and beat him into submission. Without the proof they needed, it could have gotten Linc thrown back in jail or even worse—gotten Carly killed.

The limo drove into the underground garage and pulled to a stop in front of the elevator. After a brief ride up to his condo, they walked into the entry. Linc couldn't miss the fatigue in Carly's posture or the worry in her face.

"Come here," he said softly, and she went into his arms. "We're gonna find this guy and we're going to stop him. We're getting closer all the time."

Her head moved against his chest. "I know." She looked up at him, her eyes bluer than he had ever seen them. "Take me to bed, Linc. I want to think about something besides El Jefe."

Linc softly kissed her. "That would be my pleasure, sweetheart." Sweeping her up in his arms, he strode down the hall toward the bedroom, Carly's head on his shoulder, her gown flowing over his arm, golden hair a whisper of silk against his cheek. He inhaled the soft fragrance of the perfume he had bought her, the only gift she would accept from him.

His heart beat oddly, telling him something he wasn't ready to hear.

He forced himself to focus on the present, on what they had learned and what lay ahead. Tomorrow they would start again, renew their efforts. He had the drug lord in his sights.

Linc was about to pull the trigger.

Chapter Thirty

An overcast sky diffused the sun on that cool fourth of October Sunday morning as Carly walked next to Linc into the Adolphus Hotel. Ross Townsend stood in the lobby. Dressed in khaki slacks and a yellow pullover shirt, his cropped beard shaved to fashionable dark stubble, he waited impatiently for their arrival.

"Getting them to let us view the videos wasn't much of a problem," Ross said to Linc as they approached. "Turns out the head of security is former Dallas P.D. He knew your name, said something about the contributions you made to the widows' and orphans' fund. He's got the whole thing set up and ready to go."

"Good work," Linc said.

Carly walked with the men into the security area, watched Linc shake hands with a brawny, red-haired man Ross introduced as Marty O'Toole. The security man greeted him effusively, said a polite "hello" to Carly, then left them to work through the videos.

"I went through all the footage they had and located anything you or Carly showed up in," Ross said. "Most of it's on one camera. Marty's got the video set to run from the opening of the ballroom through the end of the evening." Ross leaned down and clicked the mouse, setting the video in motion.

"This is going to take a while," Linc said, pulling up a couple of chairs.

Carly sat down next to him and focused her attention on the screen. The encounter had happened early in the evening so it didn't take long for her to spot the black-haired man who called himself El Jefe.

"There! That's him right there!"

Linc hit the PAUSE button, pointed to the images on the screen. "There's where you stopped walking."

"That's when I heard his voice. It sounded familiar but at first I couldn't remember who it was. Then I recalled where I'd heard it."

"He's standing a few feet away." Linc hit PLAY and the video resumed. "You glance down, then turn away, and start walking toward our table."

"I looked down at his feet. It was all I'd seen of him before. Big feet that turn slightly inward, like he's a little pigeon-toed. It was definitely him."

They kept watching. Linc used the zoom to zero in on the man: thick, ink-black hair, olive skin, wide forehead, long nose slightly curved. He was wearing black on black: black tuxedo, black shirt, and black bowtie.

Carly remembered the night of the kidnapping, the way he had slapped her, threatened her, the pleasure he had clearly felt, and gooseflesh crept over her skin.

"Doesn't look like he spotted you," Linc said, his eyes still on the screen.

Carly prayed it was true. On the monitor, El Jefe sat down at table twenty-three next to a buxom blonde with big lips in a strapless black dress. As the meal was served, Linc moved the recording a little faster, slowed as the bidding started. El Jefe's paddle never went up, but the man across from him bid on a couple of different pieces.

Linc moved the video ahead. He was watching El Jefe when the Botero came up for auction, zoomed in when he noticed the man's interest. When the bidding started, El Jefe made a slight nod of his head and the man across from him, heavyset, small mouth, and balding, raised his paddle. Every time El Jefe nodded, the man increased the bid until finally the painting belonged to him.

The moment the item had been acquired, El Jefe rose from his chair, the blonde stood up, and both of them left the ballroom. At the end of the evening, their chairs remained empty.

By the time Linc turned off the computer, Carly felt drained. Both of them stood up, and Ross Townsend came forward.

"I'll find out who bought the Botero," he said. "And get the names of the people at table twenty-three, figure who sat where."

Linc nodded. "The sooner the better," he said.

They split up at the front door. The valet brought up Linc's Mercedes and they went back to his apartment. The plan had been to return to Iron Springs, but Linc wanted to wait till they had the information they needed.

Since they both had businesses to run, sitting around wasn't an option. Linc retreated to his study, Carly set up her laptop, and both of them went to work.

It was hard to concentrate with so much going on in his head. Sitting behind the computer on his desk,

Linc worked online, going over updates on his New Mexico road construction project, making a couple of suggestions, then returning an e-mail from Millie, reminding him of an upcoming lunch meeting with the head of a small community college that received a substantial annual donation.

Linc asked Millie to postpone the meeting till next week and hoped to hell he wouldn't have to set it back again. But things with El Jefe were heating up and he had no idea whether or not the pot was going to boil over, or if it did, who was going to get burned.

He returned a phone call in regard to the tire re-building plant outside Pleasant Hill, found out the county commissioners would be voting on the project before the end of the month. He planned to be there along with his environmental team, hoped they got the approval they needed.

He was on the land line when his cell phone signaled. Grabbing it off the desk, he saw Townsend's name on the screen, ended the call he was on, and pressed the phone against his ear. "Cain."

"I've got what you need," Ross said. "I'm on my way over."

Anticipation poured through him as the call abruptly ended. Townsend had found El Jefe. Things could start moving now, driving toward a final resolution, whatever that turned out to be.

It was only a few minutes later that the intercom buzzed, announcing the investigator's arrival. Linc punched in the elevator code and walked out to the living room to meet him.

"Townsend's here," Linc said.

Carly rose from the sofa, where her laptop sat on

the coffee table in front of her. "He has the information already?"

"Apparently he does."

The elevator doors slid open and Ross walked into the apartment. He was frowning, not a good sign.

Linc didn't waste any time. "Who is he?"

"His name's Raul Zapata. Owns hotels and a chain of fast-food restaurants, all fairly recent purchases. Got a place on four hundred acres in the middle of nowhere out Highway 80 near Big Sandy. Built a house there about a year ago. On Google Maps it looks like a fortress. He also rents an apartment in Dallas."

"That it?"

"On the surface, there isn't that much. It's like he kind of appears out of nowhere. I'll have more once I start digging. I figured you'd want to know. I came in person in case there were some decisions you wanted to make."

"That's good work, Ross. The question is what do we do with the information?"

Carly moved closer. "I think we should call Agent Taggart. The FBI might know this man. Or once they know his name, they can look into his criminal activities. They have ways of getting information we don't have."

"She's right," Ross said. "If you're going to stop him, you need help."

"I don't like it. We went to them before and it didn't turn out well for them *or* us."

"Do you trust Agent Taggart?" Carly asked.

"Taggart, yes. Even after that clusterfuck with the cargo pickup, I think Quinn's a straight shooter. Unfortunately I have no idea about the rest of them."

Silence fell.

Linc sighed. "All right, let me call him, see if I can get him to run with the information and leave us out of it." Linc pulled out his cell, brought up his contacts and hit Taggart's number. Carrying the phone into the dining area, he put it on speaker so the others could hear and set it down on the table.

The call picked up on the second ring. "Taggart."

"Quinn, it's Cain. I've got something for you, but it has to be off the record. No county sheriffs, not your boss, nobody knows but you."

"You expect me to keep secrets from my superiors? You know that isn't going to happen."

"If you want the information, it is. I'll tell you what we've got, but it has to come from somewhere else, not from Carly or me."

"That's not the way it works."

When Linc made no reply, Taggart blew out a breath. "All right, fine. I'll figure a way to keep you out of it."

"Good enough. El Jefe was at the Dallas Art Gala last night. Carly spotted him. We went over the video footage this morning and picked him out. Ross Townsend came up with a name."

The pause was lengthy. Too lengthy. "We've already got a name."

A rush of heat hit the back of his neck. "So you've been playing me? You knew who he was all along? I don't like being played, Taggart. Not even a little. Don't expect to hear from me again."

"Wait! Don't hang up! I wasn't playing you, I swear it, Linc. We just found out this morning. Agent McKinley is still working undercover. He came up with the name."

"Which is?"

"Raul Zapata."

"That's right. If you know who he is, why haven't you arrested him?"

"Because his identity isn't much more than a rumor. Carly can't press charges—she was blindfolded. There are a million guys with a Spanish accent and big feet in Texas. We need evidence to make an arrest, Cain, which is something we don't have. Or have you forgotten that's what we were hoping you could help us get."

Linc took a steadying breath. "We know he owns hotels and restaurants. We know he owns property out near Big Sandy and an apartment in Dallas. Now tell us what you know."

"I'm not at liberty to discuss the case, but I'll tell you this. At the moment we don't have squat. No trace of any criminal activity connected to Raul Zapata. Nada."

"Then you'd better keep looking. That's what I intend to do."

"You can't do that, Linc. You'll be interfering in a federal investigation."

"Fine, I'll do my best to stay out of your way. I'd advise you to do the same." Linc hung up the phone.

"I can't believe this," Carly said. "What do we do now?"

"Exactly what we planned to do. We're going back to Iron Springs and wait for El Jefe's call. I doubt we'll have to wait much longer."

"You want me to come with?" Townsend asked.

"I've got plenty of security on the ranch. I need you to keep digging. And try to do it quietly. We don't want anyone else getting killed."

They left for home that afternoon. *Home*. There was that word again. It was making Carly more and more nervous. No way could she allow herself to think of Blackland Ranch as her home.

And the fact she had caught herself with those exact thoughts more than once made her realize how badly she needed to get back to her own house, her own life.

As the chopper lifted off the helipad at the top of the Tex/Am building, she thought of her evening with Linc. Besides her near-encounter with Raul Zapata, the night had made one thing crystal clear: her time with Linc was limited.

Half a dozen women had approached him while the two of them had wandered through the crowd, and though Linc had paid them little attention, the opportunities for him to find someone new, a woman who posed a fresh challenge, weren't going to go away.

The man was rich and powerful, gorgeous and smart, and amazing in bed. Who wouldn't want a man like that?

True, he was difficult, domineering, and he could be ridiculously controlling, but she had managed to handle him. Another woman could do that just as well.

One thing she knew about men—the grass was always greener—their interest in a particular female lasted only as long as that of a tomcat.

Sooner or later Linc would tire of her and want a replacement and she would be gone.

A sharp pang throbbed in the area around her heart. She knew what it was, recognized the feeling as longing. Linc was everything she wanted in a man, everything she had never found in anyone else. His money didn't matter. It was the man himself who appealed to her so strongly. A man she could never have.

Which made him more dangerous to her than she could ever have imagined.

An ache rose inside her, a pain that would only get worse after he was gone. She had to do something, had to find a way to take a step back.

She took a deep breath and clamped down on her emotions. For now, her worries about Linc had to be postponed. With all that was happening, she needed to stay in the present, needed to focus on the problems at hand. As long as El Jefe posed a threat, walking away from Linc wasn't an option. Until Raul Zapata had been dealt with, she needed Linc's protection.

She ignored a little voice that warned, deep down she didn't really want to leave. She wanted to stay with Linc forever, wanted to feel protected and safe, the way he always made her feel. Almost as if he loved her.

Carly shook off the thought and glanced out the window of the chopper, saw that they were nearing Blackland Ranch. Vast stretches of open grassland bisected by ravines and meandering creeks lined with foliage stretched off toward the east.

The helicopter swung around, shuddered as it hovered over the asphalt pad, settled, and the rotors began to slow. Carly sighed as the door slid open and they climbed down onto the tarmac.

Besides her problems with Linc, she had a business to run. Tomorrow was Monday. She desperately needed to spend time at the office with Rowena. It wasn't fair to abandon her friend with only the briefest instructions, hoping her new office manager would somehow be able to figure things out on her own.

She crossed to Linc's big GMC and Linc opened her door.

"You okay?" he asked, jolting her out of her thoughts.

"As much as I can be," she answered honestly.

"We're going to get him," Linc said as Carly climbed into the passenger seat for the short ride back to his sprawling brick ranch house. "I don't want you to worry."

She didn't tell him Zapata was only one of her worries. "I know," was all she said.

Chapter Thirty-One

As soon as they got back to the house, Linc went into his office, sat down at his desk, and pulled up his e-mail.

Townsend had sent him a Google Maps link showing the property owned by Raul Zapata. When he zoomed in on the satellite photos, the place looked exactly like the fortress Ross had described. A castlelike dwelling even more outlandish than the mansion Linc's ex-wife had designed sat in the middle of a big chunk of ground surrounded by an impressive wall. Tall wooden gates blocked the entrance.

Privacy Linc well understood, but this seemed a little over the top. He rubbed a hand over his face. At least they now knew where to find him.

He pulled the burner phone out of his briefcase and phoned Tag Joyner. "Tag, it's Cain."

"Hey, man, what's up?"

"We got something. El Jefe's name is Raul Zapata. Mean anything to you?"

"Zapata. No, man, ain't heard of him. You sure it's him?"

"I'm sure. Lives on four hundred acres over near Big Sandy. Owns hotels and a fast-food chain."

"So I guess we need to call off the bounty."

"I've got a name and location. Money's still there if someone comes forward with usable information."

"Right. That sounds good. I'll get the word out."

"Do it with care, my friend. We still don't know enough about this guy to predict what he might do."

"I get you, man. Stay in touch and stay safe."

"You, too."

The line went dead. Frustrated he couldn't move things along any faster and beginning to feel claustrophobic, Linc walked out of his office, down the hall to the open guest room door. Carly sat at her makeshift desk going over work invoices on her laptop.

"It's still Sunday," he said, drawing her attention. "I don't know about you, but I need some fresh air. How would you like to go fishing?" He wouldn't have thought of asking any of the other women he'd dated. But this was Carly, and since he loved to fish, it was worth a try.

Her features lit up and she grinned ear to ear. "Really?"

He grinned back. "You really want to go?"

"Of course." She shoved back her chair and stood up. "Joe took me fishing all the time. I admit I haven't been since I left home and I'm not all that good at it, but I'd love to go fishing."

Linc looked into those pretty blue eyes and something shifted inside him. He told himself it was nothing. Hey, what man could resist a woman who liked to fish?

But he was no fool and he knew it was way more than that.

The feeling had been building since the day he'd seen her standing in the graveyard, grieving for Hernandez, a man she barely knew, grieving so deeply for her grandfather. Building since he had watched her take the wheel of an eighteen-wheeler and bull it into submission.

Building every time he took her to bed and buried himself in her sweet, responsive body.

The truth burned like a neon sign in his head. Carly Drake was the woman for him.

The problem was he didn't think she would believe him.

And until he had dealt with El Jefe and Carly was safe, there wasn't a damn thing he could do to convince her.

Putting the thought aside, Linc went out to collect the gear they would need while Carly went to get ready for their fishing trip. She walked out of the house in cut-off jeans with a ragged hem and a Dallas Cowboys T-shirt, her hair plaited into long golden braids, one on each shoulder. A pair of worn, rough out leather hiking boots covered her feet.

"I'm ready," she said.

Linc grinned. She reminded him of a twenty-first-century Daisy Duke, so damned cute, he wanted to throw her over his shoulder caveman-style and carry her back to bed.

"The way you look, it's going to be damned hard to concentrate on catching fish," he grumbled. And he meant hard in more ways than one.

Carly laughed and he forced himself to focus on something besides the tightness in his jeans. "We're taking the Jeep," he said, wondering if he could find a place private enough the guards wouldn't see them, glad he'd tossed a blanket into the back.

Carly's cell started ringing just as they reached the vehicle. "Hold a sec." Pulling the phone out of the back pocket of her jean shorts, she pressed it against her ear. "This is Carly."

When the color leached out of her face, Linc knew his fishing trip was about to be canceled.

"Ms. Drake. It is good to hear your voice." Every muscle in Carly's body went tense. It was him. Raul Zapata.

"I assume you have been expecting my call," he said.

Her hand shook as she signaled to Linc, who was already striding toward her. Carly held the phone so he could hear.

"If you want the truth," she said, "I was hoping I'd never hear from you again."

"Now is that a nice thing to say to your business partner?"

The notion sent a chill down her spine. "What do you want?"

"I have something for you to deliver. You will receive instructions tomorrow, telling you where to pick up the cargo and what time. Have a truck ready to leave."

"How do you know I'm not still working with the FBI?"

"Because you know what happened to Hernandez and you are smart enough to know if you do not do as I say, it will happen again." The line went dead.

Her insides were shaking, making her stomach churn.

Tears welled, spilled over onto her cheeks. "I wanted to go fishing."

Linc took the phone from her trembling hand. "Let's go inside." As soon as they stepped through the door into the entry, Linc drew her into his arms. He always felt so solid, so strong. A fresh shudder went through her, this time one of relief.

Linc kissed the top of her head. "We'll go fishing, I promise. Let's get you settled down a little first."

"Do you think . . . think the FBI could have traced the call if we had told them?"

"It didn't last long enough. The guy knows what he's doing. Unfortunately."

She swallowed, brushed away tears as he led her into the living room and eased her down on the sofa. He walked over to the wet bar. She heard the sound of a bottle cap turning, then liquid being poured into a glass. Linc returned and pressed a heavy crystal tumbler into her hand.

Carly took a drink of the amber liquid, felt the burn of the whiskey as it trickled into her stomach and spread out through her limbs. With a sigh, she leaned back on the sofa.

"Better?"

"No. Well, a little, I guess. Thanks."

Linc sat down beside her. "You know we've been expecting this call. And picking up a load of whatever Zapata's smuggling is exactly what we need to happen."

"I know."

"Your truck is ready to go. All we have to do is make sure the equipment is working. Tomorrow you go into the office as usual and wait for the call. Who knows, maybe Zapata will be arrogant enough to be waiting at the pickup site himself and we'll nail him on the first try."

"I guess so. . . . Maybe."

He took the glass from her hand, set it on the coffee table, and to her surprise, drew her up from the sofa. "In the meantime, you're dressed to go fishing so let's go."

She looked up at him. "Really?"

"Yeah, baby, really."

God, he was the most amazing man. She gazed up at him and felt the soft, almost painful beating of her heart. It was the moment she knew she had committed a terrible error. Somehow she had let down her guard.

Somehow she had let herself fall in love with him.

At least the weather was good that Monday morning. Sunshine, low humidity, just a few drifting clouds in an otherwise clear blue sky. Linc needed to go into Dallas. He had a million things to do, appointments too important to cancel, discussions he'd planned to have with Beau, briefings with his staff, but it was too risky to leave Carly at the mercy of El Jefe.

Zapata expected a Drake truck to make a run tonight. Linc planned to do exactly that and he planned to be the man behind the wheel. It was dangerous. Hernandez had wound up dead.

But Zapata knew he was involved with Carly, might even expect him to be driving. If he followed El Jefe's instructions, he figured he'd be okay.

Unless he was willing to cooperate with the FBI and risk another failure, unless he was willing to chance

El Jefe's wrath descending on Carly—neither of which were options—he didn't have any other choice.

He spoke to Frank Marino, had the bodyguard accompany Carly to her office that morning. Linc wanted to go with her, but he wasn't a man who went unnoticed, and since they didn't know for sure who to trust, he planned to go down after Carly got El Jefe's call or as soon as the office closed.

In the meantime, he was home, impatiently waiting, trying to work, which was impossible to do.

At four o'clock, his cell phone rang. Ross Townsend's name appeared on the screen and from that moment, his worries only got worse.

"I need to see you," Ross said. "It's important."

"I plan to be at the Drake yard a little after five. We can meet there."

"That'll work. I'll be there as soon as I can."

Which left Linc a little over an hour to worry about what Ross wanted. Apparently something the investigator wasn't willing to discuss on the phone. By the tone of Ross's voice, something definitely not good.

At ten to five, Linc left the ranch and drove to the truck yard. By the time he arrived, the office was closed, most of the employees were gone when he walked through the door.

"Hey, Linc!" Rowena smiled and walked over, unaware of the latest drama.

"Hey, Row, nice to see you."

"Carly's in her office. I'll tell her you're here." While Rowena went in to get Carly, Linc went outside to speak to Frank.

The bodyguard knew nothing about El Jefe's expected call or the modifications they had made to the truck. The fewer people who knew, the less chance for a leak. As soon as Carly got a text or phone call with instructions where to pick up the load, Linc would take the truck out and Frank could take Carly back to the ranch, where she would be safe.

"Carly may be working late," Linc said to him. "Why don't you take a break?"

"Sounds good. I could use a soft drink." Frank headed for the truckers' lounge, and Linc walked back inside just as Carly came out of her office.

"We're done for the day," she said. "Everything okay?"

"Ross Townsend's on his way here from Dallas. I'll give you the answer to that after I talk to him. Anything happening on your end?"

Carly glanced over at Rowena, who was busy talking to one of the drivers. "Nothing yet."

"As soon as everyone's gone, I'll take a look at the truck." He held up the sheaf of papers he'd brought with him. "I've got detailed instructions on how all that surveillance gear operates. Let's just hope I can make sense of it."

"I hope so, too, and I hope it's hidden well enough that it can't be spotted."

For the price he had paid, it had damned well better be.

As soon as the employees were gone for the day, including Rowena, Linc went outside and located the truck they would be using that night. By the time he'd satisfied himself the surveillance equipment would work the way it was supposed to, Ross Townsend was pulling into the yard.

Linc followed him inside the office. "What's going on?"

"I'm not exactly sure, which is the reason I'm here. I've got something I need to show you."

"We can use my office." Carly led them in that direction.

Walking over to the table in the corner, Ross opened the manila folder he'd brought with him. "Remember that DNA sample we got off the manifest at the crime scene?"

"What about it?" Linc asked.

"If you recall I had it run through CODIS and came up with zip."

"So?"

"Well, I got to thinking . . . if the guy's smuggling drugs, they would probably be coming in from Mexico or South America. Maybe he's an international criminal. I called in a favor, had it run through Interpol's DNA database, and bingo, we got a hit."

"So Zapata is wanted . . . where? In Mexico?"

"No. It wasn't Zapata's blood." Ross moved one of the sheets of paper aside and pointed to a photo. "The DNA belongs to this man—Hassan Mohammed Al-Razi."

"What the hell?"

"Exactly. Al-Razi was born in Saudi Arabia. His father was an assistant to the Saudi ambassador to Mexico. Hassan moved to Mexico with his family when he was a teenager, lived there for several years before his dad moved back to Saudi Arabia. Five years ago, Al-Razi disappeared. No one knew where he went until you found that drop of blood. How he got to Texas, I have no idea, but he's a known terrorist, Linc. He's wanted in connection with everything from a truck bombing that killed twenty people in a Pakistani market to explosions at a bus station in Baghdad that killed sixty-five. He's on the Interpol terrorist list and he's wanted big time."

"I can't believe this." Carly sank down in one of the chairs.

Linc fought to stay calm. "What the hell is Raul Zapata doing with a terrorist?"

"That's what we need to find out," Ross said.

"We have to call the FBI, Linc," Carly said. "We don't have any choice. Zapata might be smuggling terrorists into the country. That might be what he wants Drake to haul. He has to be stopped before that happens. We can't afford to risk other people's lives."

Linc clenched his jaw to keep from swearing because it was true. Along with the September eleventh attacks and the Boston Marathon, there had been major terror attacks in London, Madrid, Paris, and Brussels. Hell, all over the world.

Now the DNA evidence said a known suspect was in the area, his sights set perhaps on the people in Dallas or another Texas city—or anywhere in the country.

"I'll call Taggart," he said. He turned to Carly. "You're right, baby. We no longer have any choice." Linc pulled out his cell, but Carly's phone rang first.

Christ, not El Jefe, he thought. *Not yet.* Linc gritted his teeth to keep from snatching the phone out of Carly's hand and let her answer the call.

Looking down at the blocked number on her iPhone, Carly felt a crushing weight settle on her chest. "It's Zapata or one of his men."

"Take the call, honey," Linc said, looking as if he wished he could grab her up and carry her out of danger.

She took a deep breath, pressed the phone against her ear. "This is Carly."

"Good evening, Ms. Drake." The familiar voice rolled over her, rough, guttural, tinged with Spanish, unmistakable. A chill slipped down her spine.

"This is your business partner," Zapata said. "Are you ready to take delivery of our first load?"

Her fingers trembled as they tightened around the phone, which she held so that Linc could hear. "I don't understand why you're doing this to me. Why are you so determined to get Drake Trucking involved? If the money's as good as you say, there must be other companies that would gladly do your bidding, no questions asked."

"I do not want other companies! I want Drake!" His voice steadied. "You wish to know why that is?"

She could hear the effort it was taking him to control his temper. "Tell me."

"Joe Drake is the reason! Your grandfather humiliated me. When I came to him with a simple business proposal, he laughed in my face. No one laughs at El Jefe! Do you understand me? No one!"

Carly started shaking. She felt Linc's big hand settle on her shoulder and took a steadying breath. "I understand."

"I am not sure you do. That is why I have taken out a small insurance policy." There was a shuffling sound and a new voice came over the line, one that sliced into her heart and threatened to shred it to pieces.

"Carly? It's me . . . Zach."

"Zach!"

"Men came to Grandma's house. They beat up Tom and made me go with them. I'm scared, Carly."

She tried to sound calm. Linc's face was flushed with fury, every muscle in his body taut. "Everything's going to be okay, Zach. I'm going to do exactly what El Jefe wants me to and he's going to let you go." *Please God.*

"But—"

El Jefe's voice came back on the line. "So you have finally come to your senses. This is good. The boy's grandparents have been warned to say nothing. They are waiting for your call, your assurance that the boy will be all right."

"I'll do whatever you want. Just don't hurt him."

"Listen carefully. At six-thirty P.M. you will drive your truck out of the yard. You personally, no one else. You will take Route 19 south, make your way to Waco, then drive south on 77, all the way to Victoria. Be at Big Vic's Truck Stop no later than one A.M. Do you understand?"

"Yes."

"At the truck stop, a man will join you. He will direct you to the pickup site. Once the cargo is loaded, other instructions will follow."

"What . . . what about Zach?"

"The boy will be waiting at your final destination. Alive if you do what I say."

Carly gasped as Linc jerked the phone out of her hand.

"She isn't driving," he said. "The truck can make the pickup and delivery, but Carly isn't driving—I am."

Terrified Linc was going to get Zach killed, Carly leaned up so she could hear Zapata's reply.

"You think, *Señor* Cain, because you are rich, you make the rules? The woman drives the truck—Joe Drake's granddaughter. Or the boy comes home in pieces."

Her stomach twisted. She grabbed Linc's arm, dug her nails into a powerful bicep to get his attention, and started furiously nodding, warning him to agree.

When Zach shrieked in the background, Carly forgot to breathe.

"All right," Linc said. "Carly drives the rig. But I go with her. That's not negotiable. I go with her to run your errand and bring the boy home."

A long pause, then Zapata chuckled, the grating sound sliding over her nerves like barbed wire. Carly thought he was enjoying having a powerful man like Lincoln Cain at his mercy.

"As you wish, *Señor* Cain. It is a long journey. Perhaps it is best to have another driver along. You and Ms. Drake will make the pickup, then deliver the load as instructed and pick up the boy. You understand?"

"Yes."

"Deviate from the plan in any way and the boy is dead." Zapata hung up the phone.

Chapter Thirty-Two

Carly wanted to cry. She wanted to scream. She wanted to pound her fists against the wall and tear out her hair. With a steadying breath, she battled the feelings down and fought to gain control of her emotions. "What are we going to do?"

Linc looked down at his heavy stainless wristwatch. "Barring any problems, it's a little over six hours from here to Victoria. It's ten after six right now so we have time, but not a lot. First we need to phone the Wellers, make sure they don't call the police, let them know we're going to bring Zach home."

She swallowed. "They must be terrified." Her hand shook as she punched in Amanda Weller's contact number. Her throat tightened when she thought of how scared Zach must be.

She looked up at Linc and her eyes burned. "Could you talk to them? I'm afraid I'll cry and I don't want to frighten them any more than they are already."

Linc took the phone, holding on to her hand for a moment before he let go. When Tom Weller answered, Linc asked if he was okay. Apparently he was battered and bruised but all right. Linc told him they were going to meet El Jefe's demands and bring Zach back to them. Speaking calmly, he reassured them, told them he wouldn't let anything happen to the boy.

Carly knew it was a promise he would do his best to keep, but there was no way to be sure.

She clamped down on the hysterical sob that rose in her throat. A little boy's life was at stake because her grandfather had stood up for the principles he believed in. Donna had been right. Joe would have refused to pay the money El Jefe demanded, just as he had refused to be involved in the man's criminal activities.

Carly took a shaky breath and forced herself under control. There was no time for emotion, not with so much at stake.

The trip to Victoria was pushing four hundred miles. Taking the less-traveled route El Jefe had laid out, they could be there by one A.M. but they needed to get on the road.

"I'll bring up the truck," she said. "If anyone's watching, they'll see me behind the wheel when we drive out of the yard." Earlier, she'd mentioned the Glock beneath the driver's seat. Linc hadn't seemed surprised.

"I'll talk to Frank," he said, "send him to join the rest of the security people back at the ranch."

While Linc went to find Frank, Carly locked up and went to get the rig. The big white eighteen-wheeler with the winged Drake logo on the side had recently been washed and the tank filled. Carly climbed into the cab, adjusted the seat so her feet were flat on the floor, and checked on the Glock under the seat, along with a spare magazine. She buckled her seat belt and started the big Cummins diesel, felt the rumble of the engine roaring to life.

The truck had a standard transmission instead of an automatic. Joe was old-school; he'd liked the extra control. As Carly shifted the powerful vehicle into gear, an odd calm settled over her.

She could do this. Together she and Linc could make this work. They could pick up El Jefe's load, deliver it, and bring Zach safely home. The cameras would collect at least some of the evidence they needed to stop the maniac threatening all of their lives.

She could do this. She wouldn't allow any other thought into her head.

As she drove the truck forward and pulled up in front of the office, Linc opened the door on the passenger side and swung up into the cab. She shouldn't have noticed the huge bicep with the barbed wire tat threatening to tear through the sleeve of his black T-shirt. She shouldn't have felt a tug of sexual awareness, but she did.

Clearly she wasn't dead yet.

As she eased out of the yard and turned the big semi-truck and trailer onto the road, Carly prayed they could rescue Zach and manage to stay alive.

With fear for Zach riding on her shoulders, the first two and a half hours seemed like ten. Linc had offered to drive after the first hour and several times since then. Carly told him she'd turn the rig over to him in Waco, which was near the halfway point and would be coming up very soon.

It was dark inside the cab, just the glow of the speedometer, tac, fuel, temperature, and oil gauges illuminating the dashboard. She and Linc were both too wired to nap on the twin mattress in the sleeper compartment behind the seats.

Maybe as the journey wore on . . .

The back roads they had been traveling for nearly two hundred miles covered thousands of acres of rural Texas landscape and passed through a dozen tiny towns. Turning south on 77 would be more of the same.

"We're coming into Waco," Linc said. "There's a convenience store up ahead. I could use a cup of coffee and you're probably ready to take that break."

She nodded. "I'm definitely ready. Coffee sounds good." She braked, began downshifting through the pattern, made a wide turn onto the side street, then pulled into the asphalt parking lot, which was big enough to accommodate the rig.

Jumping down from the cab, she took a moment to stretch the muscles in her neck, shoulders, and lower back, then locked the truck, and she and Linc walked into the convenience store. It didn't take long to make a pit stop, grab a packaged sandwich and a candy bar for energy, along with a big paper cup of hot coffee.

When they reached the truck, Linc swung in behind the wheel and Carly climbed into the passenger seat. Both of them buckled in and Linc started the engine. They finished the sandwiches as the truck pulled out of the parking lot and headed farther south. Linc took the turn onto Highway 77, and they settled back in their seats.

"How are you holding up?" he asked, finishing his coffee as the truck rolled into the night.

"All right, I guess. I'd feel a lot better if I weren't so worried about Zach."

"They've got no reason to hurt him. We're doing

what Zapata wants. We aren't going to give him any trouble."

"Except for the video cameras and sound equipment in the trailer."

"Zapata won't be expecting surveillance gear. I checked it out and it's very well hidden. No way will anyone notice."

"I hope that rat bastard is there at the pickup site. I hope we get the proof we need to bring him down."

Linc chuckled. "So do I, but I wouldn't get my hopes too high. Once Zach is safe, we should at least have some of the evidence the FBI is looking for."

She sighed. "I hope so. I want my life back, Linc."

"I know you do, honey. We're going to make that happen, I promise."

Traveling well south of Waco at nearly ten o'clock at night, there were few cars on the road, just the occasional pair of headlights coming in the opposite direction or a vehicle pulling out of a driveway after the truck drove past.

"You sure you can't sleep?" Linc asked. "Be good if you were fresh when we got to Victoria. We've got no idea how much farther we'll have to go to get to the pickup site."

"I know. Maybe once the caffeine wears off, I'll give it a try."

But an hour later, she was still wide-awake, still worried about Zach, and no way would she be able to fall asleep.

As the miles rolled past, Linc grew more and more tense. It was after midnight, Victoria still thirty miles away. They should make the rendezvous on time, but until he drove into the truck stop and met up with Zapata's man, he wouldn't stop worrying.

Next to him, Carly was nodding off, her head against the window. He wished she had climbed into the bed in the sleeper, but he hadn't suggested it again. It wouldn't have done a lick of good and at least this way she was resting.

Another half hour passed. The lights of Vic's Truck Stop burned into the darkness up ahead. As he started downshifting, Carly stirred, then jerked upright in the seat.

"Are we there? What time is it?"

"We made it a few minutes early," Linc said. "Keep an eye out for Zapata's man." Pulling into the lot, he found a parking spot away from the big mercury lights illuminating several acres of asphalt, and turned off the engine. When no one walked up to the window, they climbed down to stretch their legs, went in and used the bathrooms, then headed back to the truck.

As they approached, a man stepped out of the darkness, big, with black hair slicked back and a bushy mustache. Linc recognized him as the man holding the knife on Carly when Zapata's men had attacked her at the roadhouse.

"The woman drives so I can keep an eye on you," the big Latino said, pointing his pistol at Linc.

"You don't need the gun," Linc said. "You've got the boy. We're going to cooperate."

The man just grunted. Linc remembered Carly saying his name was Cuchillo—*knife*—a name she'd heard the night she'd been abducted.

Jerking open the door to the sleeper compartment, Cuchillo climbed in and settled himself on the bunk behind the seats. Linc climbed into the passenger seat while Carly eased into the driver's seat, fastened her belt, and started the engine.

"Where are we going?" she asked.

"Just keep heading south. I will tell you where to turn."

Pulling back onto the road, she followed the pavement south. A ways down the highway, the man's deep voice rumbled to life.

"Turn here. Head for Tivoli."

Carly made the turn and kept going. At the tiny grease spot in the road that was Tivoli, she was ordered to turn again, onto Road 35. The truck passed through farm country for a while, then into an area of marshes, bogs, and swamps that was completely desolate. A good place to pick up smuggled cargo—or get rid of bodies.

Linc flicked Carly a glance and her gaze caught his. He read her unease, which matched his own.

Twenty miles from Tivoli, Cuchillo ordered her to turn down a boggy lane. Linc knew roughly where they were, knew the land around here was part of the Aransas National Wildlife Refuge. Proof of that in the form of a huge boa constrictor at least twelve feet long appeared in the headlights along the side of the road.

"Did you see that?" Carly asked as the truck drove past.

"Yeah. Lots of snakes out here. Gators, too."

"Keep driving," Cuchillo said.

The road petered out, dead-ending into a saltwater bay. Just beyond, the headlights reflected on dark, murky water stretching far into the night. Linc caught a glimpse of a big rubber boat pulled up on shore. Farther out, a powerboat disappeared into the darkness, heading back out to sea.

The smugglers had delivered their cargo. Whatever the hell it was.

"Pull up here and turn the truck around—and do not get stuck in the mud."

There was a makeshift circular turn-around area. Carly pulled onto what appeared to be a solid-looking piece of earth and turned the truck around so it faced back the way they had come. So far she was doing a helluva job of handling the big rig. Linc was proud of her.

"Put on the outside lights and turn off the engine," Cuchillo said. "Mosquitoes are as thick as dog hair here so leave the windows up, and do not get out of the truck."

"Whatever you want," she said.

Cuchillo climbed out of the cab, slammed the sleeper door, and disappeared toward the rear of the trailer. Linc had purposely left the roll-up door unlocked. He could hear the rattle as someone shoved it up, then the slide of something heavy being loaded into the trailer.

Carly leaned forward to look in the side mirror. "They're staying out of sight behind the truck. What do you think they're loading?"

He glanced into the mirror, saw only the sides of the trailer. "Something heavy. Could be drugs, could be anything."

It didn't take long to complete the job, whatever it was. The roll-up door rattled back down and the sleeper door opened. A whiff of marijuana seeped from Cuchillo's clothes as he climbed into the truck, a can of bug spray in his hand. He sprayed the interior, ending the buzz of the annoying insects, and settled himself on the bunk.

"Start the truck."

Carly cranked the engine. The truck came to life and idled softly.

"Where are we going?" Linc asked.

"Back the way we came. No tolls on 77 so no cameras. There is a convenience store in La Grange. You can take the wheel from there."

Cuchillo yawned. "I need to get some sleep. Wake me when you get to La Grange. El Jefe is expecting me to call from there." Apparently satisfied Linc wasn't going to cause him any trouble or maybe just too stoned to care, he stretched his bulky frame out on the bed. "Do not do anything stupid or the boy gets killed."

Linc looked over at Carly, whose eyes met his. They were heading back toward Dallas. The cargo could be anything—from drugs to a dirty bomb.

"It's going to be okay," Linc said softly as the truck rolled along and Cuchillo started to snore. "We'll get Zach and head home."

Carly nodded. But both of them knew they might never see home again.

Chapter Thirty-Three

At the convenience store in La Grange they all took a bathroom break, bought fresh cups of coffee, and returned to the truck. Linc climbed in behind the wheel.

"Take 35 north toward Dallas," Cuchillo instructed.

Dallas. She prayed they weren't carrying a bomb of some kind.

They didn't take time to fuel up. The truck held enough diesel to reach the city, still two hundred miles away, and return to Iron Springs. If they had to go farther, they could refuel along the way.

Carly leaned back in the passenger seat. Handling the big semi had become almost second nature, but after twelve hours on the road, she was exhausted. Though the night was beginning to gray toward sunrise, Linc seemed more alert than when they'd started.

He was gearing up, she knew, mentally preparing himself to handle whatever happened when they reached the drop-off site.

"When the highway splits, take the east route." Cuchillo folded back into the bunk and seconds later, started snoring. The awful truth was, until Zach was

returned, there was nothing they could do but follow
his orders.

As the miles rolled past and Linc drove toward
Dallas, Carly's nerves kicked up, pushing away any
sleepiness. The split in the interstate was only a couple
of miles ahead. It was seven-thirty in the morning, the
sun tipping over the horizon, traffic heavy.

Linc handled the truck with the ease of a veteran
driver, moving in and out safely while holding a steady
speed. With the thick Dallas traffic, Carly was glad he
was behind the wheel.

Linc glanced toward the bunk behind the seats, saw
Cuchillo was still asleep, and turned to Carly. "You
okay?"

"Nervous."

He nodded, looked back at the bunk. "You better
wake him up. We don't want to miss the turn to the
drop-off site, wherever the hell it is."

She sighed. "Could be anywhere."

"I know. Be careful. Remember he's got a gun."

"Believe me, I haven't forgotten." Carly turned in
her seat, leaned down, and barely nudged the man's
leg with her boot. "Cuchillo . . . it's time to wake up."

The big Latino jerked awake, muttering a dirty word
in Spanish as he sat up in the bunk.

He glanced around, saw where they were. "Take
35 east. Be careful not to miss the exit."

"Be easier if you just told us where we're going,"
Linc said.

"Irving. Just listen and do what I say."

The directions got complicated after that, swinging
the truck onto one freeway and then another. The
heavy traffic kept them hidden in plain sight. Carly
wondered if that had been part of Zapata's plan.

More instructions were given and finally Linc pulled the trailer into an area of warehouses and transportation hubs filled with dozens of trucks. Being close to the Dallas-Fort Worth Airport, there was a lot of manufacturing in the area. She spotted the signs for a Frito-Lay plant and a UPS express freight center. Hard to believe they were bringing a load of smuggled goods into the middle of all this activity.

But apparently that was exactly the plan.

"Turn here."

Linc turned the truck into an asphalt lot behind a food processing plant surrounded by a chain-link fence. The gate rolled closed behind them. Following Cuchillo's instruction, Linc backed the rig up to a loading dock and turned off the engine.

"You will stay here while the cargo is unloaded."

"Where's the boy?" Linc asked.

"I will bring him to you." The big Latino opened the sleeper door and jumped down to the asphalt.

Carly could hear the rattle of the trailer door rolling up. Seconds passed, then the scrape of the heavy cargo being unloaded. Glancing out at the side mirror, she caught a glimpse of something she hadn't expected.

"People," she said. "They're climbing out of the back. He's trafficking illegals."

"And God only knows what else."

An instant later, the sleeper door jerked open and Zach climbed into the truck.

"Zach!" Carly leaned into the back to hug him. Zach clung to her and they held on to each other for several long seconds before Carly let him go. "Thank God you're okay."

"Boy, I'm really glad to see you guys."

Carly's throat swelled. "We're glad to see you, too."

"You okay?" Linc asked. "They didn't hurt you?"

"I'm okay, but I really want to go home."

"So do we," Carly said, knowing that until they got back on the road and away from these men, anything could still happen.

One thing she didn't expect was the sound of the trailer being unhooked.

"Oh, no—they're releasing the fifth wheel." The trailer contained all the video evidence they had collected, everything they needed to make this nightmare end. "What are we going to do?"

But she was talking to air because Linc had stepped out of the cab and was striding toward Cuchillo, who stood a few feet away. Carly unfastened her belt, reached beneath the driver's seat, and moved the Glock to her side of the truck. The windows were down so she could hear the conversation.

"You can't have the trailer," Linc said. "That wasn't the deal."

Cuchillo raised his pistol and aimed it at Linc's broad chest. "Get back in the truck. You can afford to buy your woman another trailer. This one stays here."

"Is El Jefe a man of his word or not?" Linc pressed. "The trailer is ours. We're taking it home."

Carly's heart was pounding, thumping faster with each hostile word. She wanted to call Linc back, tell him they would find another way.

The cab jerked a little as the trailer came free and another man walked up, tall with very dark skin and a nose that was narrow and slightly hooked. As she recognized the man in Ross Townsend's photo, her pulse pounded so hard, her ears started ringing. It was the terrorist, Hassan Mohammed Al-Razi.

Linc must have recognized him, too, because he turned and started walking back to the truck.

"Where do you think you are going?" Al-Razi asked.

Linc didn't answer, just climbed in behind the wheel, and clicked his belt into place.

As he started the engine, Al-Razi walked up to the window. "Do you think I am going to let you just drive out of here?"

Linc ignored him. "Grab something and hold on, Zach. We're leaving."

Carly's insides were shaking. Grateful she had buckled herself back in, she looked out the window to see a dozen men moving into position around the truck, pointing a variety of deadly-looking weapons at the cab.

"Time to go home," Linc said. Dropping the truck into gear, he started pulling away from the dock. A wall of men moved in from all directions, but Linc just kept driving.

When a pickup shot out of nowhere, blocking the way forward, he slammed the truck into REVERSE and cranked the wheel, jammed his foot down hard on the pedal, and the truck moved backward. Using the side mirrors to steer, he shifted again, picking up speed as the truck shot backward, scattering men in every direction, knocking one of them down. Pistols roared and shots tore through the metal sides and back of the cab.

"Get down!" Linc shouted as he shifted into high REVERSE and roared back across the asphalt. A barrage of gunfire shattered the side windows; another blew through the sleeper, missing Zach's head by inches.

From her place in the foot well, Carly yanked the Glock out from under her seat, popped up, and began firing. She hit a man in the leg, one in the shoulder, heard the thump of wheels rolling over a body, but

Linc just kept going, increasing his speed, roaring backward toward the gate, crashing through it at thirty miles an hour.

When the wheels shot into the street, he jerked the yellow parking brake and cranked the steering wheel, spinning the truck a hundred and eighty degrees, sliding it into a forward position. He released the brake, shifted again, his boot jammed down hard on the pedal and the truck shot off down the road.

Linc zigzagged, throwing off the aim of the men chasing after them on foot, firing like maniacs, their bullets slamming into the cab. He downshifted, roared around a corner, then started picking up speed again.

There was a line of cars coming toward them from up ahead. For a moment, Carly thought Al-Razi was bringing in reinforcements and a fresh rush of fear shot through her.

The most welcome sight she had ever seen were the initials FBI printed on the sides of the vehicles blowing past them, careening around the corner they had just turned, heading for the food processing plant.

"The FBI!" Zach shouted. "The FBI is coming!"

Carly grinned.

Linc didn't stop, just kept roaring through the streets of the warehouse district back toward the interstate.

"How did they know?" Carly asked.

"I have no idea, but I'm damned glad to see them."

Linc kept driving. They were rolling along I-30, heading back toward Iron Springs, when his phone started ringing. He pulled it out of his pocket and looked down at the caller I.D. "It's Taggart." Hitting the speaker, he rested it on the center console so she could hear.

"You guys okay?" Quinn asked. "You got Zach with you?"

"We're all okay," Linc said. "Damned glad you decided to show up at the party."

"We would have been there sooner, but we didn't know your final destination. Once you arrived, it took a few minutes to get the team to your location. We're mopping up now. We've got thirteen Mexican illegals, four men wounded, two dead guys, including Hassan Mohammed Al-Razi—who got his seventy-two Virgins by trying to shoot his way out. Two other possible terrorists are also in custody."

"Nice work. How'd you know what was going on?"

"You didn't think we'd swallow that BS you were slinging about cutting a deal with El Jefe? We've been monitoring you for days—McKinley put listening devices in Carly's office and a GPS tracker on the truck you had modified. Good idea, by the way. Ought to give us some really good intel. We also put a drone in the air. Heat sensors detected human cargo in the trailer."

"You knew about Zach?" Carly asked.

"Not until you got the call last night. We had no idea he'd been taken. Glad you managed to get him out of there safely. I'll call the grandparents, let them know he's okay."

"I'll have Zach call, too," she said.

"That's good. We can pick him up at your house this afternoon and transport him back to San Antonio."

"Cool," Zach said from behind the seat. "I get to ride with the FBI."

Linc chuckled. "Looks like you've got things under control. Been a long night. We're headed home."

"Technically we need statements from all of you, but considering what you've been through, we can handle that when we get out to your place later today."

"Thanks. By the way, what else besides Mexican illegals and terrorists was Zapata smuggling?"

"Sorry, that's on a need-to-know basis. Matter of national security."

Linc just grunted.

"One last thing. Zapata is still on the loose. We've put a BOLO out on him but we don't have him in custody yet. You need to be careful until we can round him up and bring him in."

"Good advice."

"Carly, you and Zach stay close to Linc."

"We will," she promised, since close to Linc was exactly where she wanted to be.

As the truck continued home, it occurred to her that her troubles with El Jefe were about to be over. Once that happened, Linc's promise to her grandfather would be fulfilled.

A sharp pang dug into her chest. How much longer did she have with him? How much longer before he was ready to move on?

Refusing to let her tired mind go there, Carly focused on the road back to Iron Springs and said a silent prayer of thanks that they were all still alive.

Chapter Thirty-Four

The morning after the shooting Linc insisted they take a badly needed day off. Late yesterday afternoon, the FBI had shown up at the ranch to take their statements. Taggart had confiscated Carly's Glock as evidence, since she'd shot two of the rotten bastards.

The good news was the action had clearly been self-defense so she wouldn't be facing any charges.

The raid was all over the news, the press giving accolades to the FBI for stopping a potential terrorist attack. The death of Al-Razi and the arrest of two radical jihadists were splashed in bold headlines across the newspapers. Since there was an ongoing investigation, there'd been no mention of Linc, Carly, or Zach's role in the event. Linc hoped it would stay that way.

Zach was back with his grandparents. Taggart had arranged FBI protection for the family until Zapata was arrested or the feds felt sure the man was no longer a threat to them.

The night on the road had been long and tiring, yesterday equally exhausting. At least he'd been able to sleep late this morning, his rest deep and undisturbed with Carly's sweet little body draped over his chest. Snuggling led to a round of sleepy, very satisfying sex, which led to showering together, which heated things up all over again.

They were both dressed now, Carly in the kitchen, Linc in his home office catching up on e-mail. Work was mounting up in Dallas, but after what had happened, no way was he leaving. He could barely let Carly out of his sight.

Something had changed for him that terrible night on the road. Though he had known the truth deep down, the danger they had faced together had forced him to admit how deeply he cared for her.

Carly was strong and determined. She was loyal and courageous. She was everything he admired in a woman or for that matter, in a man. Carly wasn't just the right woman for him, the lady he wanted beside him as his life moved ahead, he was in love with her, deeply and without reservation, the forever kind of love he'd never thought to have.

Now that he was certain of his feelings, he intended to do something about them, had already made plans. He just had to convince Carly.

Needing a second cup of coffee, he padded barefoot down the hall, following the aroma of a fresh brewed pot. Spotting Carly at the kitchen counter, Linc walked up behind her, eased her back against his chest.

"Got a cup for me?" he asked.

She turned into his arms, lightly rested her palms on his chest. "I might. You could try bribing me with a kiss."

He grinned and happily obliged. His body stirred but now wasn't the time. "Unfortunately we have to behave," he said, ending the kiss before he was ready. "Tag should be here any minute."

"I wonder what he wants."

The ranch was still under heavy security, the reason the guards out front had just phoned. They'd stopped Tag Joyner at the gate and called Linc for permission for Tag to enter the property.

Accepting the cup of coffee Carly poured for him, he wandered into the living room, over to the window. Tag, who had been to the ranch house before, rode his flame-striped, metallic red Harley up in front, jammed down the kickstand with a heavy motorcycle boot, and swung a long leg over the seat.

Settling a black leather saddlebag over one shoulder, he walked up on the porch as Linc opened the door.

"Good to see you, bro," Linc said, the men leaning in to clap each other on the shoulder in a man hug. He stepped back to let Tag in. "What's up?"

"Got something for you. It'll cost you big if it's real, but it'll be worth it."

Carly walked into the room as Tag opened the saddlebag. She smiled. "Hey, Tag."

"Hey, Carly." Pulling out a clear plastic Ziplock bag with a paper coffee cup inside, he handed it to Linc.

"What is it?"

"Guy came forward to claim the reward you offered. Rides with the Bandidos. Wants fifty thousand for what's in that bag. Says the terrorist the FBI killed in that shootout—Hassan Al-Razi?"

"Yeah?"

"Says he's Raul Zapata's brother."

Carly's eyes went wide. "You're kidding."

Tag pointed to the bag. "The DNA on that cup should prove it."

Linc's gaze shot to Carly's, then returned to Tag. "Where'd he get it?"

"Out of Zapata's house. Apparently our guy worked for him off and on. Mostly protection, nothing illegal, or so he says."

Linc held up the Ziplock bag. "If what he claims is true, he'll get the fifty thousand. It'll take a few days to find out, but if it's real, he'll have his money."

"I'll tell him." Tag flipped the saddlebag closed and settled it back over his shoulder. "You think they'll catch him?"

"They damn well better." But with each passing day, Linc worried the bastard was going to skip the country and get away. If he did, the threat would always be hanging over their heads.

"Gotta hit the road," Tag said. "See you at Jubal's."

"I owe you way more than a beer," Linc said, following him to the door. "Figure out what you guys need for the clubhouse and consider it done."

Tag grinned and waved. Swinging a leg over the seat of the bike, he grabbed the handlebars, revved the engine, and shot off down the road back to the front gate, his shaggy brown hair flying out behind him.

"You think it's true?" Carly asked.

"Makes sense. Explains the connection between the two men."

"You know, there was something very distinctive about Zapata's voice. A gruff, sort of guttural sound when he said certain words. That was the reason I was so sure it was him the night of the gala. If his first language was Arabic not Spanish—"

"That could explain it. We need to know more about Al-Razi's family."

"We need to call Taggart."

He nodded. "The FBI can get the DNA results a lot faster than we can."

Grabbing his cell, he punched Quinn's contact number, heard the agent's familiar voice come over the line.

"I've got something for you," Linc said.

"We could sure use a break in the case. What is it?"

"Physical evidence that Raul Zapata and Hassan Al-Razi are brothers."

"Jesus."

"Exactly. In return, I want to know what else was in the trailer."

Taggart cursed. "Not on the phone. I can be at your place by noon."

"All right. We can meet at the big house. I'll see you there at noon." Linc hung up the phone.

Right on time, Quinn Taggart showed up at the mansion at exactly twelve o'clock. Carly looked up to see Mrs. Delinski showing the blond FBI agent into the study, where she and Linc were waiting.

"So what have you got?" Taggart asked, wasting no time as Linc led him over to the ornate rosewood table and chairs near the fireplace and all of them sat down.

Linc picked up the Ziplock bag he'd left on top. "An anonymous source gave me this, says it came from Zapata's residence. Says it'll prove he and Hassan Al-Razi are brothers."

Taggart's features tightened. "Could be he's right.

After you called, we went back and took another look at Al-Razi, the father. Seems he had two sons—each by a different mother. Both of them lived with him in Mexico with wife number one. Eventually Hassan, the older sibling, returned with his parents to Saudi Arabia, but the younger boy, Bharat, was still in high school. He had friends there, wanted to stay, so they let him."

"What happened to him?" Carly asked.

"No idea. Nothing on him after he graduated. He just seemed to fall off the grid."

"So it's possible Bharat got into the drug trade with his buddies," Linc said, "made a little money, then changed his name to Zapata and moved into Texas to build his empire."

Quinn held up the plastic bag. "If this is Zapata's DNA, it could link him to Hassan, prove he's Bharat Al-Razi, and your theory is correct. There's no chain of evidence, so it won't stand up in court and it won't be a perfect match, but it'll tell us if we're on the right track."

Linc's chair squeaked as he leaned back. "All right, now it's your turn. What was in the trailer besides human cargo?"

Taggart sighed. "This isn't for publication."

"Agreed," Linc said, and Carly nodded.

"There were three heavy wooden crates in the back, each over five feet long. Each held an FIM-92 Stinger infrared homing, surface-to-air missile, along with the launchers, the warheads—the whole enchilada."

Carly felt the blood draining out of her face.

Linc softly cursed.

"That food processing plant is directly in the flight path of the Dallas-Fort Worth Airport," Quinn said.

"A single, shoulder-fired missile could have brought down a jumbo jet."

Carly's stomach rolled.

"Now that they control some of the richest oilfields in the Middle East," Taggart continued, "these terrorist groups have amazing amounts of money. Enough to outfit an army with top-of-the-line equipment."

"And buy anything from missiles to nukes," Linc added, "if they can get their hands on them."

"Exactly."

"How was the attack supposed to happen?" Carly asked.

"A lot of the workers in that food processing plant are Muslim, part of the resettlement program. Al-Razi figured a few radicals thrown into the mix would go unnoticed. And they wouldn't have to be there long. From what we gleaned from one of the men we captured, their attack was planned to occur by the end of the week."

Linc blew out a slow breath. "Al-Razi's no longer a threat, but unfortunately, Zapata is still on the loose."

"We're after him, believe me," Taggart said. "Within hours of the raid in Irving, we hit his compound. The place was deserted. It had been gutted and burned out to destroy any possible evidence. We're hoping he's still in Texas, but there's no way to be sure."

They talked a little longer, tossed out some ideas, all of them hoping new information would turn up soon.

Discouraged by the grim prospects, Carly was grateful when Linc suggested they break and invited Taggart to stay for lunch.

Mrs. Delinski served chicken salad sandwiches on flaky croissants, with potato chips, fresh fruit, and ice tea. Carly had no idea how the lady managed all that on such short notice but the food was delicious.

They ate out on the terrace overlooking the blue waters of the huge, kidney-shaped swimming pool.

Enjoying the mild early October weather, they were almost finished eating when the attack began.

Chapter Thirty-Five

"That sounds like a chopper," Quinn said. "You expecting a ride into Dallas?"

"Not today." Linc spotted the helicopter in the distance, flying over the ranch from the south, heading in their direction.

He looked back at the house to see Deke Logan bursting through the French doors, striding toward him.

"We're under attack," Deke said. "We don't know who, could be as many as thirty armed men."

"Zapata," Linc said, without the slightest doubt.

"I'll call for backup." Quinn pulled out his phone to make the call, but the feds were a long ways away. The fight could be over by the time they got there.

"They came in the back way," Deke said. "Wounded a couple of men who were patrolling the road. These guys are driving military Humvees. One's mounted with an M-2 heavy machine gun. Hell, one's carrying an M-30 mortar! I'm pulling my men back, Linc. We've got to set up a line of defense."

"Where are Zapata's men now?"

"They're forming up, getting ready to make a full-out assault. Fuck, who the hell are these guys?"

"ISIS, maybe. Could be Al-Quaeda or some other group. Turns out Raul Zapata has terrorist connections."

"Fuck," Deke repeated.

"The house is solid stone. Why don't you set up your defensive position here?"

Deke glanced around at the opulent stone mansion. "You sure?"

"Damn sure. Get your injured men inside and take them down to the basement. Mrs. Delinski's a retired nurse."

Deke spun and raced back through the French doors, heading for his men. Turning to Carly, Linc caught her shoulders. Her face looked pale but her jaw was set.

"Carly, honey, gather up Mrs. Delinski and the rest of the staff and get them downstairs to the basement, out of the line of fire."

"I can't believe this."

"Go, baby."

She nodded, turned, and raced into the house. Linc and Quinn strode after her. As they stepped into the family room, he could hear her shouting orders, saw the housekeeper running for the entry to bring the gardeners inside.

"There's a gun safe in the study," Linc said to Quinn, striding in that direction. "I keep a Nighthawk .45 for protection, a little .380, and a couple of hunting rifles."

Quinn jerked his pistol out of the clip holster on his belt. "Standard FBI issue, Glock .23, forty cal."

Dropping the clip, he checked the load and shoved it back in, slid the gun back into his holster.

"FBI's on the way," Quinn said. "Sheriff's been alerted. Should be some deputies out here in the next few minutes."

"Howler's an idiot. He'll be lucky if he doesn't get his men killed."

They started out of the study just as the front door burst open and armed men in camouflage and tactical vests poured into the marble-floored entry, with Deke Logan in the lead.

"Mendez, Conners, Wash, and Cisco—cover the windows across the front of the house." Deke pointed in that direction. "Ash and Castillo, get the injured men downstairs, then go with Brewster and Finn to cover the back."

Deke turned to Linc. "Cain, you're with me. We'll take the dining room."

Linc didn't argue. Logan was former special ops. He knew what he was doing, and defending the ranch and its occupants was what he got paid for.

"I'll meet you there," Linc said, regretting his decision to give Marino the next two days off, though they were well deserved. Striding into the study, he opened the gun safe and took out the weapons, checked the load in the Nighthawk, and shoved it into the waistband of his jeans.

When Carly ran up, he didn't tell her to wait in the basement with the staff—he knew damned well that wasn't going to happen. Instead, he handed her the .380. "It's this or a rifle."

She took the smaller weapon, shoved it into the pocket of her jeans, and grabbed one of the rifles, an older model thirty ought six. "I'll take both."

Linc's mouth edged up. He couldn't resist pulling her in for a quick, hard kiss. "Stay close," he said, and Carly nodded.

Linc grabbed the remaining rifle, a thirty-thirty that had been around the ranch for years. Taggart headed for the living room while he and Carly ran for the dining room, where Deke had turned over the huge mahogany table and shoved it in front of a window.

Carly surveyed the opulent surroundings the same way Deke had. "When these guys start shooting, it's going to destroy your house."

Linc flashed her a grin. "Yeah, that's too bad."

Carly laughed. He couldn't believe it. With Zapata's army bearing down on them, a helicopter armed with God-only-knew-what circling overhead, and the house about to be blown down around her ears, she managed to laugh. If he wasn't already in love with her, he'd be crazy in love with her now.

They dragged a couple of heavy wooden dining chairs up to the windows and tipped them over, then settled in to wait.

"You ready for this?" he asked.

"No." She tilted up the rifle, used the barrel to smash out one of the windowpanes, and rested the gun on the sill. "I am now."

His mouth edged up. He wanted to tell her he loved her. Almost spit out the words. Might have if the rattle of machine gun fire and a barrage of bullets hadn't shattered the window above their heads. Shards of glass flew across the dining room.

Armed with an AR-15, Deke returned fire. Linc could hear shots being fired into the house from a dozen different locations, hear shots being returned from the living room, billiard room, ladies' salon, and rooms at the rear of the house.

The fight was on. Now all they had to do was survive till the cavalry got there.

Linc hunkered down at the window and began pulling off shots.

By the time the FBI showed up, the house was a pile of rubble. With limited ammunition, Carly took careful aim with her rifle, managed to hit one of the attackers in the shoulder and spin him around, shot another in the knee. Linc took the helicopter down with a couple of well-placed shots through the bubble window, wounding the pilot, who toppled over onto the controls.

The bad news was the chopper hit the house before it exploded, blowing up several bedrooms on the second floor and starting a small fire.

"These guys have damned good equipment," Deke said, crouched at the window next to them. "But they aren't well trained—not like my guys." Ducking beneath a stream of machine gun bullets, he elbow-crawled out of the dining room to check on the rest of his men.

As the battle wore on, a mortar round demolished the laundry room and tore out the back wall of the kitchen. Some of Deke's men took care of the Humvee it was mounted on, making short work of the driver and the guys manning the weapon, ending the threat before there was any more damage.

The second Humvee exploded when one of Deke's guys tossed a grenade through the driver's window.

The whir of blades had Carly looking skyward. "FBI," she said, reading the bold letters on the side. "Thank God."

Linc raised his head up enough to look out the window. Along with the FBI chopper, both ICE and DEA vehicles were converging on the scene from two different directions, surrounding Zapata's rapidly dwindling army.

It was over quickly after that, the various entities taking charge of the attackers, who dropped to their knees and pushed their hands into the air. Carly prayed Raul Zapata was among them.

The sheriff arrived after the fight, which Linc said was a blessing. Agent Taggart had gone to join his men, while Deke's soldiers, those left inside to defend the house, laid down their weapons and walked out to join Deke and the rest of the security team.

Someone sent word to the staff, who used the outside exit to leave the basement and were now milling around on the concrete decking beside the swimming pool.

A pair of ambulances arrived. The fire department was on its way, but the fire in the far end of the house was still burning and smoke was drifting down the stairs.

Linc stayed behind to collect what few items he wanted out of his study and Carly stayed to help him.

"I don't think the fire will reach this far," he said, "but you never know. There are a couple of first editions I'm fond of and these photos." Pictures of Beau and his brother, Josh, a few other mementos sitting on bookshelves.

Linc tossed the items into his leather briefcase. "Let's get out of here."

More than ready, Carly took a couple of steps toward the door before a familiar voice stopped her. Bharat

Al-Razi, alias Raul Zapata, alias El Jefe, blocked the carved wooden door leading into the study.

"You are going nowhere," Zapata said. "You and Cain will never leave this house."

Linc should have seen this coming, should have figured a guy like Zapata wouldn't go down without a fight.

Wearing a black tactical vest over military fatigues, Zapata pointed a big .45 caliber pistol in their direction, but it wasn't the gun that worried Linc. It was the maniacal smile on his face and the grenade he gripped in his hand.

"You will die here today—both of you! You infidel dogs have caused me to fail in the task Allah set for me." He coughed as smoke began to curl into the room, drift up into the skylight.

"You still have a chance, Al-Razi," Linc said calmly, easing Carly a little behind him. "If you leave now, you can escape and try again."

Al-Razi spat on the floor. "You will die, then I will leave."

Linc should have seen it coming, should have known Carly wouldn't go down without a fight. Just as Zapata pulled the pin and rolled the grenade across the floor, Carly's little pistol appeared, a shot roared, and a bullet ripped through Zapata's throat. He screamed and clutched his neck.

Linc snatched up the grenade and tossed it back, grabbed Carly, and dived behind his heavy rosewood desk. Carly screamed as the grenade blew up. Metal fragments exploded into the plaster walls and ripped into the desk, showering the room with deadly shrapnel.

The concussion made Linc's ears ring, but the metal didn't penetrate the thick slab of wood protecting them.

Carly lay trembling beneath him, clutching his shoulders. Linc shoved himself off her, did a quick check to be sure she wasn't injured, caught a glimpse of the spray of blood that had once been El Jefe, and came to his feet.

"Is he dead?" Carly asked as the door burst open and Taggart and half a dozen FBI agents rushed into the study.

"He's dead." Linc caught her hand, pulled her up beside him, and into his arms. "But we're still alive."

Weapon in hand, Quinn surveyed the destruction. "Jesus, what the hell happened?"

Linc tipped his head toward the bloody spray of red. "Zapata/Al-Razi or whatever his name is won't be bothering us again." Linc stayed in front of Carly, blocking her view. No use putting that ugly memory into her head. "Let's get out of here."

The fire trucks had arrived by the time they walked out of the study. Hoses were being deployed, firemen climbing up on the roof. Linc slid an arm around Carly's waist, keeping her close as they walked out of the smoke-filled, bullet-riddled house. Flames licked through the ceiling in the living room. A stream of water from a big fire hose blew through the window, soaking the velvet draperies, sofas, and chairs.

It was over and they were safe. As far as Linc was concerned, they could let the damned place burn.

Chapter Thirty-Six

Two days had passed since the shootout at the big house. This morning, Linc had gone into Dallas and Carly had gone to work at the yard. It had felt good to drive herself in without a bodyguard.

Even with all the problems, Rowena had been doing a fabulous job of almost single-handedly running Drake Trucking. Today they had spent the morning catching up, going over cargo manifests and rearranging schedules, just generally getting the place back together.

The day had gone swiftly, and she and Row had accomplished a lot. Now it was after six, the office closed for the day, Carly back at the ranch house.

Linc wasn't home yet, which was good. It was time she packed her things and returned to her own home. It had to be done. There was no reason for her to stay at Linc's any longer. No excuse to continue sleeping in his bed every night.

It was time for her to go back to the real world, back to her own life. Putting it off would only make things harder, might even get embarrassing for Linc if he had to ask her to leave.

Her chest clamped down. Packing to leave was even more painful than she could have imagined. She'd been at it awhile, had one suitcase filled and was packing up another. There was still a row of cardboard boxes along the wall in the guest room, clothes Linc had brought here after her house had been vandalized.

She would have him send them over whenever he found time.

She glanced around the master bedroom. Everything from the masculine wood furniture to the big king-size bed made her think of him. The fragrance of his aftershave drifted in the air, reminding her of the first time she had met him, how unbelievably handsome he had looked that day, how strongly she'd been attracted to him.

She remembered the first time they had made love, thought of the heat that always seemed to simmer between them. Her throat ached as she walked over to the dresser and picked up the crystal bottle of perfume he had bought her the night of the gala. Holding it against her heart, she felt a wave of longing.

His motorcycle boots sat in the corner. A black T-shirt hung over the chair. Everything in the room reminded her of Linc, reminded her why she had fallen so desperately in love with him.

Reminded her why it was way past time for her to leave.

She heard familiar footsteps striding down the hall, and a heavy weight crushed down on her chest. She had hoped to be finished and ready to leave by the time he got home, but she still had another suitcase to fill and her toiletries to pack.

"Carly?" Linc called out.

"In here!" She steeled her spine, reminded herself

to keep the conversation brief, keep him from knowing her heart was breaking into pieces.

He was smiling when he walked through the door, dressed in the navy blue suit he had worn to work that morning, looking totally gorgeous. He saw the suitcases on the bed and the smile slipped off his face.

"What are you doing?"

"I'm packing," she said lightly, praying with everything inside her he wouldn't hear the tremor in her voice. "Time for me to go home."

His smile returned. Shrugging out of his suit coat, he tossed it away, loosened his tie as he walked up behind her, eased her back against his chest.

"I don't want you to go home. I want you to stay here with me."

She'd known he would object. He wanted her to stay—but for how long?

When she didn't answer, he turned her to face him. "I want you to stay, Carly. I want you to marry me."

Her heart jerked. For an instant, she thought she must have heard him wrong. "What?" In a million years, she'd never expected him to say those words.

"I love you. I want you to marry me. I was planning to ask you properly. I promise I'll do it right later, but I don't want to wait any longer."

Her head was spinning. "You aren't . . . you aren't serious?"

"Of course I'm serious." He frowned. "I thought you'd be happy."

"I don't know . . . it never occurred to me you'd even consider marrying me." She looked into his beloved face. "You're Lincoln Cain. You can have any woman you want. I'm not a beauty queen. I'm not a *Vogue*

cover model. I'm just a trucker's granddaughter from
Iron Springs."

His voice softened. "You're the woman I love, Carly.
The woman I want to spend the rest of my life with."
He ran a finger down her cheek. "I saw you with Zach.
We could have kids, raise a family."

She looked into his beautiful gold-flecked green
eyes and a rush of love for him hit her so hard, she
swayed on her feet.

She shook her head, steadied herself. "Marriages
never work. You should know that better than anyone.
Look what happened to you. Three years and it was
over. Look at your father and mother. My dad didn't
stick around long enough for me to know his name.
Even Joe couldn't make it work."

"Marriage depends on the people," he said. "You
and me, we're right for each other. We can make it
work."

She trembled. She wanted to believe him so badly.
She had never wanted anything more than to marry
Lincoln Cain.

But what if it didn't work out? What if in a few years,
or even months, he left her? She couldn't bear it. She
loved him too much. She wouldn't be able to stand
that kind of pain.

And what if they had kids? She didn't want to raise a
child by herself. She knew what it felt like to live that
way.

But what if it could work? What if they really had a
chance to be happy?

"I just . . . I need some time. I never expected you to
ask me. I-I need to be sure it's the right thing to do, the
right thing for both of us."

Linc straightened, his powerful shoulders going back. "You don't need time, Carly. It's an easy question. Either you love me and you want to marry me or you don't. A simple yes or no is enough."

She thought of Joe, thought of Linc and the beauty queen he'd married before, thought of Garth Hunter and Carter Benson, men who had said they loved her.

"It . . . it isn't that simple."

His jaw went tight. "Actually it is."

Turning away from her, he walked to the door. "You can stay here as long as you want. Just phone Millie when you leave and let her know you're gone."

"Linc, please . . ."

Reaching into the pocket of his slacks, he pulled out a blue velvet box and set it on the dresser. "Sell it. Use the money to pay off part of your loan." Turning, he strode out of the bedroom.

"Linc!" Carly ran after him. "Linc, wait!" Racing behind him down the hall, she called his name again and again, but Linc just kept walking, storming out the front door toward his truck. He slid in behind the wheel and started the engine.

"Linc! Wait! Please don't go!"

Gravel spun out from beneath the tires as he shifted into gear and pulled the truck onto the dirt road. Her heart was aching, throbbing like a wound inside her chest. Tears streamed down her cheeks.

"Linc . . ." she whispered as the truck disappeared down the long dirt road. "I love you so much."

A keening sound tore from her throat as fresh pain sliced through her, ripping her apart, making her ache all over.

What have I done? she thought. *What have I done?*

It never occurred to her to go after him. There was nothing she could say to make things right between them, no way to make him understand.

No way to tell him she was afraid to marry him because she was terrified of losing him. More afraid than she had ever been in her life.

Chapter Thirty-Seven

Beau Reese strode out of the elevator onto the executive floor of the Tex/Am Enterprises building. Passing the reception desk, he waved but didn't head for his office. Instead, he went in search of Millie Whitelaw, Linc's personal assistant.

He stopped when he reached her desk. "Where is he?"

Millie's dark head came up from behind the computer screen. The worried look on her face told him what he'd already figured out, that something was very wrong.

"I know he's in Dallas," Beau said. "I talked to the pilot who choppered him in—but he isn't at his apartment. He isn't answering his cell. What the hell's going on?"

Millie rose from her desk and led him a few feet away where none of the staff could overhear. "He's in his suite, Beau. He's been there two full days."

"What the hell?"

"It's Carly. He asked her to marry him and she said no."

Beau shook his head. "I don't believe it. I've seen them together. She's crazy about him."

"I know." Millie's eyes filled. She blinked to keep from crying, which sent Beau's worry up another notch.

"I don't know what happened," Millie said. "I've never seen him like this, not in all the time I've worked for him."

Beau brushed past her, opened the door to Linc's private office, then went over to the paneled wall, opened the door and walked into the private adjoining suite.

On the far side of the room, Linc was sprawled on the caramel leather sofa, an empty bottle of Stagg Kentucky Bourbon in his hand.

"What the fuck? I haven't seen you drunk since before you went to jail."

Linc groaned as he sat up on the sofa, set the empty whiskey bottle down on the floor at his feet.

"You love her that much?" Beau asked.

Linc's white shirt, a solid mass of wrinkles, hung open to the waist, and his tie was gone. He'd clearly been wearing the same pair of navy blue slacks for days.

"I love her," he said, not sounding nearly as drunk as he looked. "Trouble is she doesn't love me."

"Bullshit. She loves you. You said something wrong. You did something. Somehow you screwed it up."

He just shook his head.

"Where is she?"

"Out at the ranch. I told her she could stay as long as she wanted. I don't care about it anymore."

"Goddammit." Turning, Beau started for the door. "Get cleaned up. We've got work to do."

Linc made no reply.

Beau left him sitting there, walked out of the suite,

and returned to Millie's desk. "I think he's through the worst of it. Give him twenty minutes, then suggest he take a shower and get cleaned up."

She nodded. "What are you going to do?"

"I'm going to fix this. I'm not sure how, but I'm going to do my best."

Millie flashed him a look of hope. "He loves her so much."

"I know."

An hour and forty-five minutes later, the chopper set down on the pad at Blackland Ranch. He'd called ahead and had the Jeep waiting. Ten minutes more and he was pulling up in front of the low brick ranch house Linc called home—or had until two days ago.

He hoped Carly was still there, hoped to hell he could find a way to make things right for her and his best friend.

Praying he wasn't there on a fool's errand, Beau took a deep breath and climbed out of the Jeep.

Carly answered the door, surprised to see Beau Reese standing on the porch.

"May I come in?" Beau asked. With his black hair curling softly over the collar of his shirt and his brilliant blue eyes, Linc's partner was amazingly handsome. He was tall and lean and fit, the kind of man women drooled over. For Carly, though, no man could compare to Linc.

She stepped back to let him in. "If you're looking for Linc, he isn't here."

"No, he's in his suite at the office—drunk out of his wits."

"What?"

"That's right. You didn't think it was going to bother him that the woman he loves doesn't love him enough to marry him?"

Her eyes burned. She'd been crying for the last two days, didn't think she had any tears left, but fresh drops rolled down her cheeks.

"I love him. I love him so much, I feel like I'm dying."

Beau reached out and wiped away a drop of wetness. "Jesus." He led her into the living room and sat down next to her on the burgundy leather sofa. "Christ, Carly, if you love him, why didn't you say yes?"

She drew in a shaky breath. She wondered if she could make Beau understand. "I've had plenty of time to think about it. I suppose I was trying to protect myself."

"Protect yourself? From Linc?"

She swallowed. "The thing is, Beau, I'm just a woman, same as the rest. Sooner or later, Linc will get tired of me and want to move on. That's what all men do."

"Linc isn't like that. He's the most loyal man I've ever known. You think he didn't give the idea of marrying again a whole lot of thought before he asked? Linc didn't become the wealthy, successful man he is today by making hasty decisions. He made a bad call once. I think he married Holly because he thought it was time, something he needed to do. This is different. No way he would ask you to marry him if he wasn't completely sure it would work."

She sniffed but made no reply. She had no idea

what Linc thought about marriage. They had never discussed it.

"Linc loves you, Carly. I know him better than anyone. He loves you—and he needs you. You understand that, right?"

She shook her head. "Linc's the most capable man I've ever known. He doesn't need anyone."

"You're wrong. Sure, he can take care of himself and damned near everyone else, but that isn't the same as having someone who cares about him, someone who loves him. He's never had that. You didn't have a family, but you had Joe. Linc's never had anyone."

Her heart squeezed. She'd never thought of that. That Linc might need her as much as she needed him. She pulled a tissue out of her pocket and dabbed at the tears on her cheeks. "You really believe a man can love a woman forever? You think it could really happen?"

Beau glanced away, stared off in the distance above her head, finally looked back at her. "I loved a woman that way once," he said softly. "Her name was Sarah. We met in college and we were perfect together."

"What happened?" she asked gently.

"In her senior year, Sarah got cancer. We fought it together. We thought we could beat it. Sarah had so much to live for." He glanced away. "But the odds were against us from the start and finally she died."

"Oh, Beau."

"I loved her desperately, Carly, beyond all reason. There's never been anyone else for me. There probably never will be."

She reached over and covered his hand where it rested on the sofa. "Beau, I'm so sorry."

"Linc loves you like that, Carly. The way I loved

Sarah. If you love him, you have to go to him. You have to tell him."

Her throat tightened. Was there still a chance for them? "I never should have let him leave. I tried to call him back, but it was too late."

Beau smiled. "You're both pretty hardheaded. That's probably what makes you so good together."

She stood up from the sofa, wiped away the rest of her tears. "I've got a bag mostly packed. I was planning to move home this afternoon. Let me change, wash my face, and comb my hair."

Beau grinned. "Good idea. You look almost as bad as Linc."

Carly laughed. God, it felt so good. She was going to Linc and she was going to marry him. If he'd changed his mind, she would just have to change it back.

She threw a few more items into her bag, washed her face, put on some makeup, and brushed out her hair. She looked passable, not great, but it was the best she could do. By the time she'd put on a flirty little blue print dress that came to just above her knees and a pair of high-heels, she was ready to marry Lincoln Cain.

Grabbing a navy blue knit sweater, her purse, and the handle of her rolling bag, she started for the door. A quick stop to grab the blue velvet box Linc had left on the dresser and she met Beau in the living room.

"The helicopter's waiting," he said. "But unfortunately there's been a change of plans."

Her heart seemed to stop. She was terrified to think what that might mean. "What's happened?"

"Millie just called. Linc's brother was wounded in action. They treated him at Bagram Airfield. From there, he's being medevaced through Ramstein Air Base to Lanstuhl Medical Center in Germany. Linc plans to be there when he arrives."

"Oh, my God."

"We need to go, Carly. Linc's got a G-6 chartered. He's on his way to the airport right now."

"I'm ready. Let's go."

Beau gave her a quick once over, flashed a smile of approval. "Linc's gonna owe me for this. He's gonna owe me big." Beau grabbed her bag and started tugging it toward the door.

Beau deserves to find someone, she thought as she followed him out to the Jeep. But the notion slipped away, replaced by thoughts of Linc and concern for his wounded brother.

A big white G-6 private jet was sitting on the tarmac outside the executive terminal at Dallas Love Field when the helicopter set down.

"I'll get them to hold the plane and have someone take care of your luggage," Beau said as they ducked beneath the blades. "You go to Linc. He's going to need you now more than ever."

She brushed a kiss on Beau's lean cheek. "Linc's lucky to have you for a friend."

"I'm lucky to have him," Beau said and took off on the run with her bag.

Carly hurried across the tarmac and climbed the stairs to the cabin of the sleek white jet. It was roomy and elegant, with polished mahogany tables and wide butter-cream leather seats. She spotted Linc in one of them, his head tipped back and his eyes closed. He looked tired and a little worn, and more dear to her than ever.

As she sat down next to him, his eyes cracked open and he sat up in his seat. There wasn't an ounce of friendliness in his face.

"Carly . . . what the hell are you doing here?"

She started to answer, but Linc held up a hand.

"Never mind, it doesn't matter. You need to leave. My brother's been wounded. They don't know if he's going to make it. I can't deal with him and you both—not right now."

Her chin went up. Gripping the edge of the seat, she stared him straight in the face. "I'm not leaving. I'm staying right here."

"Bullshit. Get off the plane."

Her heart raced so hard it hurt. *Oh, God, oh, God, oh, God.* "I'm staying."

"You didn't want to be with me before. Now it's too late."

"I wanted to stay, but . . ." Her throat ached. "I didn't understand, okay? I'm here now and I'm staying."

One dark eyebrow went up. "Yeah, for how long?"

She swallowed past the ache. "Forever." Her voice broke, but she didn't look away. Her hand trembled as she lifted it so he could see his diamond ring, the same marquis-cut stone he had bought her to wear to the gala, reset into an engagement ring. A thin platinum band inset with diamonds accompanied it, perfect to wear to work.

"You love me?" he asked harshly.

Her eyes teared up. "I'd die for you," she said.

A shudder went through Linc's big body. Dragging her into his lap, he buried his face in her hair. "Why didn't you just say yes?"

She held on hard, couldn't make herself let him go.

"I was a coward. You're way out of my league. I was afraid of getting hurt."

"I love you, baby. I'd never do anything to hurt you."

She wiped away a tear. "I know. Beau explained things, helped me understand."

He scoffed. "Beau always was a better salesman."

"Are you sure I'm the one?"

He smiled at her softly. "You're everything I've ever wanted, Carly."

She went back into his arms. "I love you so much."

"You sure?"

"Never more certain."

With a sigh, he relaxed, settled back in his seat with her still in his lap.

"You heard about Josh?"

"Beau told me."

"I'm going to Germany. You coming with me?"

She felt the words like a warm caress. "I'm with you all the way, honey."

Linc kissed her softly. "We'll get married as soon as Josh's well enough to come to the wedding."

Josh had to get well. Linc needed him, just like he needed her. They would both be there to make sure it happened.

"Sounds like the perfect plan," she said, smiling up at him.

And it was.

Epilogue

Three months later

A lot had happened since that day three months ago. Josh was healing. He was no longer in the Marines, a decision his injury had prompted him to make. He was living in a double-wide trailer set up for him at the back of Blackland Ranch, giving him the privacy he needed. Linc wanted him to stay in Texas, wanted to build a place for him on the ranch.

In time, Josh would decide what he wanted to do.

Zach had become a real member of the family, spending lots of fun weekends out at the ranch. He had joined his local swim team and had already won his first trophy.

Carly and Linc had been married three weeks, after a simple ceremony in a beautiful little chapel in Iron Springs with all of their close friends and neighbors. Afterward, they had partied in a back room at Jubal's, then left for a weeklong honeymoon on a private island off the Florida coast. Though traveling was fun, they preferred being at home on the ranch.

The wedding was perfect. The honeymoon was perfect.

Beau was right—when the fit was perfect, everything just seemed to work.

Not that they didn't have their differences. Linc was still as stubborn, overprotective, and controlling as he had been before. The crazy thing was, now that he was her husband, somehow she found it endearing.

They were living in the ranch house, at least for the time being. Eventually Linc wanted to rebuild the big stone mansion.

"We'll gut it," he'd said, "redesign it just the way we want, and make it our own. We'll keep what we like and give away the rest. It'll be a great place to raise our kids."

Standing now at the window in the living room of the ranch house, Carly's heart gave a little leap of anticipation as she watched Linc driving up the road toward home.

He strode in like he always did, bigger than life, taking up the very oxygen in the room. He bent his head and very thoroughly kissed her.

"Hi, honey." He smiled. "How was your day?"

She grinned. She loved when he said that. "We got a couple of new accounts. Business is picking up so much I decided to hire an assistant for Row. That way I can take a little more time off to be with my handsome husband."

Linc grinned. "I like the sound of that." He held up an envelope. "I had a visitor at the office today—Joe's attorney, Willard Speers."

"Mr. Speers? I paid his bill sometime back. What did he want?"

"He came by to drop off this letter. He said we needed to open it together."

She moved closer, read the handwriting on the envelope. "That looks like Joe's writing."

Linc led her over to the sofa and both of them sat down. Carly carefully tore open the envelope and pulled out a single sheet of paper.

Carly started reading out loud. "'Carly, if you and Linc are reading this, by some great miracle the two of you are married and my fondest wishes have come true.'"

Her head came up. "Oh, my God."

Linc took the letter, started reading where she'd left off. "'I'd like to think I had some small part in getting the two of you hitched.'"

Carly took back the letter. "'Carly, you know how much I love you. You're married to the best man I know. I believe he'll treat you right and be a very good husband.'"

Her eyes filled.

Linc took back the letter. "'Linc, I wanted someone special for Carly. I know you remember me saying that more than once. I believe you've become that special man.'"

Linc paused for a moment to clear his throat. "'Knowing the two of you, watching you grow and change over the years, at some point, it occurred to me that you would suit each other perfectly. I couldn't be sure, of course, but I figured you ought to have time to find out.'"

"That's why he asked you to look out for me," Carly said. "He wanted to give us the chance to know each other." She read the last paragraph. "'So have a great life, you two, and know that wherever you are, I'll be watching over you. I love you both, Joe.'"

Linc eased Carly into his arms and just held her.

"He wanted us to be together," she said against Linc's shoulder, wiping at the tears on her cheeks.

Linc looked up as if he could see her grandfather in heaven. "I owe you, Joe Drake. You gave me the best gift I've ever had."

"He gave us each other," Carly said, and smiled through happy tears up at Joe.